w
T
A
p
p
ca
an
gro
and
cro
An
par
the
extr
great

M
volu

On

MOTHER AND SON

BEING VOLUME THREE OF

The Soul Enchanted

By

ROMAIN ROLLAND

Translated from the French by

VAN WYCK BROOKS

NEW YORK

HENRY HOLT AND COMPANY

C.

"For peace is not the absence of war. It is the virtue that is born of the vigor of the soul."

SPINOZA,

Tractatus Politicus.

MOTHER AND SON

BOOK ONE

BOOK I

PART I

AR could not frighten Annette. "Everything is war," she thought, "war under a mask. . . . I am not afraid to meet you face to face."

All her family were like herself in that they accepted unprotestingly whatever the fates brought to them.

She felt a fatalistic acquiescence that had come to her through her recent ordeal. "I am ready, let come what may." Her sister Sylvie felt a secret longing so strong that she could hardly suppress an impatient cry of "at last!" At last the monotonous round of the days was going to expand, the circle of loves and hates was going to widen. Her son, Marc, felt a sombre enthusiasm of which he said nothing, but which was betrayed by his feverish hands and eyes. It had appeared, then, the tragic ideal from which his weakness shrank but which the voice of his deepest instincts obscurely invoked, the ideal that youth will not confess, the appeal to that fettered strength that lay prone beneath the ennui of an epoch that had lost all its reasons for living. He saw his elders setting forth in an ecstasy of action and sacrifice. The flood of their enthusiasm would before long roll through thickly muddied waters, but during these first days the stream was pure, as pure as it could be with adolescents whose souls were already defiled with elemental disturbances. Marc, bend-

3

ing over the stream, drank here and there of the burning
purity of this immolation, and the slime in its depths as
well. He envied and dreaded the morrow that awaited
them. . . . When he raised his eyes he met those of his
mother. Both glanced away. They had understood each
other, enough to wish not to be better understood. But
they knew they both walked under the menace of the same
storm.

The only one who felt no share in the exaltation was
Sylvie's husband, Leopold; and he was the only one of
the group who was actually setting out. He had calculated that his class, one of the oldest of the territorials,
would not be called out at once, that the calls would rise
grade by grade. He was in no sort of hurry. But he had
a presentiment that the war would be in more of a hurry
than he, and that it would not forget him. It remembered him even more quickly than he had expected. He
had come from Cambrai. He found himself at the very
front, an honor that a man of his age could easily have dis-
pensed with. When the time came for him to leave, however, he put a good face on it. He had to; Sylvie was
heroic, and he could expect little pity in the eyes of the
other women. Each of them had her man, her husband,
her lover, her son, her brother, who was leaving. That
they were all leaving together gave a semblance of reg-
ularity to the abnormality of the affair. The hard thing
would have been if any of the men had protested. No one
risked doing so. Such an idea never even occurred to
Leopold. The acquiescence of his family was as categori-
cal as the draft order itself. The suspicious glances of
that little fox of a Marc would have spied out jealously
any weakness on his part! . . . He blustered it out. At

the farewell dinner the good fellow drank the health of
the whole workshop, heavy as his heart was at leaving it.
So far as his business was concerned, he could be sure that
Sylvie would watch over it competently. The rest! . . .
Perhaps it was better not to think about it. . . . Just at
present she was a Lucretia. . . . Confound the woman!
. . . He wet her cheeks with his tears when he left her.

"It will be an excursion," she said. "What magnificent
summer weather. Take care not to catch cold!"

Annette kissed him (that was so much gained). She
felt sorry for him but she did not show it for fear of weakening him. . . . "Why not? since it must be done!". . .
And his anxious, searching glance read nothing but inflexibility in the affectionate glance of the older sister.

It must be done.

A wall. No way out except forward.

He set off.

*
* *

From the top to the bottom of the house the swarm poured forth as from a hive. On the fifth floor was that son of the widow, an old bachelor of thirty-five. On Annette's landing, the young bank-clerk who had just been married. Below were the magistrate's two sons. Below them the only son of the professor of law. Still further down, the son of the man who kept a small wood and wine shop on the ground floor. . . . In all, eight warriors, who were not warriors from choice. But no one consulted them about it. The modern state spares its free citizens the effort of choice. And they approve. One care the less!

From the top to the bottom of the house there was perfect assent. With perhaps one exception which no one noticed, young Madame Chardonnet, the new bride, Annette's neighbor, who was too weak to protest. Few of the others understood why their complete liberty, their right to live, should have been taken away from them and placed in the hands of a hidden master who was about to sacrifice them. But with the exception of one or two, nobody tried to understand. Understanding was not necessary for assent, and from the beginning of their lives they had all been brought up in assent. A thousand souls who unite in consent have no need of a reason. They have only to watch one another and do as the others do. All the mechanism of mind and body begins to work of itself, without effort. . . . Heavens! how easy it is to drive the herd to market. Nothing is required but one poor shepherd and a few dogs. The more animals there are the more docile they are and the easier to direct, for they

6

form one mass and the units are lost in the whole. A people is a sort of blood that coagulates. . . . Until the fatal hours of the great upheavals when nations and seasons periodically renew themselves. Then the frozen river overflows its banks and lays waste the country, flooding it with its dissolving body.

These tenants of the house were all entirely different. Their faiths, their traditions, their temperaments, were unlike. Every one of these soul-cells, every one of these families, had its own chemical formula. But from them all came the same acceptance.

They all loved their sons. As in nine out of every ten French families, the sons formed the very foundation of the home. When they had hardly begun life themselves, when they were twenty-five or thirty, they had transferred to their children, at the cost of an obscure, daily sacrifice, the joys they had never experienced and the ambitions they had ceased trying to realize for themselves. And at the first call they gave them up, gave up these sons without a word of blame against any one.

There was the Widow Cailleux on the fifth floor. She was nearly sixty years old. She had been thirty-three and the boy eight or nine when the father had died. Since then, they had been inseparable. For ten years they had scarcely passed a whole day under different roofs. They seemed like an old couple; for, although he was not yet forty, Hector Cailleux, the son, had already the air of a retired official and his life was over before it had begun. He did not complain of his lot; he would not have desired any other.

The father had been a postal employee. The son had followed in his steps. There had been no advance from

one generation to the next, he had remained at the same
point. But to remain at the same point, not to fall back,
does every one realize how vast an effort this often repre-
sents? When you are weak and unfortunate, you advance
in merely not losing ground. In order to bring up her
son, the mother, who was without resources, had had to
work out by the day. This was painful for one who had
had her own little middle-class home. But she never
complained, and now they had climbed back into the humble paradise they had lost. She found her rest in her
work, for it was work for herself and her son, since she
made her home with him. A kindly, bovine, Berriot face
that went better with the white ruffled cap than with the
lady's hat that perched on Sundays on her gray head above
its white-streaked coil of hair; a wide, toothless mouth that
never spoke out loud but that had for her son and her ac-
quaintances an affectionate, weary smile; a slight stoop.
She was always the first up, and in the morning she
brought her son hot coffee in bed. While he was at his
office she took meticulous care of the apartment. She prepared the meals. She was a good cook and he was something of a gourmand. In the evening he told her what
he had heard during the day. She did not listen very
closely, but it made her happy to hear him talk. On Sunday she went to morning mass. He did not. This was
understood between them. He was neither a skeptic nor
a believer. Religion was a matter for women. She would
attend to it for the two of them. In the afternoon, they
took a short walk together, but they rarely went outside
the quarter. He was old before his time. But they were
satisfied, with few expenses and small pleasures that repeated themselves in the accustomed order. The bond
between them was so strong that he had never married

and never would marry; he felt no need of it. No friends, no women, almost nothing to read, yet he was never bored. He took the same paper that his father had read. This sheet had changed its opinions three times, but he had never changed; he was always of the same opinion as his newspaper. Few curiosities, an automatic life! The best part of it, for the two of them, was their monotonous or wordless conversations, the expected unfolding of the same daily little acts and rites. They had no intense desires—except for this intimacy which had become a cherished habit. Nothing must occur to disturb it! Things must change as little as possible! They must think as little as possible! Let them only remain together in peace! . . .

And this modest wish was not granted them. The war, the order for departure, had come to separate them. She sighed and hastened to get ready his belongings. They did not protest. Might made right. Mighty Force had spoken.

The Cailleuxs were on the floor above Annette. On the floor below were the Bernardin family, father, mother, two sons and two daughters, Catholics and Royalists from the Midi, from Aquitaine.

The father was a magistrate, a corpulent, thick-set little man, as hairy as a wild boar, with a short, thick beard that engulfed his face. He was lively and hot-tempered and stifled when he was shut in, for he had been born a jovial countryman. City life suffocated him to the bursting-point. He liked to dine well and was full of Gallic laughter, but the least opposition flung the old boar, stamping, with lowered snout, into transports of rage that were as brief as they were violent. For he would sud-

denly remember his office or the confessional and, cutting
short a roar in the middle, he would control himself and
resume his unctuous manner.

The younger of the two sons, who was twenty-two, had
just begun his law studies. He affected a small, pointed
beard, the shrewd, thin-lipped smile, the weary eyes and
the equivocal glance of the end of the sixteenth century.
He was really a very good boy who longed to possess the
perverse air of one of the darlings of Monsieur d'Eper-
non's company. The other son, who was twenty-eight,
with a round, smooth-shaven face and hair flung back
artistically and draped in heavy masses, with strands like
waves, *à la Berryer*, had begun to distinguish himself as a
barrister in the "Camelots" trial. When the King returned, he was to be made Keeper of the Seals.

The three women, the mother and the daughters, re-
volved in the background. (Annette was to know them
later.) Self-effacing, reading little, always at home,
never going to the theater but often to church, they spent
their time in pious works.

The three men had received a strict, solid, classical education. . . . *"Rome, the sole object."* [1] It was easier for
them to discourse in Latin than it would have been to ask
their way outside their own country in English or German. They would not have condescended. It was for the
Northern Barbarians to understand their tongue. They
lived in the ideal of the past. Good Christians, all three
of them, they admired unreservedly the paganism of
Maurras: he was such a good Roman. They were light-
hearted, high-livers, and, when they were alone with men,
not above a risky story or two. When the family were
gathered together, the six of them all went to mass, and

[1] Corneille: Horace.

it was a most edifying spectacle. Their horizon was narrow, but very clearly defined, like those French land-
scapes, with their sharp, well-coördinated lines, in which
the circle of hills has enclosed for centuries the unchanged,
little, old city. The parish of Paris is itself a provincial
town. Its inhabitants feel no ill-will for what lies beyond
their walls; merely, without enquiring, *a priori*, a little
irony. They ignore it. They live for their own little
circles. And above there is God, the arch of the sky where
the bells of Saint-Sulpice ring in their white towers.

But when the government of the Republic demanded
the two sons, to feed their flesh to the enemy's machine
guns, none of them objected: the "Young Hussy" had
become sacred. The six of them disliked the idea, but
they did not show it. They knew that one must render
unto Cæsar the things that are Cæsar's. God is not too
exacting. He is satisfied with the soul. He gives up the
body. He doesn't even claim any rights over action. The
intention is enough for him. And Cæsar profits by it.
He takes everything.

On the second floor Monsieur Girerd, a professor of law
and for several years past a widower, lived with his son.
He was of a very different sort, though he, too, came
from the Midi. He was a Protestant from Cévennes.
He considered himself a free-thinker (an illusion that is
shared by more than one mortar-board-covered head of
our University). But he had his notions, as the young
Bernadin said, laughing among themselves at his ungainly
air and that severe face, like the face of one of Coligny's
preachers. A very worthy man, very strict in his duties
and full of moral prejudices—the worst of all because
they have no pity. With all the esteem he felt for his

neighbors upstairs and his somewhat stiff but unfailing courtesy, he paid them back, as the saying is, in their own coin. In spite of his sincere desire to be impartial, Catholicism seemed to him a blemish, a deformity, which, whatever they might do, marred forever even the best of men. He had no hesitation in seeing in it the cause of the decline of the Latin nations; and yet he was a scrupulous historian who carefully avoided any sort of passion in what he said and wrote, at the risk of appearing cold and tedious—as he was, indeed, in the lectures, heavily documented, bristling with references and spangled all over with notes, which he intoned monotonously through his nose. Even so, although he was unaware of it, his historical criticism was falsified by preconceived ideas so self-evident to him that he never noticed them and by a total lack of plasticity that prevented him from adapting himself to any other way of thought. This widely read man, deeply experienced in books and considerably experienced in life, had preserved under his gray hairs a depth of ingenuousness that was comic, touching—and terrifying, for it authorized all sorts of fanaticism. A very high moral sense, an atrophied psychological sense. Those who differed from him were beyond his understanding.

His son was like him. He was a young doctor at the Sorbonne who, at thirty, had just sustained a remarkable thesis, but who saw the world through the spectacles of ideas. His own, of course. The glasses ought to have been verified by an optician, though this had never occurred to him. For him, as for his father, the "first thing" was never a fact. "*The first thing is the principle.*" The Republic was a principle. The advantages won by the first Revolution were as demonstrable as a theorem. And the war that was beginning was the necessary conse-

quence of the demonstration. It was to establish Peace
and Democracy in the world. They never stopped to
think that perhaps it would be better to start by preserv-
ing this peace. They never questioned that those who had
broken it were backward peoples who refused to see and
accept the truth. It was necessary, therefore, to force
them to accept it, for their own good as well as for the
good of the world.

These two men, father and son—they seemed like older
and younger brother—who resembled and loved each
other, tall and erect, thin and proud, were enveloped in
an ideology that would not admit so much as a hair's
breadth of doubt. In all good faith, their science was
placed at the service of their democratic faith. Their faith
was their conscience, and they had no other. They believed. They believed. They would have believed at the
stake. (The son indeed was going to be at the stake, in the
trenches; and the father was going to be there, in thought,
suffering with him.) . . . They believed. . . . And
these men pretended that they were free-thinkers! . . .

Young Girerd was engaged to Lydia Murisier, a
charming, spirited girl who belonged to a rich Genevese
family. She had fallen in love with him and he—reli-
giously—with her. Lydia's love was not particularly religious, in fact it was quite profane, but in order to resemble
him she strove to make it so, just as her laughing blue
eyes strove to appear serious. And profane Lydia would
have remained from the very depths of her nature, which
demanded of life only such natural joys as earth, air and
water, all the seasons, good health, sunshine and the love
of her beloved—if only the beloved had not sought his
life's happiness outside of life, among ideas. She strove
to find her own there with him. And so this little Swiss

who, left to herself, would have had no reason for taking
sides in the quarrel of the nations, meekly learned by
heart the French republican catechism, the Revolution of
the year I and the Rights of Man in arms,—the faith of
her fiancé. . . . Ah, if she had listened to her own instincts how she would have carried him off in her arms,
safe from the mêlée! How anxious this war made her!
How far it was from her way of thinking! But she reproached herself for all this, since her beloved saw and
judged otherwise: she was weak, she was mistaken. To
be worthy of him she must shut her eyes. . . . Oh, my
love, I long to believe. Since you believe, I believe. . . .

Clarisse Chardonnet refused to believe—the only one
in the house who did. She was Annette's neighbor, on
the same landing. No, no! Her love was not the sort
of love that sacrifices itself, that sacrifices the beloved to
the false faith of the beloved. . . . Even that would not
have been true! He did not believe; he had merely a
quite human respect for and fear of public opinion. He
was an ordinary enough bank clerk, an attractive boy, a
handsome boy, with delicate fair mustaches and pale,
somewhat lusterless eyes. The affairs of the world, bank-
ing, politics, even—let us admit it—his country, were
absolutely, completely immaterial to him. The only
thing in the world for him was this little woman whom he
had taken—or had she taken him?—three months before.
What months! . . . They could never have enough of
them. Their hands, clasped together, trembled when they
recalled the nights they had passed. How she held him,
this passionate creature! . . . A little Parisian working
girl, who adored him like a god, a god who belonged to
her, her treasure, her plaything, her darling, her pet ani-

mal, her soul, if she had one, her heart's heart, her everything, her own private property! . . . She was a bru-
nette, thin, frail, feverish, with velvet eyes and lips like a
scarlet line in her pale face that she painted so carefully.
Passion had sucked all the blood from it. And he oblig-
ingly allowed himself to be adored. He was not surprised; he abandoned himself to this ravenous creature.
Each in turn became the other's prey. Neither of them
dreamed that the game must end. Life had no other
meaning for them. . . .

But when the war came for him, he rose without protest. It was no cheerful matter and he was far from
courageous. He could have wept for what he was leaving
and what he was going to meet. But he was afraid of
being ridiculed and scorned if he allowed his weakness to
be seen. It was not manly to love too much. She understood and cried out to him:

"Coward, coward!"

Then she sobbed.

He bridled and sneered angrily:

"Coward! That's certainly the right word for a man
who is about to be a hero! 'To die for his country!'"

She begged him to stop. The funereal phrase terrified
her. Then she begged him to forgive her. It was a fine
chance for him to display his glittering patriotism, a means
of bolstering up his own courage. And she dared to protest no longer. She was too alone, she could not say what
she was thinking. The whole world (which was nothing)
and he himself (who was everything) would have called it
heresy. But she was well aware that secretly, deep in his
heart, the unhappy youth thought as she did. . . . "To
die for one's country?" No, no—for the gallery! . . .
Men were cowards! They hadn't the courage to defend

their happiness.　Poor things, poor things!　She wiped
her eyes.　They were before the footlights.　She had to
smile, since he wished it; she could cry later in the wings.
. . . Yes, you too! . . . You don't deceive me.　You,
too, feel death in your heart.　O coward, coward, why are
you going?

And he, who was reading her mind, thought aloud,
"What is one to do?"

But she was a woman and a passionately devoted
woman.　She could not understand.　She could not grasp
what was troubling him. . . .

"What are you to do?　You should stay behind."

He shrugged his shoulders, discouraged.

Ah, the whole world was against her!　The world was
against him too.　But she was angry with him for admit-
ting that the world was right.　He submitted.　Why? . . .

The two workmen in the attic submitted also: Perret
(saddlery and leather-work) and Peltier (electrical in-
stallation).　They were ready to march against war, but
since no one marched against it they had to march with it.
No other choice was left.　They were socialists who had
set out from the same conviction.　But when you set out
you draw apart, and they were no longer both at the same
stage.

Only eight days before, Perret had been unshakable in
his belief that there would be no more wars.　"That's all
newspaper nonsense, the bluff of those poker-players,
those diplomats and ministers over their gaming-tables.
If any of those traders in peoples come for us, we'll haul
them up short.　You can reckon on us, us of the Internationale,—Jaures, Vaillant and Guesde, Renaudel, Viviani
and all the syndicates.　The iron division.　And then all

the comrades on the other side of the wall, the German ones. . . . Listen here, Peltier!   Just these last few days we (our men) have had a meeting with their men.   Everything is arranged and the password has been given out. If those blackguards ever risk mobilization we shall carry out ours, with our arms crossed!   . . ."

But Peltier laughed and, whistling in his beard, said to Perret:

"You are young, comrade!"

Perret lost his temper.   He had passed his thirty-seventh year, and thirty-seven years of hard work are worth fifty of these do-nothings.   But Peltier calmly replied:

"Exactly!   You have worked too hard.   You have not had time to think."

And as Perret still protested, passing on to him, still warm, the article he had just read in the last number of his paper, the only paper that lied according to his particular bent, Peltier shrugged his shoulders and said wearily:

"When it's only a question of talking!   . . . But when it's a question of acting!   They'll all march off."

They all had marched off.   When Jaurès fell, as a bull falls at the blow of a cowardly, concealed matador, there had taken place all through stricken Paris those sombre funeral rites, those speeches and speeches, that rain of speeches about the man who could no longer speak for himself.   They were all there, those who wept for the man in the coffin, and those who thought: "He is better off there. . . ."

But the masses that awaited the oath of vengeance, the command that would shatter their anguish, the lightning in the darkness?   From all these mouths that poured forth their mortuary eloquence nothing came but death and renunciation.   They said:

"We swear that Jaurès shall be avenged."

But before the words were fully uttered they had betrayed him; they had become the agents of the war that murdered him. They told the people:

"Go out and kill! Let us form the *Union Sacrée* over the bodies of our brothers!"

And their comrades in Germany said the same thing.

The masses, bewildered, were silent, and before long they quieted down, they fell into step. Mere reasoning was not their business. Since those whom they trusted to reason in their place, since their guides were leading them to war, they had to go. And Perret now persuaded himself that he was going to serve the cause of the people and the Internationale. After the war, the Golden Age! The pill had to be gilded somehow. And Peltier, disillusioned, said:

"Just watch it coming! I'm fed up with the cause of the people. I'm going to try to look after my own. The best thing is to do what they are doing"—he was thinking of the bigwigs of Socialism, who had backed down— "come to terms."

Peltier came to terms.

From the attic to the cellar there were no violent feelings in the house. They were angry at the Germans for being the aggressors. (For of course they were! This was never discussed, since every one knew it!) They did not like war, but they were resolved to give those fellows a lesson. And from the depths of their grief, as they writhed in silence, with their teeth clenched, the consciousness of their sacrifice awoke their enthusiasm. But hatred was not yet born.

The only trace of it, perhaps, was in Ravoussat (Numa)

the wood and wine merchant on the ground floor. This
big, thick-chested, round-shouldered man who dragged his
gouty feet around in muddy shoes talked a great deal
about the Boches, spitting out curses; and he envied his
son Clovis, who was going to slit the bellies of those
sausages. The boy was delighted; it was a picnic. He
was going to get beer and Gretchens over there. They
laughed, they shouted. . . . But one could see the anxiety this big man was stifling with all his shouts, his anger
at the risks to which he was forced to expose his son, his
only son. . . .

"Suppose he were . . . Suppose they did . . . Good
heavens, suppose they went and killed him for me!"

No matter. Throughout, the atmosphere of the house
was full of dignity, without fury and without weakness,
full of a religious and virile acceptance. They showed
their confidence, reaching out, like an arc, to the unknown
God. Whatever troubles they had they kept to themselves.

Have I visited them all? Have I forgotten no one in
my tour of the house?

Ah, yes. On the fifth floor, in the little apartment next
to the Cailleux, that young writer, Joséphin Clapier,
twenty-nine years old, with a bad heart, who had been
discharged from service. He kept in his burrow. His
instincts warned him to stay out of sight. At the moment
people were pitying him. But pity is a loan which it is
better not to abuse. And Clapier was prudent. His conscience was not at ease. Downstairs there was that spying
eye, Brochon, who has not been mentioned. It was difficult to avoid seeing him, however, as he was the concierge's husband. He was a police agent, and he was not

called out because his eyes and his fist were needed at home. His work kept him out of the flood, on the banks. He was none the less a warrior, for he watched over suspects and enemies in the rear. But for his own house he had a fatherly regard. Its spirit was good, it did him credit. He showed a special indulgence towards the tenants. Duty, however, came before everything, and he kept his eye on Clapier. Clapier was a pacifist.

And this is really the end. We have finished our review with the house watch-dog. We have entered everywhere, except on the first floor. The first floor is shut up. The first floor is sacred. It belongs to the proprietor. And Monsieur and Madame Pognon, rich, old and bored, are away on their vacation. They received their rent in July. They are coming back in October.

A quarter of a year will have passed.

And a million lives.

*

* *

The eight warriors had gone, those who were left held their breath as if to listen to their far-away footsteps. The streets were full of noise, but in their hearts, over the house, lay night and tragic silence.

Annette was calm. This did her no credit, for she was risking nothing. She knew it and was humiliated by it. If she had been a man she would undoubtedly have gone, without a moment's hesitation. Would she have been as firm if her son had been five years older? . . . Who knows? She would have said that the mere thought was unfair to her. She was the sort of woman to blush with anger at herself and regret that she could not cast herself and all she loved into the struggle. She might have regretted, yes, perhaps. But would she have cast her son in? Truly? Was she sure of that? We must appear to believe her. If it had been denied, she would have frowned like an offended Juno. But when the young lad happened to pass near her she had to restrain herself in order not to catch him passionately in her arms. He was hers. . . . She held him. . . .

Whatever possibilities for action slept in her, she was not called upon to act. For the moment she and her son were safe. Fate had granted her respite for observation. She made the most of it. She looked on boldly and freely, for no ideology disturbed her. Up to this moment she had never concerned herself with the problems of war and peace. For nearly fifteen years she had been entirely occupied in the immediate struggle, the struggle for bread, and an even fiercer struggle, the conflict with herself. That had been the real war, renewed every day, and the truces that had been signed had been indeed merely scraps of paper. As for war outside, state politics had been very remote from Annette. The Third Republic, or rather— for this ineffectual régime never said *yes* without also saying *no* and extolled alternately dry powder and the dry olive-branch—the good fortune of Europe, of which Europe was unworthy, had maintained an uninterrupted peace for forty years (Annette's forty years) during which a whole generation had seen war only as something faraway, shadowy, as a piece of theatrical scenery or an idea, as a romantic spectacle or a theme for moral and metaphysical discussion.

With her whole attitude of mind tranquilly colored by that standard scientific education of the period before relativity had come to shake the foundations of everything, Annette was accustomed to accept the established fact as an order of phenomena which is given once for all and regulated by laws. War formed part of the laws of nature, and it had never seriously occurred to her to oppose them. They did not spring from the heart, or even from the reason, but they ruled men and women, and one had to accept them. Annette accepted war as she accepted death, as she accepted life. Among all the wants that we have received from nature, along with the wild, enigmatical gift of life, war is not the most absurd—perhaps not even the most cruel.

And as for her country, Annette's feeling was in no way exceptional. It was not very ardent, but she did not question it. In her everyday life, she had never thought of displaying it or examining it. It, too, was a fact.

But during these first hours when the war struck upon it as the hammer strikes the bell in the clock-tower, it seemed to Annette like a part of herself, a vast, engulfed

province that stirred from its sleep. And her first feeling
was one of expansion. She had been shut up in the cage
of her own individualism. Now she escaped and stretched
her cramped limbs. She awoke from the sleep of her
isolation. She became a people. . . .

And she felt in herself all the movements of a people.
. . . From the first, she was dimly aware that a great door
in her soul, a door that was usually closed—the temple of
Janus—was opening. . . . Nature was unveiling naked,
elemental forces. . . . What was she going to see?
What was coming forth? . . . Whatever it was, she was
ready, she was waiting, she was in her element.

Most of the souls that surrounded her were not made
for this torrid life. They were in a ferment. Before the
first week of August was over they had caught the fever.
It ravaged these defenseless organisms. Their skin became mottled with the flushes of a blood that had been
vitiated by the sudden inrush of acrid and pestilential ele-
ments. The sick became silent, absorbed. They shut
themselves up in their rooms, and the epidemic smol-
dered.

Annette was calm. She was the only one in her circle
whose balance was not destroyed. In fact, she became
more normal than ever. Dreadful as it is to say it, she
breathed at ease. She was probably like those women,
those mothers, in the days of the Great Invasions. When
the waves of the enemy began to beat against the palisades
of their movable city, they mounted their chariots and
rushed to its defense, and their naked breasts breathed
more easily in the wide air of the plains. Their hearts,
beating slowly and powerfully, longed for the struggle,
the smother and spray of the attacking waves of enemies;
and they embraced the ravaged fields, scarred by the

wheels of their chariots, embraced the horizon, the darkened circle of the forests, the supple lines of the hills, and the dome of free heaven that awaits free souls.

Annette, from her chariot, looked about and recognized: "This is the way it is. . . ."

As India says: *"And this is you, my child."*

The circle of the world was filled by her spreading soul. She recognized herself in it. "They are myself, these feverish souls. . . . I, these hidden forces, these naked demons, these sacrifices and these cruelties, this enthusiasm and this violence, these accursed and hideous powers that are rising from the depths . . .

"What is in the others is in me. I was in hiding; now I am discovering myself. I used to be only a shadow of what I really am. Until now the dream has filled my days and the real has existed in my repressed dreams. But this is the real now. The world at war . . . Myself . . ."

How express in words the inexpressible that swelled like must in the wine-vat, the silence and thoughts of this Bacchante's soul? This rising effervescence which she watched and inhaled—this calm vertigo . . .

A terrible drama was being played, and she was one of the players. But the time had not come for her to go on the stage; she was ready, but she had not been called. She could watch the torrent of action. She breathed this unique moment. Her glance was drowned in the current as she leaned over it, but she clung to the bank, waiting for the cue that would tell her:

"Your turn! Fling yourself in!"

*

* *

The torrent roars and rises. The dams are broken down. The flood is everywhere. Defeat, massacre, villages in flames. In fifteen days, Occidental mankind had plunged back fifteen centuries into the past. And now, as in the ancient times, came whirlwinds of people, torn from their native soil, fleeing before the invasion. . . .

The interminable exodus of refugees from the north flung themselves upon Paris like a rain of ashes, the precursor of waves of lava. Day after day the Gare du Nord, like a gutter, poured forth its mournful flood. Muddy and weary, they piled up in great sordid masses along the sides of the Place de Strasbourg.

Annette, who was without work, and devoured by a need to spend her unused energy, passed through these human herds, these heaps of weariness that were shaken, every now and then, by outbursts of cries and violent gestures, and her heart leapt with indignation and pity. Among this multitude of unknown unfortunates, where she floundered out of her depth, she wanted to find some being upon whom she could fasten her myopic eyes and her passionate desire to help.

She had scarcely entered the station when she saw, in a recess of the wall between two pillars—she instinctively chose a group, two figures—a man stretched on the ground and a woman seated beside him, holding his head on her knees. Worn out, they had dropped down close to the entrance as soon as they had left the train. The flood of passers-by brushed against the seated woman, who formed a rampart between them and the prostrate man. She let them trample her; she had eyes only for this face with its closed lids. Annette stopped and, sheltering her with her body, leaned over to look at her. She could see only the back of the neck, milky-white and robust, a shock of thick red hair, covered with dirt and trickling with perspiration, and hands that pressed the waxen cheeks of the man stretched on the ground. A man? A young boy of eighteen or twenty, who was at the end of his strength. At first Annette thought he had just died. Then she heard the woman repeating tumultuously, in her heavy, passionate voice: "Don't die! You shan't die! . . ."

And her hands, spotted with mud and bruises, fingered the eyes, the cheeks, the mouth of the motionless mask.

Annette touched her shoulder. She did not turn around. Annette, kneeling down beside her, pushed away her fingers so as to touch the boy's face. The woman did not seem to notice her presence. Then Annette said: "He is alive. He must be saved."

At this the woman clutched her and cried: "Save him for me!"

Looking directly at her, Annette saw a face peppered with freckles, composed of vigorous planes and curves, whose most striking features were a red mouth and a short nose, the line of which formed, with the prominent lips, a sort of muzzle. Ugly, a low forehead, prominent cheek and jaw bones. But the mouth was exacting, and that mass of red hair made the top of her head look like a tower as it rested on the narrow forehead. Only later one noticed the large, blue, Flemish eyes, the fleshy face.

Annette asked: "But he isn't even wounded?"

The other woman sighed: "We have been walking for days and days. He's all in."

"Where do you come from?"

"From Comines, way up in the North. They came

there, they set fire to everything. I killed them. . . .
I took down the gun from the farm-house wall and shot
at the first one from behind the hedge. We ran away.
Whenever we stopped running to breathe, we could hear
their feet galloping behind us. They were coming like a
steam-roller, the whole sky was black with them. Like a
hail-storm coming up . . . We ran and ran. . . . He
fell. . . . I carried him."

"Who is he?"

"He is my brother."

"We must get out of this dust. They are stepping on
us. Stand up! Do you know anybody in Paris?"

"I don't know a soul. And I have nothing. Everything is destroyed. We fled without any money, without
a stitch of clothing except what we have on."

Annette did not hesitate. "Come with me."

"Where?"

"To my house."

They lifted the prostrate man, the sister taking his
shoulders, Annette his legs. They were both strong and
the wasted body was very light. In the square they found
a litter: an old workman and a boy offered to carry him.
The sister insisted on holding her brother's hand; she got
in the way of the porters and jostled against the passers-
by. Annette linked arms with her. Whenever the
stretcher shook and swayed she could feel the woman's
fingers twitch, and when the porters laid their burden
down for a moment she knelt down beside it on the pavement. She passed her hands over her brother's face with
a flood of rude, caressing words, partly Flemish, partly
French.

They reached the house. Annette installed them in the
dining-room. The Bernadin family loaned the brother

a bed and they made another couch on the floor with Annette's mattress.   They undressed the sick boy, who had
never regained consciousness, and called a doctor.   Before
he arrived the sister, who had refused to rest, fainted;
and for fifteen hours she slept like a log.   Annette
watched.

Her eyes went from one mask to the other: the one
drawn and waxen, as if he might die at any second, the
other violent, swollen, her mouth wide open, breathing
in her throat: gusts of incoherent words came from her.
And Annette dozed in the silence of the night, watching
over these two slumbers, the slumber of death and the
slumber of delirium.   And she trembled, asking herself
why she had brought under the roof of her house this
torch of madness.

*
*   *

Hitherto there had been no relations whatever between the various apartments. The most any one had known had been the names of their neighbors. The first weeks of the war brought them together. These small separate provinces flung down their custom-barriers and united to form a common nation. For once their hopes and fears were mingled. They no longer passed without speaking when they brushed by one another on the stairway. They learned to look into one another's faces and began to discover one another. They exchanged a few words. Their suspicious individualism no longer opposed its reserve of vanity and pride to questions that engrossed every one: news of those who had gone and of the great threatened parent, the nation. When the postman was expected, a small group formed at the foot of the stairs and each lonely anxiety warmed itself in the mutual confidence. The spirit of compliance, which knows equally well how to create and to forget its prejudices when it chooses, tactically dropped for a time those that had served to bar out their neighbors. Monsieur Girerd had a word now for Monsieur Bernadin. And the Bernadin ladies, pious, kindly but timorous souls, responded to Annette's advances with obliging smiles. They had decided to forget for the present their doubts regarding their enigmatical neighbor and her perhaps irregular maternity. They had not become any more sympathetic or any more tolerant than they had been the day before. But what they would not accept, they pretended to ignore.

Little Madame Chardonnet alone shut herself up in her grief and refused to notice the affectionate glances of Lydia Murisier, who divined the torment she was in and was ready to mingle with it her own sorrow and her own hope.

From the top to the bottom of the house, they were all in the same boat, and the typhoon was coming. Danger made them all equals.

What if the whole world were threatened! (It was going to be.) All the peoples were going to become Humanity at last in their struggle with Nature. But two conditions were necessary: first, that no one would have a chance to escape without the others, and, secondly, that all should have one chance of escaping from the danger; for if there were no such chance man would abdicate at once. For many years these conditions had never occurred simultaneously. They had done so this time.

The great German rush was beating almost against the walls of Paris. The government had decamped. Every one in the house expressed indignant scorn for the flight to Bordeaux. Sylvie was furious. She made one think of her grandmothers in the days when King Louis took to his heels. It would not have been good for our heroes of Château-Morgaux if they had come within reach of her scissors! Aunt and nephew, Sylvie and Marc dug and pushed wheelbarrows about the earthworks that Gallieni had ordered to keep the feverish Parisians busy. There was no panic. They waited, hoping for the best, ready for the worst. Marc caressed his famous revolver in his pocket; he was quite capable of hoping the Germans would enter Paris so that he might try it. Annette, her hands burning, but calm in her manner, had never felt better in her life; at last she knew the risk she and her son were running.

The others felt likewise. The anguish of the parents

was relieved by the thought that they were associated in some degree with the danger of their sons.

Lydia Murisier came to Annette's apartment to read her fiancé's letters. The two women had been attracted to each other before they had exchanged a word. Annette had caught the secret song of the spring in the meadow, the hidden spring that was ashamed to show itself. And Lydia had seen in her tender smile, like that of a big sister, that she understood this music—she alone in the house—and it was sweet to her to be understood. But the two women never spoke of this music of the heart. It was out of place, amid all this noise of arms, to listen too much to the melody of their days of peace, the flute that bewailed their lost happiness. Lydia read the letters of her beloved, which spoke of the exalted duty of the soldiers of civilization. The young stoic admitted her to this frozen radiance, and the enamoured Lydia bathed in it with a shivering joy. The warmth of her breast melted the snow of his ideas. She was still a child, and the austere sacrifice was gilded with illusion; for her, heroism, also, was still half a game. She knew it was dangerous, but she believed, she wished to believe, in the protection of a god, of her god, who watched over her love. (Did not her love and her god wear the same face?) She appeared confident, happy, and she laughed her good throaty laugh, as children do. Then suddenly she wept and would not say why. And Annette pitied her. She saw her exaltation in the burning thoughts she recited, all in one breath—until she stumbled and hesitated. (Had she not mistaken a word?) She apologized with a glance, with a confused, charming smile. And Annette wanted to take her into her arms and say to her:

"My child, what you are telling me is not the real you.

Place your forehead against my mouth!   When you are silent, I can hear your heart . . ."

But it was not best for her to hear it.   The child was right.   Let her recite the words she had learned and that brought forgetfulness!   Ideas put the heart to sleep.

The whole house was intoxicated.   The exaltation reached its peak during the days—the five days—when the battle of the nations was bursting forth.   The natural instincts of self-defense, of mutual help, glory, sacrifice, had found their full scope.   Then came the day when on the Place Notre Dame the crowd implored the help of the Maid.   And from the gallery of the cathedral the cardinal flung forth the word:

"Victory!"

*
* *

Then everything came to a stop. The first enthusiasm was broken. The soul fell back.

From October the action slackened. The supreme danger had passed. The thorn had been driven for so long into the flesh that it was beginning to fester. Life had to be organized on this basis for years. But who could face these years with a firm heart? People lied to themselves, they lied to one another. In order to sustain the exaltation they had recourse to factitious methods, the delusions, the atrocities of the press. (They were so, indeed, for the press welcomed them, invented them with a cannibalistic joy.) And the public was shaken like a drunkard in his stupor by outbursts of red hatred.

The house stewed in its own juice of suffering, irritation, impatience, boredom. The winter dragged along. The morbid fermentation of people's souls appeared in the dismal light.

The two refugees from the north, Apolline and Alexis Quiercy, had stayed on with Annette. She had taken them in for a few weeks, expecting that the brother would grow better and that they would find another lodging and employment. But they did not look about for them. It seemed to them quite natural that Annette should take them in, and they did not bother their heads about it. It was no concern of theirs whether Annette could afford it or not. They looked upon themselves as victims to whom the rest of France was indebted; and this went so far that at last Apolline complained of their quarters. They were cramped in the dining-room. She did not quite ask for Annette's room, but if it had been given her she would merely have said, "Thank you."

Marc was exasperated. This woman repelled him so much that she fascinated him.

They were strange guests. Alexis passed part of his days lying down. Apolline scarcely ever went out, and it was not easy to induce her to air the room. They stayed shut up, without moving. Alexis was of a torpid nature and his race in the August man-hunt had been too much for him. He had fair hair, close-growing and curly, a narrow rounded forehead, small, vague blue eyes, full lips, and a habit of breathing with his mouth open. He was like his sister, but she was the man of the family. Absorbed in his glassy revery, he spoke little; he browsed over his rosary, pulling the chaplet about. Prayers are cradles to rock the slumbering spirit. The brother and the sister were devout after their fashion. God belonged to them; they settled down upon this as they had upon Annette. It was for the others to oust them out. Inert but tenacious. Alexis covered himself with his crust. He left all movement to Apolline.

A brute energy slumbered in this girl. She kept it stifled for hours while she sat bending over her needle-work, across which her impatient fingers accurately flew. Then all at once she would fling the work aside, rise and stamp. She would begin to walk, walk, walk around the narrow space between the bed and the window; she would stop and shake her fist at the enemy; she would talk about scratching his eyes out with her nails; she talked and talked in a whining, groaning, threatening, lamenting voice, with monotonous repetition. And when she had finished she would fling herself suddenly on her brother's bed and strain him to her heart with a torrent of passionate words. He would mingle his own doleful and monotonous words with hers. At last, at last they would fall silent, and it seemed as if death were in the room.

Such neighbors were far from restful, but no one dared complain too much. They pitied them; they had to try to be patient with one another. Every one was suffering. These had endured more than their share. Before their escape, they had seen their old servant shot and the house burned, their invalid mother with it. The others could understand how their spirits must have been shaken by it. Annette, who was inured to anxieties and ordeals, felt herself obliged to endure this dull, heavy presence. Of them all, she was the only one with whom Apolline was willing to be companionable. Their relations went no further. That unbalanced nature passed without transition from a sudden hostility to a rough sympathy, only to fall back to its original starting point. During those rare moments when she became friendly she seemed to feel some traits of kinship with Annette's nature, though they were not traits that it pleased Annette to recognize. When the curtain fell again between them and separated them, she was relieved. But these moments of contact were rare. More often Apolline egoistically buried herself in the morass of her troubled and violent soul. A feverish odor rose from it.

Marc, like a young dog on a leash, had sniffed this odor with disgust, with attraction. He detested it and he spied upon it, and this atmosphere of mephitic passion weighed on Annette during nights of sleeplessness.

It was as if the damp breath of a swamp were filtering along the stairway and under the doors. On the same landing, next door to Annette, Clarisse shut herself up and shivered. She would not see any one; she was angry at the whole world. All her blood seemed to be stopped. She felt like the bark of a frozen tree that was turning to stone. Hardly would the warmth begin to return in gusts when word would arrive from the man who was gone. She would read it with dry eyes, her heart congealed. When he left her, he had stolen from her the sun of her nights. And after she had read the letter she would crumple it and hold it in a ball in her fist. But she would answer him with a short colorless note in which there was no sign of what she was suffering or what she would have liked to make him suffer. She did not pretend anything; she was one of those for whom writing seems made only to express what is about them—never what is in their depths—what they are doing, never what they are thinking, what they are. She never spoke of such things even to herself. To commune with her heart she had to feel her heart beating; and her heart was shriveled by the frost. Even her suffering was rigid. And her bitterness was like an iron bar.

But in the spring the ice melted. One day Marc heard her laugh. She was walking up and down in her bedroom, looking at herself in the mirror. They met her on the stairway. She was going out late and had got herself up tastefully. She was a Parisian girl, with an instinct for dress; the lines of her body were graceful and her movements supple as those of a cat. She was full of smoldering fire, though her eyes were cold. She passed noiselessly, avoiding any occasion for stopping. She merely bowed. If any one spoke to her she would answer briefly, with a polite reserve, and go on. She intended to have no exchange of mine and thine:

"I am going my way. You go yours."

She was always like a stranger; and people will forgive anything sooner than a refusal to eat from the same
plate. The young woman was surrounded by thoughts of
ill-will, but she was quite indifferent to them, and the
others were too busy to notice where she went. One
person only watched to see when she came back at night,
and his imagination was always at work: Marc. Always
he . . . He was surrounded! To the right and left of
his bed, these foolish virgins. Their burning bodies . . .
A wind of lust was blowing over Paris, and lust is the
sister of hate.

Hate may be chaste also. In the Bernadin family it was
associated with the *Man of Sorrow and Love*. The
"Prayer for Peace" which the Holy Father had addressed
to the Christian world had been hushed up by the State
and clergy. These two confederates were in agreement;
it was urgently necessary to modify the voice of the All-
High. The faithful were in revolt. The Gallic blood
boiled in their veins. Old Bernadin, pious but fiery,
thundered against the foreign pope. Fortunately, there
were holy men in France who camouflaged the Word . . .
—"Holy Father, Your Holiness enjoins us to pray for
peace. . . . Very well! We shall explain. . . . Your
will be done,—provided it is also our will! Peace, peace,
my brothers. . . ."
"Peace is victory," the vault of Notre Dame replied,
echoing the cardinal-archbishop.
And the gilded ceiling of the Madeleine said: "Peace,
Lord, the true peace, your peace—that is to say, our peace
—but not that other, the peace of the enemy whom we
wish to kill!" . . .
It was merely a matter of "definition."

In this way, Christian consciences were reassured. The Bernadin family declared itself well satisfied with the pope and his shepherds. In the old magistrate's heart there was an odd jumble of edification and malicious joy in having interpreted a text of the law contrary to the real meaning. His head, with its devout, obstinate eyes, bowed before the altar and a furtive laugh played through his rough beard.

"That was very well done. *Fiat voluntas tua!* Holy Father, they have been making game of you. . . ."

And Père Sertillanges made the poor women weep with ecstasy when they saw Christ as a "Poilu," with their sons, in the trenches of Gethsemane. Through a frightful transfiguration, the field of carnage was presented to their reddened eyes and terrified hearts as an altar on which, in a chalice of mud and gold, pain and glory, the sacrifice of the divine blood was celebrated.

The first to drink of it, to the very intoxication of despair, was that young mouth, made for kisses, of Lydia Murisier.

Her beloved had fallen, in the early days of September. For a long time she did not know it. In the confusion of those clashing troops that charged, retreated, charged again, with heads lowered against the wall of flesh, trampling the flesh of the dead, there was no time to reckon up these matters. Lydia, full of confidence, was still reading the letters of the living man when all trace of his substance had disappeared fifteen days before. The country was saved, and no one dreamed that its saviors were not. In October the sentence of death fell on the house. Its cruelty left room for no doubt. The statement of a comrade gave the day, hour and place. The sentence fell. In the house nothing seemed changed. Monsieur Girerd had locked himself in. If it had not been for the concierge, who knew everything, no one would have known anything. Lydia passed like a shadow. She was living with her father-in-law now. But the apartment seemed deserted. No sound came from it. Annette walked past the door and went down stairs. The silence strangled her; she dared not break it. . . .

She knocked. After some delay Lydia opened the door. In the shadow of the passage her features were invisible. The two women embraced each other without a word. Lydia wept silently, and Annette felt the tears from her burning lids dropping on her cheek. Lydia took her hand and led her into the bedroom. It was six o'clock in the evening, and the only light came from another room. Monsieur Girerd must be there, but nothing stirred. Annette and Lydia sat down, holding hands, and spoke in low voices. Lydia said:

"I am going this evening."

"Where are you going?"

"I am going to find him."

Annette did not dare to question her.

"Where?"

"Where my beloved is sleeping."

"What?"

"Yes, the battle-field is open now."

"But how can you, among all those thousands? . . ."

"He will show me. I know I shall find him."

Annette longed to cry out: "Don't go! Don't go! He is alive in you. Don't go and look for him in the odor of the slaughter-house."

But she realized that Lydia was no longer free. Annette touched her hands, but it was the dead man who held them. She said, "My poor child, couldn't I go with you?"

Lydia answered: "Thank you."

And pointing to the lighted door, "My father is coming with me."

They bade each other good-by.

That evening Annette heard descending the stairs the light step and the heavy step of the two who were setting forth.

Ten days later they returned, as quietly as they had gone out. Annette did not know it until, hearing the bell ring, she opened the door and saw Lydia on the threshold, in mourning, with her heart-broken smile. It was as if she were face to face with Eurydice who had come back without Orpheus. She put her arms about her, almost carried her into the room and shut the door. The little fiancée was only too anxious to tell her about her journey to the land of the dead. She did not weep. There was an exalted joy in her eyes which was even more heart-rending. She murmured:

"I found him. . . . He guided me. . . . We were wandering over the ruined fields, among the graves. We were tired and discouraged. . . . As we came near a little wood, it was just as if he had said 'Come' to me. . . . A little wood of scrub oaks. . . . It was full of blood-stained clothes, letters and rags. A regiment had been surrounded there. I went into it. I was led. Father said, 'What's the use? We've had enough. Let's go back!' I stooped down at the foot of an oak, at one side, and picked up a scrap of paper from the moss. I looked at it. My letter! The last he had opened! And his blood was on it. I kissed the grass. I lay down on the place where he had lain. It was our bed, and I was happy. I would have liked to sleep there forever. The air was full of heroism. . . ."

There was a despairing ecstasy in her smile. Annette did not dare to look at her any longer.

Monsieur Girerd seemed to have been turned to stone. Inflexibly he had taken up his work again. He spoke to no one, but in his course, in his lectures, in vehement articles he preached an implacable crusade. He worked himself up into a fury; he destroyed the soul of the enemy, he insulted it, cut it off from humanity. In the house every one bowed to him, but avoided him: his glance, as he passed, seemed a reproach to those who were still alive. They felt themselves obscurely guilty towards him. And their instinct to find a scape-goat gathered all its arrows of accusation into one sheath and aimed them at the man upstairs who had not gone.

Clapier (Joséphin), the man with heart-disease. Gun disease! The heart of a true Frenchman is always good enough to die with when the time comes for fighting. . . . But he was one of those people who had brought down on us the war and the invasion, one of those pacifists!

A gentlemanly boy, shy, a good writer, who only asked to live in peace with his pen and his books. Every time he leaned over the well of the stairway he breathed the odor of suspicion rising up it. As he went by, doors half-opened to watch him, but people pretended not to see him when he bowed. Brochon, squatting in his office, looked the other way but, once out in the street, Clapier would discover that Brochon was following thirty paces behind him. And on the landing of his own floor, he saw the jeering insults in the eyes of the workmen's wives.

He invented more than half of this, inventing was his

trade.   He had an imagination that bubbled like a glass of champagne.   He became terrified.   He lived alone, and estheticism is not enough to enable one to endure for long the isolation of thought.   One has to have a character for that, but this commodity isn't found at the bottom of an inkwell.   Fine words invite you to carry yourself well. But if you carry yourself badly, fine words invite you to lie.   They did not have too much trouble in adapting Clapier and his pacifism to the virile task demanded of them by the ferocious influence of the house.   He enrolled in the censorship bureau, and became a letter-opener.   He was not a bad fellow.   He wished no one any harm.   But as the weak, once they leave the path, always go farther than the strong, he became fired with an exaggerated zeal.   He denounced the conspiracies of pacifism. He tried unceasingly to force his former companions to come with him to Canossa.   A renegade is always ready to abjure in company.   Woe to any one who resisted him! The good boy with the soft hands felt the claws of the State growing on the tips of his fingers.   His short-winded heart beat like that of the great Corneille.   He became a Roman.   He was ready to sacrifice, if he had had any, his own relatives.

At this price he won the favor of Brochon.   But he never understood why good patriots like Annette turned their backs on him, as she did whenever she saw him afterwards.

*

* *

Annette was troubled. She had lost her first confidence. As the days, the months, went by, her uneasiness increased. She had too little work and too much time for thinking. And she became aware, all about her, of the monstrous spirit that was taking possession of these beings—the coarsest and the most charming. Everything was abnormal, vices and virtues alike. Exalted love, hatred, heroism and fear, faith and egoism and the whole sacrifice savored of sickness. And the sickness was spreading. No one was immune.

Annette was all the more struck by this because she did not attribute it to an accidental cause. She never dreamed of accusing any one's intentions, intrigues, responsibilities; she did not know *this* war, but she did know *war*. She did not see the battles, the councils; she did not see the face of the Beast, but she felt its poisoned breath on her face. More than ever, the war seemed to her a fact of nature (decomposition is natural in the same way that integration is organic), a pathological fact, a plague of the soul. And these very people, who were not in the habit of displaying their illnesses, exposed this one as if it were the Holy Sacrament: they made it appear "ideal" and "from God" as the meat in the butcher-shop is decked out with gilt and paper flowers. Not one of these thoughts, even the most sincere, was free from falsehood and servility in regard to the monster whose leprosy was ravaging them. Annette recognized the symptoms in herself. She, too, burned with these passions of murder and immolation, of everything the heart and the senses will not confess and the lying spirit surrounds with its

43

aureole. Her nights were given over to the heavy, criminal life of her dreams.

If it had merely concerned herself, Annette would not perhaps have reacted against the poison. This condition she shared with every one. She shared it as she shared danger. Why should she repel it? She would have endured it, haughtily, with disgust, merely refusing to gloss it over to herself. But she would have endured it if she had not seen its terrifying effects upon the one who was more precious to her than the light of her eyes.

Marc was infected much worse than his elders, for his flesh was more tender. Nothing that took place in the house or outside escaped him. His eyes and his ears, his sense of smell, his whole body, were like a sounding-board that caught the nervous waves radiating from these electrically charged souls. He had a disturbing instinct, more mature than his intelligence, that scented from afar the troubled dramas of people's consciences.

Long before the others, he had read, under the murky cloud, the destiny of his two neighbors, the brother and sister, read without understanding, but read to the bottom. Long before his mother he had grasped the metamorphosis that was taking place in Clarisse Chardonnet. Annette still took for granted the despair of the abandoned woman, when he saw the molting and the new plumage. He spied upon her through the partition. When she went out, he was there on the stairway to sniff her trail of musk. He noted the smallest transformation in her appearance and dress. If he had been her husband or her lover, he could not have been more interested. It was not that he was in love with her. But he was inflamed by a far from innocent curiosity. These souls, these bodies of women.

To find out what was in them! He guessed she was guilty even before she was. It only made her the more attractive. He would have liked to follow her—no!—to be inside of her— What was going on in that breast? To taste her desires, her secret tremors, her forbidden thoughts. His senses were still only half determined. Boy or girl? And he did not yet know if he wanted a girl in order to be one or to possess one.

One night he was returning rather late with his mother. He saw, he thought he saw, in the dimly lighted street . . . Clarisse going by with an escort. He exclaimed Ah! in surprise, lowering his eyes with a strange modesty, as if he didn't want her to know that he had seen her. Annette, who had heard his exclamation, asked him what he meant. He hastened to distract her attention. It seemed to him that it was his duty to protect Clarisse. But later he regretted that he had not looked at her more carefully. Was it really she? He was no longer sure. He devoured her. . . . Her? No, the unknown woman.

This obssession filled his nights. It streamed from this house, from the atmosphere of the city at war, as the mist rises from the warm land under the white-hot lid of a stormy sky. The waiting, the anxiety, the boredom, the mourning and death all fanned this desire. Clarisse was not the only possessed soul.

Perret's daughter did not come home any longer. Her father was not there, now, to keep an eye on the poachers; and when the game had been stolen the mother could think of nothing better than to weep and put the girl out of doors. Marc had lost none of this. Her name was Marceline. It was almost as if she had been himself. The brazen-faced little hoyden, with the mocking eyes, glancing from under her crinkled lashes, her nose slightly tilted, her little round chin, her prominent lips, pointed like the mouthpiece of a hautboy! He longed to enjoy them; but the mere thought of their contact against his own sent a shiver through him from his knees to his shoulders. When they met on the stairs, she called him by his first name and looked him so full in the face that he was disconcerted. But he assumed a bold manner to hide his agitation and called her Perette. She laughed, and they exchanged glances of understanding.

Peltier had no daughter. But his honor, if he looked at it that way, fared no better. His wife, a jolly gossip, buxom and wary, wore silk stockings and laced shoes. She had earned them. She worked in a factory,—but "Lightly come, lightly go." A proverb well suited to these days of warriors! He was a good patriot; so was Madame Peltier. She never deceived her husband except with the Allies. Was that doing him any harm? Why, she was fighting with him! So she said, and laughed. This robust Gauloise only half deceived herself. But good heavens! her poor husband was no worse off for her being better off! So much the worst for the absent! And so much the worse for what had been and for what was going to be! The present had a big mug. It took everything, demanded everything, was everything. And it was nothing. It was the abyss.

Marc was revolving in it. Foolish to worry about the future! The future? There might not be any. If you counted on that you would be taken in. Accept what came your way. Serve yourself at once; don't wait for any one to serve you. You have teeth, hands, eyes, a marvelous body that is as full of eyes as the tail of a peacock,—that takes hold of life through its pores. Take and take! Love and know, enjoy and hate! . . .

He ran about Paris, missing his classes, feverish, curious, disoriented. War, women, the enemy, desire— flaming Proteus with a thousand tongues. How many intoxicating drinks there were to lap up until nausea came! How many things to become excited over—until the moment when you fell back, overwhelmed, exhausted by life! It was very hard to keep an eye on the runaway colt. Every one was the prey of his own thoughts. It was a long time before Annette suspected anything. In her growing uneasiness, she could not remain with idle hands, and there were no more lessons to occupy her. The middle class were cutting down their budgets sharply by suppressing the wages of those useless creatures—the teachers. For several weeks Annette undertook night duty, as an assistant, in a Paris ambulance.

Marc made the most of it. He stole off and prowled about, his heart beating, sniffing around him, more occupied in seeing than in tasting, too inexperienced to dare, too proud to risk being laughed at by betraying his ignorance, his legs weary, his mouth dry, his hands hot. He came, went, returned, wandered about unceasingly. He would soon have been snapped up if, by chance, on the second night when he was going his rounds in a questionable bar, in company that was not for him, a hand, a small, firm hand, had not gripped his shoulder, and a voice half angry, half mocking had not said: "Well, what are you up to here?"

Sylvie, his aunt. . . . But what was she doing there? As he did not lack self-possession he asked: "And you?"

She burst out laughing, called him a "young scoundrel," imprisoned his arm under hers and said: "You are making me lose my evening, but duty before everything. I've got you. I'm going to take you home."

He protested in vain. She consented to walk about a little before returning. Aunt and nephew, side by side, flung sarcasms at each other. She understood quite well that the young animal was longing to run about but she had enough good sense to realize the danger of a precocious liberty.

"Do you think that you belong to yourself, little sucking calf? that you can dispose of yourself? Stop! You are our treasure. You belong to your mother. A museum piece to be kept under lock and key."

She joked and scolded him. And he, full of revolt, pawed the ground. He not free? Then why was she?

"Because I am married, my fine friend?"

This audacity took the wind out of his sails. She looked at him ironically. He wanted to be angry, but he laughed: "All right. I'm caught! But you are too. I caught you."

She laughed. Each of them was guilty, and they threatened each other with eye and finger. She took him home, but she did not betray him to Annette. She distrusted the authority of her elder sister and her seriousness. In her heart she thought: "You can't prevent a spring from running. Put a stone in front of it; it will only leap over it."

Suddenly Annette opened her eyes. She saw it was not good to leave the child alone in the nest. She gave up her job. Besides, she had become disgusted with that rush of women towards the wounded man—love mingled with pity, love in the blood, love of the blood!

"Don't feel superior. You have felt it too. . . ."

Of all hypocrisies this was the wildest. The civilized human beast seasons its ferocious instincts with an odor of falsehood. She breathed it in her child. He carried it in his clothes, in his hair, in the tender down on his skin. If only the odor of death had not had time to soak into his heart!

It was not merely this troubled awakening of puberty that frightened her, this assault of the senses, this wildness of the little faun that he could not conceal. A mother who understands life expects this hour; and if she does not see it come without emotion, she is not surprised. She watches and waits in silence—sadly, proudly, pityingly—she waits for the young male to pass through the necessary ordeal, to burst the sheath and complete the separation from the maternal body. But this hour, which in times of quiet can strike like the beautiful noon angelus in the country on an April day of love, rang out hoarsely in the tempest of these delirious people.

One evening, tired of labor and the day's errands, Annette had sat down in the Luxembourg Gardens. Her son happened to pass with some school companions. They stopped to talk in one of the paths. A clump of trees separated them from the bench on which Annette sat, invisible. She heard her son's eager, mocking voice extolling the days that were coming when they would give the Boches back two eyes for one and a whole jaw for a single tooth. These gamins were scenting before the feast the sweat and blood of the slaughtered animal; they played at being strong men without useless scruples and without weaknesses. Marc, boasting of his crimes, was saying:

"The Boches have been violating, burning, cutting people's throats. They have done well. We shall do better. War is war. It will be a great spree. Of course we'll talk about civilization in the papers, for the sake of the idiots. We'll civilize all right."

This met with approval. He was proud of his success. Then they all began to lick their chops over their future exploits—"the women and girls they were going to fecundate"—more's the pity—"with the noble sperm of the French." These youngsters did not know what they were saying. They were pretending to be men. Nor do men know any more what they are doing. They do it just the same.

It was like a blow in the face for Annette. The out-rage issuing from the laughing mouth of her boy struck her to the heart, to her entrails—*Feri ventrem!* It was to this she had given birth! This young wolf! "He didn't know. . . ." But wouldn't it be even worse when he did know? How was she going to snatch him from the vile call of the Jungle?

Then another day she heard him—this time to her face—shamelessly making fun of those panders of peace and war, the men of God and the Law. His sharp eyes had lost nothing of the heroic hypocrisy of the Girerds and the Bernardins, who, in order to win the game, cheated people with the *Cross* and the *Idea*. He had never be-lieved in them, he believed in nothing (for the moment). These children had taken a disgust for words, for the words that fell from grown-up lips, for the sticky tongues of their elders, *Justice*, the *Republic*, God, words, words, words. . . . Churchmen or laymen, they were all tarred with the same brush. . . . (Ah! that's a good one! They don't take me in!)

But instead of becoming indignant, Marc burst into laughter. He thought the trickery a good thing; he was in on the game. Idealism and religion were capital dust to throw into people's eyes, good asphyxiating gas. The one who was the greatest cheat was the strongest.

Good for us! We don't lack preachers, professors, charlatans of the Church, the Press and Parliament! It's a good thing to lie "for God, for the Czar, for the Fatherland!" (Michael Strogoff). Of all man's inventions, the finest is that of the Gods!

This schoolboy Machiavelli boastingly displayed the cynicism that amused him. Annette was indignant. It would have been better if she had remained calm. But he had touched her to the quick and she cried out indignantly: "Enough!"

Marc was astonished. "Why?"

"One doesn't make a joke of such things!"

He said slyly: "That's just what one does do."

"One dies for those things."

"Ah, I forgot that you belong to the period that swallowed all those things. I beg your pardon."

"And I don't give it to you," said Annette, whose anger was rising. "Stop your irony."

"It's my way of being serious," said Marc. He had an unpleasant look and a pinched smile at the corners of his lips. He went on: "I would have you notice that I am rendering homage to *those things*."

"That is what I don't forgive you," said Annette. "*Those things*, their God, their faith,—I don't believe in them. It is a misfortune. But I respect those who do believe. And when I see men scheming and cheating with their faith, that faith that is not my own—I am ready to defend it. I suffer for it."

Marc answered: "You waste your time. It is more practical to make use of it. It is a force, like human stupidity. Let's use it! Let's use it! Everything must be made to help towards victory. It's all right for me to make use of it—since I don't believe in it."

Annette lowered her head and, placing it close to his, looked him in the eyes. She said: "Don't force me to despise you."

Marc recoiled a step.

She stood there with her eyes full of irritation, her face thrust forward. She was once more Juno, the heifer, ready to charge, the Annette of former days. Her nostrils quivered, and she said roughly: "I can endure a great deal, the seven deadly sins, vices and even cruelty. But one thing, one thing I don't forgive, hypocrisy. To pretend to a belief one does not have, to lie to oneself and to one's ideas, to turn faith into a Tartuffe—it would be better never to have been born. On the day when I see you degrading yourself that way I will shake you from me as I shake the mud from my shoes. However bad, however low you may be, be true! I would rather hate you than despise you."

Marc was silent, choking. Both were trembling with anger. The hard words had lashed both his cheeks. He would have liked to lash back in turn, but his breath failed him. He had not expected such a storm. Mother and son stared at each other like enemies. But in spite of himself the son's glance fell. His eyes dropped, to hide the tears of rage that he repressed. He pretended to laugh, he exerted all his strength so that she should not see his weakness. She left him abruptly. He ground his teeth, he could have killed her!

Her words had branded him like a red-hot iron.

Annette had hardly gone out when she regretted her violence. She had thought she had mastered it, but the storm had been gathering for several months and she felt that this explosion would not be the last. Her words now seemed odious to her, and their brutality shamed her almost as much as they did him. She tried to win his forgiveness. When they found themselves together, she was familiar and tender, as if everything were forgotten.

But he did not forget. He kept her at a distance. He considered himself insulted, and to avenge himself, since she liked people to be frank, he affected to do and say everything that could wound her. "Ah! If you prefer cruelty? . . ."

He deliberately left about on his table letters or notes for his "Journal"—atrocious things about the war or the enemy, or bits of licentiousness. He watched for the effect on his mother's face. Annette suffered, discovered his game, and restrained herself, but a moment came when she exploded. He had his triumph. He said: "I'm being sincere."

One night, while his mother was asleep, he left his bed. He did not return until lunch time the next day. Annette had had time to go through all the degrees of anxiety, anger and pain. When he appeared she said nothing. They had luncheon. Marc, surprised, relieved, thought: "She's conquered!"

Annette broke the silence: "You ran off last night like a thief. I had confidence in you. I have lost it. That was not the first time you have abused it. Now I know it, I shan't lower myself or lower you by watching you day and night. You would use deceit and that would make you slyer than ever. I can't protect you here. The very air is sick, and you are not strong enough to resist it. For several months everything you have done and said has shown me that you are catching all the contagions. You will go away with me."

"Go where?"

"Into the country. I am applying for a position at a college."

Marc cried out: "No!"

He had lost all his fine assurance. He did not want to leave Paris and condescended to beg his mother. He laid his hand on hers, urging, coaxing her: "Don't insist on it!"

"It's already done."

He withdrew his hand, furious that he had humiliated himself to no purpose. Annette was already weakening. The least sign of tenderness overcame her. She said: "If you would promise me . . ."

He interrupted, dryly: "I shall promise nothing. In the first place you wouldn't believe me. You have just said so. You think I would deceive you. I should deceive you so little that I tell you to your face, I shall do it again. You haven't the right to prevent me."

"Indeed!" said Annette. "I haven't the right to watch over your nights?"

"No one is less qualified than you to lay down the law to me. My nights, my life, are my own."

He had said a terrible thing. Did he know what he had said? Annette turned pale, Marc also. Both had been more violent than they had meant to be. But perhaps their violence did not exceed that savage spitefulness of instinct that knows the blows it is dealing and deals them deliberately. Those terrific, silent passages at arms; the hand strikes before the brain has calculated, and through a tacit convention, no one says "touched." But the blow has gone home and the soul begins to fester.

From this moment onward every word of discussion only increased the distance between them. Annette saw the boy's faults too baldly and humiliated him over them. Consequently he boasted of them and denied that she had any authority. That imperious tone, that mortifying severity would have driven him to say or do any insanity. He refused to yield. Annette put the decision up to him; he could go with her into the country or she would shut him up in a Paris lycée as a boarding pupil. He cried out in anger. This absolute power that was used against him seemed to him abominable. And in a fury, through animosity, he chose to be shut up.

"Which do you prefer?"

"Anything, so long as I am not with you."

A harsh farewell. There was hatred between them. But love was at the bottom. Love drunk with bitterness. Wounded love that suffered, bled and wished to avenge itself. . . .

PART II

THE decimated University was having recourse to women. Annette, duly armed with her two licensed diplomas, had been appointed to a boys' school in a village of central France.

She left in the early days of October, 1915. How lovely the autumn was! At the long stops that the train made among the fields the thrushes were to be heard piping among the vines; and the calm rivers, wandering over the meadows, seemed to carry in their hands their long trains bordered with golden leaves. She knew the country and the people, their nonchalant speech with a breath of irony passing over it. It seemed to her that she had been delivered from the plague-stricken Soul she had fled from, and she reproached herself with not having torn her son away also.

But it was not long before she found it again. Across these rich, sleepy provinces the shadow of the storm was creeping. At this moment furious battles were taking place in Artois and Champagne, and convoys of prisoners were being brought back to the rear.

As she passed through one of the stations, Annette saw, not far from the depot, a crowd pressing noisily about the fence around a wood-yard. They had been penned up there like cattle for several hours or days—a herd of Germans whom they had been carting about for nearly a week, without any too clear idea as to where they were taking them or when they would arrive. There were so many other things to think of. The entire population of

the little town, men, women and children, had rushed to
see the animals in their cage. One would have said it
was a passing circus. A free spectacle. The prisoners,
broken with fatigue, were falling on the gravel. Most of
them, silent, half-conscious, looked mournfully about the
circle of jeering eyes that peered at them through the
slits in the enclosure; jovial jaws threw jets of saliva at
them. A few of them had fever. They were beaten
dogs, ashamed, frightened, full of hate and trembling.
The cold nights and the rain had brought on dysentery.
They relieved themselves on a dunghcap in a corner of the
enclosure, in plain sight. Every time they did so, an
enormous laugh roared up from the spectators. One
could hear the shrieks of the women and the sharp cries
of the children. Striking their thighs, beating their
haunches, half-doubled over with laughter, they displayed
their gaping jaws in their transports of delight. This was
not wickedness; it was a total absence of human feeling.
The animal was amusing itself. . . . The laughter of a
crowd in a merry mood is always bestial; and this was
horribly so. On both sides of the palisade nothing remained but the gorilla. The man had disappeared.

As she climbed back into her carriage, Annette stared
with fascinated disgust at the hairy jaws of her neighbors
and the fair down on their arms.

This obsession pursued her during her first days in the
old school where she had come to teach in a sort of hole
of a Jardin des Plantes. . . . "Jardin des Plantes!"—
what irony! The smallest tuft had been rooted out of
the soil which was as yellow and rough as the desert of
Toledo. In the long court, which you entered through a
gate like the wicket of a guillotine and which was strangled
by four prison walls with blear-eyed windows, a single
tree, an old plantain, puny, sickly and twisted, had man-

aged to persist. The nails of the little animals had torn
off the bark. Not a leaf remained within reach of their
claws, and the trunk was scarred with kicks. It seemed as
if big and little alike were conspiring to destroy life. The
State had taken the men away from the children, and they
had revenged themselves upon nature. Destroy! Destroy! Peace saw to that as well as war. It is half of
education.

On the other side of one of the four walls ran a street
that was reeking with tanneries. The stale odor found its
way into the damp class-rooms where the little cattle,
penned-in, stank. Their noses were stopped up. There
were a dozen of them—twenty at most—twisting about on
the hard benches in an atmosphere that was yellow with
the soot that filtered in through the greenish windows
from the court, smoking with the mists of late autumn.
A cast-iron stove stuffed full of fuel (for wood abounded
in the country) roared away. When they were almost
suffocated, they opened the door. (The window was
never opened.) Then the fog entered and the odor of
hides, hides that were being tanned; and this seemed
positively refreshing after the odor of the living skins.

But a woman, no matter how accustomed she is to the
healthy odor of cleanliness, adapts herself more easily than
a man to the most repulsive necessities. One often sees
this in cases of sickness; her eyes, her fingers show no
disgust. Annette's sense of smell resigned itself. Like
the others, she breathed this odor of a wild beast's den
without wrinkling her nose. What she found it harder
to accept was the odor of these souls. Her spirit was less
pliant than her senses.

*
* *

But it was no longer the Soul made feverish by passions—struggle, hatred, torment. She had escaped from that. Well, she ought to have been satisfied. She found indifference here.

The soft earth had not suffered. Rich and mellow, it dozed in the valley, as on a feather bed which its body had hollowed, its head resting on the cushion of its hills, so that it might snore better and without dreaming of anything that lay beyond its pillow. A peaceful soil, a temperate race, a practical untormented spirit. God did not die for all men. Not for these was humanity being crucified.

Annette had known the country from her childhood; her father's blood had come from it. Formerly she had enjoyed its restful tranquillity. But to-day? She had once envied its healthiness. But to-day? Tolstoy's saying recurred to her—a saying that is not true of women alone: "A being who has never suffered, who has never been ill, a people that is healthy, always healthy, too healthy,—is a monster! . . ." To live is to die every day, and every day to struggle. This province was dying, but it was not struggling. It was slipping away peacefully, like its unrippled rivers, like the river banks and the days, in a secretive, egotistical common sense.

The time came, however, when this land caught fire. This old Burgundian city, with its three proud churches, its Gothic towers and spires of white stone, darkened and eaten by the weather till they were like rusted armor, lifting their silhouettes like knights of Christ above the river that stretched out like a serpent—their rows of

statues of decapitated saints, their gaping windows like
drops of blackened blood, the treasures of the cathedrals,
the tapestries of Haroun, the massive Goldsmith's work
that had come down from the emperors Charles, the son
of Charles and the father of Charles, the ruins of the
pointed towers and the encircling walls of the times of the
English wars—all attested the vigorous life of other
days, the red blood, the golden cross of the great bishops,
the epic struggles, the Duke, the King—the kings (Which
was the real one?)—and the passage of the Maid of
Orleans.

Its streets were depopulated now. Between the walls
of the middle-class houses, with their narrow doors, raised
up one step and tightly closed, one could hear, ringing far
away on the old pavement, a listless step approaching.
Overhead, the rooks were crying in their heavy flight as
they formed a black circle about the bell-towers of the
cathedral.

The race was dying, but it was happy. It had room
enough; the land was savory; their appetites were satisfied, their ambitions limited. From one generation to
another, all the adventurous souls had set out for the
conquest of Paris. Those who were left found all the
more space to stretch out in. When the bed is empty, you
can turn about in it. The war was to make it still larger.
It took the sons, but not all of them. And people's
imaginations were not lively enough to worry beforehand,
while their practical sense reckoned up the profits. An
easy life, with good food, the moving pictures, the café,
the bugle of the barracks for the ideal and the animal fairs
for the real. They were jovial; they were not much
affected by the ebb and flow of news, the advances, the re-
treats. They were no fools. Of the Russians, who were

always taking to their heels before the Germans, they said: "Well, if those fellows keep on they'll take the Trans-Siberian railroad and come back by way of America!"

Comfort had smoothed out their angles, their hardness, their cruelty. (Stop! . . . Look out, brother! Don't be too proud of it! . . .)

It was quiet. It was sleepy. Annette, are you not at ease? Isn't peace just the thing you have been looking for?

Peace? . . . I don't know. Peace? . . . Perhaps. But this is not my sort. This is not peace. . . .

"For peace is not the absence of war. It is the virtue that is born from the vigor of the soul."

Peace engulfed the old province, wrapped up in the circle of its hills, vines and fields, in that prosperous center of France—where the guns of the war sounded only dully, from which the flood of armies turned aside, as a river flows around some immovable block—(until two years later, when the Americans were to establish a camp there, the bustle of which was first to entertain and then soon weary the sleepy boredom of the inhabitants). But this peace had the odor of these college class-rooms where, with the odor and the windows shut and the stove roaring, the bodies and the souls of the little men stewed in their own juices.

*
* *

Three-quarters of them were the sons of small merchants or well-to-do peasants, master-farmers from the surrounding country. A few, two or three in a class, were the sons of notables, of old legal families, or officials, the élite of the town. These could be picked out fairly quickly, although they were all covered with the same glaze of slyness that the teaching of the school and their tacit understanding in the face of the professor, spread across their faces. But however different they were, these little mugs all bore the mark of the thumb of the sculptor who had modeled the race out of the clay of the land. It was he who had cut the faces out of the stone of their churches. One recognized them at once. Their rough heads might easily have been placed on the decapitated saints (What saints!) in the niches, without any damage being done. They were the authentic grand-nephews of the cathedral, and this was consoling. "The little fellow is still alive!" But it was not very reassuring. For, between ourselves, the saints of the cathedral were often famous blackguards. Or holy touch-me-nots. Annette found both types in her classes. Merely less strongly marked. The old wine had been too long in the bottle.

But what struck her most, at first, in these boys' faces— boys at the awkward age, bony, chub-cheeked, out of shape, rudely modeled, pushed awry—were two traits, rudeness and slyness. They were of the soil. The long, crooked Valois nose, the small, bright, secretive eyes, the precocious lines on their foreheads when they laughed, the jaws of young foxes, with yellow teeth protruding at the sides for joking or gnawing, gnawing erasers, their nails or balls of paper. Annette, in her chair, felt like the hunter facing the terriers—the hunter or the hunted? Which of them was going to be the game? She and they watched each other. One had to keep one's finger always on the trigger. The side that first lowered its eyes had to beware!

Theirs was the side. After a first examination, with stares, titterings, murmurs, elbows thrust into sides, the lids had dropped. But the eyes continued to watch; and this was still worse. One couldn't reach them and they had one. They let none of one's movements escape without marking them by a grimace that passed as if by wireless to the other end of the class. They had a motionless, innocent air (innocent in both senses); but their legs twisted under the table, their feet scraped the floor, their hands fumbled about the bottoms of their pockets or the thighs of their neighbors, their eyes winked and their tongues made lumps in their teeth. They saw nothing and they saw everything. If the master's attention relaxed for a moment a shiver passed over the whole class.

All this is an old story to teachers; and, although Annette was just beginning (for hitherto she had given only private lessons), she found that from the very first she was self-possessed; the instinct for government was in her blood. It made no difference when she fell into a revery. At the least stir that warned her of danger she was fully armed; and these little wolves and foxes who, counting upon her abstraction, crawled towards her, with their jaws secretly opening, were stopped short at the fire that blazed up in her imperious eyes. And they had expected to get so much fun out of this woman who had been set over them as a shepherd!

To these small males, woman had her appointed place

in the home and at the counter. There she ruled. You
saw her head (she had a pretty head) and sometimes the
palms of her hands (she had nimble hands). If she
emerged, what was interesting was the lower part of the
body. What a scent they had for that! Most of them
knew nothing, or almost nothing. Very few of them had
had their first experience; but there wasn't a single one
of them who wanted to appear ignorant. And they talked
about it, these young clowns! If women only suspected
what was said about them in these studs of adolescent
boys—about them, about those who attracted and stirred
their excited imagination in the narrow circle of their
days, sisters, married or unmarried women, mistresses or
servants, any one who wore a skirt, even if the skirt came
from God! The mother, alone, is by a tacit truce, almost
—not always—spared. And when one appears who has
no ties, whom no man protects (possesses, rather: nothing
for nothing!), no husband, son or brother—then the
stranger is fair game. Their intention and their plan is to
make a fool of her.

Yes, but when the prey is Annette it's a big mouthful.
Who is to begin, and how?

A strange female! They jeered behind their hands,
probing her with their eyes, but she had a keen, hard or
mocking glance that nailed the coarse joke to their lips.
They were astounded when she said, with a flash of diaboli-
cal insight: "Now, Pillois, wipe your mouth! That smells
badly!"

"What does?" he asked.

"What you have just said."

He protested that he had said nothing, that he had
spoken too low for her to hear.

"I saw it just the same. Go outside when you want to

relieve yourself! If you can't control your thoughts, at
least I want your mouths to stay clean."

They were paralyzed for a moment. Where had she
got hold of that bold tone and glance, those answers that
fell like a slap in the face? Without any impatience,
with a perfectly just hand that now was calmly stroking
her blond eyebrows? The circle of jeering eyes gathered
again about her. She felt them exploring her from her
ears to her heels; but she faced them, and by ceaseless,
unexpected questions, that fell right and left, she kept
their thoughts always occupied. She knew only too well
what was going on in these empty little skulls, the swarm
of flies that rises from the glycine plants in the spring.
She knew. If she had not known, they would have seen
to it that she learned.

That big Changnois, the son of a horse merchant, was
only fifteen. But he seemed seventeen, squat, massive,
his face peppered with freckles, square-skulled, his hair
pale blond and shaved like a pig, enormous hands with
nails bitten to the quick, rough and sly, always joking
and quarreling: when he whispered you could hear his
stomach rattling like a big fly at the bottom of a pot.
He leered at Annette; he appreciated her figure and her
charms; he licked his tongue like a connoisseur and
wagered "old fellow" that he would make her a declaration. When she spoke to him he rolled fish-eyes at her.
She made them all laugh at his expense. Then he swore
furiously that he would have the hussy's head! He had
arranged to be caught while he scrawled some dirty
pictures. And now he was awaiting the effect. His air
was impassive, but his waistcoat was shaking. He was
laughing in his stomach. And the other puppies, who had
been forewarned, were yelping in advance, their eyes

fastened on the victim, on her forehead, her eyes and those long fingers that held the pad of paper. She gave no sign of surprise. She folded up the paper and resumed the dictation she had begun; and Changnois, sneering, wrote with the others.

When it was finished, she said: "Changnois, you are to go back for a few weeks to your father's farm. You are sick here. You belong in the fields among your horses."

Changnois laughed no longer. His hindquarters had no desire to renew acquaintance with his father's foot. He protested, he argued. But she was inflexible.

"Come, off with you, my boy! Your stall is too narrow here. Out there you will be in the open and they will curry you well. Come, here's your pass for the censor."

She wrote on the sheet of paper: "To be sent back home. Expelled."

Then she said to the class, who were sitting there open-mouthed: "Boys, you are wasting your time. You think you can intimidate me because I am a woman. You are several centuries behind the times. Nowadays women share in the work of men. They can hardly replace them, for men have their own lives; but they don't lower their eyes to them. . . . You want to become men? No need to be impatient. That ambition is within the reach of the most limited. The whole question is whether you are going to be honest and capable men in your own trade. We are here to help you, but if you are unwilling we shan't force you. Fair play! It's up to you, yes or no; are you willing? Very well, then, come ahead!"

After several attempts they became convinced that they were not the stronger. Then without a word, a treaty was signed. Of course the frontiers would always have to be guarded; otherwise the treaty was only a scrap of paper. They were guarded; and upon this normal relations were organized. They ceased to dispute the established authority; and as their coalition had no longer any object, they showed themselves disunited, as they naturally were. Annette began to distinguish individualities out of the tribe. There were a few, not many—three or four out of all the six classes—who won her sympathy; but it would not do to show this. They were little boys of a finer fiber, who did a little thinking. One saw their intelligences blushing under their skins; they were sensitive to a word, an attention, a glance. In almost every case they were objects of suspicion to the others, even persecuted. Their relative aristocracy drew down upon them the natural hostility of the tribe, and their very sensitiveness was all the better reason for making them suffer. It would have done them harm if any preference had been shown for them; they would have paid for it. Worse, they would have exploited it, these little comedians. If one interested oneself in them, they would believe themselves interesting; they would desire to be so and their natures would be falsified. After all, they belonged to the same species as the others, naïvely cynical little rakes. Annette had to constrain herself to be impersonal, however much she felt the need of taking one of them in her arms, for lack of the one she missed! The absent Marc was always there. She sought for him in every one of them, she compared them with him. And though she did not find one of them—this mother!—who equaled him, she tried to deceive herself. She imagined him in their place, before her. She saw him. She read in them so as to read in him. For lack of a better, they served as mirrors that reflected, without too much distortion, the lost

son, the prodigal son who was going to return.   But what
did they reflect?

Alas, they reflected their elders!   Their ideal went no
further than to be and to believe what those who had preceded them by a generation had thought and been (which
is called "progress," this force of the past that walks backward!).   They may have had their own characteristic
features, before entering school, but it was hard to tell
them apart.   They were stamped with the seal of their
proprietors, their fathers, who were themselves stamped
with that of their relationship and the community.   They
no longer belonged to themselves.   They were part of
that nameless Force that for centuries had been gathering
these prairie-dogs into cities, repeating over and over the
same gestures and the same barks, building exactly the
same thought-huts.   The school was the workshop that
taught the fingering of the thinking machine.   What
could an isolated initiative do to enfranchise them?   The
first thing necessary was to teach them not to put on the
thought-shoes of their elders.   And they took such pride
in disguising themselves as their elders!   The less they
thought for themselves, the happier and prouder they
were—and, heaven knows, it was the same thing with their
elders!   They expanded when they abdicated their personal judgment (that nuisance!) for the belief of the
crowd, whether it was called School, Academy, Church,
State, Fatherland or had no name and was merely the
Species, that lifeless-eyed monster to which people
attribute a providential wisdom and which creeps about at
random, plunging its gluttonous trunk right and left into
the slime of the marshes from which it once sprang and
which is going to engulf it again.   (So many thousands of

species have already perished there! Is it possible we are not going to be able to save our own?)

The *ignis fatuus* gleams over the marsh. One had the illusion of seeing it shine for a moment in the eyes of some of these children. Annette tried to catch it. What did they think of life? What did they think of death? This war, these storms that were beating against the gate of the hills, down there, on the horizon—what echo did they find behind these little secretive foreheads?

There was no echo but the ratatata, the bugle calls, the fire-crackers, and the pictures from *L'Illustration,* a far-away spectacle which, when it was prolonged, ended by boring them. (They were blasé.) Their marbles and their bets interested them more, or the tricks they played in the class. When they were older it would be business, the gains and losses of the household.

And yet they had relatives out there in the trenches, many of whom had been hit. Didn't they think of them?

Without feeling. Usually to boast of them. They became heroes by proxy. The news that came from the front had been previously filtered. They saw all the misery from a comic angle. Boudin said, rolling with laughter: "Old fellow, my brother out there says they are up to their nozzles in dung."

Corveau said they bled the Boches with their knives. He showed how it was done. He had seen a pig killed.

They described to one another, with mocking eyes, the effects of the shells. Church-towers, trees, intestines and heads flew about in their minds like barbaric playthings. They stopped short with the scenery. Oh, they pictured to themselves the flesh and the blood; they even felt the sort of pleasure that boys have for messing about in filth.

But the protest of the soul beneath it all never occurred to them.

Those who returned from over-there did nothing to awaken it. Corveau's elder brother was home on leave. He said to these youngsters: "I had a good pal who made a little money selling the fuses of the shells that hadn't exploded. He was as clever at unscrewing them with his ten fingers as a monkey, and he would go and pick them up when they were hardly cold. I said to him, 'Look out!' He answered, 'They know me.' One day I was following twenty paces behind him, getting safe behind a tree. 'Let that one alone,' I yelled. 'It might go off.' He answered: 'Oh, you've got cold feet!' Bang! the shell went off under his nose. He caught it, all right, poor chap. There wasn't anything left of him."

He roared with laughter and the boys with him.

Annette listened, stupefied. What was behind this laughter? The memory of a good joke? Nervous excitement? Or was there nothing behind it?

She took him to one side and said: "Come, Corveau, is it really so pleasant out there?"

He looked at her and tried to go on joking. But she did not laugh. Then he said: "To tell the truth, it isn't as nice as all that."

And, after a few moments, he began to pour out some bitter confidences.

"Why don't you tell about them?" asked Annette.

He made a gesture of discouragement.

"You can't. They wouldn't understand. And besides, they wouldn't like it. And besides, what good would it do? It can't be helped."

"Because you don't want to help it."

"It isn't up to us to want."

"Who is it up to, then, if it isn't to you?"

He was nonplussed: "Why, the people that run the show."

It was useless to go on, to remind him that these people had been put in charge of the show by him. It was he who had chosen them.

That very evening Annette heard him beginning to brag again. He felt some need of it. It was not the others he was trying to deceive, it was himself.

If these men were not capable of seeing and desiring the truth, how reach those who had been spared the ordeal —these children?

They did not understand things. They were the victims of words. As long as the words made a fine noise, they paid no attention to the meaning. Annette had asked them to write down their ideal of life. Bran wanted to be an officer, as one of his great uncles had been. He wrote proudly: "Does not the river always rise again to its source?"

They swaggered about the war. The older ones, those who, if it lasted one or two years more, might be called, repeated the blusterings they had heard proclaimed by a few old veterans: "The bullets go through you, but they don't hurt! Up, you dead! . . ."

Heroism-to-come enabled them to dispense with effort in the present. They "didn't give a damn." They said: "After the war, we shan't have to bother about money any longer. The Boches will do the paying. We'll hitch them up. Listen here! My father says he's going to buy half a dozen of them and nail horse-shoes on their dirty feet. Ha, ha! . . ."

The best educated, the sons of the president and the lawyer, filled their mouths with the fustion of the newspapers. Lavedan was Corneille and Capus ˙was Hugo. The others were satisfied with the faked pictures of the small illustrated sheets.

Annette tried an experiment. She dropped a sounding-lead. She read them a chapter of *War and Peace*—the death of little Petia—those beautiful pages, drenched with October mist and the dreams of the young tree that was never to awaken. "It was an autumn day, mild and rainy; the heavens and the horizon melted into a single tint of dull grey. A few big drops were falling. . . ."

At first they scarcely listened. They laughed at the Russian names. That of the small hero had the gift of throwing them into convulsions of merriment. Then, little by little, the swarm of flies settled on the edge of the bowl; they became silent, and made the chatterers keep still. One single boy, who blew out his cheeks every time the name recurred, persisted in this same coarse pleasantry to the end. The others were held. When it was ended, a few yawned. A few roused themselves from their trance with a noisy commotion. A few, awkwardly dissatisfied, tittering, played the connoisseur: "Those Russians are half-wits!" A few, without being able to explain, said, "It's stunning. . . ." Some said nothing. These were the ones who had been touched. But how far, and why? It was very hard to tell. One couldn't get them to say a single word out of their hearts. It was their own affair. They weren't going to hand it over!

Annette looked eagerly at one listener, a thin, fair little fellow, with a long nose, fine, well-cut features and a narrow chest, who coughed and looked the other way. He was intelligent, timid and not very frank, like children who know they are weak and are afraid of exposing themselves. She suspected that his soul had been stirred.

During the reading, when she lifted her eyes from the book, she had met the saddened eyes of the child who had hastened to thrust his nose back among his papers. This little fellow had often thought of suffering because he was himself sickly and nervous, and egoism is often the key to pity. He who suffers himself has a chance of awakening to the suffering of others.

Annette detained him after the class. She asked him if he liked Petia, that young brother. He blushed, he was disturbed. She recalled the dream of the sensitive child's last night. How beautiful life was, vigorous, fragile life! The life that would have been, the life that was not going to be. . . . Had he understood? He shook his head and turned away his eyes. But she had caught sight of them, the light had burned in them.

"Did you think, suppose you were in Petia's place?"

He protested: "Oh, I shan't have to go. I'm not well. They've told me that I am to stay in the rear."

He was comforted and proud of his poor health.

"How about the others, your comrades?"

He was quite indifferent to them! He hastened to find in his memory the phrases that he ought to think. *To die for one's country.* The others could go and get themselves killed. He had found his balance again. The light had gone out. . . .

Who knew?

*
* *

Annette was unfair. She saw no reasons for hoping. But there were plenty of them.

This race of kindly folk, egotistical, ruminating, had a right to slumber a little. They had been on the march a long time. They had fought the Crusades and the Hundred Years' War. This had not made them younger, but it vouched for their stock. They had seen so much, done so much, endured so much, suffered so much! And they laughed! It was marvelous. Whoever laughs lives and is not ready to renounce life.

In this world of people who are discontented with what exists, what exists satisfied them. They felt no hatred or envy for their neighbors, they were convinced that nothing was better than home and nothing finer than to stay there. They disliked the war, they were used to taking their ease after forty-five years of peace. And on a day's notice they donned the uniform of war without sulking. How docile they were, these debaters! They were ready to sacrifice everything—without any fuss—because "It's done." "It always had been done." According to the angle from which you looked at them, they were absurd— or they were touching. Their basis of good-natured, indifferent acceptance had its element of emptiness. But there was something grand about it also.

As for the children, what could one know about them? What appeared on the surface was only a game. The true work went on underneath. The eyes of teachers and parents saw no further than the youthful bark. All one knows about a child is what makes him considered a child. One doesn't see the eternal Being who is ageless and whose fires smolder in the depths of every soul, big and little. One can never know whether or not the fire is going to spring up. Confidence! Patience!

But Annette had none. She was like a robust swimmer who wishes to cross a river and swim against the current. Or like those migrating birds that fly against the wind.

When she had felt the odor of fever about her in Paris, she had let the air in. She had opposed to it her desire for calm. When she saw the heavy indifference here, she heard the rising call of suffering.

She was restless. If she was discontented with others, it was because she was also discontented with herself. They were what they had to be, according to their nature. But was she in accordance with her own? For more than a year she had given herself up to the fate that was sweeping along her people. At first she had found in it a violent pleasure; before long, a habit. Now, weariness. Some secret, inner, remote force within her protested. She was not clear about it, she suffered confusedly, she felt guilty towards herself. And this obscure remorse weighed over everything she saw, over the whole little world that was bounded by her horizon—this humanity in miniature. She saw the defects of men in these children's faces. She foresaw their destiny, their commonplace future, the cul-de-sac of life. She saw her own son lost in this nameless crowd, in this swarm that flowed like a river and knew not whither it was going. She saw herself, a working ant, childless, who went through her mechanical task without joy. It seemed to her that these children, all—even her own—were born of a monstrous, stupid queen ant, Nature with a wicked mouth and a withered soul.

She lacked everything. It was not only that she missed her son, cruelly. She missed herself.

*
* *

And her son missed her, though he would never have admitted it.

He had withdrawn from her, furious that she had deserted him and left him chained up in jail. Chained! They would see!

For four weeks he did not write to her. She wrote to him once, twice, three times, maternally and severely at first, letting him understand that if he was willing to make amends she would forgive him. (Forgive him! Him! That was just what *he* would not forgive!) Then she wrote angrily because he had not written, then anxiously. She was very much disturbed. He ground his teeth. He could not be brought to make up his mind to answer until Sylvie, from whom Annette had asked news of the boy, came to the school parlor to urge him. Then he ingeniously manufactured a masterpiece of dryness. Not a word of reproach or complaint. No bitterness. (This would have been expressing his heart to some extent!) A cold politeness, a *pensum*, to which he pretended, henceforth, to force himself punctually every fortnight and which told her nothing about his life except the externals—stripped of all personal accent, all savor and color. Vainly Annette insisted, demanding details. She understood perfectly that he meant to show his resentment. She tried to disarm him; then she affected the same inflexibility. But there always came a moment when her repressed love overflowed in her letters. The boy watched for these hours and triumphed in them. She always repented of them later, for he merely wrote in a still briefer and more detached manner. She opened his letters now with noth-

ing but pain at the thought of what she was going to read.
Yet always, in spite of everything, she hoped, and always
she was disappointed. She grew weary of suffering and
waiting. When the day came to write (he only answered
afterwards, letter for letter) she would put it off a day,
then two days, then three. Then would follow one of
those explosions of reproaches and love, which she could
not control. She would be silent for a month. Since it
made no difference to him!

Her silence of a month almost made him ill. It was
vain for him to pretend that he was a strong man, that he
disdained her letters. How he waited for them! It was
not merely his pride that enjoyed the vengeance of saying:
"She can't get on without me!"

He could no longer exist without these whiffs of love
which the wind brought him from far-away fields. As
long as they had arrived regularly, on the expected day,
he had pretended to receive them with the indifference
they deserved. When they began to arrive at capricious
intervals he realized that he missed them: he was filled
with impatience, and, with it, desire. When they came
at last with the expected letter, he enjoyed them madly,
wildly. (Of course he refused to recognize this! Pretended! He preferred to attribute his pleasure to the
pride that said, insolently, "Once more I've 'done' her!")

But when she ceased to write, he had to admit the humiliating truth that he needed her. Admit it? No! No!
"I have seen nothing, I know nothing, I have nothing to
confess. . . ."

At night he dreamed of her, dreams in which she cease-
lessly returned, never tender, never loving, but haughty,
hard, sarcastic, wounding and humiliating him. He
awoke detesting her, burning furiously to do . . . What?

To say cruel things to her, to get her into his power, to make her suffer, to avenge himself. But the imagined contact of his hands made him tremble. He drove away the image. The image returned. That beautiful, scornful mouth . . . He tried to outrage it in his memory. He thought of the free life that she must have led and that she denied him. He also saw in his dreams other women who resembled her in no way, neither in features, appearance or age—and yet he unhesitatingly identified them with her. They permitted him to satisfy with them, against her, in the dark abyss, his repressed feelings—the hundred-headed hydra . . .

What months! Feverish and bound fast in this menagerie! Locked up! . . .

*
* *

Locked up, these thoughts and these burning young bodies! For them the prison, the boarding-school, was more dangerous than the street. Boredom depraves the spirit. Anxiety, waiting, lust, fear, cruelly tormented these little animals. The cloud of suffering that hung over the besieged City dulled their brains and poisoned their limbs. It brooded over the sweating dormitories where the surveillance had been relaxed. The proctor set the example. He went out every third night, with the connivance of the watchman. The general-superintendent snored in a room to one side. As long as everything took place in silence, the gallery was unchained until dawn. Marc listened, stifled, and escaped, nauseated. He jumped out through a window into the garden of the school—the prison.

Dark night. Four walls. Overhead, an overcast sky. The ray of a search-light passed and brushed the shadows. Marc had stepped into another prison.

He approached the wall that skirted the deserted street. Dark houses. Everything slept in this middle-class quarter, far from the center and the noise. Many of the inhabitants had fled from Paris. Marc leaned over. Too high! He was in danger of breaking his legs. None the less, a fury drove him to escape. His leg was over the ridge! He hung by his hands and sought with his feet for some crack that would serve as a foothold. In the street he heard steps coming. He tried to climb back. Too late, he was seen. From below him, in the shadow, a voice asked: "You want to jump?"

He asked: "Who are you?"

But already two hands at the end of two raised arms had grasped his feet, and a voice said: "Come on! I've got you!"

He found himself in the street, his feet on the pavement. About him were the sombre walls of the houses. Overhead, the night. A third prison. It was like a nightmare. A box of compartments. You went out, you returned, you passed from one to the other; but the big cover on top remained closed.

An unknown man was close to him, touching him. They were almost of the same size. A match was lighted, and for a moment the flame illumined the two faces. He was a young workman, hardly older than Marc, beardless, with a grayish skin, delicate features, a sharp expression, lively eyes under arched eyebrows, a curious, fleeting glance that brushed by without settling, an equivocal smile at the corner of the pale lips. The darkness had fallen again between them. But they had had a good look at each other. The workman took Marc's arm and said: "Where are you going?"

Marc said: "I don't know."

"Then come along with me."

Marc hesitated. His instinct warned him. He knew the dangers of the jungle. He knew nothing of the other; but he had a feeling that the other came from the jungle. His heart was beating. But his curiosity overcame his fear. And besides, if he was not yet brave he was reckless. (One learns bravery later, when one is able to weigh one's strength or one's weakness. He had not yet tested his.) He was curious enough to take the risk. He freed his arm from the hands that grasped it; and, holding the other, in turn with both his hands, but at a distance, he said, "Let's go"—without asking him where.

All night they ran about. As their hands had done at first, their spirits felt for each other. Awkwardly, a little roughly. Each was afraid of the other; but neither of them knew that the other was afraid. It was not physical fear. The first contact had almost dissipated this in Marc. But it came back in gusts as they walked in silence, side by side. Marc touched his knife in his pocket, a harmless weapon that he wouldn't have known how to handle. They hastened to talk again. Words reassured them.

In the daylight they would have been slow to approach each other. But at night, in these streets that had gone into mourning, where the lights were veiled as if for a catafalque, differences were effaced; they belonged to the same herd. The same desires drove them, the same dangers menaced them. Tired of walking, or rather because they wished to study each other before going further, they sat down on a bench in a shadowy square.

He said his name was Casimir. He rolled a cigarette and offered it to Marc. Marc, who disliked smoking and was most fastidious, took it and began to smoke. Shame! He had nothing in his pockets, neither tobacco nor money. What was he going to do when his turn came? This preoccupation at first prevented him from listening. But he heard just the same and his curiosity returned. Confidence for confidence! They told each other all about themselves.

Casimir was an electrician who worked in one of the war factories. The sum that he earned every day overwhelmed Marc, who possessed nothing, earned nothing and was fitted to do nothing but spend. Casimir did not abuse his superiority. He had long been used to it; perhaps he would have exchanged it for that middle-class inferiority he had despised and envied since he was born.

But to-night he thought neither of scorn nor of envy. The attraction was too strong. This face he had caught a glimpse of just now, this unknown human world. It was the same with Marc. They longed to explore each other. The barriers were down. Had not Marc just run away from his own class? (What class did he belong to, this child without a father?) They were equals.

Casimir was the older. It wasn't a question of age. A few months more, and it would not be worth talking about. He was older in his experience of the crowded life of the working-class.

Marc was silent, confused, eager to hear. His silence was the thing that served him best. He had the air of knowing what the other was ignorant of. And when he ventured to speak, it was in brief, broken words, an ironic, detached tone that deceived the other.

But the deception did not last long. It could not stand a close scrutiny, nor could his own girlish face by the lamp-light of the café into which Casimir dragged him. His embarrassment and his naïveté lay revealed to the other's gaze, that keen furtive gaze that clutched him like the tendril of a vine, from the side, watching him, spying on him, embarrassing him and attracting him at once. He wanted to flee and he wanted to brave it out, but, hesitating between the two, he did neither the one nor the other. He betrayed himself, he surrendered. . . .

*

* *

He shared Casimir's prowlings through the jungle. If Annette had suspected what the eyes, the hands, the body of her child had touched! But there is a pardon for these hard little souls, whose tough little cores can be touched by no defilement. They are saved by what ought to destroy them, by their curiosity. They wish to see and know, they wish to touch. Yes, but *"Noli me tangere!"* They will not let themselves be touched.

"I have touched and I pass. I remain a stranger to you. I was that already, before I knew you. I am even more so now. I am disgusted with you, with myself, especially with myself. I have soiled my body, my hands, my eyes. I wash them furiously. But my heart is intact. The mud has not touched it."

". . . And what bits of precious metal I have picked up in this Paris mud! . . ."

In this boy of the streets and the workshop, among his companions, in this conglomeration of souls formed by the people of our monstrous cities, virtues and vices are mingled. Corruption and salty air.

A sexuality aggravated by the hot fever of the herd—senses that are aroused, scorched, blunted before their time, a savage curiosity that outstrips, provokes, exhausts desire, a frenzy that relapses before fecundating—everything attempted, everything used up—the flesh blighted in its flower, the soul's down brutally crushed, the grass trampled everywhere, the body defiled by pleasure without joy—like the woods near a town after a Sunday in Spring. This is its devastating aspect, the charnal demon

that drains and exhausts the udder of the race, the cancer
that eats into its stomach in its strength of action and its
fecundity. But over the ravaged fields the winds pass;
after that which consumes, that which renews. Only a
shower is needed for the trampled grass to rise in patches,
for the grain and the dog-grass to turn green again. Liberty is the lance of Achilles. It kills and it brings to life.

Precociously overheated by the glowing breath of the
social forge into which his birth had cast him—in the
mephetism of this chaotic fountain of pleasures and pains,
equally brutal and equally murderous, under this destructive regimen of barbaric hygiene, infected lodgings,
physical and moral dirt, unhealthy food and drink, hard
work and outbursts disproportionate to his age, Casimir
was burning his candle at both ends.

Erethism of the spirit was no less dangerous than that
of the body. But it was less fertile, and together they
formed a monstrous equilibrium that dominated the being
before its maturity and left it foundering in the sink of
carnality. Yet this same mad tension of all the desires,
this hysterical liberty, without the least moral restraint,
but also without the prejudices that are the price of ordinary social morality, enabled the leaping, frisking spirit
to reach, with a sudden bound, the green bushes in the sunlight, on which were strung the buds of thought. The
young goat did not stay there; it descended with one leap,
but between its teeth it held the tonic bitterness of a
healthy mouthful.

Casimir was an anarchist. The pride of those who are
self-taught, swollen by a badly chosen and worse digested
learning, a dogmatic egoism and a love of low comedy, a
taste for empty debates, sexual aberration, the maniacal
destruction of all established values, and great romancing

and bragging about immorality, the mutual violence of groups and individuals that envy each other—have always wrought havoc in the lofty edifice that cannot be built without the pure hearts and hands of a Réclus or a Kropotkin. Only the stoical élite can dwell there. The crowds that rush through it degrade it, as they have degraded the basilicas of Christ by peopling them with those disgusting little gods, the go-betweens of God.

But the mere word Liberty has a magic virtue, even for souls that are sunk in the bog of their own desires. It is a breath of Heroism (An illusion? . . . What matter!) that abjures servitude, all the servitudes by which it is bound. . . . Lamentable Epigoni of the Titan that has risen against the *sic volo jubeo* of the Tyrant. In these castaways there burned again the sacred fire of Prometheus.

Marc watched its spark crackling along his steps.

It was an exceptional time when all the estranged brothers, anarchists, socialists, syndicalists, all who were in revolt against the war, forgot their private quarrels in order to unite on this platform. There were so few of them! Hardly a handful! All the rest had deserted, through weakness before public opinion, through fear of detection, through the reawakening of old instincts of national pride or the lapping of blood, above all through confusion, the frightful confusion of those oratorical ideas with which democracies are stuffed like turkeys. No Jesuit, in the flourishing times of casuistry, made so fatuous a use of the *distinguo* which, when applied to everything, results in befuddling everything; war and peace, the rights of the individual, liberty and the abdication of all liberties. The surest result was that the minority of minds, which had just painfully begun to liberate themselves, returned to the convict-bench and rowed with their backs bent under the whip. There were not a dozen in Paris, towards the close of 1914, who had succeeded in keeping clear of the chains. Their number had gradually grown since, uniting into two or three small groups, the shrewdest of which was that of "La Vie Ouvrière."

On Sundays Marc attended a few of their reunions. What he heard there aroused him.

Hitherto he had never questioned the war. He was too clear-sighted not to have grasped its cruelty, its injustice, perhaps even its absurdity. But he thought it was all the more virile to accept it. He was at that age when the supreme virtue is summed up in this word, virility. And an unjust force secretly exerts an even greater appeal than a just one, because it seems more forceful: all brute, pure brute and more dangerous. He made it a point of pride to exalt pitilessly the law of the struggle for survival that shuts men up in the crab-baskets of eternal strife. No sniveling! Be the stronger! Just because he himself was weak he assumed this sneering cynicism that had revolted Annette.

"So much the worse for me as well as for the others! So much the worse for those who fall! It is for me, either by strength or trickery, to manage to get on top!"

It amused him to despise his mother's indignant protests against this blustering inhumanity. He accused her disdainfully of "sentimentalism." This settled everything.

"Insipid twaddle! Woman's stuff! Filling your mouth with it! It sets my teeth on edge!"

It was true that at the time Annette was engulfed in a complete confusion. She still accepted the war, while she refused to accept the ignominy of the foul breath of the slaughterer. She stopped half-way on her road to thought; she dared not look to the end. Also she had difficulty in finding reasons, detached from herself, for her revolts. Her inner voice was all she needed to guide her. It was too little for Marc. A man needs clear ideas, whether they are true or not, to help him to label his passions.

Marc found them by the handful among the logicians of working-class thought. All their revolts were rigorously deduced and built up on carefully formed structures of figures and facts. The unstudied speech of Merrheim, slow, groping, monotonous, seeking the exact word, never exceeding the thought, a grand honesty that was, like Phocion, the ax of eloquence; the tranquil good nature of Monatte, who detached his interest from you and from himself in order to follow exactly the succession of observed facts; the steel-like precision, the compressed passion of Rosmer, who was afraid that if he let himself go he would betray the idea; this frozen heat had an overwhelming effect on the skeptical, feverish, violent adolescent. The clandestine character these meetings were forced to assume, the incessant danger that hung over these little catacombs, the oppressive sense of the enormous mass of nations that held in their power these "thieves" of justice, these seekers of truth, with their veiled light, breathed a religious spirit into the revolt, in spite of the coldness of its leaders. Like the gleams of a revolving lighthouse, it transfigured these dull faces, these weary eyes.

And the proud little bourgeois felt himself shamed by so many of these workmen who surpassed him in bigness of heart.

*
* *

Pitan, old Pitan, as they called him, although he was not yet forty, was a thin, spry little man with a head too large for his body. The first thing that struck you about him was the beard that covered his whole face, his thick lips buried under its hair. His complexion was yellowish, his nose flat, his eyes of a velvety brown, the pupil mingled with the iris like the eye of a water-spaniel.

When Marc looked about the room at the meetings he met these eyes with their grave smile. Pitan was one of the few, among all these comrades, who seemed to be interested in men not merely for the idea (or for his own interest) but because they were men, through human love —like a dog. The young bourgeois attracted him; he saw his embarrassment. And Marc's instinct told him that the Newfoundland dog was swimming towards him across the current. They came together.

Pitan was an itinerant mender of china and porcelain. He had a small shop in the suburbs where he did his delicate work; and his ingenuity led him to add to his repairing trade objects of all materials, wood or stone, as well as fragile knicknacks. As a free worker, he could dispose of his time better than his companions in the factories and workshops; and he lavished it on the cause. He was ready to carry notices of meetings and pamphlets from one end of Paris to the other, to rouse up the forgetful, to waken those who slept, to sound the call to arms. Marc took advantage of several free afternoons at school to go with Pitan. He was soon tired. Neither bad weather nor distance made any difference to Pitan. He came and went with his halting step, the hard, brisk step of an old campaigner. He scarcely stopped for a minute till the task was ended; and he never took a drink. They joked him about his vow of temperance and chastity, for he had no love affairs and he was not married. He lived with his old mother, whom he concealed jealously and who tyrannized over him. His father had been a drunkard and he had seen as a child the ravages of that disease. He carried the marks of it in his invisibly undermined constitution. This was the reason he had not married. Although his life was far from gay, he seemed happy. Sometimes, however, there was a shade of melancholy in his spaniel's eyes. He had periods of intense fatigue when he would run off and hide, lethargic, incapable of speaking, his tongue tied, his brain paralyzed. After a few weeks he would appear again, with his devoted smile and all his old activity. Then his comrades, who had not thought of him while he was away, found it quite natural to load him down with all the tasks for the cause which they were avoiding. And Pitan set off on his rounds, returning at nightfall, or in the middle of the night, when the last sheet had been distributed, staggering, drenched with rain, satisfied.

Marc was not strong enough for this. Pitan was sorry for him, and without letting him see it, found reasons for stopping to get their breath.

Pitan's conversation was slow, calm, unending. It spread like the solid water in a canal between the two locks of his speechlessness. Marc impatiently tried in vain to interrupt Pitan. Pitan, smiling, let him talk and then tenaciously returned and wound up his thought. Irony had no effect upon him. He did not overrate the value of his speech. Speech to him was the need to clear his thought. He could only do so by pulling it out of the mud of silence

in which his mind was stuck fast. He had to air this
heavy, inner life, choked with mud during its eclipses of
biennial hemiplegia. Thinking for him meant thinking
out loud. And besides he needed some one else in order
to think at all. This solitary man had been born with a
fraternal instinct.

Talking did not hinder him from observing and listening. Marc became aware, long afterward, that Pitan
had remembered everything he had said, had meditated
on it and turned it over and over as if with a spade.

He thought it becoming to parade before him as well
as before the others his difficulties as a small bourgeois,
his revolts as a schoolboy who was emancipating himself
from the prejudices and obligations of his class. Casimir
and his companions had laid these down to his credit—
without departing from their attitude of superiority.
They had an air of giving him a good mark, which flattered Marc but mortified him as well. Pitan showed
neither praise nor disdain. He shook his head while
Marc told his story, then he went on with his soliloquy.
But several days later, while he was waiting for the workmen to come out, at some distance from a factory, between
the lines of high walls above which stretched the red
necks of the gigantic chimneys and their heavy rings of
smoke, Pitan said, without any preamble:

"Just the same, it would be better for you to stay at
home, Monsieur Rivière."

(He was the only one who did not address him familiarly.)

Marc was thunderstruck: "Home? Where?"

"In your school."

He protested: "But, Pitan, do you think I do wrong to
come with you, to learn what you are thinking and how
you live?"

"Surely not. It can't do any one any harm to find out how the rest of us are made. But you see, Monsieur Rivière, you will never know."

"Why?"

"Because you aren't one of us."

"Ah, do you say that, Pitan? I come and you repulse me!"

"No, no, Monsieur Rivière. You come and I am glad to see you. We thank you for your sympathy. But that doesn't alter the fact that you are and always will be a stranger among us."

"You don't seem a stranger to me."

"Come. There are workmen behind these walls. What do you know of the lives of these workmen? We can tell you what they do, we can tell you what they want, what they think and even what they suffer. But do you feel it? When I have the toothache you are sorry for me, but if you have no trouble you can't feel my trouble."

"I have my own troubles too."

"Of course. I don't ridicule them like the people who say that compared to the real sufferings of those who are condemned to a life of poverty, the suffering of the middle-class is a luxury, manufactured for the idle. It is a luxury, perhaps,—aside from sickness and death, of course. Even so, sickness and death are not the same for all."

"They aren't the same?"

"No, my boy. To be sick and die peacefully in one's bed without having to think of what is going to happen to one's family—that's luxury, even that. But those who live in luxury never notice it; and whatever suffering may be, whether it's real or manufactured, it's still suffering. So I'm sorry for them all, yours and ours alike. Each has his own troubles, made to his own measure. Only they aren't alike."

"We are alike, Pitan."

"But life isn't. Come, what does work mean to you? You say, your people do—the best as well as the worst, yes, even the blood-suckers that live on the troubles of others—you say that work is beautiful, that work is sacred, and that whoever does not work hasn't the right to exist. That's perfect. But have you ever even formed an idea of forced labor, labor without relaxation, without any hope of getting away from it, blind, poisonous, stupefying work, work that fastens you to the mill-stone like an animal in a treadmill—till the hour of liberty comes, the hour when you croak? Is that sort of work beautiful? Is it sacred? Can't you see why the people who live off it, after having dishonored it so, always seem strangers to us?"

"But I don't live off it!"

"Yes, even you, with your youth sheltered from fear of hunger, your school, your leisure to study peacefully for years, without having to think of your daily bread . . ."

All at once, to defend himself, Marc remembered what he had never thought of before: "I don't owe that to your work. I owe it to my mother's work."

Pitan was interested. He started him talking about his mother's courageous life. And in describing it Marc discovered it. But his pride was mingled with a confusion that Pitan lighted up with a word.

"Very well, my friend," he said tranquilly, when the boy had finished. "So she's the one that's exploited."

Marc did not like to have any one teach him his duty. "That's my affair, Pitan. That doesn't concern you."

Pitan did not insist. He smiled.

The workmen were coming out of the factory. He got up and went towards them. He knew several of them and exchanged a few words with them while he distributed his pamphlets. But they were in a hurry to straddle their bicycles and get home to supper. They scarcely opened the pamphlets, merely saying: "That's right, that's right . . ."

They put their hands in their pockets and did not even take the sheets. Three or four stopped to talk. Marc remained at one side. He felt only too plainly: "I am a stranger."

When Pitan returned to him, Marc walked along beside him for a few minutes and began to talk again: "You didn't break any news to me, Pitan. I had seen it already. Casimir and the others are never comrades with me. Sometimes they flatter me; at other times they humiliate me. They seem to be proud of me and against me. Proud of having me as a hostage from the middle classes so that they can despise me."

"Hoho!" (Pitan laughed gently.) "You mustn't go too far the other way, now. But there's some truth in it. And it was because I felt it that I told you."

Marc stopped short, stamped his foot and exclaimed: "It's unfair!"

He turned aside so that the other should not see his weakness: his tears were starting. Pitan silently took his arm and they went on walking.

"Yes," said Pitan, who had been meditating, after they had taken a few steps, "there are many unjust things. Almost everything in this society is unjust. That is why it must be changed."

"Can't I work at that?"

"You can, you must. Like us. Every one has his own way and his own gift. But the new society, the order of the proletariat—I'm sorry, Monsieur Rivière, but you can't enter it. It makes me sorry for you. But so things are. I shall not enter it either, for that matter, for I shall be dead."

"But your people, the people of your class?"

"The people of my class, yes. They'll enter it."

Marc withdrew his arm from Pitan's and said: "Pitan, you and the others are nationalists. You fight against the country, but it's for the sake of another country. And this is just as jealous as the old one."

Pitan said good-naturedly: "As for me, I'm not jealous of anything, my boy. One may be fair or dark, big or little, white or yellow. It's all the same to me. Every one bleeds and dies just the same. I am for all the countries. None of them bothers me. But there you are! They don't allow ours, the country of the proletariat, the right to live. It will have to be taken by force, from yours."

"And you will take our lives too."

"We are not angry with you, but your class steals our sunlight."

"I don't take much of it," said Marc, sadly.

"You have the means to go and find it. In your books, your studies, in the free and peaceful labor of your spirit. Go and find it, and then afterwards give it to us, who haven't the means to pay for these costly excursions. That is what you can do best. Go home and work for us there!"

"It isn't very pleasant," said Marc, "living without companions."

"You are the companion of all, not just the companion of one."

"Ah, what loneliness!"

Pitan stopped and looked with smiling compassion at the boy's face, which he was trying to conceal. He straightened his back, took a good breath of the air that was poisoned by the reek of the factories, and exclaimed: "Yes, it's good, it's healthy."

Marc rubbed his nose. Pitan tapped him on the shoulder: "Look!"

For the first time he spoke to him familiarly.

From the circle of fortifications they looked out over the vast, bare plain, the long lines of smoke from the factories which the icy wind of winter twisted heavily, like linen in the boiler, in the tub of the muddy sky, and behind these the swarming houses, the thousands of lives, the City—the austere tragedy. Happy and serious, Pitan breathed deeply. Then he said: "Solitude shared with all means that all are the brothers of all."

"And they all devour one another," said Marc, bitterly.

"They have to eat," answered Pitan, simply. "It's the law. So let's feed them! Let's feed the others with ourselves. That is what we are born for. And of all good things that is the best!"

Marc looked at the earthy face of the little chinamender, illumined with its inner fire; he was struck by that silent happiness that dreamed of offering itself as food. He was thinking that the Christian God, himself, had come to give himself as food. Oh, what a barbarous humanity! He saw plainly the grandeur of all this, but he was still too young to aspire to it.

No! Not to be eaten! . . . To eat!

*
* *

Shaken, but disappointed by these men of the other shore, where he could not find a footing, he was like a bird, poised between earth and heaven, who did not know where to alight. He had fled from the nest; he did not want to return to it; he was still too young to build one of his own—where would it be? While he waited for the time to come when he could establish his own abiding place, where was he to find shelter? On what branch was he to alight? Doubt had overtaken his former prejudices, and although he persisted in them, since he had nothing to put in their places, he knew they were ruined. In this world of ideas, which has a vital importance to the over-heated brain of a city boy, this youth of fifteen was alone and lost. There was nothing to which he could attach himself.

He had come across Perette again—like him she had escaped from home—Marceline with the pouting lips. This time he had a taste of them. They took up again, but more intimately, their old meetings on the stairs. He had sought her arms as a refuge. Detached as she was from what she had left, he was for her a messenger from home. They had come from under the same roof, they had played by the same gutter. In the immensity of the City, the fugitives clung together and warmed their feathers. Marceline pecked the faltering mouth of her young lover. This boy was very ardent! He was burning himself at the lamp. He gave himself over furiously to this world of pleasure, this world of suffering which he had just discovered. It amused Marceline; but while this girl had no scruples, she felt for the blushing, shameless Cherub who devoured her something that troubled and astonished her, something maternal. She had taken her family sentiments lightly enough but she felt responsible towards the young lad. She held him on her breast, she scrutinized his pale cheeks and feverish eyes. At first she laughed at his nocturnal escapades. Then she was anxious when he went back damp and frozen in the icy dawn. He was lightly clad, he was imprudent, he had a dry cough, he was violent, he was burning. A gust of wind might have made one mouthful of him. Marceline was troubled; and at the same time she blew on the flames, she played with him. He was jealous and she tormented him; she did not intend him to bother her. She had scruples, but she ended by nearly being the death of him.

Just then, just in time, Pitan intervened. He knew every one, every one knew him. His kindness and simplicity, which they teased him about, had given the odd old fellow the privilege of telling people the sort of truths they did not want to hear. . . . They listened; and, whether they heeded him or not, they never thought of taking offense. Pitan said to the girl: "Mamselle Marceline, you can keep your little brother, but you won't keep him long. He's getting ready to go."

Marceline answered: "I know it, Papa Pitan, and it troubles me. I can see plainly enough that he's using himself up. But what can I do? That youngster won't listen to anything. He is blind and deaf. He's nothing but a hungry mouth; he's just like a sucking baby, and you can't stop his thirst. He's unhappy. He's distracted. He's sick, and there's no way of consoling him."

"He isn't in his right place with us. What he needs is his own home."

"He doesn't want it."

"I know, I know. He's at the age of revolt."

"We all are."

"Don't flatter yourself, Mamselle Marceline. At the bottom of your heart you are looking forward to the time when you can paddle a whole nestful of little rebels."

Marceline laughed and said: "I have some paddlings to pay back, all right."

"Let's attend to this rebel."

"Oh, this one. It wouldn't do to get after him against his will. The minute you begin to lecture him he's like a pony that kicks you on the nose."

"You know him. Isn't there any one you can put him in charge of?"

"His mother is a long way off."

"I know. The brave woman is earning his bread for him. She doesn't know what's going on. I thought of writing her, but from what I can see they don't get on very well. They've had a row, I know. They are probably too close to understand each other. She has her hard work and her troubles, that woman; it wouldn't do to worry her needlessly, if there is any other way. Hasn't our cub any other relative here, on the spot, who would be able to take him and look after him?"

"Yes, of course! Wait, Pitan! There's his aunt. I know her. She's no prude. She'll understand."

"Well," said Pitan, "you must go and speak to her."

Marceline made a wry face. She did not like to let go of her young pigeon. But she was a good girl and she said: "In his mother's absence, I'm a sort of mother to him. What would I do if I were in her place? It's true,

I can't keep him. My little scamp. There's only one way
to save him. I'll have to go. . . ."

She kept him one more night in her arms. Then she
went to see Sylvie and turned him over to her.

*

*   *

Sylvie was going through a crisis—the severest in her life since the death of her little girl. This woman, who had tried madly to forget, and whom the war had flung into a frenzy of excitement and pleasure, had just been recalled to reality by a blow. She might easily have foreseen this blow, but she had not foreseen the effect it was going to have on herself. Her husband, Leopold, had died, a prisoner in a German hospital. And this was the letter in which the poor man announced the news in advance:

"My dear wife, forgive me if I trouble you. I am not very well. They have put me in the hospital, but I can assure you that I am very well cared for by the Germans. I have nothing to complain of. The rooms are heated, for it is still cold outside. They say you are having trouble keeping warm, back there, that you haven't any coal. I can see you in the workshop, with the windows covered with frost: Celestine's fingers are numb, she is rubbing them on the cat's back. You yourself are never cold. You go around poking with your feet, shoving the others about to warm them up. But in our big bed, when the time comes to go to sleep, the sheets are clammy. At least during the day you can walk about, come and go; and it's something to be able to move around. If I could move! I am obliged to tell you that the doctors think that they will have to cut off my leg at the thigh. Well, what can I do? I don't know anything about it, and I let them do as they please. But I am so weak that I am afraid of dying under their hands, so I wanted to write to you first, to embrace you. Although one always hopes he'll get through. Perhaps I shall come back, perhaps I shan't come back. I beg you, my dear wife, not to upset yourself. It's not my fault, and you may be sure I shall do all I can to get through. But if misfortune comes, well, you are still young, you can marry again. I am not an unusual kind of person. Men like me can be replaced. If only he is honest, a good worker and respects you. Not that it gives me any pleasure to think of you with some one else. But I must have you happy. And no matter how it comes about I say in advance that it will be all right. My Sylvie, we've had our ups and downs together. We've worked hard. Sometimes we've quarreled. But we were always good comrades. I've often irritated you. I know well enough that I wasn't the one you ought to have had; but we are what we are, and I have done my best. Don't be angry with me if I haven't succeeded as I wished. Embrace Annette and Marc. We have not always been what we should have been to them. I would like you to pay a little more attention to the boy. We have no child. You ought to try to connect him later with our house. I can't go on. I'm not strong enough. And what can one say on this paper? I embrace you. Ah, Sylvie, I wish I could hold your hand! Good-by, or au revoir. Your faithful husband who thinks of you, of all of you, and will think of you from far away, under the ground. Near or far, I tell myself that it's the same earth and that your feet walk on it. Good-by, my dear wife, my dear old friend, my sweetheart, my love. Thank you for everything. Have courage. My heart is full at going. Ah, my God!

"Leopold.

"There is a note to Cribelin, one hundred and fifteen francs, due the eleventh of June, 1914, that has never been paid."

The last lines were smeared. A drop of moisture had fallen on them which the thumb had brushed.

The news of Leopold's death arrived at the same time.

It was then that Sylvie discovered how much she loved the man who had shared her life for twelve years. She had never appreciated him as anything but a good soul and a good partner in business. Death revealed to her that their association had gone far beyond their business. Mingling their days together, they had interlaced them so closely that the fingers of the expert dressmaker were unable to disentangle them now. She could not make out whether the thread that was broken was his or hers. The whole skein was broken.

And suddenly she became aware of the wrong she had done this man who had been a part of herself. The parsimonious love she had measured out to this affectionate heart! The infidelities of which he had perhaps never known, even if he suspected them. That he had not known of them took away none of her remorse, for she knew about them herself; and she was he now. She had the superstitious feeling that in dying he had turned the key that allowed him to read her heart. And what completely overwhelmed her was to recall, by comparing dates, what she had been doing that night when he had sought her hand in his death-struggle. In vain she said to herself: "I could not have known . . ."

In vain she said, "He didn't suffer from it . . ." In vain she said: "What's the use in thinking of it? You

can't change the past! . . ." That was just it. The
harm you do the living you can make up for. "My poor
husband, if you had come back I shouldn't have reproached myself! It isn't so much what I've done.
That's not so important. If you had come back I could
have made it up to you in affection. But now you are
dead. I can't pay you back now. Whatever I do, I shall
never forget this wrong. I am left with my debt. I feel
like a thief."

Like most people in Paris, Sylvie had a very strong
sense of injustice. Especially, of course, the injustice that
has been done to oneself. But also, very strongly, one's
injustice to others. It was painful to confess to herself
that she was left in debt to her best comrade.

When she was younger, she would have shown more
elasticity. She would have made the best of what she
could not change. When life still stretches far before
your feet if you stumble, you say that you will make
up for it. Somebody else will benefit from the injustice
you have done. But when the longest part of the road is
the part you have left behind you, the mistakes you have
made remain on your hands. You have taken the wrong
path; it is too late to change; you will never get there
now.

She went seriously back over her past life. It all spread
out before her, from the first days of her marriage, the
birth of her child, the quarrel with Annette, Yvonne, the
catastrophe, the life that went on again, Leopold's goodness, which had seemed so natural she had never thought
of noticing it, the war, her lovers, and the poor man who
had died over there, alone and betrayed . . . No, it
wasn't pleasant. And she tried instinctively to warm herself with the two that remained, Annette and Marc.

She had reached this point in her thoughts when Marceline came in and made her unvarnished confession.

And that very evening, alarmed by this story, as she was just going to look for Marc at his school, Marc came in. He had been expelled.

*
* *

Matters had moved quickly. One night when he had been stealthily reëntering the school he found himself face to face with the guilty superintendent, who was coming in also. Caught in the act, he replied as equal to equal, with a cold insolence. The master found himself trapped between the duty of dealing rigorously with him and fear lest the boy, who seemed ready for anything and who threatened him with his eyes, would ruin him also if he were denounced. He had a bad conscience but duty, aided by pride, carried the day. Marc was called before the head-master and dismissed. He said not a word. He did not deign to say anything either by way of excuse or accusation. In his heart he thought the better of the master for not having flinched.

Sylvie was transfixed at seeing him enter. She herself felt no small degree of responsibility. Annette had entrusted him to her. She had promised to watch the lad and keep her informed of his health and his behavior at school, to take charge of him on the days when he was allowed to go out and to hold the reins tight. Sylvie, who disapproved of her sister's puritanical severity and tacitly took the boy's side against her, had left the reins loose on his neck. She had told herself that youth must have its experiences, that nothing teaches it so well as its idiotic mistakes, that it was healthy for it to leave a little of its fleece on the bushes and that it was not so stupid that it couldn't find its feet again after its capers. She had even been imprudent enough to say to the boy:

"I knew how to pull myself out of things alone. You have a beak and claws as much as I have and you are no

fool. You know how to defend yourself. You have
eyes to see with, even if you have nothing to look at but
those monkeys at their desks, their eyes glued to the
black-board. You have legs to run about with even if they
are tied to your bench six days out of seven, before your
rack of Greek or Latin. Well, on the seventh day enjoy
your arms and legs. Run about, my dear, and see what
pleases you! Find out about things! If you burn yourself a little you will get out of it by blowing on your
fingers. And at least you will be insured against a conflagration."

She never stopped to think that it is a strange method
to take out insurance after the house is burned down. She
was repeating what she had always heard about her among
the common people: "Let nature have its way."

Also, she was not sorry to get her nephew off her hands,
so that she could go about her own affairs. She had plenty
of these and Marc knew what sort they were. She said
nothing about them, but she made no secret of them.
Sometimes Marc, coming to see his aunt on a Sunday
morning, would find that she had not come home. When
she did not see him, she contented herself with a letter.
She gave him money to amuse himself with. Sometimes
three weeks went by without his seeing her.

Sylvie was no more a hypocrite than she was a prude;
these were the least of her faults. Thinking of the way
she had carried out her sister's instructions, she did not deceive herself about the excuses she had made in regard to
her nephew, excuses that had just been brought back to
her. She told herself that she had completely lost her
head. For six months she had been thinking only of herself; and in her mania for amusement she had totally forgotten the boy who had been entrusted to her.

When she saw his pale face, his nervous gestures as he

told her, with a forced laugh, of the conclusion of his exploits, she said her *mea culpa*. Marc, who expected a fit of nerves or reproaches, or both, was astonished at her silence: "What do you say to this?"

She answered: "I have nothing to say to you for the moment. I have too much to say to myself."

Marc was not used to seeing Sylvie wasting her time in meditation. "What's the matter with you?"

"The matter is that I've ruined my life, that I've ruined my husband's life and that I'm in a fair way to ruining yours."

"How does that concern you? My life is my own. I do what I like with it. And besides, what is life worth, anyway?"

"It is worth what you are worth. Even that isn't true. It is of infinite value even for one who is worth the least."

"What are they doing with it out there? Go and look in the trenches! Life isn't worth much."

"I know. It doesn't cost them much. They have just taken Leopold's."

"Leopold!"

Marc had not known. The news was a blow. He understood Sylvie's seriousness. But he had never thought that the dead man had held such a place in her heart. He was astonished to hear her: "That's just why, because I understand now all the value of that life and what a murder they have committed—I have committed also."

"You?"

"Yes, what did I do with that life, that affection? Shame! Well, there's no use dwelling on what can no longer be undone. But what one can still do one must. You are still here, and I have to make reparation."

"What?"

"For the harm I have done you—let you do. (It's all the same. Don't interrupt me!) You know, my child, you needn't try to put on airs before me. I'm not your mother. The silly tricks you've been up to, the tricks you are so proud of—I know all about them, to my cost. They're nothing to brag about."

"Or to blush for either."

"Perhaps not. I'm not trying to shame you. I'm not entitled to, for I have done worse than you. I know one can't always resist; it would be inhuman. But I know the danger; and I have always known how to stop myself in time. You don't know, you never will know. You belong to another species. You are like your mother. You take everything seriously."

"I don't believe in anything," said Marc, drawing himself up.

"That's the most serious thing of all. I don't worry about anything, or about everything. I live in the present moment, which satisfies me fully. But this means that I am always looking at my feet, and if I happen to fall it's never from very high. But you are as you are; you never do anything by halves, and if you are lost you will be entirely lost."

"Of course I am as I am. I can't help that, and it's all the same to me!"

"But it isn't all the same to me, and I shall prevent it."

"By what right?"

"By right because you belong to me. Yes, to me, my child! To your mother and to me. She would never tell you, she who's always sacrificing herself; but I tell you myself. We didn't bring you up, we didn't labor for you for sixteen years to have you destroy, in a day, like an idiot, all we have manufactured. When you are a man,

after you have paid back all you owe us, you can do as
you choose with yourself. Until then, my dear, you have
a debt to pay. As the quail in the wheat says, 'Pay your
debt.'"

Marc angrily cried out that he had never asked for
any loan, that he had never asked to live.

"But you do live, my boy. Be as angry as you like, but
walk straight! I am here to watch."

And, without allowing the discussion to drag on, she
said: "Enough about this! It's closing time!"

Then she deliberately discussed with the boy, who was
quivering with helpless rage, what she was going to do
with him: "Without doubt the best thing would be for
you to go and join your mother."

"No, never! I hate her!" cried Marc.

Sylvie looked at him curiously, shrugged her shoulders
and did not even answer. She was thinking: "Idiot!
Family of idiots! . . . What has she done to make him
love her so?"

She said coldly: "Then there is only one solution. You
will stay with me and go to another lycée as a day pupil.
As for what has happened, I imagine you are not anxious
for me to tell your mother about it? Very well, I'll
manage somehow. But as for the future, remember I am
the government and I know all the tricks. Don't try to
hide! You will be free at your own hours, which means
at the hours I think best for you. I shan't tyrannize over
you, I know your needs and your rights. I shan't ask
more from you than you can give. But what you can, all
you can, you are going to give, my boy; and I shall send
in my bill for it. I am your creditor."

*
* *

She wrote Annette that the boarding pupils of the school had been sent home because of an epidemic and that she was taking her nephew in with her. Annette, who was only half reassured to learn that Marc was under her sister's roof, escaped from the country over a week-end and came to see with her own eyes. Sylvie knew quite well the reason for her visit. She was the first to admit that Annette had doubts as to her educative value as a guide for a growing boy. But she avowed so sincerely her previous mistakes and her keen sense of responsibility that Annette was quieted. They talked a long time about Leopold and, sadly turning over their old memories together, the two sisters found themselves closer than they had been in years.

Annette did not find in her son the same reasons for reassurance. His unhealthy appearance frightened her, but Sylvie undertook to have him in good shape again in three months. As for obtaining the least intimacy from the boy, it was not to be thought of. He held his mother off with the same air of obstinacy and reserve. Sylvie, taking Annette aside, made her promise not to insist. She had had enough trouble in getting him to agree not to bolt away from the house over Sunday, so that he would not have to talk with his mother. She had got him to promise at least to keep up appearances. As for the rest . . . they would see later! Her instinct told her that sometimes it is best to treat diplomatically the obstinacies of children. It was a sore point. Sylvie promised herself to cure this also, but the first necessity was to pretend not to notice it. Annette was too intense to be able to admit her sister's wisdom, so Sylvie did not speak to her of it. She looked upon her as another wounded person who was in equal need of care, but this cure she could not assume. Annette alone could be her own doctor. All that Sylvie could do for the moment was to see that the trouble between mother and son grew no worse.

Annette resigned herself to not discovering the reason for her son's hostility, and on Sunday night she set off again from Paris. In her affliction she at least carried with her the reassuring sense that she had left the disquieting boy in wise hands.

*
* *

Sylvie needed all her experience, all her intuition and her shrewd diplomacy, backed up by the firm grasp of an energetic and artful Parisienne, to hold in check, during the three months that followed, the young ocelot she had promised herself to train. She had put him into the room next to her own, at the end of the apartment. A door opened into the outside passage; but Sylvie kept the key and unlocked it only during the days and hours when she allowed her nephew to receive his friends in his room. Then Marc was sure that no indiscreet eye supervised his visits: it was the truce of God, or perhaps of the devil. Sylvie never failed. In the same way, she never tried to find out what he was doing, reading or writing in his room. He was sure of his own territory and she respected it. But he could not go out, except during the hours of the truce, without passing Sylvie's bedroom. All other exits were blocked. It is true that once he was out he might not have returned. He had threatened her with this, half laughing, half seriously, to test the ground and his Cerebus. In the same ironical manner she answered him, drawing her lips back over her teeth: "My dear boy, you would smart for it."

"Ah, what could you do?"

"I would have you posted up among the lost dogs. You can be quite calm: wherever you may be I have my men. I would have you taken into custody."

"So you have relations with the police, now?"

"If it were absolutely necessary I should not stop at any means. But I have no need of them. I have my own police. Your friends, my dear, will refuse me nothing."

Marc leaped up indignantly: "Who? Who? It isn't true! So I've been sold? I haven't any one, any one I can trust!"

"Yes, indeed, my fine fellow. You have one right under your hand."

"And who's that?"

"Myself."

Marc, with a gesture of anger, repelled her.

"That doesn't suit you? I understand, little pasha! Well, that's your penance. Come, I don't dispute your right to love and be loved. That's the daily bread of every living soul. But you must first earn this daily bread. Work, be a man! You wouldn't want to be the only useless one of the three Rivières, the parasite? Look at the ends of my fingers. Covered with needle-pricks. It makes no difference that I have loved my hands and loved having others love them, I haven't spared them. I'm not a prude. I've thoroughly enjoyed life. But it wasn't given to me. I bought it, day by day. I've worked hard. You do the same! And smooth out that offended mug! I do you an honor when I fill your ears with my song! I treat you as an equal. Say thanks! And shut up! Scamp!"

Marc boiled and fumed at hearing himself treated so casually. He would have liked to bite the hand that shook him so insolently by the leash, reminding him that he was under obligations to these two women, that he ate their bread and had no right to free himself from this humiliating servitude before he repaid them. But the most maddening thing of all was that he too had a sense of justice, that stupid sense, so deeply rooted in the Rivières, and that he admitted to himself that it was true.

He had nothing to reply to Sylvie's insolences. He had his honor as a man to save.

And then, there was another reason which he admitted less freely. This hand he would have liked to bite was not without charm. Sylvie aroused in him an irritated fascination.

Sylvie knew it. It was one of her weapons and she was careful not to neglect it.

The women of Paris have two or three youths. They would have more if they were not French and did not know how to limit themselves. Sylvie was in her second, and it was not the least appetizing. She could have turned the head of any one she wished. She did not wish to turn Marc's head except just so far as was useful to establish her government. Her measure was honest. One line more, and it would have risked not being so. It took a Sylvie not to go beyond it.

She knew the thirst in which the soul of the young lad languished, parched with desire, pride and that intellectual balderdash they stuffed him with at school, a thirst for the caress, for darkness, and the source that irritates and calms—a need to lean in dreams his feverish forehead against a soft, round throat that was warm, that was fresh, that breathed the aromas of a garden in spring and the queen of the flowers, the beautiful feminine body. She knew also the famished curiosity about life of these young wolves. Enjoyment for them is three-quarters knowing, and knowing often dispenses them from enjoying. To know! The chase! And life is the game. . . .

"Well, run, my boy. I am going to take you out for a walk. The chase will make you forget the game."

They were both together in Sylvie's room, in the evening, sitting by the table. He had finished his work, and

they didn't want to go to bed. Her fingers, always in
movement, were shaping the curves, softening the pro-
tuberances of a gallant and martial helmet. She did not
look at him; she knew she was being looked at.

Look! I am good to see, but I am even better to listen
to. . . .

The boy's eyes could take in at their ease every detail,
from the tips of her feet to the points of her ear. (Her's
were a little long and tapering, like those of a goat-
woman.) But she did not allow his mind the time and
silence to ripen its forbidden fruits. Her tongue never
stopped. She held him and led him by a golden chain.
She was careful not to question Marc and did not try to
find out his secrets. The way to make him tell them was
not to ask him. She reeled off at random her past adventures, humorous accounts of her mad—and wise—
pranks in which she sometimes lost her virtue but never
her bearings. Her malicious tongue, even while it
moistened the thread she broke between her teeth, caught,
in passing, the silhouettes of people, their gestures, the
ridiculous things about them—without sparing her own.
She treated Marc as a confidant. She carried him through
risqué situations, but her good humor saved everything—
along with the laughing judgment that dissected these
follies and agitations of the senses. Her naturalness was
perfect; one never stopped to think whether the tale were
moral or not. It was a staggering spectacle in which the
wit was stronger than the heart or the senses. Marc
followed—captivated, rebelling, laughing, shocked,
pleased and subjugated—the comic romance of life as this
unequaled observer told it. She seemed quite disinterested in her adventures and misadventures; it was all a
fairy-tale. What good company! One evening he had

felt a furious desire to kiss her face! But the fancy passed before he had time to formulate it. His impulse was dampened in the twinkling of an eye by that mocking spirit that pierced him to the quick. No illusions! He was enraged that he could never take himself seriously under her gaze. And while he raged he laughed. Laughing together and understanding—it was delicious! Laughter a remedy of pride, as it is of the morbid dejection of young people who at one moment claim every right for their ego and the next deny its existence. His inflated passions, which had grown too quickly, like his body, in which the child and the man disproportionately overlapped, the turn for tragedy which he had by nature and which he cultivated before his mirror, were like the curves of the velvet hat, corrected by the thumb of the skillful French sculptress who knew, through having experienced it, the tonic virtue of intelligent laughter. We do not recommend her method to others. Each method has only the value of the one who applies it. Any one who ventured to imitate Sylvie's method without having her dexterity would repent of it. It was an *article de Paris*.

The aunt and the nephew were both Parisians. They got along together very well. The tranquil liberty and the healthy irony of this unshadowed confidence gradually won Marc's confidence. He began to tell about his own experiences, even presenting them in a light that was not to his advantage. The moody boy was not offended when she laughed. And before long he not only confessed the past but the present as well, asking for her advice when he was about to commit some folly. It did not always prevent him from doing so, but at least if he was an idiot he no longer had any doubts about it. When she was convinced that nothing could turn him aside, she said: "Go ahead, but look out, you big silly."

And after it was done, she would ask: "Well, did you see, silly?"

He replied: "I saw, I was an ass. You were right."

They came and went about Paris together. Sylvie was ignorant of nothing, and she concealed nothing: "I call a cat a cat. . . ."

No false modesty. Her bold speech, the seriousness of her work, her vigorous honesty, formed an equilibrium between order and liberty, in which the unbalanced spirit of the young boy regained its breath and self-control. And thus, from this constant intimacy, which to timorous eyes might not have seemed without danger, there sprang up a frank comradeship, with nothing equivocal about it, between a novice and an initiate.

And although this affection was not of the utmost importance to the young boy, it was a diversion from other thoughts.

*

*   *

Sylvie never spoke to Marc about Annette. The two sisters wrote each other, and Marc suspiciously imagined that Sylvie drew up a weekly bulletin about him. But the clever mouse, knowing what an inquisitive fellow he was, played a trick on him. She left one of the letters open upon the table, quite certain that he would read it. And Marc discovered that there was no mention of him in it. He ought to have been pleased, but he was annoyed. Not to count at all was more than he asked for. "But what are you always writing to each other about?" he said impatiently.

"We love each other," replied Sylvie.

"A queer taste."

Sylvie burst out laughing: "For which?"

"For both of you."

Sylvie pulled his ear: "You are jealous!"

He protested haughtily.

"No? That's a good thing, for there wouldn't be any remedy."

He shrugged his shoulders. He only half believed her, but he was curious. How could two such different women be sisters and love each other? The enigma of his mother began to occupy him again.

Annette had resigned herself. She no longer tormented Marc with her anxious affection. Acting on Sylvie's advice, she confided only in her. Marc, no longer disturbed by her interest, began to feel confusedly the lack of this disturbance. And when the summer vacation came, he accorded Sylvie the grace of going to join his mother.

But the test was premature for both of them. From a distance Annette could moderate her affection. She could not do so from close by. She had been too much deprived of it. For months she had been dying of thirst, and in her heart she cried out for a drop—no, for torrents of love. In vain she repeated Sylvie's wise advice to herself: "If you want to be loved, don't show your love too much. . . ."

Could it be concealed? If it could, one was only half in love. Nothing by halves! For both of them, mother and son, it was all or nothing; and since it was all for Annette, for Marc it was nothing.

And yet he arrived full of conflicting feelings, a rancor and an attraction that were equally burning and that longed only to discharge themselves, like a cloud that is filled with electricity. When he met her, however, this woman whose soul had the breadth of a great wind, the fire retreated under the cloud and the sky emptied itself. With the first meeting of hands, words, glances, this absorbing affection that threatened to clutch him made him draw back, hurriedly. . . . Stop! . . . Once more it was the *Noli me tangere* of the Gospel.

"What, even for those who love you?"

"Those most of all."

He could not have explained himself, but Nature knew. He must not yield. The time had not come.

She drank him in greedily. "Look, the water has fled. Dig in the sand with your fingers, search with your mouth. . . ."

She looked at him too much. He felt this anxious glance inspecting all his features one by one. Like all mothers, she was worried first about his health. Her minute questions made the young lad impatient. He put them aside with a disdainful smile. As a matter of fact, in spite of appearances, his health was holding out well. His body had grown longer, his figure thinner, his face wan, hungry, tormented. A few lichen threads were beginning to prick above his feverish lips. His sickly appearance came from troubles of the spirit. His mother, who had lost touch with him, could no longer read what was going on in him. She saw on this mouth, on this adolescent forehead, traces of a precocious experience, hardness, irony; and she asked herself, her heart contracting: "What has he done? What has he seen?"

She trembled lest this sacred young flesh had known corruption. She felt herself responsible. Why had she abandoned him? But he would have none of her. How can you protect one whose soul is tightly shut? Enter by force? Already she had wounded herself against that obstinate lock. The hard metal was her own. And besides, what would she have seen if she had entered? She was afraid to think of it.

And he, feeling himself spied upon, closed the shutters again over his soul. Yes, what his mother's glance had caught was true. These blemishes were the shadows on the virgin skin of the tree of knowledge. Yes, he had seen and known too soon. But she did not see the reactions of the newly sown soul, the healthy disgusts, the loyal sorrows, and that relationship between revolt and passionate outbursts which was concealed under his bashfulness, the virile instinct that demands that the young of man shall fight alone, without help.

Consequently, since he refused to allow her to enter his life, she had to resign herself to their living side by side without any intimacy. And this was far from pleasant. Annette no longer noticed the austerity of the life she was leading; but Marc felt his skin scraped by it as if by a rough towel. He felt this tragic seriousness, which she had ceased to perceive, weighing upon him. He did not reflect that he was refusing her the only ray of light that could have cheered her, that he was freezing in its bud the flower of maternal love. Thrown back into the inner drama from which she was trying to escape, she betrayed, without meaning to do so, the disquietude of thought through which she was passing. And Marc caught in this, perhaps, too much of a resemblance to his own not to keep out of its way.

In the sleepy atmosphere, in the flat existence of the little town, he could find no resources for amusement away from the shadows of the house. The countryside, rich and blooming in its yellowish maturity, dozed in the August sunshine. It would have been good to clasp it with his growing arms. But the small Parisian was not yet sensitive to Nature. Too many other objects solicited his spirit and his senses. The hour had not yet struck when his eyes would open and read the silent music written in the book of the fields. One must be more mature to discover the value of the unstudied fields and their odor of violets. If the body feels, it does so unwittingly. The charm works later.

Annette took him out for several walks. The presence of another person was enough to interrupt the soul's colloquy with nature. Annette thought out loud; she enjoyed so keenly the earth and air that she placed herself between them and the young boy:

Keep out of my sunlight! . . .

She loved to walk. He saw her strength, her youth

awakened by the rapid rhythm of her step and her blood. He saw her run, exclaim, full of enthusiasm over a flower, an insect. Later, when he was in Paris again, these images would return to him; this joy, this flood of life, this mouth, these eyes, this humid throat. (Once, in her joy, she clasped him madly, and he played the man, ruffled by this familiarity.) For the moment everything shocked him. This woman tired him. He was quickly out of breath. He was humiliated. He could not endure having her slacken her pace so that he could keep up with her. He put an end to the walks by a flat refusal.

So nothing remained for him but to be bored. He did not hesitate to show this. Never by complaining. No! He said nothing. He was sacrificing himself.

Of all attitudes this was the one that Annette could least endure. "Sacrifice, my dear? I don't want it. I would rather do without you. . . ."

She made a last attempt: "It's Paris he misses. Well, we'll go to Paris!"

She spent the last three weeks of her vacation there with him, in spite of her secret repulsion at returning.

For almost a year, her only connection there, except with Sylvie, had been with the little mourning widow and virgin, Lydia Murisier, whose letters kept growing more and more distant. The two women liked each other, and yet it was as if, in their exchange of thoughts, they were constantly stumbling against word-barriers of the heart—an embarrassment they did not wish to plumb. Each kept a tender memory of the other, and it would have been sweet to throw their arms about each other. But they had no desire for a meeting that would have forced them to explain themselves. When, on her arrival, Annette learned that Lydia was away from Paris, for a fortnight, she was both disappointed and relieved.

But this was the least apprehension she felt in returning to the house. There were others! She preferred not to think about them in advance. And this return to her apartment was even worse than she had feared.

As she no longer needed it, she had left the use of it to the two refugees, Alexis and Apolline, reserving for herself only her bedroom and that of her son. They had invaded all the rooms and now looked upon themselves as the owners of the apartment. Annette seemed to them an intruder: it was as if they were doing her a kindness in allowing her to lodge under their roof. That word "thanks" did not go well with Apolline's sulky features. They only lightened a little when she learned that Annette was not going to stay longer than two or three weeks. She showed, moreover, that she expected to give them the use of only one room. She considered that for three weeks the mother and son could sleep quite well in the same chamber. Marc indignantly asserted his rights, *manu militari,* by throwing Alexis' belongings out of his room. Most painful of all was the condition in which Annette found her apartment. Dirt and disorder, broken plates, kitchen utensils burned and befouled, walls spattered with water that had rolled down, here and there, and spoiled the hard-wood floors, the wear and tear of curtains and furniture. They had respected nothing. The best coverings and bedding had been unceremoniously taken out of Annette's room to serve the invaders. The portraits and engravings of which she had made her domestic horizon had been moved or replaced, some set on the floor, turned against the wall, others carried in a heap into the storeroom. Apolline had substituted for them photographs of her own family with astonishing jaws and bigoted expressions. Even the books and papers, except the few that had been safely locked up, had been touched, less through curiosity (Apolline did not read) than because of mere idleness and itching fingers. Traces of the latter were scrawled everywhere on the spotted leaves and dog-eared pages. Through all the rooms trailed the odor of a wild animal's burrow. Marc, disgusted and furious, talked of throwing the creatures downstairs. Annette tried to calm him. She made a few severe observations to Apolline, which were badly received; and at the first words she was struck with an oppressive sense of the spiritual disorder, the tragic crisis into the midst of which she had fallen.

The brother and sister avoided each other. Between them there seemed to be hostility, aversion, anger or fear. Annette's sudden return had again obliged them to room together. At night you heard heated altercations in stifled voices, a stormy recitative from which emerged Apolline's gusty apostrophes and excited breathing. A heavy silence followed. This went on for a week. Then, in the middle of the night, Apolline came out of the room, screaming. Annette got up to insist upon her being silent. She found her in the corridor, almost naked, tearing herself with her nails and lamenting; she had lost her reason. Annette brought her into her own room and tried to calm her. She got back into bed. Apolline, in a heap beside the bed, poured out a torrent of savage, violent words. Annette put her hand over her mouth so that the boy in the next room should not be awakened. (He had been listening for a long time.) And in the tumultuous flood Annette, frozen, read the truth. . . .

The night passed. Apolline, crouching on the carpet,

just below Annette's pillow, groaned, fell silent, then furiously began reciting prayers. She ended by going to sleep with her mouth open, snoring. Annette did not sleep. At the first light of dawn, leaning over the edge of the bed, she looked down at the woman sleeping against it, with her head thrown back and her savage, frightened, hunted, animal face. It was like an antique mask, with its heavy features, terrible and grotesque, the mask of an eyeless Gorgon with a mouth in an attitude of silent clamor. Under Annette's gaze, the Gorgon awoke. Hardly had she caught sight of these eyes scrutinizing her from above than she rose, fiercely, and started to go out of the room. Annette held her by her wrist. She groaned:

"What do you want, now? Let me go! You have snatched out of my mouth the bread that was covered with excrement, my shame, my treasure. What more do you want? You hate me, you despise me. I return it. I'm a piece of filth, and I'm better than you!"

"I don't hate you or despise you," said Annette. "I am sorry for you."

"Spit on me!"

"It's not for me to judge you. Your God will take care of that. And you are mad, and I'm sorry. The whole world is mad. One doesn't know whether one won't be struck down oneself to-morrow. But you can't stay any longer in this house."

"You are going to turn me out?"

"I have to protect my son."

"Where do you want me to go?"

"Work; look for something to do! How could the two of you, for two whole years, stay here without doing any useful work with all the distress the country is in?"

"Our distress is as bad as the country's. Let the others pay!"

"Who will help you if you don't help yourselves? Your trouble, the canker that devours you, is caused by doing nothing. Only work can save you."

"I can't work."

"What? You with all your strength, accustomed to the hard country work, you who are suffering from the energy you ought to be spending? You shut yourself up in idleness, like a wolf in a cage, and then you howl through the bars at God! God is work."

"I can't do it any longer. I need my possessions, I need my land. They took everything, destroyed everything, my property, my land, my people. Nothing is left to me. He's all that is left to me. (She pointed to Alexis's room.) And I hate him! And I hate myself! And I hate God, who wanted it to happen."

"And I, who don't believe in him, pity him. I pity him. You have betrayed him. Hate, hate, the only word that fills your mouths! You don't know any other. If there is a God he gave you your will. What are you going to do with it?"

"I am rolling it in this dirty den, in this flesh he has given me. I revenge myself on him. He is in me, and I am destroying myself."

"Your God is like the scorpion. If he can't destroy, he destroys himself."

"He is the God of Verdun, the God of to-day."

"You make me ill. Leave me! Do you want to destroy me also?"

"I shan't weigh on you any longer."

She ran out.

During the day they moved out of the house. The

whole house breathed more freely. Their presence had been the source of endless complaints. Annette, who wished them to go, felt disturbed to see them leave. She tried to discover where they were going. Apolline refused to tell her, as she refused with a brutal "No" the offer of money that Annette made her.

This same week their neighbor on the landing, young Chardonnet, returned on a leave of forty-eight hours.

He spent these hours shut up in his rooms. No one saw him. But on the other side of the wall Marc heard footsteps; and with his sharp gaze he followed the silent drama of this return.

Clarisse was no longer the Clarisse of the year before. The whirlwind of madness had passed over her, had passed away. And she once more found herself within the four walls of her apartment and those still more tightly sealed walls within which thought burrows, coming and going noiselessly, from one room to the other, without causing a sound from the furniture or the floor. The cat! And neither in her slits of eyes, velvety and shining but without any inner light, nor under the fresh-colored rouge that masked her pale cheeks, could any one have read her memories and dreams. But the starving husband, who had returned to eat the fruit of his garden, did not find the same taste in the soul he had left; and although he was, on the whole, a poor observer, he saw at the first glance that behind the façade the house had changed. Something had happened. What? And how could he find out? The smiling façade did not yield up its secret. It was in vain that he embraced her. He did not hold her thought; he held only the body. And what had this body done? And this witness for the body, this mind—what had it seen and wished? What did it know? What was it hiding? It would never tell anything. He would never know.

They talked calmly about ordinary things. And suddenly the man's voice became angry. Without any apparent cause. He had felt it. She bowed her head. They were silent. He was ashamed of having betrayed himself and enraged that he was not able to draw out her secret. They were fastened together, and yet walled up against each other. He rose without a word and went out, slamming the door on the landing. Clarisse had not moved; but after a moment Marc heard her using her handkerchief. He knew that she was weeping.

When the husband's leave expired and he left, they had nothing to say to each other. What they did have to say would have knocked down in ruins this façade of life that both of them—he as well as she—feared to shake. For how could they have lived if, in that field of ruins, like a bombarded plain, which their life was at present, they had not been able to attach their nest to that façade of the past, the illusory image of what they had once been! They said good-by to each other. Their lips were dry. They embraced. They loved each other. They were strangers.

During this same week, the last that Annette had to spend in Paris, Lydia Murisier returned.

Seeing each other, the two women felt again all their old affection. And their lips met before they had said a word. But the moment they began to speak they spoke from behind a wall, and they both knew that even if they had the key they would not have opened the only door they had to pass through. It was very painful; a barrier between them. They wanted each other, and yet they could do nothing to lift the barrier.

Lydia had lost that flower of frankness and spontaneity, the poetic grace of which had perfumed every one of her movements. She had severely repressed it, covered it over with her mourning veil. She had offered to the dead her sacrificed nature. The rapturous, sorrowful mysticism of the first days had not lasted. Its heart-rending, morbid charm had failed. Such states can be prolonged only by factitious methods. The heart begs for mercy, the heart wishes to forget. To be forced to remember, it must be put on a chain and tortured. It is the slave fastened to the grindstone, under the whip of the will. Lydia had lost her flexibility, thinking of the dead.

"Think of him! Think of him!"

And this was not enough: "Think like him!"

She had entirely forsworn her own way of thinking to espouse that of the being whom she wished to snatch from oblivion, from *her* forgetfulness. . . . (The tragic struggle of souls, in the silence of the night, against the death that is encroaching upon the treasure of their love!) She was enveloped in this idealism of dry, burning ideas that had formed the tissue of Girerd's soul; they spoke through her mouth—that young mouth broken with tenderness. And it was so strange and painful to hear her! Annette listened, frozen, and could not answer. She felt the deliberate insincerity, the heroic, mendacious effort of the dear girl to believe in what she did not believe. And she could not answer, for she knew how inhuman it would be to pull off the mask. It was this armor that kept the delicate, broken plant from falling! But though Annette said nothing to betray her thoughts, Lydia read them on her closed lips and she drew the bolt of the door already closed in the wall that separated them.

She exalted this war that had taken away her happiness and her life. She thrilled as she extolled the problematical future this fighting was preparing, this misty Messianism of future justice and peace, through the slaughter and iniquities of to-day, and these millions of bereavements—no! her own, the body of her beloved, springing from his blood (this was the only one that counted!)—the mocking future of this reign of God: the formless God of those who no longer have one, of the men of the Occident who have lost their God and want one at any price: universal Democracy.

Oh, tender, heart-broken mouth, how false these words sound coming from your lips! Your withered smile is like a wound. . . .

She displayed her faith. She paraded it, for she guessed that Annette no longer felt it. (Had she ever felt it?) She had divined her disillusionment with all these ideas and her withdrawal from all the passions that in these days held the countries united. And Annette, who had not realized it until this moment, became aware of it through the instinctive opposition that separated their paths and said to the two women:

"Alas, we shall never meet again on this earth!"

But where could one flee on this earth? What had they made of this world?

The atmosphere of Paris, the atmosphere of the world, was unbreathable during these last days of the summer of 1916. The earth was an open jaw, baying after death. Its furious breath stank with the corpse of humanity. The tumbril-loads of flesh, ground up on the Somme and at Verdun, could not satiate it. Since the time of the religious slaughtering of peoples by the Aztecs, heaven had never inhaled such hecatombs. Two new neighboring nations had just joyously entered the dance of death. It was the thirty-second declaration of war in two years. The dancers were stamping their feet. The press, crouched on its heels about the circle, clapped its hands, beat the bones against the kettledrums and howled. In Germany they were singing the new Canticle of Saint Francis, the hymn to our sister Hate:

"Faith, Hope and Hate have been given us. But the greatest of the three is Hate. . . ."

In France, Science, jealous of the Ninety-three Intellectuals, wanted to have her own and published that monument to dishonorable insanity, *The Germans and Science*, in which the greatest leaders of thought—two names excepted—not only cast the Germans out of the European family, but doctorally analyzed their brains, their bones, their excrement and cut them off from the human race. One Master of Science wanted to see Berlin razed to the ground, "so as to leave in the center of that proud land an avenging oasis of ruins," A Doctor of Laws established the legality of reprisals. One honest and respected mouthpiece of Liberal Catholicism in France congratulated French Catholics, "for not having hesitated in the name of Christ, not to forgive the Catholics of Germany." Another chorus-leader demanded the Emperor as his share of the spoils, so that he could put him in the bear-pit in the *Jardin des Plantes*. For the grotesque and the horrible were mingled, Tartuffe and Père Ubu. And perhaps the worst of all was that, of the two, the grotesque had the leading part in the drama. Among the local fiddlers, the leaders of the dance, shameless hypocrisy rose to Himalayan heights. One canting minister, at a sitting of the Assembly, exalted in a tearful voice, to the applause of his enraptured associates, the august disinterestedness of the newspapers that he was himself bribing. And the Welsh boaster, Lloyd-George, that petty Cromwell, holding a Bible in one hand and a sword—somebody else's sword—in the other, preached to his Baptist brethren the new Genesis. Comparing the first Creation with that of the war, of which he was the Lord, his thunder burst over those sons of iniquity, the pacifists: "For no inhumanity, no absence of pity, could be compared to their cruelty in holding up the war"—midway. Meanwhile, impassive America, rounding out her note, flooded the Old World with her articles of death. For the right hand is not supposed to know what the left is doing; and if it is written, "Thou shalt not kill," it is nowhere written that thou shalt not honorably manufacture instruments for killing, provided they are of good quality and are well paid for.

Annette, stopping her ears, scornful, heartsick, took refuge with her sister. But Sylvie never troubled herself about the times or the misfortunes of others outside the narrow circle of those who belonged to her, those whom she loved, her own. The charming girl said:

"Darling, you mustn't bother about it. There's nothing to do but to be patient. Look at me! I'm waiting. It will surely end by ending some day. But we mustn't hurry! It's got to last a while longer. One of my good friends, a good-looking chap with three stripes and the *croix de guerre*—he's just been killed—said to me: 'We've got to kill a million Germans.'"

Annette stared into Sylvie's eyes. Was she talking seriously? Yes, she was serious. Oh, not deeply! She put no passion into it. She felt no anger at those she was killing in advance. But since it must be it must!

"You know," said Annette, "we shall have to reckon at least half a million of our own for their million."

"Well, what do you expect, my dear! You have to pay something for it!"

The fashionable world had come to life again. The tearooms were crowded, and beautiful customers were beginning to flock to Sylvie once more. The tension of the past years had ceased, as well as that virile bearing of the first days of the ordeal and those morbid reactions of hate and pleasure that had shaken the senses like attacks of intermittent fever. It was much more terrifying; human nature was getting used to it. It had adapted itself to the new conditions with that ignoble, marvelous plasticity that permitted man to slip like a worm through the smallest cracks by which life escaped during the convulsions of the earth in the millenniums when all the species that were less capable of forswearing themselves and bending so as to pass, perished. And if one must admire the art of reëstablishing a normal existence in the midst of the abnormality of the most monstrous times, then Paris was marvelous.

But Annette was not disposed to do homage to it. She saw its reflection on her son's face and the mirror frightened her. Marc no longer showed the quivering excitement, the fits and starts, the violence, the grimacing laugh that had disturbed his mother the summer before. He no longer showed anything; he was indifferent. His pale face was like a pond in which the fever that had left him had sunk to the bottom. The water was troubled but there were no ripples. The motionless surface reflected nothing beyond it. And nothing from outside was reflected in it. He was asleep.

He seemed to be asleep. And he seemed to see, feel and hear nothing of the storm that was twisting the forest about him, the falling trees, the gusts of death, the stench and the uproar—and this mother was leaning so anxiously over the edge. But who could be sure? Under the oily slime that covered the pond a life was in travail. The time had not come to disclose it. And if he did disclose it, it would not be to his mother's imploring eyes.

It was only in talking to Sylvie that he revealed himself at all. He was at ease with her and talked calmly. With Annette he watched himself and he watched her. But there was no more of the insolence and irritation there had been in their former relations. He was polite. He listened without answering. He waited without impatience for her to leave.

*
* *

She left, frozen out. He was more a stranger to her than when they had clashed. One is still bound to one's adversary. One is not bound to one who is completely indifferent. She had become unnecessary to him. The others, Sylvie, sufficed. Who leaves his place loses it. There was no longer room for her.

No longer in her son's heart, no longer in the universe. For she saw everywhere people who were alien to her and nowhere any one to whom she was akin. All their reasons for living, for wanting to live, for believing, for wanting to believe, for fighting, for wanting to conquer, had fallen from her body like outworn garments, as the summer leaves fall from a tree. And yet she *wanted*. She had no experience of those neurasthenic states in which energy dissolves and timorously flees. She was charged with energy. Her depression sprang from her inability to use it any longer. What was she to do with this force, this need for action, this need for struggling, this need for loving, with this need ("Yes, I also . . .") for hating? Love what they loved? No. Hate what they hated? Never! Fight? For what cause? Alone in this mêlée, towards whom, towards what could she turn?

A week had gone by since she had resumed her work in the college. One cold, rainy October evening she was going home, tired and absorbed. As she was about to enter the house she noticed an unaccustomed agitation in the streets.

A new hospital (of misfortune) had just been opened not far from where she lived. The charnel-houses of

Verdun were disgorging their wounded. They could find
no more stalls in which to hang this martyred meat. For
the first time the little forgotten city was receiving its
load, and the first ones they were sending them were
Germans! Up to the war they had not even had enough
hospital room for their own people. They had piled up
their sick, wrecks of over-work or laziness—in the end all
come to the same rubbish heap!—in narrow, sordid, dilapi-
dated quarters, where infection and dirt had been collecting for centuries. No one bothered about it, neither
the sick nor the doctors. They were used to it. And
now, with progress (that is, with the war) new thoughts
(or rather new words) had appeared—hygiene, antiseptics.
The problem was to make death healthier, while they
multiplied it. So, for the new hospital they had white-
washed the filthy walls of an old boarding school, united
the odor of phenol with the odor of mold, rearranged the
class-rooms, while they invoked Ambroise Père, and put in
an endowed bathroom—a real rarity!

And the Boches were to get the first taste of all this
luxury! The little town protested furiously. It had
just been very severely tried. The battles of the past two
months had decimated the children of the country.
Nearly all the families were in mourning. The customary
apathy had been shaken to the point of exasperation.
Even the personnel of the hospital were divided. One
party had decided to refuse their help to the enemy. A
petition had been drawn up and was going about from
hand to hand. The arrival of the convoy came before
the matter was settled. They knew nothing about it until
it was there. The news had brought all the people out
of their houses.

The wretched herd had already been driven out of the

station. The street that led from it was filled in a few
minutes like a gutter after a heavy rain. Most of the
people were inoffensive beings, good-natured, indifferent,
a little coarse, not bad hearted. But their worst instincts
blazed up on the spot. The appearance of the procession
was announced, from a distance, by roars. They came
along, two cart-loads of living débris, bundles of rags on
litters, with their heads thrown back. The arm of one
hung over the edge and his nails were scraping the dust of
the road. A small group, less severely wounded, walked
in front, with bandaged faces or arms. In the front rank
was the tall, thin silhouette of a German officer. The
escort was inadequate. With fists raised, the crowd—the
women with their claws stretched out—rushed to meet
them. *Union Sacrée!* For the first time all sorts of
people were mingled together, small shop-keepers and
middle-class folk, and even, a few steps behind, several
society women. The unfortunate men who were walking
along stopped for a moment but those who were behind
forced them to go on. They moved forward, pushed,
with terror on their faces. They thought they were going
to be massacred. Stones were thrown. The crowd
bristled with canes and umbrellas. Cries of "Death!"
Hisses! The officer, of course, attracted most of these
attentions. A fist struck him; a hand snatched off his
helmet and threw it down; a shrieking woman spat in his
face. The man staggered from a blow. . . .

Annette sprang forward.

She had been three rows back in the crowd, staring with
petrified eyes. She had not foreseen or intended what
followed. She had not even had the time to be aware
of what was going on in herself. She dashed forward,
her head lowered, pushing aside the furious men and

women who blocked the street in front of her. She broke her way through. And the people learned what the fist of a Rivière meant. She reached the German officer and, turning to face the crowd, with her arms stretched out, she called out to them:

"Cowards! Are you French?"

The effect of these words was like the double blow of a whip.

She continued in the same breath: "Are you men? All wounded people are sacred. All those who suffer are brothers."

She dominated the crowd with her voice and arms. Her violent glance, sweeping over them, struck every one between the eyes. They drew back, growling. Annette stooped down to pick up the officer's helmet. This single second was enough to destroy her domination over those who surrounded her. The snarling mob, undecided, was gathering itself together to spring at her throat when a young woman, wearing the costume of the Red Cross, stepped up to Annette's side and said in a frail, firm voice: "This lady has said the honorable thing. Wounded enemies are under the protection of France. Whoever fails them, fails her."

Every one knew her. She belonged to one of the most respected aristocratic families of the neighborhood. Her husband, an officer, had just been killed at Verdun. Her gesture was decisive. Two other ladies, nurses, took their place beside her. A few of the bourgeois hastened to urge those about them to be calm. The woman who had just spat in the officer's face began noisily to pity a wounded boy. And the crowd, grumbling, but making way, let the convoy pass escorted by the young widow and Annette, who supported the staggering officer with their arms.

They reached the hospital, and no one dared to make any further protests. Professional duty and humanity resumed their rights. But in the confusion of the first hours, aggravated by the lack of nurses (the wavering ones returned, one by one, during the night) the staff were overwhelmed and Annette was able to remain, without any one's noticing her, until the middle of the night. With the help of that fury of a few hours earlier, that female fanatic, who now turned out to be a good-natured soul, ashamed of her violence and anxious to have it forgotten, Annette undressed and washed the wounded. And when one of these unfortunates was pushed aside, as beyond hope from any operation, she consecrated herself to his last dying hours.

He was a stripling, thin, nervous, brown-skinned, of that half-Semitic, half-Latin type of the Rhineland. A frightful wound. His abdomen was open, and already the worms were stirring in it. He was shaken by convulsions and gritted his teeth in his pain; then he would howl. His eyes opened and closed, seeking some person, some object, no matter what living thing, some firm point to which he could cling in his shipwreck. He met Annette's eyes and caught hold of them. . . . Those pitying eyes. . . . Oh, what an unexpected light in his distress! The waters were swallowing him up. Struggling up from the depths, he cried:

"*Hulfe!*"

She bent over him. She put her hand under his head, which was straining to rise. She murmured pitying German words in his ears. They fell like rain on his dry, burning skin. He gripped her other free hand and sank his fingers into it. She felt to the very depths of her own flesh each quiver of the dying man. She whispered

patience to him. The brave boy held his breath to stifle
his cries and took a firmer grip of this hand that was
holding him above the abyss. Annette's eyes grew more
and more tender as she watched him going down. She
said:

"*Sohnchen! Knabelein! Mein armer lieber Kleine!*"
He had a last convulsion. He opened his mouth to
call her. She kissed him. She did not free her hand
from these anguished, dying fingers until she had seen him
delivered.

She went away. It was three o'clock in the morning.
An icy fog. A dull sky. Empty streets. There was no
fire in her room. She did not go to bed until the daylight
came. The horror of the world was in her. Her heart
was swollen with pain. And yet it was eased. It had
found again its place in the tragedy of humanity.

*

* *

All that weighed upon her had fallen away. With one motion of her shoulders she had shaken it off. And now that she saw it at her feet, she understood at last the weight that had been crushing her.

She had been lying. She had been lying to herself. She had avoided her own eyes. She had shrunk from looking in the face the monstrous ideas that had oppressed her. She had accepted passively the fatal war and the country. She had accepted timorously the excuse of a "fact of nature." And suddenly there had risen against this brutal nature her own nature, denied and gagged, her betrayed, unsatisfied nature that was avenging and liberating itself. And her breast, restrained by savage bonds, broke the bonds and breathed freely. She reclaimed her right, her law, her joy and her suffering also, but her own suffering—Maternity.

The whole of Maternity. Not merely that of her son. You are all my sons. Happy and unhappy sons, you are wounding yourselves. But I clasp you all. Your first sleep, your last sleep, I rock in my arms. Sleep! I am the universal Mother. . . .

When day came, she wrote to the other mother, that of the dead boy whose eyes she had closed. She sent her his last kiss.

Then she took up her class-books and her note-books. And she began again her day's work without having rested, but with new strength and with peace in her heart.

PART III

NNETTE'S action made a great stir. It was discussed in all the houses. If it had not been publicly approved by young Madame de Marëuil it would have been unhesitatingly condemned. But as she had this security behind her, there were a few who acquiesced. Many were scandalized. All felt a concealed irritation. Even admitting that she was right, they could not endure a stranger to the neighborhood coming and giving them—and in such a tone!—lessons in dignity.

They were silent, however, when they learned—everything is known in a few hours in a small town—that Madame de Marëuil had called on Annette the next day and, not finding her at home, had left an invitation for her. Annette was under the ægis; so they postponed their resentment until the next occasion. The principal of the college, who had sent for Madame Rivière, contented himself with giving her a discreet warning; no one questioned her patriotism, but she must abstain from expressing it *extra muros!* "Do your duty in your own place, when and how it is asked of you—*Ne quid nimis!*" At Annette's first word of reply the principal drew back with an affable gesture. "I'm not reproaching you. It's just a little advice." But Annette knew that a master's advice is a first summons.

For the moment, there was nothing to do but resume the yoke and go back into her niche. She had done what she had had to do. To-morrow would suggest to-morrow's duties. To-day she was spared the trouble of choosing between them, for when she presented herself again at the hospital door she found it closed against her. A sign forbade any one to enter the wards who was not a member of one of the two local organizations, the Red Cross and the Women of France. (These, incidentally, were as bitter rivals as the dog and the wolf.) Later she discovered that the prohibition had been intended especially for her.

But if this door was closed to her need of serving, another door opened where her new maternity could find employment. And no one could have foreseen the dangerous roads along which these obligations her newly awakened conscience had assumed were going to lead her.

At her first call on Madame de Marëuil, the young widow, without departing from a somewhat cold reserve, expressed an affectionate esteem for Annette. She told her that one of her brothers-in-law, who was severely wounded and was being cared for by his family, had a great desire to see Madame Rivière. Annette at once availed herself of the invitation.

*
* *

Germain Chavânnes was only related to Madame de Marëuil, née Séigy, through the marriage of his sister to one of the Séigy brothers. But the two families had long been closely connected by ties of sympathy and interest. Both of them had taken root in the land long years ago. Their lands adjoined. Their differences of opinion had always been more apparent than real. The republicanism of the Chavânnes was of a pale shade; the cautious red of the early days had gradually faded. What remained of it was a pink, which, if it was not entirely white, combined very agreeably with it. Their solid, honorable wealth contributed not a little to fill the ditch that limited rather than separated their estates. (At all times, and everywhere, property is related to property.) They cultivated their land themselves—about twenty farms— plundering the country like a flock of chickens; and their love of the soil and their worship of order which, if it was not their religion, was quite half of it—of course we are referring to the only religion which is a power for order in the Occident, that of Rome—these essential traits, which the de Marëuils, the de Thésees, the de Séigys shared in common with the small landed nobility of the region, had left only enough difference between them to flatter the pride of each by persuading him that it was a mark of superiority over his neighbor. This is the weakness of all men. The de Séigys and the Chavânnes were too well-bred to allow any of this to appear. The proper thing was to keep the secret for one's own special enjoyment.

That Annette Rivière should be invited into this circle

was a surprise, and for a good reason. Not to Annette, who had no feeling for social distinctions. But to the neighborhood, actually, she was invited only by these two single members of the Chavânnes and de Séigy families, to whom present circumstances had given undisputed rights in their homes: Madame Louise de Marëuil and Germain Chavânnes. Both had paid heavily the debt to their name and their country. And both had a special place in their circle. It took Annette only a few days to realize this.

The Chavânnes house was an old dwelling with gray walls in a tortuous street that ran down from the cathedral. Silence surrounded it, broken from time to time by the melancholy sound of the bells and the polished oak door with its well-rubbed ironwork, which alone shone coldly in the dusty façade; one crossed a paved court before arriving at the main body of the house. The windows of the living-rooms looked out on this gardenless court, without a leaf of a tree, without a blade of grass, shut in by the four gray walls. It was as if the bourgeois of the province, after the long months passed on their estates, in their country-houses, wanted to wall themselves in when they came to town so that Nature could not find them. The Chavânnes usually lived here only for a few months during the winter; but events, the war, the duty of taking an active part in public affairs, the illness of their son, had decided them to stay in town until the future brightened.

At the moment, the family was virtually reduced to women. The father was dead. All the men who were strong enough, the sons and sons-in-law, had left. There remained a boy of seven, the son of young Madame Chavânnes de Séigy, who spent long hours with his nose against the window-panes, watching for the entrance door to swing ajar for the rare visitors, and day-dreaming to the sound of the bells and the cries of the rooks. He dreamed of flags, cake and graves. His was the first face that greeted Annette on her entry into the house. She met him as she went by, and every time she returned, watching alone, eager and idle, stealing out of sight.

Shadows filled the room on the first floor, with its high ceiling and deep alcove, where a young man, seated by the window on this bleak November day, rose from his armchair and bowed to Madame de Marëuil and the visitor she presented. But although at the first glance one could see that death had woven its shroud in this room, its shadow had spared the head of the wounded man. His face was one of those faces of central France that seem all luminous: a kindly face, with regular features, an aquiline nose, a well-defined mouth, very blue eyes and a blond beard. He smiled at Annette and thanked his sister-in-law with an affectionate glance.

The courteous conversation began with vague remarks about health and the weather. They clung to cautious statements. Then, after a moment, Madame de Marëuil discreetly vanished.

Upon this, Germain Chavânnes, whose piercing eyes had studied Annette's features in rapid glances, held out his hand and said:

"The good Louise has told me of your valor. You are not one of the people who prolong the fight, when it is over, against a beaten enemy. You are soft-hearted enough to spare the conquered. So I dare to hope that you have a little heart left for the conquered one you see here."

"You?" said Annette.

"I. Severely wounded. Badly beaten. I have all the vanities."

"You will get well."

"No. Leave that illusion to others and to me! There are enough of us for the task. That isn't the reason I need you. The defeat for which I ask your indulgence is not of the body but of the spirit. It would be nothing to be conquered if one believed in the conqueror."

"What conqueror?"

"The fate that sacrifices us. . . . No, that isn't the right way of expressing it. The fate to which we sacrifice ourselves."

"Do you mean the country?"

"That is one of its faces. The mask it wears to-day."

"I am conquered too, and I don't believe in the conqueror. But I don't surrender. It isn't over yet."

"You are a woman. You are a gambler. Even when she loses a trick, a woman believes she is going to win in the end."

"I don't believe it. But, win or lose, as long as there remains to me a pound of flesh to play with in the game of life, I shall play it."

Germain looked at Annette, smiling: "You don't come from about here."

"And where else, if not France?"

"What province?"

"Burgundy."

"There is wine in your blood."

"There is blood in our wine."

"Very well, I should love to drink a glass of it now and then. Will you grant me a quarter of an hour's conversation occasionally, when you are impatient and have too much energy on your hands?"

Annette promised and returned. They became good friends. They talked about everything except the war. At her first questions, the wounded man had stopped Annette with a gesture. Road closed. No passing that way!

"No, don't let's talk about it! You couldn't understand. I don't mean only you. All of you who are here. Here: out there. . . . Two worlds: this side, that side . . . we don't speak the same language."

"Couldn't I learn it?" asked Annette.

"No, not even you, with your warm sympathy. Love doesn't take the place of lack of experience. You can't translate what is written in the book of the flesh."

"Why not try? I have such a desire to understand, not out of curiosity but in order to help. I should like to approach, humbly, your trials."

"Thank you. But the best way you can help us is to make us forget them. Even among comrades from 'out there,' we avoid 'out there' by mutual consent in our conversation. Stories of the war, in the books and papers, disgust us. The war isn't literature."

"Nor life either."

"That's true. But man needs to sing. And life is a theme that lends itself to variations. Let's sing!"

He stopped, coughing. Annette held his head. He recovered his breath, apologized and thanked her. The smile had returned to his hollow features. There was a drop of sweat on his forehead. They waited without speaking, looking at each other affectionately.

Germain Chavânnes was a little under thirty. He had grown up in this milieu of bourgeois provincialism— right thinking, liberal but imbued with prejudices that were sound and healthy enough which, together with work and the love of the soil, form the bony structure of these central provinces. (If they did not have these prejudices, the ease of their life, their *laisser-vivre* would get the upper hand.) Germain knew all these things well. The dough of his body was from this water and this flour. But the unknown baker had added a leaven that did not come from here.

This rich young bourgeois, whose future had seemed fixed from his birth, happy, easy, grazing in the rich pastimes of his estate, had gone to Paris to study in the School of Oriental Sciences and Political Science. The career of a consul attracted him much less than the opportunity for traveling. Nevertheless, he loved his country as an epicure, the sky, the air, the speech, the food, the good earth, the good people. And he thought of nothing but escaping from it! While he waited for a distant appointment, he had taken a look around Europe, in every sense. A singular taste, in the judgment of his stay-at-home fellow-citizens. But it is useless to discuss tastes and colors (especially when they are those of a rich man). The war had come to interrupt his traveling plans. And now his illness. He had been gassed; the inner tissues had been slowly eaten away. Nothing remained for him now but the *voyage au tour de sa chambre*. (Not even that! For several days he had had to lie down.) The journey within himself—this was not the least distant nor the least mysterious. An unknown country. He explored it, with all his consciousness. But whence had he received this vocation, this taste for flight?

He explained it to Annette in the playful, mocking tone in which he clothed his thoughts: "I lived in the country. I loved hunting, less for the sake of the hunt than for the contact with the earth and the living animals and plants.

Loving the animals did not prevent me from killing them. But killing them did not prevent me from loving them. When I held a partridge, still warm, in my hand, or squeezed the belly of a white-rumped rabbit to make him give up his dewy luncheon, I felt closer to them than I did to myself—to man. I didn't feel sorry for them. One is always pleased with a good shot. And I think that if they had been in my place, and I in theirs, they would not have lost the chance of a shot at me. But I was trying to know them and myself. Afterwards I ate them. Why do you turn up your nose? So that you can smell them better? A plate of partridge and cabbage with a well-browned rasher of bacon is a feast for the gods. You wouldn't have turned it down. But the gods, let's confess it, are strange creatures."

"Frightful creatures!"

"Don't let's judge. Let us eat or be eaten. (Just now, it's my turn.) And let's try to understand. The gods? They're too far away. But those I have under my hand, men and beasts. My first discovery was that men and beasts have lived close together for millions of years without making any effort to understand each other. Oh, their skin and their flesh. But what they think, what they feel, what they are—men have never thought about that. They are not curious and they don't like to be bothered. To ensure respect for their own thought, they deny that animals can think. But when I opened my eyes, I was amazed to discover that among themselves men don't know one another any better. It makes no difference whether they come together or not. Each one is full of himself and has no thought for you. My neighbor, if your rhythm is in harmony with mine, all is well; you are my fellow-creature. If our rhythms differ, you are a stranger. If they clash, an enemy. Upon the first I generously bestow my own thoughts. The second has a right only to thoughts of the second rank. As for the third, as in *Malbrough*, *'le troisieme ne portait rien'*—so he has a right to nothing. I deny him thought, just as I do to the animals. (Are the Boches men?) However it may be, whether the *other* belongs in the first, second or third grade, in all three cases I don't know him and I don't even try to. I see myself, I hear myself, I talk with myself. I'm the frog. 'Mo-a' . . . When passion or the feeling of my own importance puffs me up, the frog becomes an ox and I call myself Nation, Country, Reason or God. This is a dangerous state. Better go back to our pond! Alas! I have never known how to croak there in peace, buttoned up to my neck in my impervious skin. Since the day when the demon of curiosity (or sympathy?) touched me, I have wanted to know them. I don't say understand them (Who could flatter himself that he did that?), but at least touch them, finger the living flesh of their spirits as my fingers did with the warm, soft body of the partridge. I have touched them, I have tasted them. Loving them and killing them. For I've killed also."

"You have killed!" said Annette, drawing back.

"I had to. Don't be angry with me. They've paid it back well."

*
* *

Thus he talked on, veiling with Gallic irony the tragedy of his thought. It seemed hopeless and beyond pity. It was the land of shadows. But over the earth laughed the sunlight of the living. The contrast made his vision of the universe all the more sombre. He saw the original error of creation, and he did not think it could be atoned for. Annette's passionate instinct revolted. She believed in evil, in good, and she projected them ardently from her own heart over the sky of space starred with life. She had her own side in the great conflict. She may not have believed she was going to win. Winning was not her aim. Her aim was to fight. What she believed evil was evil; evil was the enemy. And she would make no compromise with the enemy.

But it is quite easy to fight when one puts all the evil on the other side and all the good on one's own. Germain's blue eyes, that affectionately caressed this positive, fiery soul, was thinking of a very different battle-field! Krishna was fighting Krishna; and he was not at all certain that the fruit of the combat would be life or death— total destruction. Germain realized their mutual incomprehension and saw it as universal, saw it as eternal. It was not for him to participate in it. He had the fatal gift of saying "yes" to his own thought and not being able to say "no" to the thought of others, for he understood it. And he was more interested in understanding it than in trying to change it.

He had not always been like this. He had started off in life with a whole soul that had no desire to understand but only desired to take. His eyes had been opened by the calamities that had befallen him. He calmly told Annette about one of these. (He felt no embarrassment with her! She seemed to him an intelligent comrade who understood life and had passed through experiences similar to his own.)

He had loved a woman, loved her tyrannically. He had meant to love her according to his own heart, not according to hers. What he thought good for himself he thought good for her. Since they both loved each other, were they not the same? She was in love with him, and she became tired of him. Returning home one day, he found the cage empty. She had fled. A few lines of farewell explained the reason. The experience was harsh, but it struck home. He had learned that others wish to be loved by us not for what we ourselves are but for what they are.

"Insolent, isn't it? But I had to accept it. And since then I've tried . . ."

He related the adventure, making a joke of it, as always.

"To accept everything from those we love," said Annette, "is by no means difficult, when one pays the cost alone. But when it is they who pay, or one's neighbors, can one be a party to it?"

"You mean the war?"

"War, peace, what does it matter! This forest of Bondy where the strong devour the weak and find that they are devoured in turn by those who are still stronger!"

"You mean that every one is weak. In the end they are all devoured."

"I am on the side of those who are devoured."

"Ha, ha! You are alive, and you have beautiful teeth!"

"I wish I had only lips so that I might kiss all living

things. But since the *Unnamable* has placed these knives in my mouth, let it be only to defend my children!"

"But that's the war itself, in person."

"No, I shall protect them against the war."

"They are all like you. Let us say nine out of ten! And without the nine others the teeth could do nothing."

"Yes, war for the sake of peace. That's not at all what I meant. I don't suppose you believe in this sinister mummery?"

"I don't believe in it. No. But they believe in it. I respect their faith."

"Their faith? A mask behind which they hid their instincts for ill-doing, jealousy, pride, covetousness, pillage and lechery."

"Don't put anything more in!"

"There is something more."

"What do you know about all these commodities?"

"I know all the commodities. I have them. I keep them in my chest."

Germain stopped speaking, enveloping with the eye of a connoisseur the woman beside his bed who breathed fire as she spoke of peace. Then he said—(though he did not utter exactly the words he was thinking):

"You have good blood. You have plenty of that! But tell me, Madame Judith, since you allow the Philistines a portion of your virtues, why stop half way? Make them a present of the others, the best!"

"What do you mean?"

"Why, to be sure, your love, your sincerity. You reject these people, you reject them en bloc, as liars and evil-doers. That's easy, alas! If it were true, life would be too easy; they would not be so strong. Look at them from near by."

"I don't want to see them."

"Because?"

"Because I don't want to."

"Because you have seen?"

"I have seen."

"But you have not seen them dispassionately. I understand you. It would hinder your activity. But whether you act or not, see first. I will lend you my glasses. Look! You can arrange it with yourself later."

*

*   *

She did see, in spite of herself. Germain made her no eloquent speeches on humanity. That was not his style; and in his eyes, man in general was not worth a radish. He was interested only in what passed away, a person, an hour. In his eyes, what did not pass, what did not die, did not live; it was already dead.

He talked to her simply of the little town and the countryside. Ever since his childhood he had been collecting in his portfolios a store of "chalk drawings," in the old French sense—portraits roughly sketched, taken up again, hollowed out, in which the artist had caught the spirit under the skin. Townspeople, countryfolk, his own people . . . Ah! he knew them outside and inside, from top to toe. He had only to choose. He showed her a few from his collection that Annette thought she recognized—whose narrow-mindedness and egoism stifled her. The men and women, for instance, who had behaved like mad wolves on the day when the prisoners arrived. Yet they had their own sort of goodness, their domestic virtues. Under the opaque envelope, these dull lives had not been incapable of acts of devotion. And each one of these sacks of bones, for whom no God seemed to have died, carried its cross. Annette knew this quite well! But she too had hers to carry, and like them she had a tendency to believe that hers alone was the true one. On one side she saw the executioners, on the other the victims. Germain forced her to see that every one is both victim and executioner at once. This unbelieving Frenchman brought up before her eyes the picture of an extraordinary ascent of Golgotha, a whole people bearing crosses and flinging insults and stones at the Man on the cross!

"But it's frightful," she said. "Can't one remove the bandages from their eyes? Instead of stoning one another, they should turn their united strength . . ."

"Against whom?"

"Against the great executioner."

"Name it."

"Nature."

"Don't know it."

Germain raised his shoulder a little. He went on: "Nature? It would be easier to have to do with a God. A God would be capable of reason. (At least, we please ourselves by hoping so!) But Nature—what is it? Who has seen it? Where is its head, its heart, its eyes?"

"Here. My eyes, my body, my heart. It's myself, and my neighbor."

"Your neighbor? Wait, take a good look. . . . No, don't go away. Wait a moment!"

A visitor was coming in. A big, ruddy-cheeked boy. He had the fresh-colored, good-natured face of those chubby angels on the portal of Bourges Cathedral. He wore the blue cloak of a soldier. One of Germain's comrades, the son of a rich landowner of the principal town of a neighboring district. He was on leave and had walked twelve miles to come and see Germain. He embraced the sick man and bowed respectfully to Annette. Then he began to chatter. He was bursting with good humor and health. He brought news of this and that person whose simple, laughable names were like those of the footmen in a farce. Their comrades "out there." Some of them were dead, some living. The funny, singsong, nasal accent of the country enlivened the tale. The visitor tried to soften the vigor of his expressions for Annette's ears. (Respect the ladies!) He kept watch over himself. When he addressed her, it was in an affable, unctuous, old-fashioned tone. But his heart opened as he spoke freely of his own people—his mother, the little sister whom he adored. He was like a big child, affectionate, well-behaved, perfectly frank.

After he had left, Germain asked Annette: "What do you think of him? Isn't he a butter-ball? You could spread him on your bread!"

"There's no fraud about him," replied Annette. "Pure milk with all the cream on it. He smells of the rich grass of your fields."

"What would you have said if you had seen this big chubby baby, this good boy, good brother, good comrade—they would give him the Eucharist without confession, and he would take it without a moment's hesitation; he's never told a lie; he's as honest as gold—if you had seen him, as I have seen him, in the trenches, on the day of an attack, having a grand time with his butcher's knife?"

Annette made a gesture of repulsion.

"Never fear! You shan't see him. I spare you. I close the shutters. Everything safe. The night's outside. There are only the two of us in this room."

Annette, still horrified, said: "And he can laugh! He's at peace!"

"He's forgotten all about it."

"It's impossible."

"I have seen others who have done unnamable things during the day sleeping at night like children. Not a trace of remorse. And they would have been ready an hour afterwards to embrace the enemy they had stabbed. And they would have forgotten their kindly impulse just as quickly as they forgot the other. It's too difficult to get everything in harmony; they haven't the time. They must save all their strength for the present moment, live as they can, in broken scraps, at haphazard, disconnectedly, like some wild puzzle."

"Poor things!"

"Don't pity them. They get on very well."

"It is myself that I pity in them."

"Always that blessed egoism! Keep your ego for yourself, and leave them theirs!"

"No, I can't believe it is their real nature. . . ."

"*Homo Edditus naturae.* Nature, an edition revised and augmented by society. It seems as if war were the normal exercise of a natural instinct, consecrated by custom. And who knows? Perhaps it is also an outlet for the destructive forces placed in the human being. After having satisfied them he finds he's appeased."

"Did you?"

"I'm outside the question. I'm out of the picture."

"No! I want to hear you speak."

"Not yet! Wait! Germain Chavânnes' turn is coming. First, in order to know him, you must see with his eyes."

"I would like to see inside of him."

"Patience! I have had plenty of it! Imagine how much it required for one who saw himself caught in the net and was not in the least deceived as to what had caught him!"

"If it was like that, how were you able to join in the fight?"

"I might answer, 'They didn't leave me any choice.' But even if they had left me one, it would have been just the same; I should have chosen the net. I don't want to flatter myself, but I didn't think then as I do now. My unhappy gift for being porous, so that souls outside filter through me, has too often made me forget my own. We are French, we all live together, we are curious about one another, we listen to ourselves thinking out loud, you think in twos, in twenties, in thousands; and we become nothing but sounding-boards for every echo. You couldn't imagine, no one could imagine the marvelous enthusiasm that uplifted us during the first days. The *Chant du Depart.* It didn't spring from us; we sprang from it. It soared over us like Rude's screaming angel on the *Arc de l'Étoile.* But it was a hundred times more beautiful; and one would have given one's skin to rub it against oneself. It enveloped us with its wings. We didn't walk, we were carried, we soared forward to deliver the world. It was like the intoxication in love before the embrace. What an embrace! And what a frightful sell! Everything is a sell, Love too. It sacrifices us to those who are to come, to the future. But this frenzy of faith in war—what is its aim? To what, to whom does it sacrifice us? When we sobered down and began to ask this question, the sacrifice had already been consummated. One's whole body was caught in the grist-mill. Nothing was left but the soul, and the soul was cut to pieces. What can you do with the soul without the body, the soul against the body? Make a martyr of yourself? There are plenty of other executioners! There's nothing left but to see, know and accept. You have taken the leap. You have played the fool. One, two . . . Come! On to the end! Life doesn't hand out return tickets. Once you have gone you will never come back. And even if I were able I would not come back alone. We are together. We die together. I know it's absurd, that this death is for nothing. But to save yourself alone? No! That isn't done! I belong to the herd. I am the herd."

"And the herd follows you."

"The sheep of Panurge."

"When will one of you refuse to leap?"

"He won't come from our fields."

"Who knows?"

"Perhaps it will be from yours, Annette? One of your lambs?"

"My son! Oh, heavens! Don't make me think of him!"

"You see! You wouldn't dare advise him to."

"May the war spare him—spare me!"

"Amen! But it is not we who say the mass. We are only asked to say the responses. The bloody rite is performed. And we are taken."

"I am quite willing to be. But not he!"

"You will learn the wisdom of the good mothers of France, Germany, eternal humanity. They resign themselves at the feet of another, the *Dolorosa*."

"Never! I have my child. I shall keep him."

"In spite of every one?"

"In spite of every one."

"And in spite of himself?"

Annette dropped her head; her breath stopped short. He had touched her in her sensitive spot. Her fears, her troubles, the secret doubts which she did not wish to admit to herself—of these she said nothing. She had never spoken of this son; Germain merely knew that he existed. But her silence spoke for her. Germain pretended not to hear it.

"I know them, our little brothers! Those of the class of '18. . . . And what will those of the class of '20 be like? They are not bothered, as their elders, those hot-house plants, were by illusion. No danger that they'll be taken in. They accept the war as a matter of business. No question any longer of such nonsense as right, justice, liberty. The only question is winning. Each for himself. Self entirely. Self the flesh-eater. *Struggle for life. Life for struggle.* The scent of woman, glory and blood. And scorn for everything. The dream of the awakened tiger."

"You are the devil," said Annette.

"A poor devil," said Germain. "I am leaving the table without having eaten."

"Do you regret it?"

"No, I belong to the species that has made its own times. I don't complain. We must understand, understand everything."

"That's too much! To understand everything is not to act any longer. My heart protests. I am a woman. What is left for me?"

"Indulgence."

"That's not enough! I want to help, I want to save."

"But whom? If they don't want to be saved?"

"Whether they want it or not, I want it. I know perfectly well that I am nothing, that I can do nothing. But I want to do everything. I must. If all the gods and all the devils, and the worst devils, men, if the whole world said, "No!" I should say, "Yes!""

"You are a martyr. You want to be beaten!"

"Don't imagine that. I can strike blows."

"All your efforts wouldn't move a grain of dust on the hard stone of destiny."

"Perhaps . . . No. . . . But it's a relief."

"I've told you, you are Bellona. Your name, Anne, is a false name."

"It's the name of the grandmother of Him who conquered death."

"And he died."

"But on the third day he rose again."

"You believe that?"

Annette stopped, taken aback: "I never did believe it before. . . ."

"But now?"

"I don't know. . . . It has pierced me through and through."

Germain contemplated this strange woman, who was visited unexpectedly by mysterious guests. Sitting beside the bed, on a low chair, she was leaning her head against the sheets as if she were prostrated. He placed his hand gently on the fair helmet of her hair. She lifted her brow. Her eyes were surprised but calm. In a low voice, Germain asked: "So you believe?"

"In what?" she asked.

She was sincere. She no longer knew. She went on: "I believe that I must act, help and love."

"Good," said Germain. "That was the reason I asked you to come. I didn't want to tell you at first. I wanted to see you and see in you. Now I have seen. I've talked enough about what isn't the real me. Forgive this irony I dress myself up in. I open the door. Sister Anne, come in!"

*

* *

"When fire has broken out in a quarter and you know you are too weak to save everything, you let the fire have its share; you abandon what has to burn; you cut the bridges and take up your position in the keep, where the most precious things are locked up. Either you save your life, your deepest life, or you wait for the fire to bring the house crashing down among its ashes. I saved mine. But the fire is coming. Anne to the rescue!"

He could not help keeping up his jesting manner, but his tone betrayed anxiety. She took his hands: "What must be saved? Here are my hands. They will search in the fire for it."

"My joy, my faith, my I. The one I love."

"A woman?"

"A man. My friend."

"Where is he? Why doesn't he come?"

"He is a prisoner."

"In Germany?"

"In France."

"He's an enemy?"

"You said it. My brother, my friend, my better self. They have taken him away from me and said to me: 'Forget and kill! He is an enemy.'"

"And you fought him?"

"Never against him. When I faced the frontier, I knew he was not on the other side. Before I left, I had embraced him in France. He stayed here."

"They arrested him?"

"He is in the West, shut up in a prison-camp. And for three years—so near, so far!—I have heard nothing from him, I have known nothing about him. Does he still live? And I am dying . . ."

"What! Can't you get any news?"

"I can't ask for it here."

"Your people love you. How could they refuse you anything?"

"No, I can't speak to them about it."

"I don't understand."

"You will understand. Now I have found you. It makes me happy to speak to you about him. Talking about him with some one else who can love is almost like talking with him. Will you love him?"

"I love him already in you. Make me see him. Tell me about him!"

"His name is Franz and mine Germain. Germain, the Frenchman, and Franz the German! I knew him two years before the war. He had been living in Paris for several years. He was painting, and we were in the same quarter. Our rooms looked out into the same garden. We had spent years near each other without having spoken to each other. Once, absent-mindedly, at a street-corner one evening, we ran into each other. But it was only later that I remembered this. In the whirling current of Paris, which carries men and women away like leaves, you meet and touch long before you see each other. But any little encounter makes you realize that you have seen each other before. One day a common friend took me to see him. And I recognized him.

"He was twenty-three but he seemed much younger. He still wore the look of the woman, the mother he had lost as a child. A sensitive face, easily moved, restless, given over to all the winds of hope and suspicion.

Shadow and light passed over it, without any transition.
Confident abandon, and gloomy discouragement. Sometimes it offered itself completely, and then again it would
draw back, hostile, inaccessible. But I was the only one
to see it and to look for the cause. None of the people
with whom he was in contact had suspected it. You love
or you don't love. People haven't the time to know those
whom they love. I had not cared about such things very
long, myself. But life had just made me pay for it
heavily. (I have told you about that.) I had learned
to my cost that you must never love your neighbor as
yourself but as the other that he is, that he wishes to be,
and that you must discover him.

"No, he wasn't like me at all, this young stranger.
That was just it! I needed him. He needed me.

"He had been cruelly repressed in his environment and
his education as a child: a school of military junkers,
clericals, with all the rigorism and abnormality of their
antisocial caste. His feminine nature had been brutalized
by it. Too weak and too alone to revolt, he had had to
bend under this constraint of custom and thought. And
he had borne the mark of it through life, like a girl who
has been violated. He had remained timid and suscep-
tible, without self-confidence, without will, badly ad-
justed to life, a misanthrope with a starved need of loving,
of being loved, of giving himself—and the constant pain
of being made game of. For these natures are made to be
abused. They show their lack of armor too naïvely. People can't resist the pleasure of pricking them with the
points of their blades, just to make them cry out. Better
not to be armed at all than half-armed.

"At his father's death, Franz escaped from his native
land. He came to Paris and tried to forget the nightmare

of his childhood. But a past from which you suffer is a
peau de chagrin. Time makes it shrink, but the flesh is
only the more hurt by it. Then Paris exercised its usual
charm over the young lad who had been so deprived of
poetic and plastic beauty. It is the natural element where
one breathes at ease; its very lack of morality is one benefit
the more. But Franz was too used to the inner life not
to feel the lack of it around him. He suffered from that
irony and dryness of heart. He had beliefs, but they were
all tottering. He was incapable of defending himself
alone against skepticism and the breath of pleasure. They
were not dangerous to his friends, who made a game of
taking things seriously, for nothing takes hold of them.
But this wasn't so with him; he took everything seriously.
He was sinking to the bottom, with a mortal disgust at not
being able to resist.

"It was at this time that I met him. The friends, good
fellows, but far from sensitive, who introduced me, were
very fond of him. With men of their sort this was a
good reason for treating him roughly. They laughed at
the confidences they had extorted from him, and the jolly
souls did not keep their amusement to themselves. Their
whole circle had the benefit of it. Franz was handed
about as a sympathetic and rather comical curiosity. Naturally his 'patrons' (as they considered themselves) exploited his kindness and his timidity. Madame sent him
about on errands, or took him into the big shops for his
advice or to get him to carry her bundles. Monsieur
obliged him to read his lucubrations and turned over to
him the unpleasant task of approaching the editorial offices. He was the *famulus* at every one's beck and call.
In return they polished him up, put him through his paces
or crammed him with advice he had not asked for, bur-

glarized his thoughts, picked the locks of his hidden feelings, and spread them out before everybody, in their absurd nakedness, for his good. He would have had to be an ingrate to complain.

"He complained of nothing; but, thank God, he was for his own good ungrateful. I saw it at once. Under the constrained smile with which he received the flattering and mocking things that were said to him, I read his irritated suffering and the shadow of his deep discouragement. I needed no explanations to understand. At one glance, I had measured the distance between his patron and himself. And when the former spoke to me, I addressed myself, without replying, to the one who had remained silent—with all the pity and respect I would have felt for young Orestes, when he had fallen into the hands of the barbarians of Tauris. I wish you could have seen the light that shone in his eyes, at my very first words. He recognized the language of his own country. The country that survives all the Iliums, that of *Friendship*. And that respect which the soul of every human being owes its comrades, but which it grants them so grudgingly, touched him to tears. I pretended not to see these, and I went on talking so as to give him time to master his agitation. He understood my intention, and when he had regained his self-control our conversation went on, gravely and tenderly, under the eyes of Thoas, who heard nothing. We spoke of indifferent things. But the voice was everything. To the glance that asked, 'Is it you?' it replied, 'It is I, brother.'

"He had barely had time to return home when he wrote me an enthusiastic letter. I saw him again the next day, alone. Truly, I had not imagined how the outburst of sympathy I had shown him would thrill this starved heart.

I guessed still less the place the newcomer was to take in my life. Like every one else, I had had two or three friendships. I had never given much or expected much of them. It had been a real pleasure to see my friends, or render them some service, but we had tacitly understood the limits it wouldn't be wise to overstep. The egoism of young men considers this quite natural. You don't expect from others what they don't expect from you. A Frenchman takes life and men as they come. Nothing too much. Know how to be satisfied. . . .

"He was never satisfied, this young Orestes whom I had unchained! He had never known it. He had never measured his feelings about life. He brought me a friendship cut to the size of a vanished species. In order to adjust it to my own, I had to grow. I have not succeeded any too well, but I have done my best, since he wished it. For he gave me everything, and he demanded everything. And, God knows, I believe that, big or little, he has taken it all."

*
* *

After this long recital, which he had delivered without haste, to himself more than to Annette, slowing the pace at certain moments in order to relive them better, he stopped and fell into a reverie.

Annette leaned towards him, but she did not make any movement that would break the charm. Her eyes, which reflected the passing mirage, continued to listen after he had finished. Germain looked at them. Several minutes rolled by in a mute conversation. She heard it very clearly. A little embarrassed, Germain said, as if he were replying to what was in Annette's mind—as if he were apologizing:

"Isn't it a funny thing? From the moment one is born, one lives with oneself, one knows oneself, or one thinks one does. A man seems so simple and all of a piece! They are all alike; they seem to have come out ready made, complete, from the warehouse. But when you come to deal with them, what different beings they are, under the same material! Who would have thought I had a soul like an unoccupied mother or a loving sister? You are laughing . . ."

"I am laughing at myself," said Annette. "I, too, have plenty of unemployed souls."

"You are right. I can see a few of them. You are the shepherd of a whole little flock."

"I am lucky when it is not the sheep that lead me!"

"Every one must live," said Germain. "Let them have their pasturage!"

"And the keeper?"

They laughed.

170

"To the devil with society!" said Germain. "It understands nothing but the Code."

He reflected a moment and then went on:

"Look at our poor friendship. Is there anything more human, when you see a drowning man and hold out your hand to him and he seizes it, than to carry him in your arms and watch over him? From his childhood Franz was severed from all true affection, and his own was heaped up behind a dam of suffering. When he met me, the sluice-gate opened: it was like a torrent. I wanted to resist. But who can refuse the gift of a noble, ingenuous heart that believes in us? One feels grateful for that faith which one has never had. One tries to render oneself worthy of it. As a matter of fact, this great affection has made me realize how much I have lacked it also! When one has never had it, one gets used to living on a modicum; one grows wise through deprivation and expects nothing more of life. But when it appears—the affection that makes of two spirits a complete harmony— one sees how sadly one has been waiting for it; and one can't imagine any more how one has been able to live without it—Friendship . . . But this discovery we can share only with those who have made it. There is no way of understanding the reasons why we are intimate. . . . The reasons? There are no reasons! Each needs the other in order to be himself. One is not complete without the other. . . . That is exactly what other people cannot forgive! For if we are complete together, the others feel hurt."

"I haven't that feeling," said Annette. "In default of the love that I have never had, I adopt that of other people. All those who love themselves love me."

"What an appetite!" said Germain.

Annette replied: "I have nothing to eat."

"That's just the reason. Happy are those who have nothing, for everything will be given to them."

Annette shook her head, with a disillusioned air: "That is what the rich say. They try to make the poor think that they are the fullest of all."

Germain touched her hand. "You are not so poor! Your granary is full."

"Of what?"

"Of the love of giving."

"That amounts to nothing."

"Give me one sheaf of it! I should know how to use it."

"Take it. In what way can I help you?"

*
* *

The Chavânnes family had never looked kindly upon this abnormal friendship which did not rest on the community of any social interest—nation, place, career—and very impertinently showed that it could get along without it. Even before the war they thought this intimacy with a German was in very bad taste in their provincial circle. They attributed it, like Germain's other ways, to his desire to be singular. Rather than take the trouble to understand, the jeering inertia of country people puts down as a poseur any member of their family who avoids their habits and customs. Up to the war, however, it was the habit and custom, allowance being made for inertia, to tolerate what one did not understand; for nobody cared much about these things. But after 1914, farewell to that beautiful indifference that rendered life in society endurable! Every one arrogated to himself the right to mind every one else's business, and even people's feelings were subjected to a visé. It was forbidden to love anybody without a passport! It was no longer permitted to confess a German friendship. In the eyes of Germain's brother-in-law and sister, it would have been less outrageous to sleep with a highwayman. They were honest souls, solid and narrow-minded.

Madame de Séigy, *née* Chavânnes, between seven and eight years older than her brother, possessed the decision of mind that Germain lacked. She was never embarrassed in making her choices: upon every object she was provided with one—just one—thought, distinct and limited. One read it, at the first glance, on her firm, clear-cut features, the long, thin nose that went straight ahead, that didn't deviate by a line, and when it stopped had made up its mind: it held the nostrils tight. The forehead was round and unwrinkled, the hair drawn back, with not a lock out of place, leaving the ears and the temples uncovered. The eyebrows were narrow and arched, the eye precise, the mouth small, a narrow gate that seemed as if made to be closed. The chin was plump but firm in texture: not a stitch had given! There were no wrinkles on this face, nothing but straight lines that were full of will. All over it, from top to bottom, was written: "There's no use discussing it!" For the rest, she was polite and reserved. No hope of irritating her! She was sure of herself. She was a stone wall. One doesn't discuss things with a stone wall, one goes around it. It limits things and shuts them in; this is its rôle. And what it enclosed was not for you: it was a private domain, private property. Every one for himself, and you were outside!

"For himself" was Séigy-Chavânnes, first of all—then the town, then the neighborhood, then France. Of all these things the war had formed one bloc, the fatherland. And Séigy was in the center of it. She was president of the local organization of the Women of France. She therefore thought she was authorized to speak in the name of all women. And what woman says in France, the household says. Madame de Séigy-Chavânnes was no more a feminist than most Frenchwomen, because, having the power, they have no need of the right: the right seems to them a crutch for the infirm. Madame de Séigy-Chavânnes held herself responsible for all the males of her household. They gave her satisfaction. One had got himself killed (Monsieur de Marëuil), another had been severely wounded (her brother); and as for her husband, a commander of artillery, he had been for six months in

the storm of Verdun. It was not that she was a Cornelia.
She loved her Horaces. She was not anxious for them
to die. She took care of them devotedly. If she had had
her choice she would have shared their fate. But she
would not have spared them one of their trials. France,
the country, the town, Séigy, were right. She was anxious
to prove the right by her deeds. The right was nothing
without the deed. And *my* right, just or unjust, was *the*
right. All the Séigys—and France—may die, but I shall
not surrender. She was of the line of the heroic litigants
of old days. The war, life, death, were lawsuits. I may
lose everything I have, but I shall not compromise. . . .

One could scarcely imagine going and talking to such a
woman about the rights of the other party! She was
proud of her brother. He had defended France, and she
defended him vigorously against the death that was coming. But she would have let him die rather than counte-
nance that shameful weakness, a friendship with a German. She would have been aware of this—if it had
pleased her. But it pleased her to ignore it. And Germain agreed to this. There was a tacit understanding between them. Whoever loves, avoids exposing to any
slight—not only in words (Madame de Séigy was mistress of herself) but (what was worse!) in thoughts, the
name of the one who is dear to you.

Madame de Chavânnes, the mother, was alone aware
of the persistence of her son's attachment; and because
she was fond of him she closed her eyes to it. But she
did not approve of it; and her silence avoided the confidences that Germain was not tempted to grant her. She
was an old woman who had made it a law of prudence all
her life never to contest the reigning opinions, usages or

prejudices. Perhaps her heart was free, or had been, or might have been. But it had been so long since she had allowed it to speak! She had lived an active life in which her moral lassitude, which was disposed to quietism and fled from everything that might disturb it, had accorded little place for the heart. Her heart had not lost its deep tenderness; but it was submerged under an immense need for rest. And she clasped the hand of her big sick boy as much because she knew what he was thinking about as to beg him not to speak to her about it.

Annette was the first person to whom Germain had been able to confide the affection, the anxiety, that filled his mind much more than the outcome of the battles. And when Annette said in surprise, "But Madame de Marëuil?"—she was attracted by the young woman, who was so reserved, attracted by her sad smile—Germain feebly moved his hands in discouragement: "To her less than to any one else."

She was good. She was pure. He liked his young sister-in-law. They felt a chaste affection for each other which they had no need of expressing. But a whole world separated them.

He said: "Take a good look at her!"

"I have looked at her," said Annette. "She is like the good Dame du Marthuret."

Germain smiled: "That tender bird, with the bent neck, whose mild, myopic eyes, blinking a little, brood over the Child, while she strokes his little foot! She has the same open brow, the delicate nose, the long chin, the fine smile, with its youthful look, the slender lips. But sadness has spread its veil about her. Where is the Child? She is seeking for it. She is waiting for it. It is in heaven. All her love has gone after it. What remains for us here below? She is patient, she does not complain, she does her duty down here. But, without wishing it—for she doesn't want to make us sad—she shows all too clearly that this world is only a passing place for her. And for her we are only transitory too."

"What does it matter if to these transitory souls she offers the charity of her smile?"

"She does offer it. But I know its price. Don't be deceived by it."

"It is wisdom."

"It is not yours."

"I am not one of these transitory people."

"It says: 'Accept everything—fate, death, the disappearance of those you love!' She has no hatred for anybody, but she believes that the war, just because it has come, comes from God; and she honors it. As you have seen, she doesn't permit any one to dishonor it by cruelty, disloyalty, the abuse of force against the vanquished. She is truly noble. But she is noble in the ancient sense. That which has been should be and always will be. For that which has been—bad or good—has its quarterings of nobility. It springs from the race. It springs from God. She would do nothing to change it. The honorable thing is to accept it."

"I don't accept it. I don't spring from the race. I reject, or I take."

"Take my cause! It's lost."

"The lost causes are just the ones I love."

"Defeatist!"

"No! Winning them, in spite of fate, warms the heart."

"But suppose you lose?"

"I shall begin again."

"But I'm in a hurry, Annette. I can't begin again. I haven't an unlimited life, as you have."

"Who knows?"

"No. I can't nourish myself on chimeras. I am on the earth. I am not here for long. For me it must be to-day or never."

"Well, we shall gamble everything on to-day. And I am the stake. Show me the game!"

*
*   *

Annette undertook it; she threw caution to the winds. This woman, who needed to act, for whom pure thought, intention, was never enough, and who, since the beginning of the war, had failed to find her own way of acting, suddenly discovered it here in the absolute gift of herself to the cause of the eternal affections—disinterested love, the most disinterested of all, a friendship between two strange young men. The boiling energy that was in her she placed at their service, with the passion that was all her own and the rather mad nature of which could not be dissembled. She herself was grateful to him. Her reason said to her: "You will pay for it!"

"I shall pay later. For the moment, I am purchasing . . ."

"With more than you possess."

"We shall see. . . ."

Folly! But what of it! She had to give herself; and she asked for nothing, she expected nothing in return. It was enough for her happiness to give happiness—and to risk. Risk! She was a born gambler. . . . (Germain had seen her clearly.) At other times she had gambled with her life, enthusiastically.

And—let it be confessed—from the moment he saw it, Germain, in spite of his generosity, abused it. He wasn't going to spare her any longer. He forgot the risks it involved. Sickness has no pity.

Annette set to work and succeeded in tracing the young prisoner. He was shut up in a concentration camp near Angers. Through the mediation of the Agence Internationale des Prisonniers at Geneva, she contrived to send him a letter; and the thread of life was tied together again between the two friends. Under her own name, Annette sent and received the letters from one to the other. She went secretly and got them and brought them back to Germain.

When her eyes fastened upon the first lines of the first letter from Franz, she could not take them away: it was such a cry of love that she was captured by it as if the two arms had been thrown about her. She tried to free herself, but she hadn't the strength: she read on to the end. And when she had finished it, with the letter on her knees, she found herself out of breath, as if she had been assaulted. It was all she could do to conceal from the Chavânnes the radiance that surrounded her. But when she was alone with Germain, such a joy illumined her that Germain at once understood it; and, holding out his hands to her, he said, in a commanding voice, trembling with impatience: "Give it to me!"

She stood aside while he read it. Silence fell in the room. Annette, standing there, looked through the window, without seeing anything, into the sunless court. She heard the rustling of the leaves of the letter, the heavy breath. Then there was no sound. In the street, behind the walls, an ox-cart passed slowly. It seemed to rumble without moving forward. It suggested the motionlessness of the plains of Central France. Time had stopped. The cry of the cattle-drover, the cry of a bird as it hovered in front. The rumbling slowly grew indistinct. The old tottering walls resumed their immobility. And in these two souls time began to flow again. Germain's voice called:

"Annette!"

She turned round, she went to him. He was lying with his face to the wall, away from the light. The letter lay open on the bed. He said: "Read it!"

She confessed: "Forgive me! I have read it already."

Without looking at her, he held out his hand to her: "You had the right. It was yours. I owe it to you."

And without a word that betrayed his emotion, he took a hem of Annette's dress and kissed it.

At his request, she read from this time onward the letters of the two friends. The flood of tenderness passed through her. She mingled in it her own color and her fire. These two loved only for themselves. She loved for both and for herself. She was the tree on which the two birds met each other. She heard amid her own leaves the song of their burning friendship. A new air, a more youthful sky, bathed its tender branches. The times and the war were effaced.

A strange, marvelous duet! When Annette closed her eyes in order to hear it better, it seemed to her that one of the voices was that of a young girl, the other of a maternal woman. The latter held out her arms. The former threw herself into them.

Franz's first song had been of his lost deliverance. His refuge, at last! For three years he had been suffocated in the disgusting promiscuity of these crowded bodies and souls. Not one of them had a more aristocratic disgust than he. Never to be alone! The worst kind of solitude! One lost one's own self! He did not have the overflowing humanity of these rich hearts who, just because they have so much, spread it about them. Whether it is wasted or not . . . "Herds, drink it or flounder in it. If you do not it will sink into the ground. . . ." He was afraid to share his vision of life with these eyes incapable of reflecting it; and, on the other hand, he lacked that magnificent plenitude of the great solitary artists which is sufficient to itself because itself is a world. He was a delicate boy of twenty-seven who had remained adolescent, who was devoured with the need of discharging into a welcoming and stronger heart the stream of his own repressed heart. The stream was too feeble to reach its end unless it found the river of love that would carry it. It gave itself by egotism. For to be taken is to take. It is to replenish with its own flood a soul that hollows the valley for us. It had found this, and it exulted.

For a little while. In a few days this first joy was exhausted, and the impatient heart felt nothing but the distance that separated them. It cried out its desire and its deprivation. His letters described little and without precision; they called. No doubt the censorship, in any case, would have prevented any precise description of the life of the camp. But of all the constraints this was the one that weighed least heavily on the young prisoner. His absorbing ego had little time to think of the egos of other people. He talked about himself, with a naïve, touching, excessive confidence. He had that feverish, indolent, rather doleful sentimentality that is characteristic of some Austrians, a little over-delicate, a little querulous, which is saved by grace and youth. His song was a *lied*, a perpetual *rondo*, of an elegiac tenderness. The nightingale flung all his heart into it. But he listened to his own song. His heart was bleeding. He wept over his heart. Even the one he loved more than himself he loved in himself— the living echo and the response that welcomed and prolonged his fragile song.

Germain's song was firmer. His melody flowed out in a single breath, without breaking. The clear line did not adorn itself with these vocalizings and these trills. It rose above them. Germain spoke little of himself. He said nothing—almost nothing—of his own condition; for he was thinking more of the other than of himself and he was afraid of alarming him. But his letters were full of questions about his friend's health, about his hygiene, about his conduct with the officers in command and with his companions. He consoled him, advised him, soothed him; he was never weary of repeating his tender, patient, earnest admonitions to the big child who only half listened to them. This meticulous insistence was a little absurd. But this jesting soul did not mind being laughed at. And if Annette smiled as she read, it was because she found in this man her own obsessions, that maternity of the heart which puts no limits to its anxious need to give protection. She discovered in these two boys the eternal woman who is in every being, although the education of man stifles it and he blushes to confess it. She was touched by it, for she recognized its purity.

There was nothing equivocal about it. A crystal clearness. A passion as natural, as much a matter of fate as the law of gravitation. Two souls, two worlds whose orbits about the sun were interlaced, like a thread in the hands of a ropemaker. Two solitudes that were conjugated in order to make a rhythm and breathe. The solitude of one who did not understand the human herd, who was lost in this forest of apes and tigers and was calling for help. The solitude of one who understood everything, who understood too much; he clung to nothing, nothing clung to him; and that a single being, one only, needed him in order to exist gave his life a redemptory value. The savior saves and is saved by that which he saves.

And how could they both help looking for this refuge in the arms of that which nature has given us, to pour out the burning flood of our desires and our anxieties—or to mingle its own with ours? Woman . . . That was their secret. Annette could not but perceive it. In Franz, distance, fear. In Germain, perhaps an excessive readiness to be disappointed, a bitterness. (He was not the only one to know this feeling among the comrades of the trenches!) In both, the instinctive feeling, true or false, powerful, that woman is a different world. Germain had an affectionate esteem for Annette; he trusted her. But Annette was not deceived by this: he trusted her because she was the only being to whom he could have recourse; he was certain of her loyalty in serving him; he was not sure that she understood him. More than once Annette divined that the words he addressed to her were not for her but were directed over her head to the invisible friend. And when she read their letters she compared the difference in the harmonies between her conversations with Germain, which were a counterpoint of different motifs, cordially woven, and the duet of the melodious friendship in which every note awakened by its harmonies a fraternal accord. She was not jealous of this. She was pleased by it. There are times when one enjoys more satisfaction in listening to a beautiful concert than in taking part in it.

But she did take part in it—and without suspecting it, because it was in her that the two voices joined. She was the soul of the violin.

*
* *

The Chavânnes family did not want to know anything about this mysterious exchange of thoughts that passed under the veils of the messenger, who came in and went out.

The prying eyes of the bored little seven-year-old, who was always spying and speculating, had seized upon this exchange of the two correspondents. He had said nothing about it. He carried on his own hidden life, without having much to do with the grown-ups. Without knowing what was going on, he took note of everything he observed, building up strange romances upon it. He believed there was some furtive love-affair between Annette and Germain; and, as he was attracted by this blonde-haired woman who brought her light into the house, his heart was strangely troubled over it. He detested her, and he loved her madly.

Madame de Séigy-Chavânnes haughtily averted her eyes. She simply would not know anything about it.

Madame de Marëuil really did know nothing about it. Her loyal soul could not suspect what her rigid conception of duty would have condemned. She had too much esteem for Germain not to believe that, like her, he would sacrifice his heart to the exclusive demands of the country. And yet, of them all, she was the nearest to understanding the imperious sweetness of these ties of friendship. But how could Germain have dared to vindicate his rights before her, deprived as she was of what she loved, and stoically, without complaint, offering to her God her sorrow and her renunciation?

Madame de Chavânnes, the mother, was the only one

who shared Germain's secret. It was impossible to keep
it from her. She saw him writing and reading the letters
over and over. She was a discreet depository. She could
not approve, but she could not reproach. She saw this big
son, ravaged by his illness. She couldn't criticize him any
longer. She was willing that he should have at least this
one joy. She trembled lest the secret should come out and
there would be a conflict between the sick one and the rest
of the family, in which her heart would be equally trampled upon by both sides. For, on the one hand, she
thought the family were right as against her son; and on
the other, her son was her son. There was the law. And
there was something above the law.

Intractable as Madame de Séigy-Chavânnes was, she
also recognized, without confessing it, that privileged right
which goes against the right. She was a sister. She saw
death on Germain's face, and she kept silent before what
was approaching. It was impossible for her not to know
that something was being concealed from her. But she arranged it with herself that it should remain concealed
from her. Before entering the sick man's bedroom, she
took care to announce herself in a loud voice so that he
would have time not to allow her to see what shouldn't
be seen.

Her resentment turned against Annette, whose visits
were becoming longer and more frequent. She betrayed
nothing but a glacial coldness, never failing to observe a
strict politeness. This was enough between two women
who were quite well aware of what such silence means.
Annette was held responsible for the adventure in which
she was only an instrument. She accepted this without
flinching. She only came into the house to see Germain.
The others were indifferent to her.

But she could not be indifferent to her powerlessness to aid the two friends.

All of a sudden, the letters from the prisoner stopped coming. An epidemic in the camp, some matter of reprisals, blocked the whole correspondence for several weeks. This disturbing silence made the sick man very anxious. To have lost his spring, after having found it again, exasperated his thirst. He was as burning dry as a desert. Every day he greeted Annette with a furious, demanding look. He was angry with her for disappointing his hopes. This moral excitement increased his illness; and the latter, in turn, redoubled the excitement. After a period of apparent immobility, in which the poisoning seemed to moderate, it resumed its work with an increased vigor, attacking the inner organs. A few days of deceptive respite were followed by a brutal recrudescence; and one never knew from which side the destruction was going to come, for it took all forms. When it seemed to have been driven back at one point, it rushed in at another. It was like a fire devouring the heart of a house. One drove the flames back when they emerged, but there was no way of reaching the fireplace before the house was ruined. It was evident to all that there would be no stop to it.

Germain knew it better than any one else. He was wearing himself out in secret struggles against the hidden enemy, and he felt vanquished. In this futile combat his character was changing. The sick man, thrown back upon himself, in a perpetual attitude of defense, had no regard for others any longer: his egotism was his refuge. He ceased to think of anything but himself, his illness, his desire. During those nights when Germain, on his funeral-pyre, helplessly watched the mounting of the flames, he was seized with a furious desire to see his friend once more before he was consumed.

Reluctantly, his mother allowed Annette to enter the bedroom, since the sick man insisted on it; but they could scarcely talk to each other. The calls now were at a long, silent standstill. The moment Annette entered, Germain's eyes ransacked her, and then died out in disappointment; and all his strength gathered back upon his suffering. Annette vainly tried to distract him. Nothing interested him. She interrupted herself in the midst of what she was saying. But when, feeling herself useless, she would get up to leave, he would hold her back with a gesture, with some harsh reproach. And this reproach she could not rebuff. She accused herself of having aroused a hope that she was not able to realize.

One day, when they were alone—the mother had gone out with the doctor who had tried once more to delude him—he took Annette's wrist and said:

"I am lost."

She tried to protest. He repeated: "I am lost. I know it. I want, I want to see him once again."

She made a discouraged gesture. He did not give her time to speak. "I want it," he said harshly.

"Who are we to want?" she said.

"Is it you who say that? You?"

She lowered her head in confusion. With a harsh bitterness he went on: "All your protests! That female boasting! You lied!"

She did not defend herself. "My poor friend, I would do anything you ask me, if I could. But how? By what means?"

"Find the means! You are not going to let me die without seeing him again."

"You are not going to die."

"I am dying. I don't revolt against death. There's nothing to be done. It's the law. But the bestiality of men I don't accept! He is there, near me, he, my one friend; and I can't see him, touch his hand, embrace him for the last time! It's monstrous!"

Annette did not speak. She was thinking of the thousands of unhappy souls who were holding out their arms, of the state of the trenches in which their lives were dripping away, of their far-away homes, where their loved ones were tossing in sleepless agony on their solitary beds. Germain read what was in her mind. He said:

"Others may submit to it, but I, no! I have only one life, and it's only going to last a moment longer. I can't wait. I want what is my right."

Annette's heart was rent, but she still said nothing; her compassionate hands tried to calm him. He pushed her away angrily and turned his back on her. She went out.

When, after a night of feverish struggles with herself, she returned the next day, she found the sick man lying motionless. In a calm, sad voice—the calmness was more oppressive than the fury of the previous day—he said to her: "I ask your pardon. I was mad. I talked about justice, about my right. There is no justice, and I have no right. Bad luck to those who fall! There is nothing for them but to bury their faces in the earth and fill their mouths with it to stifle their cries. The worm squirms under the foot that crushes it. Folly! I hold my tongue; I no longer resist."

Annette, placing her hand on his forehead, which was covered with perspiration, said: "No! You must resist. Nothing is lost yet. I have just met your doctor. He advises your mother to have you taken to a sanatorium in Switzerland. The air is too relaxing here, too mild and humid, and the moral atmosphere is not less depressing: whatever one may do, one is infected by the war here. Over there, in the breath of the mountains and the oblivion that thrives upon the peaks, you will find your health again without a doubt. He told me so."

"It's a lie! Yes, he told me the same thing. He knows I am lost, and so he sends me off to die at a distance. He wants to get rid of me. But I say, No! I shall die here!"

Annette did her best to convince him, but he repeated: "No!"

And he clenched his teeth, refusing to speak, burying himself in his obstinate resistance.

Annette, leaning over the bed, said, with a sad smile: "Is it because of him?"

"Yes. If I left France I should be still further away from him."

Annette said: "How do you know?"

"What do you mean?"

Annette leaned still further over him: "Suppose it were just the other way?—a way of being nearer to him?"

He seized her wrists and held her down: "What are you talking about?"

She tried to escape, but he would not let her go. They were breathing into each other's faces.

"You must go to Switzerland. My friend, accept it!"

"Speak! Explain yourself!"

"You are hurting me. Let me get up again."

"No. Explain first!"

Bending close to his ear, almost tottering, leaning her two palms against the body of the sick man, so as not to fall, she said, in a low, hurried voice: "Listen! This isn't certain. It's only a chance. I may have made a mistake in speaking to you about it. But I am going to try. I am ready to risk everything."

He grasped her wrists: "Tell me, tell me!"

"It occurred to me last night. And, coming in here, after I had heard about the plan for the journey to Switzerland. If he were able to escape."

Germain threw his arms about Annette. She fell on the bed, her face against his. He kissed her eyes, her nose, her neck, furiously, at random. Amazed, overcome, she was unable to move for a moment. She slipped to her knees before the bed, then at last she rose. He had no consciousness of what he had just done. Rising up in his disordered bedclothes, he cried: "You are going to help him to escape! You are going to bring him to me in Switzerland!"

They were silent, overwhelmed, recovering their breath.

When she was able to move and speak again, she signed to him to lie down again. He obeyed her. She smoothed the bedclothes and the pillow. Without resisting or moving, he let her do so. When she had finished, she sat down at the foot of the bed; and both forgot what had happened. (It had been too much for her! It had been too much for him!) In whispers they began to discuss the plan that had just been suggested.

*
* *

Annette returned to Paris. She went to see her old friend Marcel Franck, who was wearing a very beautiful uniform. A high functionary of the Beaux Arts, he had come back from some mysterious mission to Rome that was without danger but not without glory; and he was for the moment attached to a comfortable bureau in which, at the rear and quite without anxiety, he was occupied with the preservation of works of art. He did not bring any excess of zeal to the service of this war, which he regarded as stupid—that is to say, natural: for stupidity seemed to him the normal measure of humanity. Without any undue enthusiasm, he was ready to be interested in Annette's proceedings.

He received her at once with that secretly understanding smile, the smile of the old days. He was superbly bald now, for he made of his baldness one elegance the more. His face was youthful, his eyes animated, his teeth beautiful: he was very much at his ease in the soft blue costume of a warrior, which was very becoming to him.

They were alone together. After they had exchanged greetings, Annette explained in a somewhat roundabout way the object of her call. She looked at Marcel's teeth: they were smiling. Friendly and absent-minded, he let her talk, and his glance wandered over her, from top to toe. She interrupted herself: "But you're not listening to me."

"Naturally not," he said. "With a chance to see you again, one has something better to do. Forgive me! I am listening, just the same. I know perfectly well that

you haven't come to see me, that you've come because
you have something to ask of me; and I shall be only too
happy if I can give it to you. That's understood in advance. So I look at you, I pay myself in advance."

"Don't look at me too closely! I am old now."

" 'High noon, king of summer.' "

"You may as well call it autumn."

"The richest plumage is that of the trees in autumn."

"One likes the flowers better."

"I like the flowers and the fruits."

"Yes, yes, you like everything. Will you listen to me?"

"Speak! I am all eyes!"

"You have seen all too well that I have come as a beg-
gar. After such a long separation, I ought to be ashamed
that my first call is to ask you for help. But it isn't for
myself."

"There's no excuse for that!"

"So be it!" she replied. "But as it concerns some one
else in whom I am interested, I have swallowed all my
shame."

"Some one else who interests you is still you."

"Perhaps. One never knows where one's self begins or
ends."

"The communism of self! Well then, whatever concerns you concerns me. Let's share it! Tell me your
story."

Annette told him about the young prisoner. Marcel
knew his name. At some exhibition he had seen two or
three of his little "whatever they were," although he had
no special remembrance of them. But a painter, whoever
he might be, belonged to his department. It did not displease him to reveal this fact to Annette, along with the
extent of his own influence, the largeness of his intelli-

gence. He obtained for her a permit to visit Franz in the prison-camp.

Annette took advantage of her Easter holidays for this little expedition. Instead of spending them with her son, as he had expected her to do, she went to Angers. She had to reconnoiter first, and, before everything else, become acquainted with Franz; for any plan for the future depended upon what he was himself.

She had seen him so long already through his friend's love that she was not without anxiety at the idea of meeting him. As a result of having shared Germain's thoughts, she had espoused his affection; she was coming charged with it; her eyes no longer impartial, she saw with his eyes. The tender plasticity of the feminine spirit, which woman realizes, which she combats and cultivates: she knows its dangers and she feels its sweetness. And when she relaxes the control of her will she languishes and abandons herself to the slope. . . .

In her compartment in the train, as it approached Angers, Annette stilled in her breast the beating of Germain's impatient heart.

*

* *

Franz had little to suffer in his captivity. The camp where he was enjoyed a certain liberty. Many of the prisoners worked in the town, and they were not under much compulsion save that of being punctual at the morning and evening roll-calls. The surveillance was slack: they were regarded as harmless and so far from the frontiers that they would be unable to reach them if they were seized with a fancy to escape. As a matter of fact, this never did occur to them. The majority of these good people had been established in France before the year 1914 and suffered from being separated from their relatives in Germany, but they had no desire to be restored to their dangers and their combats. And this the country-folk—the people of that rich country of the sleeping West—perfectly understood. They made no secret, in fact, of telling them so.

Franz was busy doing odd jobs at painting. The wife of the commandant had requisitioned him. He repainted the white walls between the windows of her drawing-room and freshened the obliterated pink of the shepherdesses sporting with their cupids with which an old pupil of Boucher had brightened the ceiling. The task would not have been disagreeable if the commandant had not regarded it as one of his prerogatives to treat as a servant a Boche who was in bondage. Proud and shy, hypersensitive, the aristocratic young man suffered from these affronts, which made no impression on the hide of his companions. Perhaps that was why the lady took such a fancy to him. However vulgar she may be, the female is always subtle enough to understand her victim when

195

there is any question of satisfying her instinct for cruelty.

Franz, when the day was over, left the house with a galled feeling. Instead of taking a good whiff of air and a pipe, uttering an "Ouf!" and throwing off his weariness, with the smoke, in the sweetness of the twilight, —the sky, this evening, was warm and tender, like the cheek of an apricot—Franz was walking along in utter dejection when Annette approached him.

He made a sudden movement to avoid her. He felt towards women a shyness that was mingled with attraction. Annette called him by his name. Without interrupting his walk, he gave her a slanting look, his eyes troubled and his eyebrows gathered, anxiously and irritatedly, as if some one were making an attempt on his chastity. Annette smiled at the young Joseph, who was defending his cloak. She said: "Germain has sent me . . ."

He stopped in astonishment. He stammered:

"Germaine Chavânnes. . . ."

He sought in her eyes. And with her eyes Annette said, "Yes." Franz seized her hand and hurried her along.

He went ahead, dragging her by the arm, like an importunate child, and Annette, in her surprise, though she was aware of the danger of being noticed, did not attempt to withdraw her fingers. But the hour was late; they met no one but a little peasant girl who laughed as she saw them. By a lane that ran off to one side, Franz reached the open fields. A half-fallen wall surrounded an orchard. In a breach of it, protected from eyes passing on the road by the shelter of an angle, they sat down close together, their knees touching; and, leaning towards Annette, without letting her hands go, Franz begged: "Germain?"

In the shimmering twilight that precedes the night

Annette felt herself seized by these demanding, imploring eyes. In the very act of pressing her to speak, they forbade her to speak.

She observed these changing eyes which now suspiciously refused themselves, now delivered themselves imperiously, and suddenly died out—vague and somnolent. His hair was light brown, his forehead open, his nose delicate, the lip a little full; a peurile expression played indecisively over the face, as if in a perpetual expectation of joy or suffering. A child. She compared him with the image of him that Germain had evoked, and she was astonished that he had inspired such an attachment.

The impatient pressure of the hands that gripped her recalled Annette to the reply that he was awaiting. She spoke of his far-away friend, but every moment she was interrupted by his questions, stopped in her account of the sick man by the other man's anxiety, which she strove to reassure. Her solicitude for the one who was absent turned towards the one who was present and who had to be treated cautiously.

The camp bugle rang out, and they both remembered that it had already sounded once. They must separate immediately, but it was all Annette could do to make Franz go back, promising him a long talk for the next day. As they dropped each other's hands, at parting, Franz became aware of Annette's, which she had left in his since they had first met. He looked at them. He looked at his own. He said: "These hands have touched him. . . ."

And, with his face against the palms, he inhaled her hands.

*
* *

Annette was not long in discovering Franz's incapacity to combine a plan of practical action with its execution. It was not that he lacked audacity. He was ready to risk everything; and in fact one had to take care that he did not run at once into the maddest and most desperate expedient. At the first words which Annette uttered in regard to a plan of escaping, he caught fire with such extravagance that Annette cut him short and kept to herself what she had in mind: Franz's heedlessness and temerity would ruin everything. It would all have to be prepared without him, and he could not be told of the affair until the moment had arrived for them to act. It was still doubtful that he would be able in any respect to act alone. He would have to be led, step by step, by the hand. The chances, feeble enough already, had become almost nil. And yet Annette refused to give it up. She was a prisoner of the promise that she had made; she was in the grip of that strange passion of friendship that beat her with its double current, like an islet at the confluence of two rivers. The islet remained motionless, but in the boiling of the waters it was she who seemed to turn. Unconnected herself with the agitation, Annette submitted to its vertigo.

It was an exaltation of the spirit, in these two friends, which had lost contact with reality—a tie of chivalry, created by the passionate soul against a world that denied it, under the sway of an exceptional revolt of the heart against an exceptional oppression. This chivalry had a heroic character in the elder, the stronger—in Germain—who protected the weaker in the struggle, and, wounded, succumbing, carried back to his young companion whatever attachment to life he still felt. In the younger, isolated in an enemy world, it assumed a color of mystic adoration for the protecting friend whom distance rendered almost supernatural, like the patron saints on the altars. It had required the war to give to their feelings this deformation that magnified them. In a normal period, they would have been able to maintain themselves at those middle heights where everyday life pitches its tent. Danger and fever had raised them up to the spheres one only reaches by the wings of prayer. For whole hearts, which are already more than half detached from life, friendship, like prayer, is one of the roads that leads to the divine. Not one of the three who communicated in it—Germain, Franz and Annette—believed in God. And not one of them failed to see that, in his metamorphoses, Jupiter, God, had taken in them the form of friendship, and that they were filled with him. They burned to sacrifice themselves to this.

Of the three, Annette was in the most singular situation. Hitherto she had felt neither for the one nor the other anything that resembled love. Her personal feelings did not pass beyond a fraternal pity, that penchant which every rightly made woman has for an unhappy soul who is in suffering and who needs her—especially when that soul is a man; for his broken force has for her a most touching attraction. And in Germain's and Franz's incapacity to join forces and act, she participated in the emotions which they exchanged through her intermediation: they loved each other in her, by proxy. And they had delegated action to her, to her alone.

A heavy undertaking! Was she not mad to charge herself with it? She quite thought so when she was alone; and she would have liked to put on the brake. But the machine had started, and every turn of the wheel involved her more.

In the returning train that was carrying her back to
Paris, Annette became terrified. The difficulties and the
dangers seemed to her almost insurmountable. She could
not see any way of fulfilling the obligations she had
tacitly assumed with the two friends. She was like an ant
that tries to drag out a straw that is buried under a block.
Even though she might succeed in disengaging it, this
block, suspended over her, was always in danger of crushing her along with her booty. But this risk has never
stopped an ant. And for Annette perhaps it was one
stimulus the more, for a part of herself, the part that
would not endure the brutal menace. The other, the
weaker self, had its moments of fright:

"My God, what have I undertaken? Can't I disavow
it, renounce it, escape from it? Who is holding me
back?"

"Myself. I must."

She was alone, face to face with that mountain, the
State. She was confronting the threatening visage of the
nation. She felt herself under the feet of the great angry
Goddesses. But although they might destroy her, they
could not make her yield. She no longer believed in
them. From the moment she had seen the primitive,
sacred affections, friendship and love, trampled upon by
the inhuman colossi—all the rest had disappeared. The
rest was force. Against force, the soul!

Madness? So be it! For when it comes to this, madness is the soul also. It is by this madness that I live,
that I walk over the abyss, as the apostle walked over the
waters.

*
* *

She arrived on the Tuesday before Easter; she had only five more days of vacation to give to Paris. The indifferent Marc was bitterly disappointed by this. Six months earlier, one would have said that he was simply missing his victim, who suffered for him. (And this was only human! A heart that loves is made to be abused.)

But Marc was no longer disposed to abuse it. Nor was Annette any longer disposed to yield to such treatment. The situation had changed. In these last six months, he had harshly sifted his affections—his loves and his friendships. What remained of them was more chaff than wheat. He had a hard look, singularly keen, without pity for the object upon which it rested—himself or other people, it didn't matter! Not those rather myopic, warm, illumined eyes of his mother. Nor those malicious sparrow's eyes of his aunt's that pricked on the wing every absurdity that passed and for which everything was good to laugh at and to eat. He was not accommodating; he tore the object to pieces. After the operation nothing very weighty remained of his chance friendships. Marc was determined to pull off their husks and find at the bottom of the grain the worm, the void or the dirt. And amid all this waste one grain alone had resisted: the heart of his mother. In vain had he battled against it with his beak: he had not been able to cut into it. He did not yet know what the meal was worth. But that it remained intact, without a trace of corruption, inspired him with respect, with the unconfessed desire to have access to it. He was very fond of Sylvie; but he had a

touch of affectionate contempt for her that she did not fail
to reciprocate. He knew that he could count upon her
complicity, and he was grateful to her for this, for he was
quite willing for people to be unjust for his benefit. (On
condition that they were not taken in. He had no pity
for fools.) But there was a difference between Sylvie and
Annette. Annette was a soul whom it was worth taking
pains to win. For he had come to realize also during
these last six months that his mother loved him but that
he did not hold her. Maternal love is a strong, sure
instinct, but Marc wanted something more, more than
love. He wanted to understand and to be understood, to
possess—the more inwardly the better—not the mother
but the being. The mother is the mother for all: the
anonymous incubator. But every being has its hidden
essence that resembles no other and makes its own perfume. He perceived the perfume. He wanted to reach,
under the sheath, one grain of incense: you are you, and
you exist only once. . . . I want your secret! . . .

What would he do with it? Reject it, after he was
satiated? Those little rodents—the hearts of adolescents,
are greedy to possess and do not know how to keep anything. It is well to keep whatever precious things they
long for out of reach of their teeth.

They were, with Annette. In vain had she offered
herself, with her beautiful smiling lips; she did not herself possess the key of the casket in which rested the secret
of her being. She could not make a gift of it. This was
fortunate for her. Many a time, in her life, she would
have squandered it! The inviolate sanctuary held at this
moment, for Marc, a sacred attraction.

He was counting on these Easter holidays to make himself master of it. When she did not come, he bit his

nails. And when at last she appeared, more than a week
was lost! He had to make haste to renew the intimacy,
so many times offered by her and by him refused. He
waited for her once more to furnish him with the opportunity, as she had done during the last vacations; and,
after having let her entreat him, this time he would con-
descend to yield. . . .

But this time Annette's mind was filled with other
thoughts. She did not make any advances. He had his
secrets? Very well! He could keep them. For she had
hers, and she was keeping them.

Nothing remained for Marc but to observe the "strange
woman"—the closest to himself—the furthest away—
his mother. To try and see from outside, through the
shutters. Only the other day it was she who wished to
see, and he who had barricaded himself. A humiliating
change of positions!

She did not barricade herself. "Look in, if you wish!"
She was simply not concerned with him. That was the
most humiliating thing of all! He was obliged to swallow
this innocent affront, since his curiosity, the loadstone that
attracted him, was more powerful than his *amour-propre*.

What struck him especially to-day in this woman was
her calmness and her solidity among the dusty souls that
whirled about in the wind. The house was like a ship-
wrecked vessel. The machinery was broken, the tackle
worn out; there was a typhoon in people's hearts. The
sign of death was inscribed anew, in red and black, on
the doors. Apolline had killed herself shortly after
Annette's last visit; but Annette did not learn this at the
time. Sylvie had deliberately omitted to mention it to
her. Towards the end of November they had found in
the Seine the body of the distracted creature. Of Alexis

there was no trace: he had vanished in the gulf of oblivion.
The two Bernardin sons had also disappeared, but in that
other gulf that people call glory—those epic quicksands
in which, in Andalusia, they roll the corpses of the horses
which the bulls have disemboweled. Nothing of them
remained in the mud of the Somme which the infernal
thumb of the two artilleries had not long since kneaded
away. In a whirlwind, sorrow had fallen upon the Bernardin family. A few seconds had been enough to
destroy their race. The blow had come a fortnight ago.
Monsieur Bernardin, the father, was like a beaten ox with
a bleeding eye. His fury and his faith had been exposed
to a cruel assault. There had been moments when he
wrestled with God. But God was the stronger; and now
the man, crushed, with his head hanging, held out his
thumbs in surrender.

During the night that followed the day after her
arrival, Annette found herself with the decimated herd
in the cellar of the house, where the alarm of an air-raid
had tumbled them all together. There was no sign now
of the cordial animation of those first times when they had
sought one another and pooled, in order to multiply them,
their faith and their hope. In spite of the effort they
forced themselves to make to preserve the forms of
courtesy and the appearance of a mutual interest, it was
evident that each family group—as in each group each
individual—was isolating itself at the bottom of its own
dry cell. Every one seemed to be weighed down with an
exasperated weariness. The most commonplace exchange
of courtesies betrayed by its accent the atrocious suffering
they felt. Almost all of these poor people had a long
credit of griefs, disappointments, mournings and tribula-
tions. . . . But to whom could they present the bill?

Where was the Debtor hiding? In default of him, each neighbor paid his part of the bitterness.

Blind discontent was ripening through the whole of France in this April of 1917. The Russian Revolution had just broken out. With this aurora borealis the sky was bleeding on the horizon. The first news of it had reached Paris three weeks before; and, the preceding week, on Palm Sunday, the people of Paris had acclaimed it tumultuously at a meeting. But there were no leaders; it was not directed. The common action amounted to nothing; it was simply a multitude of contradictory reactions, egoisms that were in suffering and did not know how to unite. They were easily broken. The spirit of the Revolution crumbled in isolated revolts. In these weeks of April, they were at work secretly in the armies. What these regiments, these insurgents, wanted they knew no more than the poor people of the house; and their executioners had the profit of it. But what all knew was that they were suffering; and they looked for some one upon whom they could avenge themselves.

This resentment found expression more in the gestures and the voices than in the words of the "cellared" ones. Instead of uniting their burdens, they seemed to be comparing them, accusing their neighbors of leaving the heaviest to them. Bernardin and Girerd each turned his grief against the other. They saluted each other coldly, but they did not speak. Sorrow has its frontiers. They did not cross them.

Annette expressed her warm compassion to Ursule and Justine Bernardin. These reserved girls, who had never exchanged a word with her, were almost overwhelmed by this outburst of sympathy; they blushed with emotion and gratitude. Then timidity and distrust resumed the

upper hand; and, drawing away, they passed again under
their veils of mourning, into their shells. Annette did not
pursue them. If others needed her, she was ready; but
she had no need of others. She did not seek to impose
upon any one either herself or her ideas.

About her, in this cellar, they were exchanging coldly
fanatical remarks. Clapier described the first performance
of the film, *Debout les Morts!*, exposing the crimes of
the Germans, which was adorned with this legend:

"Whoever your enemy may be, brother, parent, friend,
kill him! Know that every dead German is one plague
the less for humanity!"

Madame Bernardin gently talked to a neighbor about
the League of Remembrance for piously perpetuating
hatred against the enemy. Annette listened in silence.
Marc watched her face. She did not flinch. Nor did she
betray any feeling when Sylvie retailed in her usual light,
chattering way the jingoistic stupidities and the various
scandals of the neighborhood. Annette let her talk, smiling without answering, and spoke of other things. She
did not reveal what was going through her own mind.
Even the death of Apolline, that terrible piece of news
that would ordinarily have overwhelmed her, only
brought a gleam of pity into her eyes. Marc, whom this
tragedy had stirred to the depths, was annoyed by his
mother's reserve and tried to force her out of it. He began to describe very excitedly and crudely what he had
seen and heard. With a gesture Annette bade him be
silent. She did not take part in discussions unless it pleased
her. All efforts to drag her into one were vain. But
she had her own ideas about it all; Marc was certain of
that. A few calm words had sufficed for him to divine her
intimate detachment from that which filled the others
with passion—the war and the country. He wished he

could know more about it. Why wouldn't she speak?
Marc had been greatly stirred by the Russian Revolution. He had gone to the meeting on the first of April.
He had gone out of curiosity, but he had been overcome
by the contagion of the crowd; he had acclaimed Séverine
and reviled Jouhaux. He had seen the Russians weeping
and listened to the hymn of their Revolution; and, much
as he despised the tears, he had not found them lacking in
a certain virile grandeur. But he did not know what to
think. A few attempts at conversation with these Muscovites had immediately shocked, bewildered, irritated him;
their geometrical intolerance, their national vanity, which
revealed its ass's ear under the liberty cap, their galling
irony against France and the French. "Ah! I have had
enough of that!" Marc, who was never backward in
exercising his irony at the expense of his own people, did
not like it when people assumed it for him and against him
. . . and then that humiliating free-and-easy familiarity!
Marc was instinctively aristocratic; he was not tempted
by the ideal of promiscuity with these herds of "Judeo-
Asiatics." (These were the little animal's own words.)
Having entered eagerly, he drew back hastily. He suffered all sorts of reactions of which some were perhaps,
and others certainly, bad. He would not discuss them;
they were what they were, and he was what he was. The
dictatorship of patriotism or of the protelariat was for him
a choice between two tyrannies, between two insanities of
the reason that decides things. And his heart was not
sufficiently human, not sufficiently generous, to decide in
favor of the people—if it were at his expense. He needed
to prefer in order to understand. And Pitan and his
comrades were not the ones to help him! Pitan, of course,
was busily at work on the new raft, but for reasons so
vague that they turned young Rivière away instead of

attracting him: the mysticism of catastrophe and destruction, jubilant pessimism, the intoxication of sacrifice.

"Go and take the air! Let him who has nothing to lose sacrifice himself without knowing why! I have something immensely valuable to save: myself, my intelligence, my future, my spoils of life. When I have taken everything that belongs to me, when I have clearly seen everything and experienced everything, then! Then to sacrifice oneself in the light. Yes, perhaps. But in the night, under a bandage? Thanks, old fellow! The sacrifice of moles is not for me. Offer me some other candle than the 'reign of the proletariat!' "

Did Annette have some other light? Marc tried in vain to discover it. In order to provoke her, he boasted in her presence of several enormities. She did not seem to hear, and the bricks fell in the void. Nothing was left for Marc but the shame of having spoken. So this woman wasn't thinking of anything? For Marc, thinking was like the breaking out of nettle-rash, an irritation of the skin. The only way to alleviate it was to scratch it, to rub it against others. For him thinking was always an aggressive act. Thinking was projecting his thought, driving it into others. As long as it got into them, by consent or by force! It seemed to be unimportant to Annette whether other people thought as she did or not.

Indifferent, no, she wasn't that; but she felt instinctively that thoughts were like the shoots of plants. Let them ripen slowly! If they anticipated their time they were nipped in the bud at the first frost. In all these souls about her it was still winter. It was not the time for them to emerge from their lethargy. Their lethargy lulled to sleep their sufferings and their doubts. A premature awakening would annihilate them.

From her doorstep Annette heard Perret, the workman, vociferating on the floor above. He was in a violent discussion with one of his comrades. He had come back embittered on a few days' leave. Everything he had seen at the front, everything he had found in the rear, the botching of people's lives, the waste of property, the loss of illusions, the demoralization of his own household, his daughter who had become a prostitute, the women who made fools of themselves squandering their money as soon as it was earned in the murder-mills, had filled him with a rage of revolt against his companions, against his officers, against the world. And yet he angrily persisted in his "To the bitter end!" To his anarchist comrade who was taunting him and trying to unsettle his resolution, he shouted:

"Shut up, or I'll throw you downstairs! What do you want me to do? Haven't I enough on my hands already? It would do you a lot of good, wouldn't it, you idiot, if you proved to me that they have all been taking us in, that patriotism is just one more sinister humbug like everything else, that they are killing us for nothing? What do you want me to believe in? I don't believe in revolution any more. I don't believe in religion. I don't believe in humanity. That's even more preposterous, even emptier than the rest! If I didn't have my country any more, what would I have to cling to? I should have nothing left but to blow up the ammunition-wagon!"

Annette understood Perret. Marc did not understand him. . . . "Let him blow up his ammunition wagon!" . . . Youth has no pity for the misery of the weak, which has to compromise with life in order to live. Marc didn't compromise. And as his youth wanted to live in spite of all, he and his comrades, anarchists, dadaists, were avenging themselves now by a measureless and unbridled ridicule of everything that existed. By a derision that ran to the extreme of extravagance, an excess of the absurd, they avenged themselves by their irrationality for the murderous inanity of reason.

And here was the one he understood the least—his mother—free, he would have sworn, from everything that surrounded her, with no need for attacking in order to defend herself. She did not criticize anything. She did not find fault with anything that any one else thought. She had her own mind, her own reasons, her own house, and she kept to them. She stood on her own foundations. What were they?

Annette was a woman. Her heart was filled with one passionate thought. It never occurred to her to extend it to the universe. Her field of vision was entirely occupied by one definite, arduous, limited activity. It was not her affair to resolve the tragic enigma in which the world was floundering. For her this enigma and this tragedy were summed up in the peculiar duty that was assigned to her, or to which she was assigned—to save the sacred sentiment that filled her, this Friendship. Not even that—to save the two friends with whose fate her own was entwined. She did not generalize on the lot of other men. She had her own share in destiny. This part was enough for her; she consecrated her whole being to it. In order to respond to this appeal, she was ready to forgo people's respect and transgress every human law. A higher law had spoken. If every one did the same, in his own restricted domain, it would be the greatest Revolution of humanity.

*

* *

She left Paris without having breathed a word of her
secret to any one—to her son, least of all. For, in spite
of his desire to come closer to her, Marc, in his usual
manner of self-defense, had constantly belied the sentiments he supposed her to hold: he proclaimed a humiliating sarcasm against the pacifism he attributed to his
mother.

She had no desire to debate this subject. Peace, war,
were not her affair. They were too far away! She held
in her hands the hands of these two men who had been
entrusted to her and whom it was her duty to bring together again. It was no question of ideas. It was their
life and her own. And her own was at stake. An absurd
stake! From the point of view of reason, yes. But the
heart has its reasons. And the heart had spoken.

In passing through Paris she had caught just a word
that might help her plan. Marc had incidentally spoken
in her presence of the Russian revolutionists in France who
wished to go and take their places in the battle-line over
there and to whom the Allies were refusing passports.
But they were getting through without them. Secret
colloquies were also being exchanged, by indirect ways,
between the French resistants of the war who were in
Switzerland and their comrades in France. In the barbed-
wire network that encompassed the French mind and prevented it from breathing, a few links had given way, and
through these impoverished life was beginning to circulate
again: letters and newspapers came and went through
these mouse-holes on the frontier. And Pitan held the

thread of this perilous game—which was inoffensive enough except in the eyes of those in power, for a few free words had no chance of penetrating the stony ears and the thick shell of that great saurian, the nation in arms. They were enough, however, to feed the illusion of those who, under their chains, were trying to convince themselves that they still possessed their liberty. Annette made a note of Pitan's name. She must have a talk with him. But she had no intention of asking Marc's help in finding him.

She had returned to her post in the country. She had long private talks with Germain. She had brought him the direct message, the invisible presence of his friend. They discussed the great plan together. She did not tell him her doubts. She did not as yet see any way of carrying the scheme through. But Germain must not know anything about this! Her task now was to revive in him the will to live and make him agree to the departure. Little hope as this change of air offered, it was the last chance, and he must try it. Germain was slow in making up his mind to it: he did not want to leave until the eve of the event, when it was entirely certain. And the project still remained very vague. It took all the egotism of passion to prevent him from seeing the mortal dangers into which it was going to throw Annette and even his friend. If he saw them, it was not with the eyes of a living man: death had already mounted to his shoulders. To calm him, he had to be offered, in the meanwhile, some suggestion of what was being done to bring about the problematical event. Through Marcel Franck, Annette obtained for the young Austrian the benefit of a specially favorable treatment. He was removed from the camp for reasons of health. He was authorized to live in the town, without

any strict control, under the pretext of studies that were of
some importance for French art. Leniencies of this kind
were less rare, during the war, than is generally supposed.
One *privat-docent* of Berlin was allowed to go about without any surveillance at all in a certain town of Central
France. Sixty interned Germans of distinction were com-
fortably quartered at Carnac, with their wives or their
mistresses, and had free scope over a domain of two hundred and fifty acres. After the mad excitement of the
first years of the war, which was like the bubbling of a vat
of wine, this became customary with prisoners in some
regions; they were on the way to becoming an integral part
of the normal life of the countryside. A tacit order was
established, and the surveillance was relaxed. Franz
reaped these advantages. In Germain's eyes, they were
the first beacons on the road of liberation.

Urged by the doctor, by his family, by Annette, he
consented to leave the country. Annette made him realize
that he must lose no time in establishing himself in
Switzerland, so that he could receive the fugitive there
after the escape. But Germain was still suspicious:

"Annette, don't deceive me! It would be better to let
me die here. It's base to abuse the confidence of a dying
man, to make him go away by deluding him with promises
that can't be carried out."

"Nobody can promise to succeed," Annette replied.
"But I take it upon myself to risk everything for you—
for you two. Don't you believe me?"

He did believe her.

In the last days before the departure, he began to realize
what all this meant to her.

"Annette, I release you from your word. I renounce . . ."

But his passion was too much for him. No! He couldn't renounce! As long as one chance remained!

When the time came to bid her farewell, he said merely: "Forgive me!"—without explaining for what. Let her risk her own life for him! He had only one hour of life left.

He set out at the beginning of August, in the care of his mother and Madame de Marëuil.

And Annette found herself alone, with the impossible plan she had undertaken to carry out.

It was the worst possible time for a secret undertaking. The danger had increased. The relaxation of power in the first months of 1917 had been followed by a régime of constraint and accusations. The government, which had shown itself pitifully weak before the revolutionary strikes and the insurrections of the spring, was avenging itself for its cowardice and fear after these had been quelled. This was the period of the false "defeatist" plots which the hypocritical sytem pretended to discover everywhere in all the Allied countries. A vast calumny-factory filled with its reeking fumes the sky of Europe and America. This was not one of the least industries of the war! "Intercourse with the enemy"—that cliché, that lie which authorized all those base denunciations! The "Union Sacrée against Treason," the new league founded in September, cultivated its shameful maladies of mutual hatred and suspicion. Everybody was in arms against his neighbor. Every word, every step was spied upon.

During the whole summer Annette felt her way, in the darkness, without moving forward. She lacked every sort of means. She could not go back to Franz without attracting attention. And letters were read. How could she arrange a plan with him? And what plan? There could be no question of his crossing France on foot: he would be arrested the day after he started. He would have to go quickly and make his way under cover. He would have to travel on some main-line train and join Annette, who would accompany him to the frontier. But the trains to Switzerland were sifted on their departure and arrival. And who was going to conduct Franz from the town where he was interned to the train that was to carry him to freedom? And who would be his guide across the frontier? It was too much for one person alone to carry out such a plan. And Annette had nobody in whom she could confide.

Chance came to her aid. She had returned to Paris during the vacation months. She was in her apartment, and she held in her hands a piece of Chinese porcelain that had been broken, one of those few souvenirs that had remained from the elegant furnishings of the house of the past, the Boulogne house, where the two sisters had spent their honeymoon of friendship. And, appropriately enough, Sylvie was there. The beautiful broken plate, with its deep tints of horizon blue, brought up again the scenes of other days. Sylvie gave her sister the address of a skillful workman who would be able to repair the damage. And Annette recognized the name of Pitan.

She set out in search of him. There was little chance of her finding him. Sylvie had warned her that Pitan was always out, that the shop was more often closed than open. But Annette went to the address, which was in the suburbs, and it so happened that Pitan was there.

He was very much surprised by the visit. He was not deceived by her pretext in coming—although the moment

the pieces of broken china were placed between his big
hands he took delicate and competent hold of the petals
fallen from the fragile flower of the furnace. No one
would have come so far for a mere matter of repairing
china! But Pitan politely greeted her, without any sign
either of haste or surprise. Politely, he offered Annette
a chair, and, standing before her—standing, he was
scarcely taller than Annette sitting—he listened to her
and looked at her with his kind, velvety eyes. This man,
in whose life woman did not seem to have any place, was
never embarrassed when he talked with a woman; he
found himself quite naturally on her level. Their child-
like and instinctive qualities, even when they were most
artful, brought him close to them. This ingenuous soul
was able to read like an open book their ruses and their
desires, however adroitly painted over; and he was not
surprised by them. He never criticized them; and when
they lied to him he did not even contradict them. When
it was "no" and they said "yes," his head, as he listened
to them, shook benevolently. But his grave eyes showed
clearly that he understood the "no"; and, face to face
with his affectionate smile, they never thought of taking
offense. They saw in him a comrade—not a dupe, and not
an accomplice—sincere and indulgent, who accepted them
as they were and whoever they might be—who respected
them.

There was immediate understanding and confidence
between these gentle spaniel's eyes and those other eyes
that were equally clear—windows without curtains. And
the name of Marc, uttered by Annette, quickly thawed the
silence. Pitan's ocher-yellow, bearded face lighted up.
He said: "You are Madame Rivière?"

He respected Marc's mother because of everything he knew of her and everything he had divined, and he hastened to show it.

"You know me?" she said.

"I know your boy."

"He is not like me."

"Naturally not. He is like all boys. He takes great pains not to be like you. That's why I recognize you."

"I embarrass him. He runs away from me."

"Don't run after him! Life is like a race-track. It turns in a circle. All you have to do is to wait for him. The further he goes away from you, the closer he approaches you."

He was beaming. Annette laughed. They were in the land of understanding—Marc. They were friends. After having spoken of him, Pitan said to Annette: "In what way can I be of service to you, Madame Rivière? Is it something that concerns him?"

Annette blushed a little because he had unmasked her deceitful pretext. "No, it is not for him. But it's true that I've come for some advice that you can give me. Excuse me for beating about the bush instead of speaking straight out!"

"Oh, I saw that clearly, at once. You have no need to apologize. With their Union Sacrée, they have succeeded in making everybody suspect everybody else. 'Don't speak! Mum's the word! Be careful who may be listening to you!' When you came in—a mutual confession!—I also held my tongue."

"I shan't hold mine any longer," said Annette. "You can make anything you like of me."

Pitan had no conceit. He merely said good-humoredly:

"There is no danger with me. Speak, Madame Rivière! We were not made to conceal our thoughts from each other."

Simply, without veiling anything, Annette explained her plan. When he heard it, Pitan started a little; but he let her talk without interrupting her. After she had finished, he coughed and said: "But, Madame Rivière, do you know the danger you are running?"

"That isn't the point," said Annette, calmly.

Pitan coughed again. He asked himself what motive could drive this woman to compromise her life and her honor. He hesitated to speak. She divined him.

"Tell me, Monsieur Pitan, what you want to ask me?"

"Excuse me, Madame Rivière. But as for this young prisoner in whom you have interested yourself, wouldn't it be better for him to remain where he is, in shelter, instead of exposing himself?"

"It isn't a question of his security or mine."

Without any circumlocution Pitan went on: "Are you in love with the other one then?"

Annette blushed again. (How young her blood still was!) "No, it's no question of love, Pitan, I assure you! I am too old a woman. Such things are not for my age. I haven't even dreamed of it! I am thinking of nothing but their friendship—not the friendship they have for me —I don't count in their eyes—their mutual friendship."

"Is that really it?"

Pitan had not finished his thought. Annette said: "Isn't that worth the trouble of sacrificing oneself?"

Pitan studied her. She added, as if to justify herself: "One of the two is dying. So there's no use discussing it, Pitan."

Pitan did not discuss it. He had understood. The very

madness of the generous plan was made to persuade him. His eyes brooded over Annette with veneration.

"You can't do it alone," he said, after reflecting a moment.

"If I have to," she replied.

Pitan reflected again; then, stooping down before her, he took up a pinch of dust from the floor. He touched his forehead with it.

"What are you doing?" said Annette.

"I am enrolling myself in your battalion. You see, Madame Rivière"—he had taken a stool and sat down beside her, so as to speak in a whisper—"it is physically impossible for you to do everything at once, here and there at the same time. One helper is not too many. And I must add that you have other duties to think of. You have your son. You mustn't run any risk, if you can possibly help it, of compromising him, his name and his future, in case you are caught. He wouldn't thank you for that. As for me, I have nothing to risk but myself. A single man to-day is very cheap, sells for nothing. Let me—since I know how—arrange this affair for you! At my risk and peril! What can be done shall be done."

"But, Pitan," said Annette, touched, "you don't even know these people for whom you are willing to expose yourself!"

"I know friendship," said Pitan. "They are friends, those two. You are all three friends. The four of us are friends. Friendship is a magnet. One would have to be harder than iron to resist it."

"The world of to-day resists it very well," said Annette.

"Every one knows," said Pitan, "that the world of to-day is a world of giants. But we, Madame Rivière, don't look so high. We are merely ordinary people."

They discussed the project. And Pitan took upon himself—he would listen to nothing else—the lion's share. So it was arranged that he was to place himself in direct communication with the young prisoner. And when the moment came he would be his guide and turn him over to Annette in the train for Geneva. Through friends of his he would also arrange the crossing of the frontier. But first it would be necessary to study the terrain. There must be no undue haste. In the approaching weeks, Pitan would invent some pretext to go to the town and reconnoiter the prison-camp. He would meet Franz and cautiously lay the foundations. Pitan spoke of caution, but he was full of passion. The enormous risk he was running of being accused and summarily condemned for espionage and high treason in case he was caught did not bother him at all. He realized it, of course, but he paid no attention to it. (Who knows? To his inmost self this may have been positively attractive. Pitan, as we have seen, liked the idea of being "eaten.") The sentimental, chimerical side of the scheme had won him. He was carried away; his head was lowered, his eyes were shining; he was on the scent of a truffle. Then suddenly he stopped, laughed in his beard and said:

"Madame Rivière, excuse me! We are both of us mad—one as much as the other. At a time when everything is going to pieces, cities and men, I am busy myself patching up broken porcelain. And you, you are trying to glue together the fragments of friendship. It's all laughable! So let's laugh together! That old gossip of a Colas said: 'The madder people are together, the wiser they are!' Who knows? Perhaps later we shall be the wise ones!"

*

* *

The next day Pitan set to work. But the patience he had learned in his trade had taught him to measure his movements. He went step by step. The whole summer rolled by. When Annette returned to Paris from her post, they had not yet been able to fix upon the date for acting. But the threads were solidly attached between herself, Franz and Pitan. And when the time came for Annette to go back to the country, Pitan left for the Swiss frontier to arrange the other end of the affair.

Germain, in his sanatorium at Château d'Oex, was naturally growing impatient. He could not express himself freely in his letters. Tormented and feverish, he said all too much. Annette wrote to him: "Do you want to ruin everything?"

Then he obliged her to repeat twenty times over: "Swear! You have sworn!"

"I have sworn. Yes. I stand by it. You dying man, who drives us on, you hold our lives very cheap. Poor boy. I understand you. I am not trying to get out of it."

She had begun her third year of teaching. But for her the situation was changed. The Chavânnes house was closed. She had not merely lost the society of friends to whom she was attached. Their presence had been for her a protection which had meant more to her than she realized. That she had been admitted to their intimacy had perhaps aroused the jealous malevolence of the little town; but this malevolence had no way of showing itself. Now that the shield that covered Annette had been taken away from her, it was no longer necessary to be careful. It was known that Germain's sister, Madame de Séigy-

Chavânnes, who was still there, had no sympathy for Annette; and since her brother's departure she no longer saw her. The slander that had been repressed was able to come out into the light. For two years, grain by grain, the female race had been amassing, like the ant, a pile of patient and uncharitable observations of this nature. To the public granary every one brought his own contribution; they made a common store of them. They brought together their doubts about Annette's private life and her suspected maternity, remarks suggested by the equivocal coldness of her patriotism and by the friendly feelings she had been at no pains to conceal in regard to the enemy. Although no one knew what was going on, her journeys of the past year, her obscure doings, began to cause chatter. It was time indeed for Annette to hand over to Pitan all the active part of the operations, for her movements were being spied upon. She herself only saw that she was being treated with an increased coldness that was accompanied by a sickly smile and a honeyed politeness on people's twisted mouths.

But we never lack the sort of friends who inform us of the evil things that are being said about us. There is no pleasure like telling a bad piece of news to some one who is ignorant of it. It does everybody so much good! Besides, it's not merely comforting; it's a matter of duty.

This duty La Trottée cheerfully took upon herself. La Trottée—the widow Trottat, or, more exactly, Tortrat—was the washerwoman who had boxed the ears of the German officer and then, suddenly struck by Annette's energy, had noisily repented to the latter at the hospital. She was about forty years old, a good woman but a great lover of her bottle. Since that memorable day she had displayed an aggressive pacifism under the very beards of

the good-natured gendarmes; and she testified an enthusiastic sympathy for Annette which the latter could
have done very well without. But they lived next door
to each other. La Trottée had her trade. And there
was no way of escaping from the washerwoman and her
bottle.

Annette was willing to concede a good deal to her because of her old mother-in-law, who lived with her. No
two women could have been more different: La Trottée,
with her sharp tongue and her clumsy shape, big-boned
and brawny, with a great Burgundian nose that pushed
through people's doors, and the Mother Guillemette,
slight, slender, calm. The latter had passed her seventieth
year. Married a second time to a farmer of the region
of Arras, she had received copiously during the war the
baptism of fire. Everything she had, her house, had been
destroyed; and her old husband had died of grief over it.
She had accepted it. For weeks she had lived by herself,
under the bombardment of her own countrymen, with the
German soldiers; she had shown no resentment either
against those who had destroyed her possessions or against
those who had drawn the disaster down upon her head.
She was sorry for these enemies who were encamped beside her, who shared her dangers; and she surprised them
by her dignity. When she realized that all efforts were
vain to escape her fate and that her life of laborious
economy had all gone for nothing, she showed her guests
the place where she had succeeded in concealing the little
that remained to her of her provisions, her little treasure,
saying to them: "My poor boys, take them!—if they are
of any use to you, as long as you are still alive! As for
myself, I'm too old now. I don't need anything any
longer."

Annette had learned of this through one of the wounded Germans who was convalescing at the hospital and was permitted to go out for short walks in the town. He had been one of Madame Guillemette's passing guests near Arras; and he was overjoyed to find again the old woman whom he had remembered with an astonished respect.

"Your newspapers and your scarecrows, Barrès and Poincaré," he said, "can talk all they like in the name of France! I know the real France better than they do!"

Annette liked to talk with Madame Guillemette—as much as that terrible trumpet of her daughter-in-law, La Trottée, allowed. The old woman, with her fine blood and her reserved manners, had certainly enjoyed hearing the trumpet no more than Annette. But she showed nothing of this save through a mischievous smile that lent her old face a charm of youth. She did not claim the right to protest. Every bird had his own song.

Annette's constant visits to the two women had soon become known and were soon a subject for comment. Of the two, one was disliked and the other was regarded with suspicion because, having spent three years in the occupied territory, she had come back without any animosity against the Germans who had evacuated it. Nor was it unobserved that sometimes, in passing, a German prisoner stopped in to see Madame Guillemette, and that Annette had taken part in one or two of their conversations. This was one note the more that was added to the score against her. But Annette, before whom La Trottée had unpacked the whole basket of slanderous remarks that had been made against her, cared nothing for one censure more or less.

All Souls' Day was approaching. The sacred day. The true religion of the French. All the other holidays are merely superfluities, tardily added and of passing importance. In this one cult, connected with the bowels of the earth, all those who have come out of it, all those who will return to it, participate—people of all the confessions and those who have none. It was no more alien to Annette than to Madame de Séigy-Chavânnes, or La Trottée. And when the day came, she joined, almost unconsciously, the stream of walkers who were going with their families to make the tour of the cemetery.

Just before she reached the gate, she met Madame Guillemette limping along. She gave her her arm. They went in together. All the graves were covered with flowers, and the avenues had been raked. But in one corner, at the far side, towards the crumbling wall, among the weeds, there was a stretch of naked earth, without a sign of a flower, covered with wooden crosses. The field of the outcasts. They were the enemy dead, who had been removed from the hospital. As they were Christians, a place had been provided for them in the Valley of Jehosaphat; but they had been shut off by themselves to await the Judgment that was going to separate the sheep from the goats.

Old Madame Guillemette had not reserved in advance her own place in paradise. She confided to Annette: "One of my boys is over there. A little fair-haired fellow, with spectacles. He was very polite. When I was doing my cooking, he would go to the well and draw the water for me. He talked to me about his father and his fiancée. I am going over to have a little chat with him."

Annette went with her. The old woman could not read the names on the crosses. Annette helped her. At last they found the one they were looking for. Madame Guillemette said: "My poor lad, so you are there? You haven't had much luck! But you are having as much here as you had there! You see your old woman hasn't forgotten you. It's true she didn't remember to bring you a flower. But I am going to say a little prayer for you."

Annette let her kneel down. She was touched by the shivering nakedness of these graves, poor relations, deliberately forgotten by the family of the dead on their holiday. She went back to the entrance of the cemetery, bought from the keeper an armful of flowers, and, without realizing that her sudden impulse might seem ostentatious to the eyes that were watching her as she passed, she went back to the disgraced dead under their naked earth and strewed flowers over them. The old woman was tranquilly finishing her prayers. She stood up and Annette took her arm again, and they returned.

Then they saw a group of people, at the edge of the outlawed plot, observing them. A few women of the people with their children pointed at them, talking animatedly. At some distance to the rear, two or three ladies watched the scene, without joining in it. Madame Guillemette and her companion were obliged to pass through this hedge in order to get out, and it was not without thorns. One gossip exclaimed: "Imagine going and taking our flowers to those blackguards!"

Annette's blood began to boil. She made an effort to hold her peace and pass with a proud air. No one dared to insult her. But they were not embarrassed by Madame Guillemette. They shouted out: "You old slut! Selling yourself!"

"By Jove!" said the gossip. "As if everybody didn't know she had had intercourse with the Boches!"

The old woman mildly answered: "A fine sort of intercourse! She's lost everything!" Annette was not equally wise. She came to her defense, in her usual way, by attacking. She said it was ignoble not to keep silent with their spiteful remarks in the presence of death and that under the earth all were equals: there was no difference between those who were here and those who were there! They protested. Driven beyond endurance, she declared that she honored the German dead as much as if they had died for France. They were all equally sacrificed and all victims.

She said enough for the three local newspapers, of the three colors, from red to white, to honor her with virulent articles in their issues of the following day, relating the scene and the scandalous remarks of a professor at the University, a functionary of the State; and they called down upon her the disapprobation of the government.

The result was not long in coming. Annette was called before the principal of the college, and a summary investigation, the rigor of which she did not try to attenuate, led to her suspension from the professorship. She made no reply. She got ready to leave. She was tired out.

Besides, the hour for action had sounded. She had to have her hands free.

*
* *

Pitan was ready. His plan was arranged. He had verified it on the spot in every detail. He took it upon himself to go and fetch Franz from his camp and lead him to the train, where Annette would pilot him to the last station before they reached the French custom-house. There a friend of Pitan's would come and take the bird and guide him by an indirect route to the frontier. There was an inn there which, by singular good fortune, overlapped the two countries: one door opened into France, the other into Switzerland. The game was to slip through. The greatest risk was the morsel that Pitan had reserved for himself. Annette was cautious, but her rôle too was not without danger. She had provided herself in Paris with two tickets for Switzerland; but, in order to obtain them, she was obliged to present at the station-gate two passports, regularly stamped for the destination and the date arranged for. Pitan had undertaken to procure for her one passport, the description in which corresponded with that of Franz. But, for some reason or other, Annette did not receive it. Time was passing. The day arranged for was approaching. Annette took it upon herself to ask for two passports, one in her name, the other in that of her son. This was a mad idea. Marc was not as old as Franz and did not resemble him at all. But she couldn't wait any longer. She was going to risk everything for everything! Besides, she was counting on using the passport only to obtain the ticket.

She had no difficulty in obtaining it in Paris through the mediation of Marcel Franck—although many others, with more justification than herself for making the same journey, were losing weeks going begging for an authorization which they were refused in the end. Those beautiful regulations! They only make things awkward for innocent people. But Annette was not even aware of her good luck. When she wanted something she wanted it so much that it seemed to her natural that the thing should be accomplished; and her assurance infected those upon whom its realization depended. The pretext invoked in the present case was the health of her youngster, whom she was going to take to Switzerland. Marcel did not look into this more closely; but saw to the necessary steps.

Annette left her place in the country on the evening before the day agreed upon with Pitan. She had arranged that one move should follow immediately upon the other. During this brief lapse of time she was like the bird on the branch, established nowhere: she would escape the surveillance of people's eyes in the country and in Paris as well. For she did not inform her family that she was passing through Paris. Sylvie merely knew that her sister had just been dismissed, and she had learned the cause of it; but she did not know when she was returning. Annette only remained in Paris for just the number of hours that were necessary to prepare for her expedition; and she was going to wait until the latter had succeeded before announcing herself to her family. (If it was unsuccessful they would learn it soon enough.)

She arrived, consequently, without any one's knowing it, on the evening of November 9th, after night-fall; and she engaged a room in a little hotel near the station. Chance favored her again. The Franco-Swiss frontier had been constantly closed since the end of October, after the Italian disasters. It was still closed on November 9th. On the 10th, it was opened again—they said, for one

day; and this was the day agreed upon. Annette fever-
ishly passed the morning and almost the whole afternoon
in formalities and waits, interminably standing about at
the Prefecture of Police, then in the Foreign Office,
obtaining the passports and having them viséd; and she
bought the tickets at the station. When this was finished
the dull, drizzling day was declining. Annette returned
to the hotel to rest in expectation of the adventurous night.
But her room was as cold as ice. Now that she had nothing more to do, she was tormented with anxiety. In her
fatigue she kept thinking of the chances of the failure of
the expedition. Would not Franz's escape be very quickly
noticed? Would he arrive in time to catch the train?
And she, with her two tickets—would they let her pass?
A truce to all this! She would see soon enough. She
wasn't going to borrow to-morrow's troubles. Silence to
thought! She remembered that she had not provided
herself with any food. Franz would arrive hungry. She
went out again for a few minutes.

Four o'clock struck. The candle of day was extinguished. A damp, sluggish breath weighed upon the city.
She was drenched by a light, persistent rain that did not
stop and seemed to come from the ground and the walls
of the houses, like an invisible sky. Paris was engulfed
in the fog, as a sleeper under the bedclothes. She couldn't
see four steps ahead of her. From the streaming veil
passers-by suddenly emerged, darted past and plunged
again under the cloud. For one who wished not to be
seen this was a protection. It was also a trap.

Suddenly the pane of fog was broken by a young astonished head, by a cry; and, so quickly that Annette's heart
did not recognize it, a swift hand had seized her by the
arm. Marc was in front of her.

"Mamma! It's you!"

She stood there mute with the shock. The last person she had expected to meet! He looked at her, happy and curious. And under Annette's umbrella he embraced her. Their lips and their cheeks were drenched with rain. She had difficulty in recovering her self-possession.

"So you've come back? You are coming home?" he asked.

"No," she replied. "I am only passing through Paris."

Marc was astonished. "What? But you're staying for to-night?"

"No, I am going away again this evening."

He still did not understand. "What? You are going away again this evening? Where, why, for how long? When did you come? And you came back just to go away again, and you didn't even tell me?"

She had recovered her self-possession. "Forgive me, my dear! But I didn't know it myself until the last minute."

He began to question her again with an irritated insistence.

"I shall explain it to you later. We can't do it here, in the street, in the rain."

"Well, let's go home! There's still time before evening."

"No, I've got to go straight back to the station."

Marc observed gloomily: "Well, I'll take you to your train."

She had to go back to her hotel again. She did not want her son to know that she had stopped there. She could not entrust her plan to him. For a thousand reasons! He must not be compromised in this affair. And what would he think of it? She had no confidence in him, in his character; she thought he was incapable of understanding her ideas, that he was hostile to them. No, she could not speak of them! Another life was at stake. But not to speak was to authorize all sorts of suspicions. They were already aroused. What was he imagining about her clandestine visit to Paris? She blushed before her son.

"Go home, my dear," she said. "It's beginning to rain harder. You will be soaked to the skin."

He shrugged his shoulders. "You didn't come without any bags. Where have you left them? I will go and get them and carry them for you."

"I don't need any one."

He felt hurt, but he pretended not to have heard her. He wanted to know where she was going. "Have you bought your ticket?"

She did not answer. He walked along beside her. She felt that he was spying on her. She tried to think of a reason to give him, but she couldn't think of any. At a street-corner she stopped and forced herself to assume a tone of authority: "We separate here!"

He repeated, obstinately: "On the platform of the station."

"I beg you to leave me," she said dryly.

He continued to walk along. She became irritated. She grasped his shoulder. "This is enough. I forbid you to follow me."

He stopped as if he had been struck in the face. Annette knew that he would not forgive the offense. But she had begun and she would have to go on to the end, since this was the only way of getting rid of him. Hurt himself, he said, to hurt her: "But what are you going to do? Do you distrust me?"

"Yes."

He turned on his heels.

She called to him: "Marc, kiss me!"

But he did not turn around. With his hands in his pockets and his shoulders raised in anger, he marched off, bitterly. The veil of fog covered him again.

Annette, stunned for a moment with emotion, darted after him. "Marc! . . . My God! . . ."

He had disappeared.

She ran, jostling the passers-by in the fog. She wanted to say to him: "Forgive me! I'll explain it to you. Wait! . . ."

Too late! He was gone. The night, the cloud, had swallowed him up. After a few minutes, she retraced her steps. She had to think of the other one. The other one would not wait.

*
* *

The question of her departure prevented her from thinking any longer of Marc. She had to have the two tickets stamped at the gate of the platform. But one by one the guards sifted those who entered. There were nine chances out of ten that they would be willing to punch only one ticket. For a third time luck was on her side. A family was just passing through. Father, mother, three children, one on the arm of the father, another with his hand in his mother's. The third, a little girl of twelve, was just behind. Annette took her by the hand, and, smiling, held out the two tickets to the guard, who, in his absent-mindedness, did not observe the exchange. She passed through, uttering a few affectionate words to the child, whom she restored to the parents.

They crowded into the carriages. The compartments were already full. Annette remained standing up in the corridor. After a very long time, the train set out into the night, with all its lights extinguished for fear of enemy aeroplanes, for there had been warnings of a threatened raid. The train stopped in the dark country. The persistent rain fell, fell on the roof and the windows. Nothing stirred. It was as if they had been forgotten in the middle of the fields. It was damp and cold. Annette went to sleep on her feet, wedged between the partition and the other passengers who hemmed her in. Her knees and her ankles were aching. She was dying of fatigue. She fell into a dream; she was reawakened by the jolting of the train as it started again; then she fell back into another dream.

She was dreaming of Marc and Franz. She was in a bedroom, her bedroom in the country. Franz had come to meet her. They were going to set out together. They closed their bags. They were ready. The door opened. Marc. Franz disappeared into the adjoining room. But Marc had seen him. He was smiling unpleasantly, and his expression was firm. He offered to go with her. But Annette knew that he wanted to betray the prisoner. He turned towards the room into which Franz had withdrawn. Annette placed herself before the door.

Marc said: "Let me in, Mamma! I want to see that dear Franz. We have something to say to each other."

Annette cried to him: "I know what you want. And you are not going to get in!"

Breathing into each other's faces, they stood there, defying each other. Marc frightened her. His ironical eyes had a cruel gleam in them. Pushing her aside as she barred his way, he said: "Come now! I am going to get him, your lover!"

Indignation and fear aroused a nameless fury in Annette's brain. She found herself with a kitchen knife in her hand; and in the next second the knife would strike. . . .

In her convulsive effort to arrest herself in her crime, she found herself standing there in the darkness of the train, panting with horror and shame. . . . She was suffocating. . . . Her son's insult, her own attack at him, the dishonoring suspicion that branded them both—he, she, they were the same person!—the wind of murder, overpowering their trembling limbs. She said to herself: "Can it be? Can it be that I have only imagined this thought, that it has been in me?"

She felt a criminal twice over, in her son's infamous

suspicion, in her own attempted crime. And she could not prevent her mind from insisting: "If things had happened so, would I have killed him?"

The idea that she had spoken too loud, that her neighbors might have heard her, struck a chill into her delirium. She mastered herself, drove back the sobs that were rising in her throat. And then she became aware that the train was rolling again through the night. No! Nobody had noticed her fever. Every one else had his own. And in the protecting darkness, she wiped away the tears that were burning her. The remarks of two neighbors brought her back to the present.

They were saying that the train had changed its course, that it was turning to the left instead of following the Bourbonnais line. She trembled. She had missed the rendezvous! With her forehead pressed against the windows, her eyes ransacked without seeing the masses of shadows that sped past, and she did not recognize the road. But at the first stop she started. It was the station they had agreed upon.

She looked out. Two peasants. A few soldiers. No one got in whom she was expecting. She was sure the affair had miscarried. Devoured with anxiety, she tried to run through the corridors of the coaches. But she could scarcely make her way between the crowded bodies. The train had started again, then it stopped once more between stations because of some work that was being done on the road; and once more the lights were put out. Groping her way, with her head down, Annette tried to ascend the coagulated current; she found herself caught as in an ice-pack. The train got under way; the lights came back; and Annette saw, in the reeking glimmer of the lamp, standing against her, in the corridor, the one she was looking for. Face to face. In the joy that illumined them, their lips rushed together. There was too much to say! The spirit failed them, and the body spoke. The lost brother had found the sister again.

He thought he was hopelessly lost; and all by himself, incapable of knowing where to go, when to get out, how to steer himself, he was distracted. Annette appeared to him like an angel sent from heaven. He threw his arms about her like a child. And she, happy, brooded over him as a hen broods over its chicks. One against the other, they told each other, in lowered voices, in whispers, of their escapade. That rogue of a Pitan had avoided the ambush of the station and had taken him across the fields to the embankment where the work on the track would oblige the train to stop; and there, in the darkness, Franz had climbed in.

An hour later they changed trains. Their tickets were examined. The greatest danger was passed. There remained, of course, the perilous leap over the frontier. But confidence was restored in their hearts. Franz now had no doubts at all. He had passed without transition from one extreme to the other. And the light-heartedness of this great big boy had conquered his companion. She had forgotten all about her fatigue, her cares, her bad dreams, her dear boy, and the white hairs on her own head. Excitedly laughing and talking, they were like two school-children, enjoying themselves in a good farce. They were brother and sister. And Franz even amused himself inventing a conversation about their trade of watch-making and the ridiculous names of their neighbors over there in the little Swiss Jura town. Any one who had known the truth and seen them laughing would have thought them mad. But their nerves had been strained too much. There would be plenty of time for anxiety later!

After a while, still talking, they grew drowsy. Suddenly Franz's head leaned on Annette's shoulder; and Annette fell asleep with her cheek against Franz's hair. But from the midst of a dream that was as silky as her pillow, duty reawoke her.

"Get up!"

(She resisted.)

"Get up! They are knocking."

"Who?"

"One whom you love. . . ."

(She saw Marc; but she designated his face under a series of different names.)

"They are after him. Get up! Open!"

She made a great effort but fell back as if among her bedclothes; she drew her breath, she leaped out of bed. Her eyes opened. It was day. The train had just stopped. This was the place where Franz was to get out.

Hastily she awoke him. She got out with him. They sauntered into the refreshment-room. A gray-haired peasant came up and sat down at their table. He was slow and placid in his speech and movements. He asked for news of Pitan. They drank their black coffee together. In a minute it appeared as if the two men had come up together from the country to greet Annette as she passed. They took their leave and turned towards the bar. The peasant knew the place and the people. Calmly, he exchanged a few drawling words with the bar-keeper. Then, without haste, he went out through a side door. Franz carried for him a crate of bottled beer which he had just bought. Annette climbed back into her carriage. The train started again.

Under the extinguished sky, among the fields that were gleaming with snow, encircled by the hard barrier of the mountains, she saw from the window of her compartment the white road and the covered cart rolling away, seeking the crevice in the hedge between the nations—those prisons—and carrying the friend towards his dying friend.

PART IV

THE great town, stretching out in the sun-light to meet the clear, cold lips of Lake Geneva, was swept by the chilly north wind.

Annette entered the first hotel she saw as she left the station, and engaged two rooms for the night. She was very tired, but she had little hope of resting. Her agitation was so great that nothing of the kind would be possible until she knew that Franz was safe. Although he could not be expected to arrive before evening, she spent the afternoon waiting for him in the square near the station which she had mentioned to him. She sank down on a bench, but she could not stay still. She walked to and fro, benumbed by the gusts of wind, her legs giving way beneath her, but she only quitted her post to avoid making herself an object of observation. The day passed, night fell, she returned to the hotel. From the window of her room she saw the corner of the public garden, the gate. With an anxious face she studied, under the electric light, the shadow of every passer-by. Towards ten o'clock she went out again. The icy wind rushed into the avenue like some chariot of war. The lights in the sky seemed to stagger under its breath, and Annette felt as if these torches were going to be extinguished.

The clock was striking half past ten when he appeared.

His bearing was uncertain and he hurried along with the air of a big bewildered child who wants to cry and bites his lips instead.

He passed her without seeing her. She called out to him and he cried out with joy. With a gesture she bade him keep silent. She was radiant. He was covered with the mud of the roads. In a corner of the avenue she brushed him off with her hand; it would not do if his appearance attracted attention. Without apologizing, he let her have her way; he was so happy not to be alone any longer, to be able to tell his story. She begged him to wait till they were indoors before speaking. The chill of the night and the day's journey had given her a cold in the head, but in her joy she did not notice it. A crowd of travelers streamed out of the station. Franz's entrance into the hotel was not observed. Annette had registered him as her brother.

Annette made Franz eat. He fell upon his food, talking, talking, never weary of recounting all the details of his flight. In order to make him speak in a lower voice, Annette, leaning towards him, plied him with cakes. Her eyes streaming from her cold, her head heavy, blowing her nose, sneezing, she was overcome with sleep. He did not notice it. He could not stop eating and talking, and in spite of her fatigue, Annette did not want him to stop. Raps on the wall reminded them that other people existed, and Franz at last became silent. Suddenly fatigue overwhelmed him; he threw himself on his bed, vanquished, and fell asleep. Annette, in her fever, turned over and over again, listening to the slumber in the room beside her. The door was open. Annette rejoiced in the regular breathing of her young comrade, the rapture of having saved him. Her throat was on fire, her chest heavy, and she covered her mouth with the bedclothes so that he would not hear her cough.

Early in the morning she got up to clean their clothes. Then she went out and telegraphed to Germain's mother: "We have arrived."

When she returned, Franz was still asleep. She hesitated to waken him. She looked at him, she looked at herself also in the mirror, she saw how red her face and eyes were from the cold and the wind. Her nose was swollen and this annoyed her. But it was only a shadow. She shrugged her shoulders and laughed.

The train for Château d'Oex was leaving in the morning. She awakened the sleeper. Franz was not surprised when he saw her standing before his bed. The young caveman with women! Already Annette was no longer a woman to him; he had adopted her. It seemed to him very natural that she should be anxious about him. He was ready to give her his confidence. (Ready also to take it back again.) When she told him they were going to see their friend that evening, his mobile face darkened: so close to his object, he was afraid! Then he became impatient. With one leap he was out of bed and dressing under Annette's eyes; she did not count for him.

They left the hotel. He let her do everything, settle the bill, buy the tickets, find the train, choose their seats. He did not even offer to carry his bundle. He did stop, however, to buy her a bunch of violets. He had no practical sense, not even any power of resistance. The mob of passengers jostled him on the platform. If Annette had not turned back to signal him and wait for him he would have lost her. He was the sort of man who never knows what he is about. His mind was filled with the emotions he was about to experience.

Annette vainly tried to distract him.   During the long
journey he saw nothing, he listened absent-mindedly.
She had plenty of leisure to watch him.   He lived in one
thought only, full of expectation, eagerness, happiness,
fear.   It was not Annette but Germain who was in his
mind.   Every turn of the track was bringing him nearer.
Annette saw his lips stirring as if they spoke to the friend
he was approaching.

When they reached Château d'Oex, she begged him to
walk slowly while she went ahead of him to the Chavânnes
chalet so as to prepare Germain.

The invalid, who had heard the news, was lying
stretched out, fully dressed, in the *chaise longue* on the
balcony.   His mother was beside him.   He had tried to
get up but had not been able to hold himself on his feet.
In the four months since Annette had left him he had
changed terribly.   Annette was shocked at the havoc
wrought and, quickly as she concealed this, her first glance
had shown it.

When he saw Annette coming in, he started up to meet
her, but seeing at once how impossible this was he resigned
himself.   Annette spoke to him; he looked at her.   But
she was like a screen that concealed the only thing that
really mattered, and he drew his eyebrows together as if
to dispel the obstacle.   Then Annette moved aside and,
turning towards the half-open door, allowed him to see
what his eyes were looking for.   Franz staggered in; he
stopped, he saw, he ran forward.   They were together
again.

For days and nights—twenty times—they had pictured
to themselves—acted out in imagination—this moment
when they would meet each other again.   And nothing
had happened as they had imagined it.

They did not shake hands. They did not embrace each other. They did not utter any of the words that had been on the tips of their tongues a moment before. At the first glance Franz, his excitement suddenly arrested, collapsed at the foot of the *chaise longue,* his arms outstretched over the body that was lying there, his face hidden in the blankets. He was transfixed with fear at seeing this friend whom he had left so full of life and whom now he could hardly recognize. And Germain, perceiving this flash of terror, saw himself in its light. Death was opening between them and separating them.

Pale and rigid, he felt his friend's head pressing against his legs, and he stroked it as if to defend it against the unconfessed terror. But this terror had mastered Franz. They both knew they stood no longer on the same shore, they no longer belonged to the same epoch. The slight difference in age that separated their paths had become infinite. One of them belonged to the generation of the dead, the other to that of the living. Resigned, frozen, Germain accepted it as an unanswerable fact. It was for him, the elder, the man who was on the further side, to console the one who was on this side. Heavens, how far apart they were!

Franz was sobbing now. Germain said to the two women, whom he had waved aside at first with an impatient gesture and who were waiting in the shadow, at the entrance to the balcony: "You see how he is suffering. . . . Take him away."

Annette hurried Franz back into the room. She made him sit down, she whispered consolations and maternal reproaches into his ear. Ashamed, he wiped away his tears and gradually became calm.

With his head on his pillow again and his back turned

to the room, a look of death in his eyes as if his life was exhausted, Germain gazed at the terrible face of the desolate mountains, and he did not hear his mother when she spoke to him.

*

*　*

After this first shock, their wills began to act again. Their spirits set to work rebuilding on the new basis. Their hearts hastily dressed the wound to the illusion without which they could not live and die.

As the more instinctive of the two and consequently the more guileful in deceiving himself, Franz succeeded more quickly in forgetting what he did not wish to remember. In the evening, in his bedroom—they had taken lodgings in a neighboring chalet—he poured himself out in a letter to his friend in which he fooled himself and tried to fool Germain in regard to the emotion he had shown when they had first met. The next time he saw him, he succeeded fairly well in making Germain resemble the image he had mentally sketched of him. Their old intimacy was completely restored, and even Franz's youthful exuberance came to the surface again. But if he had forgotten, Germain had not forgotten. No longer possessing the future, he could not lose sight of the past. He could not attenuate what he had perceived; he retained a burning image of the horror his appearance had at first imprinted on his friend's features. He kept catching sight of it again, as if in flashes of lightning. As they talked a shadow would pass over Franz's animated face, a contraction of nose or eyebrow. That was enough! Germain's sharp glance had read beneath the veil of flesh; Franz had caught the scent of death and turned away from it. He would react afterwards, but it would be too late. He could not conquer his aversion in the presence of the grave.

Germain said bitterly to Annette: "He is healthy. He is right."

Gradually, however, they succeeded in closing the holes in the spider's web of their illusion. Franz ceased to see on the face of the sick man the thumb that models the face of the dying. In the end he forgot all about this hour that was approaching and saw nothing but the friend he had seen in the old days, the friend he loved. And Germain revived in his presence; his lips became red again as if he secretly used rouge. Annette joked him about it. He said to her: "You think it's a joke, but it's the truth. I'm an old coquette. That poor boy! I am afraid of frightening him."

And when he felt his agony coming on, the agony he could not master, he begged Annette to take Franz out for a walk so that he would not see him.

At first Annette had not intended to stay at Château d'Oex for more than a day or two. She had hoped to bring the two friends together and return to Paris the next day. But when she saw how serious Germain's condition was she postponed her departure. She could not leave him alone on the threshold of the shadowy door. Unwilling to ask her, for he hated to be a burden, Germain allowed her to see how anxiously he wished her to stay. He was afraid, now, of being left alone with Franz. Feeling that the two friends needed her she put off her return, in spite of all the duties that were calling her back to Paris. The most imperious of all duties seemed that of relieving the poor emigrant, who was quitting our Old World of a part of his burden.

She accepted the heavy load. She became the confidant of both. She was the sole being into whose hands they could commit their secret thoughts, for they neither dared nor wished now to confide in each other. Franz was the more outspoken. From the moment when he began to confide in her there was nothing he did not confide. He blurted out everything that most people keep to themselves.

Annette did not deceive herself. She knew that Franz and Germain had not opened their hearts to her because she was Annette, but because she was there, near them, an anonymous woman, and they needed a willing and trustworthy ear to which they could commit themselves. There was no affection for her in all this. They were both concerned with each other and with themselves alone. Although aware of this she allowed herself to be enveloped by the invasive breath of this strange intimacy. The invisible rays of their mutual love, passing from one to the other, passed first through her.

As they were walking together, Franz said to Annette: "I love him, I love nobody else. I can't tell him this. He gets such a severe look. He won't permit it. He says he can't stand sentimentality. But this is not sentimentality and he knows it; he knows perfectly well what I think, but it annoys him to hear it. He says it isn't healthy. I don't know what is healthy or unhealthy, but I do know that I love him, and that it's good to love him, that it can't be bad. I love him alone, and I don't love anybody else. I don't like women. I have never liked them. Oh, I like to look at them well enough, when they are nicely turned out, as I like to look at anything that is well-made. But there is always something in them that repels me—I should say a little attraction mingled with disgust. They belong to another species. It wouldn't surprise me if they were like those insects that devour their males after sucking them dry. I don't like to touch

them. You are laughing. What have I said? Ah, forgive me, I forgot . . ." (He was holding her arm.)
"You are not a woman."

"What am I?"

"You are yourself."

("You mean," thought Annette, "that I am you, that I am yours. I don't count. Little egoist!")

Franz was reflecting: "It's funny, but since I have known you I have never thought of you as a woman."

"That's a questionable compliment, but thank you just the same, after what you have just said."

"You aren't angry with me?"

Annette laughed: "*Ti voglio bene.*"

"What does that mean? I don't understand."

"That's just as well! You'll have to keep a sharp ear out."

"Say it again."

"No, no!"

"You are so strange! I don't understand you. I ought to be embarrassed, but I never am that with you. I feel as if I could say anything."

"That's because I can listen to anything."

"And that's the best thing of all, the only good thing in life. There are not many good things. I have only one friend myself, but when I love a friend I love him altogether. I want to possess him entirely. Isn't that natural? But one can't talk about it. Even he doesn't want to hear it. In this world one is only allowed to love by halves."

Annette could not help pressing the arm she held.

"Do you understand me?" asked Franz.

"I understand all the crazy people," said Annette. "I belong to the family."

Stretched out on the balcony, with his head thrown back, gazing at the hard, blue sky, Germain said to Annette: "What will become of him without me? He loves me too much. He is like a woman. Not like you. The rough lesson of life has virilized you. He is at the mercy of an uncontrolled heart. Where can this visionary, weak, violent heart lead him? I can't tell you the dangers I have saved him from. He never suspected it, for he is incapable of seeing them and judging them. He is too innocent to have any morals in the ordinary sense. Our ethical values haven't the same meaning for him that they have for us. He has often perplexed me and I ought to have been severe, but when I saw the sadness and astonishment in his honest eyes I couldn't help wondering if it was I who was mistaken. Is he an aberration of nature? Or is he truly natural in being unconscious of our narrow dogmas? However that may be, these dogmas govern the world which our reason has made, and since we are forced to live in it we are obliged to submit to these dogmas, even if we don't acknowledge them. He can't acknowledge them; I have never been able to make him understand them, and I have given up trying. He would pretend he did, to please me, but it would only result in his losing his sincerity. I would rather have him abnormal than hypocritical. He is purer so. But while one can't expect to convince him intellectually, one can win his heart over to any discipline, however painful, that is dictated to him by love. This is a precarious support, and if it fails everything fails at once and the soul is adrift. When I am not here any longer what is going to become of him? He must be taught to get along without me."

He ceased speaking, but he continued to gaze at the sky, so deeply blue and so hard that it seemed like a mineral.

The density of this compressed light corresponded with that of his thought. He resumed, with a bitter smile, but with the same firm, cold, measured tone, as if he were talking to himself. (Not once, in speaking, had he looked at Annette; it was as if he had forgotten that she was beside him.)

"Of course I know that he will learn. He will get along without me. We all think we are necessary, but there isn't a soul in the world who is indispensable. When he has lost me he will think he has lost everything. But what we have lost no longer exists, and we go on existing ourselves. We can't at the same time exist and not exist; and we soon make our choice. The living loose the ties that bind them to the dead, and that only impede them. And if the ties still hold they cut them innocently, on the sly. They aren't aware of it, but the dead man has fallen away and they can live. Franz will live."

Annette placed her hand on the hand of this disillusioned soul: "Where Franz lives the thought of you will live."

He withdrew his hand: "He will forget. When forgetfulness is slow in coming you go to meet it. But there is nothing bad about Franz. He will not have to bother."

Annette was about to protest, but Germain said: "I am sure of it."

But it was plain enough to Annette that he wasn't sure of it, that he didn't believe it. She had no difficulty in persuading him that he was mistaken. Though he listened with an ironical smile to the arguments of this woman, he still enjoyed listening to them. His clear-sightedness was in conflict with the need of every human being for some illusion. To yield to this need was, he knew, a defeat, but he was glad to be vanquished. After all, why should the truth that kills be truer than hope?

He gave in to Annette. "His heart will not forget. Perhaps. No, not at once. Time will have to pass. But who is going to direct this heart that is used to being directed? His very sorrow over his loss will add to his confusion. Grief instructs some but it bewilders others. They don't make any resistance, they simply allow themselves to be crushed. And then they accept any diversion to save themselves. I am afraid for him. Who loves him and will be able to advise him? Don't abandon him, Annette. He trusts you. Guide him. You will have to be indulgent. You must expect surprises. There are plenty of things in him that may scandalize you. There are in every man."

"There are in myself too, my poor friend," said Annette. "It takes a good deal to scandalize a woman, I mean one who is free, who has lived, as I have."

Germain looked at her skeptically: "A woman can live a hundred lives without learning anything from life."

"So you think we are hopeless?"

"Women have been the same ever since the beginning of the world."

"You are not so far from the cavemen yourselves."

Germain smiled. "By Jove, you are right! We are no better than you. We are all the same. We think we are very strong in the face of life and death, but they both catch us unawares. We have learned nothing. My own disadvantage is very slight at present because I have finished with school, but you who are left, Annette, still have time to feel the ferule on your knuckles. Beware, you with your nose in the air! That ripe experience you are

so proud of may play you more than one trick.   But the
one-eyed are kings in the country of the blind.   I leave
my boy to you, even if you have only one eye."

"But I have two fine ones," said Annette, laughing.

"They were not made to see with; they were made to
be seen.   But if you don't see for yourself, try to see for
him!   It is always easier to be wise for some one else.
Guide him, love him. . . ."

"Don't love him too much," he added.

Annette shrugged her shoulders.

*
* *

Annette was closer to Germain than to Franz. He belonged to her race; she understood him better. Their experience of life had come from the same mold, the same sky had ripened their thoughts. There was nothing obscure either in the sentiments she divined in him or in those she felt for him. His friendship, his fears, his stoicism, his judgments on life, his spontaneous attitude in the presence of suffering and death, his regrets at going and his detachment—everything in him was clear. If Annette had been a man with the same destiny, she would have thought as he thought, she would have been like him. So it seemed to her at least, for nothing in Germain was surprising to her. (Would she have been able to say as much of herself?) In other circumstances they would have made a capital husband and wife, with the greatest mutual esteem and affection, sure of each other, loyally entrusting each other with all the keys of their doors—all but one small key that no one ever thought of, which, if the lock had been found and opened, would have revealed the fact that they remained strangers to one another. But happily the occasions for opening this lock scarcely ever occur, and good friendships, which are honest and direct, never ask for this little key. The friendship of Germain and Annette was unexacting and uninquisitive. Each gave the other what the other expected.

But from Franz one never knew what to expect. This was the thing that made him seem remote and attractive at the same time. It was useless to try to know him. One couldn't know him; he didn't know himself. He seemed so childish, so simple, and he was. But once you were

inside him, you had not taken ten steps before you lost
your way. You found yourself walking in the dark in an
unknown land. Annette tried her whole bunch of keys
in a vain endeavor to open his doors; they would not turn
in the locks. None of them. Except one, the little one
precisely that Germain had not tried, the key of "*Je ne
sais quoi*" (as people used to say in the times of the Great
King, when they had to take care not to look too closely!).
Annette took little pleasure in making her inventory of the
corners of the soul, but from this room at the back of the
shop, unknown to passers-by, there emerged for her a
mysterious aroma, a humming as of bees, that she alone
perceived as she came and went, arranging the shop. That
some one else heard this whirring of wings—fascinating,
menacing—established between them a sort of complicity.
Between these two strangers there was a remote tie of kinship. (In matters of race the remote ties sometimes count
for more than the close ties.)

In this way she had got in touch with him and they
were able to communicate, without words, with antennæ
as of blind insects in the half-darkness. A whole tribe of
human beings have this subterranean life, but living in the
broad daylight atrophies their faculties. When the occasion comes for them to make use of them they have a feeling of pleasure which they can not explain, and they are
grateful to those who enable them to exercise these faculties.

All the time as they discussed, in the broad daylight, a
thousand matters, usually at cross purposes, Annette and
Franz listened to the rippling of the water in the valley,
and at the bottom of their souls they touched each other.

*

* *

The destruction was increasing rapidly, like the crumbling of a façade. One would have had to be blind not to see it. No rouge could remedy the distress of that face. Germain had given up using it and Franz avoided looking at him.

He would come in. With him would come the breath of life and of the fields. He brought a few snowdrops, he brought some of his new drawings, in chalk and charcoal, he brought the frosty air in his garments and healthy hands that hastily drew back from the moist touch of the dying man's restless fingers. He spoke with animation, and Germain was galvanized by the emanation of his young life. In their conversation the two friends avoided any mention of disease. Franz merely asked a few hasty questions which Germain turned aside with hard indifference. They discussed art, abstract, eternal questions—that which has never existed. (Annette listened silently, marveling at the madness of men in the grip of ideas.) Often Franz, speaking for both, talked about his imprisonment, the years in the camp, all the hardships that, looked at from a distance, almost seemed pleasant, or about the people he had met during the day, or his plans, what he would do when the war was over. His oblivious glance, gliding lightly over everything, avoided the cavernous tapestry of those hollow cheeks that seemed as if hung from the peg-like cheek-bones . . . and fled away timorously, seeking with awkward haste some other, more reassuring object. Germain stoically smiled, helping him to regain his foothold in the land of the living.

"You've talked enough!" he would say. "Now, Annette, take this child out for a walk. He mustn't lose this beautiful day."

He added, when she came up to him to say good-by: "You must come back for a moment this evening. I need you."

She went out with Franz, who said hurriedly: "He is much better to-day, isn't he?"

He did not wait for an answer but marched on with great strides, his chest thrown out, his hair on the wind, breathing with all his lungs the uncontaminated, the uncorrupted air, the pure air. In spite of herself, Annette's strong legs also rejoiced in this race, this revenge of the living animal after the oppression of the body, drugged by the bedside of pain, by the atmosphere of illness. But Franz, striding ahead, almost always outdistanced her. He was seized with a childish frenzy; he ran, he clambered up the steep slopes, clinging to the snow-covered tufts of the pines. Then they both tied on their skis and took their winged flight over the white fields. When they were thoroughly restored, almost intoxicated by the fresh air, and waves of blood had swept away the last shadows from their thoughts, they sat down in the sunlight, on an overhanging rock, and gazed out over the valley. The laughing Franz named for her the notes and chords that composed the harmony, the tail of the peacock in the sky that spread out in the West. While he talked he drew; he drew with great strokes, covering one page and then another with lines and planes, with outlines of trees and peaks, like faces of recumbent men with shriveled lips and sharp noses—not thinking about what he was doing, talking all the time. And Annette watched his fingers as they talked, listening to the idle words that fell from his

mouth. She replied absent-mindedly. Without mentioning his name she was thinking of the man they had left
lying down there. And suddenly she was hypnotized as
the fingers drew, quite mechanically, a head that she recognized—the head of a dead man. She said nothing.
Franz went on with his chatter. A cloud passed over the
sun and the silence was like a black cavern in the light.
Franz stopped, looked at his fingers, drew back in horror
as if a snake had risen beside him. His hands shrank and
closed over the sheet. He tossed the sketch-book aside
and it rolled down the slope, and with a bound Franz, who
had risen, resumed his wild flight over the snow-covered
fields. Without a word Annette followed him.

In the evening, after supper, when, faithful to her
promise, she dropped in to see Germain, the sick man
welcomed her with a face of ice. He had struggled
through a cruel day, and he was angry with those for
whom the day had been sweet. He reproached Annette
for coming so late and asked her unkindly if they had
had a good time; he complimented her on her fine appearance, her coloring, the rich blood that ran under her
skin. He seemed to be upbraiding her.

She did not reply. She understood. She apologized
humbly: "My friend, forgive me!"

He was ashamed and asked her the news of the day in
a calmer voice. She told him, but it was depressing. Far
from being exhausted after four years, the war had taken
on new strength. The threat of a monstrous spring of-
fensive was hanging over France. They talked about the
tragic morrow, and Germain projected his own agony
upon the world. He felt that the evolution of man had
been a transitory success, due to a prodigious effort and

exceptional luck, a sudden "variation," the result of genius and abnormality (two words that were almost identical), which could not be maintained. The conquests of genius, the progress of man, were a bloody laurel for its Pyrrhic victories. But the end of the epos had arrived to-day; the ascending curve had reached its climax, and the Titan was toppling over into the abyss, exhausted by its effort to surpass itself—like Rolf, the dog of Mannheim, that learned to think like a man only to relapse, after two years, pouring forth blood, into the dismal night! For man is not the only creature that has attempted the prodigious adventure. All nature has attempted it. On every side one perceives the formidable ascent of living things trying to escape from the grave of the mysterious forces. They climb, they climb desperately, leaving some of their blood on every projection of the wall, but sooner or later the moment comes when they let go and roll back, glassy-eyed, into the nightmare. The nightmare has two thresholds: the slumber of the beginning and the slumber of the ending.

"Who knows," said Annette, "if the tumultuous dream of life is ended when you fall back."

"Haven't you had enough of it?"

"The night is long. I am going to sleep again to wait for the day."

"Suppose it doesn't come?"

"I shall go on dreaming."

Germain was too detached from any sort of faith to discuss this. Nothing contributed more to his disenchantedly fatalistic vision than the wide, impersonal understanding that accompanied his own destruction. He denied nothing, neither the pro nor the con. All the madness that fills the masses of mankind with passion—religion, one's country—measure the march of destiny. The creature fulfills itself in destroying itself, and the end of human effort is Nothingness.

Annette said to him: "My friend, you mustn't always be looking at the swelling flood about you, that giddy whirlpool, those masses of people climbing up and falling back again! Look into yourself! The only *one*, the *I* is a world. In my own world I hear an eternal Yes."

"Mine," said Germain, "is a coffin. I see worms in it."

"You let life escape from you into the universe. Call it back from the universe into yourself! Gather it together on your own breast with your own hands!"

"As I shall soon gather my grave-clothes."

"You are not merely here, in this bed; you are everywhere, in everything that lives. This serene night is in you and with you, this night whose long black wings brood over the sleep and the dreams of thousands of beings. In your destitution you possess the wealth of those you love, Franz's youth, Franz's future. I myself have nothing but I have everything."

"You have the beautiful blood that warms you."

"Ah, if I could give it to you!"

She said this so eagerly that the blood which the dying man envied seemed to pour into his whole body until it was like a cup filled to the brim. Heavens, how she longed to pour it into him!

He was touched. He tried to speak but he choked. He was nearly gone. She remained beside him the whole night, supporting his head on the pillow. Her presence gave him the strength of soul to endure. Since he had nothing to conceal from her he also had nothing to reveal to her. It was unnecessary to show her how much he suffered; she felt it under her fingers. In a moment of respite, his mouth contracted into a smile and he said: "It's hard to die, just the same."

She wiped away the sweat from his forehead.

"Yes, my dear. Happily I am going to die also. One could never forgive oneself if one had to go on living when others died."

When morning came he sent her away. During those hours when he had not been able to speak he had had time to think of her, of her goodness, of the uncalculating way in which she had given herself, and of how much he had taken advantage of it. He begged her to forgive him.

"You don't know," she said, "how good it is when a friend takes advantage of you. What kills us is not being used by those we love."

She was thinking of her son. Up to this moment she had never mentioned him to Germain, and he had never thought of the boy. But during these last days when, piece by piece, he was shedding his grief along with his life, he found that he wished to know about the grief his friend was keeping to herself.

He lay awake most of the night, every night. He might have telegraphed for his sister, but he wanted no one but Annette. He still took advantage of her, but to calm his conscience he told himself that it would not go on much longer. How happy Annette was that he did take advantage of her! But he knew that a generous heart is sure to be exploited and he was uneasy over the trouble she would inevitably meet with in the future.

He talked less about himself. It was more and more difficult for him to talk, so he made her talk. He wanted to know her inner life and now that he was going to die she had nothing to conceal from him. She told him everything, soberly, simply, with a veiled emotion, as if it were the story of somebody else. He listened without a word. She did not look at him but he watched her lips. What she did not say he read. He read it more clearly than she herself. As his own life escaped, this life flowed into him. Finally it filled him completely. So that, close to death, he loved her for the first time. He loved her entirely, and in the secrecy of his heart he married her. She never knew this. She felt for him only as a sister feels, and the wing of love did not touch her being. The face of the dying man called out her pity, her passionate pity, but instinctively love averted its eyes. Germain knew this quite well and he asked for nothing. He had risen above himself.

He did not betray, however—or scarcely betrayed—the change that had come about in his relations with the woman who, all unknown to herself, had become his wife, save through the right he assumed to direct, for the first and last time, Annette's uncertainty in regard to her family life, her son. Although he had never seen the boy, his masculine intuition led him to understand Marc much better than she. He grasped the misunderstanding that had arisen between the son and the mother, and although he hadn't the time now to help her in solving it, he collected his last energies to trace for them the road they should follow.

"Annette, it's a good thing I'm going. I belong to a race of spirits that has no longer any place in the order that is coming, a race without any illusions about either the future or the past. Understanding too much has killed in me any desire for acting. One must act, take a good hold! The instinct of your heart is surer than my for-and-against, but even that is not sufficient. You have your limitations. You are a woman, but you have made a

man. You have a boy. He clashes against your limitations just as when he was born he clashed against the walls
of your womb in order to fling himself forth. He will
hurt you again more than once. Sing, like Jeanne d'Al-
bret, the song of *his* delivery. Sing the song of the breach
through which he came out of you! Tell him, in my
name, not to be satisfied with understanding everything,
like me, or with loving everything, like you. Let him
make his own choice. It is all very fine to be just, but
true justice does not sit down before the scales and merely
watch the plates oscillate. It judges and carries out the
sentence. Let him decide and strike! Enough of dreaming! Let the awakening come! Farewell, Illusion!"

One couldn't have said whether he was talking to himself or Annette.

After taking a long look at her for the last time, he
turned over in bed, as if he withdrew from the living.
Locked in silence, he stared at the wall and did not open
his mouth again save for the last moan of death, which
kneads the agonized body.

*

* *

Annette had no time to think of her own sorrow. Franz's grief absorbed everything. It was frantic. She had no choice but to devote herself to it or run away from it. It monopolized her.

During the first hours, the expression of his measureless grief embarrassed every one. It made no attempt to check its manifestations as a well-bred grief should do. It was the despair of a child or a lover. Nothing could induce Franz to leave the body of the beloved one, and as his love cried out, like his distress, Germain's family were scandalized. At last, to put an end to these excesses and avoid the "What are people going to say?", they insisted upon keeping Franz out of the house. They placed him in Annette's charge while they went through the funeral ceremony at the little country church, before taking the body to the baggage van of the train that was to carry him to his native land.

The Chavânnes set out, the living and the dead—(the most alive of them all, the extinguished light of their family). It was like one of those catafalques of the past in which the torch was borne, inverted, at the rear of the car and behind the coat-of-arms. The farewells with Annette were brief and stilted. Madame de Séigy-Chavânnes, the sister, forced herself to express the sincere gratitude they felt for her devoted attentions, and in spite of her secret antipathy she made an effort to embrace her. But after such an effort, the debt seemed paid.

Madame de Chavânnes alone—the mother—dampened Annette's cheeks with her tears and called her "My daughter." But she did so stealthily. She had been rather disposed to like her, and, strange as Annette's thoughts were to her, she had tolerated them: outside of religion, everything that any one thought was indifferent to her. But she was weak. Her own peace of mind came first! Nothing must be done that would risk agitating the family. They said to each other, "Au revoir." And on both sides it was perfectly understood that they would never see each other again.

Annette was shut up with Franz while the double ceremony of the church and the departure was taking place. She followed it in thought. She saw herself walking in the middle of the procession on the frosty road where, under the troubled sky of the end of February, the primroses were beginning to blossom. Very far away she heard the slow funeral-bell tolling softly in the silence. She listened intently, but Franz did not hear it at all; and as she lulled him with her words she caught the sound of the whistle of the departing train, like the point of a needle in her breast. He was gone. . . . The dead friend was twice dead.

She had to think of the one who remained. The other no longer needed her. Up to that moment he had absorbed Annette's pity. There would be no more compassion for him now. Her pity flowed back again to the living. The dead man had left him in her care.

"I bequeath him to you. Take my place. He is yours."

With Franz, pity had a free swing. He was not like Germain, who hardened his heart against it, not wanting to be commiserated. Franz demanded it. He had no shame in showing his weakness. Annette perceived this. It was as easy for him to ask for her help as it was for her to give it. It was a joy of which she had been deprived. Her son, like Germain, had begrudged it too much! This race of proud men who clamp their teeth upon their emotions, who are ashamed of their hearts and conceal, as a kind of dishonor, their nostalgia for the milk of tenderness which they once drew from the maternal breasts! Franz did not conceal it at all. He naïvely claimed his mouthful as his due. Like a baby that is born blind, he groped with his lips and his hands.

"Well, drink, my little one! Drink from me! I place the tip of my breast between your lips."

And this scorner of women, who had missed the maternal milk—he had lost his mother when he was in the cradle—never thought of the woman whose breast he was draining. He did not love the woman, he loved only the breast. He had to quench his desperate thirst. Annette was quite aware of this. For him she was nothing but a nurse for his misery, rocking it and lulling it to sleep. And she felt for him only a maternal love that increased every day, as every day his need for it increased. But maternal love includes all the loves. If it does not recognize them all by their names, there is not one that it does not secretly caress.

Franz told her everything, he opened himself entirely. With a strange lack of modesty, he thought it natural that she should devote herself to everything that concerned him—his bitterness, his grief, his bewilderment, as well as his body, his health, his food, his room, his clothes. Foster-mother and nurse, confidante and servant at once, —he wanted nothing else from her now, and she was nothing else for him. He seemed to expect from her the solicitude and attentions that she knew so well how to give. To Annette, as to him, it all seemed quite natural. He scarcely thanked her, and only as a matter of courtesy.

It was she who thanked him, tacitly, for needing her.

His egoism delighted her. There are some charming egoists and women often have a predeliction for them. One is grateful to a man who loves one for oneself, but how one cherishes a man who loves one for *him*self! . . . A man who thinks only of himself, who does not give himself, who takes you, devours you and finds you good.

"How good he is!" said this foolish creature.

Franz devoured Annette in the prettiest way imaginable. He was tender, cajoling, innocently seductive; he allowed himself to be pitied and pampered; he granted her the favor of expressing his wishes, and she hastened to carry them out—when she did not forestall him—running up and down stairs ten times a day to buy oranges for him, or a newspaper, or some object of which he had spoken, or to carry some urgent letter to the post-office. She was well repaid when she returned to the house after a brief absence and he impatiently reproached her for having taken too much time about it or when, on the balcony in the evening, in the dusk, sad and mournful, he came out and sat down close beside her, as if he needed to warm himself against her limbs and suddenly wept. . . . Annette, throwing her work aside, drew the big child's head over on her shoulder. And after he had had a good cry—(what happiness! this man who unblushingly let you wipe away his tears!)—he began to talk. He emptied his heart of its secret sorrows, those he had been repressing ever since his childhood and had never dared to confide openly, even to Germain, down to the grief that still continued to bleed night and day, for now he reproached himself with having avoided his friend in his last illness, for not having loved him enough, for having let him see it. She listened so well! He felt encouraged by the mere

contact of this woman's cheek against his head, by this consoling voice that never interrupted him and mingled gentle
words of pity with his laments. He confessed what he
had never expressed before out loud. And she was never
surprised, she welcomed, without being shocked, as if she
had already had a personal experience of it, the unveiled
recital of this inner life, these often scandalous confessions,
these moral deviations that would have aroused disgust,
perhaps, if they had been read in a book. She listened to
him actually as if in a confessional, the secrecy of which
is sacred, and where the listener is purified by divine love
—by charity. Such a listener is neither defiled nor revolted by the confessions; he participates in the weaknesses
of human nature, they are his own. He pities them, he
takes these errors upon himself, and he loves the other
all the more for having washed his feet with his own
hands.

*

*   *

After the first fifteen days of this total abandonment of his soul to grief, this sudden prostration of despair that passed all bounds, taking the man by the throat and crushing him—more than once, at night, Annette came in from the adjoining room to calm the sobs that were suffocating him on his pillow—he began to relax. At first there was a period of bruised half-torpor and silent tears, like the sky in transition between winter and spring, motionless and fatigued, with its hidden sun and its silent showers. Then came the shy awakening of convalescence, ashamed of getting well and wishing to conceal the insolent sense of well-being in returning to life, when they had low-voiced conversations for hours, for the heart needed to unbosom itself of its reviving flood, but would not admit it save secretly, when it was sure of a sympathetic ear.

Then they went out together, Franz leaning on Annette's arm, walking very slowly, through those mild, misty afternoons when, amid the dead leaves, under the burning thickets, the first violets were lifting their heads. Already the timid spring was announcing itself on the hills, while the valley slept, benumbed, in the sombre blue of the haze and the shadows. They thought of their friend. He was with them. It was as if he waited for them to be together so that he could be with each of them. Each of them felt his presence in the presence of the other, but when they were alone, by themselves, they felt him only as it were far away; the invisible presence was like a distant shadow. As they walked Franz pressed against Annette, so as to find Germain. He hung upon the arm of the living in his fear of losing the hand of the one who had disappeared. He overwhelmed her now with his affectionate attentions, revealing the innate gentleness of his aristocratic nature. He was attached to Annette, and he taxed his ingenuity to prove it to her. He could not get along without her any longer. Annette was touched, but she had no illusions about this. She was a Frenchwoman and she saw other people very clearly, even when she liked them. But a Frenchwoman is a woman, and what she sees least clearly—for she is not interested in seeing it—is herself.

Her duty was calling her back to Paris, where her son was. She had left him too much alone. Germain's long agony, the exigency of Franz's grief, had engrossed her whole attention. For three long months she had surrendered herself entirely; she could not have freed herself without being inhuman. (This, at least, was the excuse her conscience gave itself.) But it was no longer her duty to remain; her duty lay the other way. She felt her son's reproachful eyes upon her; he was never out of her thoughts. Having nothing to do during the day, she never passed a night without seeing him, and always with remorse. She tormented herself over the dangers he was running. On the day following the air-raid of January 30, she almost set out to rejoin him. She had much to reproach herself for. They scarcely ever wrote to each other, and their letters, at long intervals, contained very few endearments. She had written little because she lacked the time and because of a certain frigidity that sprang from her secret embarrassment; in staying away from him she knew that she was doing him a wrong, and she was unwilling to admit this to herself. So she attributed her constraint to the wrong he had done her.

He himself could not forgive their last meeting, the outrageous distrust that had been like a blow in the face.
During the nights that had followed, when he saw the
scene again, he could have bitten his pillow with rage.
But naturally, he would have let himself be killed rather
than allow any one to suspect this. In his letters to his
mother, cold, haughty, distant, he did his best to show her
that he did not depend upon her. The worst of it was
that Annette, absorbed in her very painful anxieties, did
not appear to notice anything! She would reply with
some commonplace, hasty note. The post lengthened the
delays. Her letter of January 1 was more than fifteen
days in arriving, and one of Germain's terrible crises, last-
ing for twenty-four hours, so absorbed all of Annette's
emotional energies that she totally forgot Marc's birth-
day. In vain had he proclaimed his contempt for sentimentality—he could have wept over this. His tears dried
quickly, but they still burned; and he could not have said
whether this was because of the outrageous disappointment
or because of another sentiment which his sense of outrage
would not allow him to confess. Annette knew nothing of
all this. When at last she realized how forgetful she had
been, she was very sorry, but it seemed useless to confess
this to him, since he appeared—a new proof of his insen-
sibility!—not to have noticed it. Ah, if he had been like
Franz, expansive and affectionate! In spite of the differences in their ages, she made frequent comparisons between them, for she liked to consider Franz as one of her
children. She used this as a pretext for excusing the absorbing affection that bound her to him. But her excuse
was a deceit and Annette was deluding herself. A salu-
tary but unfortunately tardy instinct urged her to punish
herself for thinking too much of the pain she would feel

in going away. But the demon of the feminine heart is expert in finding ways of revenge. It whispered in her ear that if she stayed she would feel remorse for not having left, and that if she left she would feel remorse for not having stayed. The latter course allowed her to encourage her secret feeling. One sacrifices one's unconfessed desire in order to have reasons, afterwards, for making up for it.

For Franz the question was much simpler. He uttered loud cries when Annette said she was going to leave him. He would not see that she had other duties. He simply felt hurt. She had become a necessary habit for him and he was completely upset at the thought of losing her. Annette, not at all shocked at the unreasoning demands of his heart, secretly flattered at being monopolized in this way, offered a very feeble resistance. She put off her decision from day to day. Franz artfully concealed from her the newspapers from Paris, and Annette forgot to ask for them. On the 8th and the 11th of March there were two more air-raids over Paris, and Franz, who knew about them, took care not to mention them. The closing of the Franco-Swiss frontier during the first fortnight of March served him as a pretext for the lack of news. Annette was guilty of not making any enquiries. She was well punished for this. On March 22, a double thunderbolt fell upon her. The stop-press note of one of the newspapers informed her of the explosion of La Courtille, the German blow at Paris. And a letter from Sylvie, dated ten days before, informed her that Pitan had been arrested.

Annette was overwhelmed. She did not doubt for a moment that Pitan was paying for her in the affair of the escape. And in these times this was the crime of high treason. What had been happening in the interval of ten days since the letter had been dispatched? In these days of harsh dictatorship, all the more feverish because of the approach of the enemy, sentences were pronounced without any delay and no one troubled about justice; justice was nothing but the procuress of vengeance. For months Annette had had no interest in politics. In her concern for two persons she had forgotten all the rest of the world. She condemned herself. . . .

Hastily she made her preparations for departure. She knew that in returning she was running to meet the fate that threatened Pitan. But she did not fear this fate as much as the thought of having betrayed Pitan, of having appeared to flee from her share of the responsibility. She hadn't a moment to lose! With the German advance, the road to Paris might be cut off any day. Her son, her own people were in danger. Her place was near them.

Franz protested in vain. Anxiety on his behalf had taken a second place in her mind. He must live alone now with his grief. His sorrow had become calmer; he had reached the moment when he was once more in tune with the harmony of life; his grief had become an element of it; it was no longer in danger of destroying it; it filled and nourished him, it was even a companion for him in his isolation.

And Annette was not going to abandon her friend. She realized what dangerous suggestions a too complete solitude, following months of complete intimacy, might have upon an anxious, unsteady spirit. She looked about for some discreet companions who, without being obtrusive, might watch over him a little and keep her informed from a distance about his condition.

There were two ladies living in a nearby chalet, a

mother and daughter. They lived very much by themselves. The mother, who was still in mourning, was large
and strong, with an aristocratic air. The daughter,
twenty-six years old, was an invalid, almost always lying
down. She had an abundance of fine, thick, plaited, pale
golden hair. She was not pretty. She was tall also, with
a wasted face and an elegant figure. She suffered, however, from tuberculosis of the bones, although, having
undergone drastic treatment for two or three years, she
was on the way to recovery. She limped a little. The
two women took a short walk every afternoon. They
never went very far. Annette and Franz, returning from
their excursions, often met them not far from their house;
and they would all walk home together. Leaning on her
walking-stick, the lame girl, whether from pride or indifference, made no effort to conceal her infirmity. They
only exchanged a few commonplace words. Neither the
one pair nor the other showed the slightest curiosity about
each other's secrets. But the two households rendered
each other certain friendly offices, and they lent each other
books.

Annette asked Madame de Wintergrün if she would
be willing to watch over her young friend and help to distract him in his grief, about which she told her. She did
not mention this to Franz, for he had not appeared to enjoy his meetings with the two women. If she had expressed any wish for him to become acquainted with them,
he would certainly have refused to do so; for he could not
bear her going away, and he could not have endured her
seeking for substitutes and forcing them on him.

Up to the very hour of her departure he hoped she was
going to stay. He wasted the last day sulking and making passionate entreaties: "*Aennchen*, you're not going?

Tell me it isn't true, your going? I implore you, I want you. . . ."

"But my dear boy," said Annette, "when my own people are waiting for me?"

"Let them wait! A bird in the hand is worth two in the bush. I am the bird in your hand."

Useless to try to convince him! He was like a child who says over and over, "I'm thirsty," and will not listen to you.

When he saw that Annette's decision was irrevocable he shut himself up in his room and refused to open his lips. He would not answer any more questions. He left her to do all her own packing, arrange everything, tire herself out. She thought she would be obliged to leave him without his even saying good-by to her. But at the last moment, when she went into his room in her traveling costume, he was sitting dismally in the corner. She leaned over to kiss his forehead and he lifted his head so suddenly that he struck Annette's mouth and cut her lip. She did not feel the cut until long afterwards. He, of course, noticed nothing but kissed her hands, plaintively repeating: "*Aennchen, Aennchen!* Come back soon!"

She stroked his head, promising him, "Yes, yes, I shall come back soon."

At last he rose, took her bags and went with her. Annette was the only one who spoke. To distract his mind she made a few suggestion, on the way from the house to the station, about taking care of himself. He heard nothing but her voice. He helped her into the railway carriage, climbed in and sat down beside her. He still did not speak; he sat there without looking at her. She was afraid he would allow himself to be carried off by the train, that he would come with her. But five minutes

before the time came he suddenly got up and, without a
word of farewell—for fear he would not be able to master his emotion—he sprang out. Leaning over the car-
riage-door, Annette saw him striding away. She waited
for him to look back, but he did not turn round. He disappeared. Annette found herself alone in the motionless,
soundless, almost empty train, with her lip burning. And
she licked away the blood. . . .

*
* *

At the frontier she came back to the present, the red shadow of the war and the perilous duty she was about to face. She wondered if they had not taken her description, if she was not going to be arrested the moment she set foot on French soil. Sylvie's cautious letter had not stated anything precisely; according to the way she read between the lines, she had everything or nothing to fear. But the examination of passports took place and nothing happened; and Annette passed on.

She reached Paris. No one met her. She had preceded by several days the letter that announced her coming. Her anxious mind had been running all night ahead of the train. It was Palm Sunday; and the news she had heard on the way of the bombardment of Paris by the mysterious cannon, which seemed like something Jules Verne had imagined, alarmed her about her son. The quarter where he was living was within the range of the gun. It was a relief already to have returned to Paris, under the enemy's fire. But Annette did not begin to feel really calm until she saw that the house was intact. Hastily climbing the stairs, she knocked on the door and heard (oh, joy!) her son's footstep as he came to open it.

Marc was astounded. For an instant his mind, his self-control, utterly abandoned him. The artificial wall they had raised between them vanished completely. They fell into each other's arms; and each was astonished by the passion which the other threw into the embrace.

But this was only for a moment. They were so little accustomed to these effusions that they were embarrassed

280

by them, and, letting each other go, they resumed their conventional manner.

There was a secret between them. Annette, entering the room, explained her return as best she could. Marc listened, saying nothing, but observing every one of her movements. It was she who had to undergo inspection this time. Annette, embarrassed, forced herself to talk. She had a confused sense of discomfort, a fear of being judged by her son. In more than one respect she was not blameless in her relation to him. Accordingly she appeared less tender with him and more sure of herself than she was. In her anxious circumspection she failed to observe him. She did not see that he was no longer the boy she had left three months before. How different the person we know always is from the person we used to know! We never know anything but an image that has passed. And the new image is of a stranger to whom we do not possess the key.

On the eve of his arrest, Pitan, who knew that the authorities were on his trail, had sent a letter to Sylvie in which he asked her to tell Annette not to be anxious, that he was taking everything on himself. Nothing more, but that was enough. Sylvie, without having any precise knowledge of it, had suspected the strange adventure ever since summer, and she was alarmed. In what sort of escape was her madcap sister engaged? Impossible to discover, for Pitan was in solitary confinement. By innuendo she had confided her secret to Marc. He had guessed that his mother was in danger, and the memory of his mysterious meeting with her, near the Gare de Lyon, in the previous December—(he had not breathed a word of it to any one)—came back to him. He had built up a whole romance on this. Without taking his aunt into his confidence about it, he taxed his ingenuity trying, with her, to put the story together. Sylvie told him for the first time what she had learned about the reasons that had led to Annette's recall, the scene in the cemetery, the interest she felt in a certain prisoner. Upon these data Marc had been working for a long time, and the figure of his mother appeared to him under a new light. He revised all his ideas.

In becoming a passion, in becoming dangerous, the pacifism which he had despised as maudlin, good enough for women and weaklings, had taken on a strong flavor. He imagined some adventure of heroism and love, a romance; it filled him with a smarting jealousy and a disquieting sense of attraction. He understood now that suspicion of his mother's which had so hurt him! And the worst of it was that after having been furiously indignant at it he had to recognize that his own attitude had given some reason for this suspicion. It was staggering. But he was not thinking of himself now. His mother was in danger. Seeing her in Paris again, he hadn't a moment's doubt that she had come knowing the danger that she was running. This thought supplanted all others in his mind. He was brooding over it. He besought her mentally to tell him about her danger, knowing very well that she would not do so. He was in agonies over it, and he admired her. He admired her pride, her calmness, her silence. He had discovered at last what she was! Now that she was threatened he trembled at the thought of losing her.

Annette noticed nothing of all this. One single duty filled her mind; she was very anxious. She scarcely waited to change her clothes and take a little food before she went out, not even waiting to see her sister. Marc timidly stammered an offer to go with her. She waved it aside with a gesture, and he did not insist. He was mortified and he dreaded incurring another rebuff.

She went to Marcel Franck's. He had become an important wheel in the governmental steam-roller. He had insinuated himself into a special secretaryship in the cabinet.

Without going into useless preliminaries, she told him the story. Marcel was astounded. His first feeling was very far from friendly. For the first time she saw a Franck who had lost his smile—that ironical cosmetic which his face had assumed as a second nature. During the first few moments he came very near losing even the most elementary courtesy. He could see only one thing in the affair: that this infatuated creature had got him into a fine mess. That she was in it with him did not make him laugh. He was no longer disposed to be satisfied with a play upon words; he was annoyed with Annette for having jeopardized him. But Annette's ironical glance, following the thoughts that passed over his face, recalled him to his rôle as a man of the world. His dégagé attitude returned. The pluck of this woman who was braving every risk made him ashamed of his pusillanimity; and it was the old Marcel who presently added:

"But, Annette, for the love of heaven, what devil has got into you! When you were perfectly safe over there in Switzerland and nobody was thinking of you at all, what devil put it into your head to come and throw yourself into the wolf's mouth?"

Annette soberly explained that she had come to substitute herself for Pitan or at least share in the accusation that had been brought against him.

Marcel raised his arms. "You're not going to do that!"

"I have come to ask you the name of the magistrate who has charge of the affair so that I can present my declaration to him."

"I won't permit it."

"Do you think I am going to allow an innocent man to be condemned for me?"

"He is not innocent. He is a professional at this game of smuggling mail and helping people to escape. He's an old hand at it. You are denouncing yourself without saving him. Besides, he hasn't mentioned your name."

"That's because he is generous. And I don't see why I should be less so than he."

"You have a child."

"Exactly! I don't want him to be a coward."

"You are absolutely mad."

"Absolutely. Now, my dear friend, please tell me the name I've come for. And be calm! You are not going to be involved."

He was thinking: "You are fooling me! Once they get on the track, it's absolutely certain that justice will climb step by step until it reaches my name!"

But his pride was nettled. And he resisted. "It isn't a question of myself. I am anxious on your account. You don't know the 'boss.' " (He was speaking of "the Man Who Made War.") "One summary judgment more or less is nothing to him. No woman is going to stop him! As a matter of fact, he enjoys outraging all the old conventions, the kind attentions, the sacred traditions of respect and gallantry."

"It doesn't displease me to be treated as an equal. Even in the presence of the gallows!"

Marcel did not insist any longer. He knew Annette. "Very well! But first let me look into this affair."

"Time presses."

"It won't be lost."

"My evidence is a heavy burden to carry."

"You are strong enough to carry it a day or two longer. If there is any chance of having the charge dismissed, wouldn't that be better than having the two of you sacrificed?"

"Who is going to guarantee that I shan't hear to-morrow, or the day after, when it's all over, that Pitan has been the victim of one of those summary judgments you've just spoken of?"

"I know the magistrate. I shall keep you informed. I am not trying to deceive you. I shouldn't take the risk! At the worst, if a sudden arrest were to take place without my knowing it you would still be able to give yourself up. No one has ever been able to prevent a woman from going to her ruin."

"I am not afraid of that, Marcel. But I am not anxious for it. I haven't any taste or desire for useless heroism."

"Thank God for one word of common sense! Ouf! And as for useful heroism . . . Annette, let's speak frankly. I want to do what I can for you. Why haven't you told me that he was your lover?"

"Who?"

"That handsome young fellow you've saved."

"What nonsense!"

"Come, you're not still going to try to hide it from me? I don't blame you. If it's your pleasure you are perfectly right!"

"But I assure you it isn't!"

"Come now!"

Annette blushed. "No, no, no, no!"

Marcel smiled. "All right, don't be angry! I shan't

ask you anything more. But, between ourselves, you Mysterious Creature, you must admit that it would embarrass you very much to explain why, if you didn't love him, you saved him."

"Because——" she began impetuously.

But she stopped. She saw that, however she might express her true reasons, he would not believe them: he wouldn't understand them. Well, so be it! Let him believe what he liked!

Marcel's smile had won the day. One couldn't conceal anything from him!

But he was a good sort. Love gave a certain piquancy to the affair. Just the same, this Annette . . . Damnably compromising . . . But deep down he was proud of it!

*
* *

He set to work at once. He saw the military magistrate. The latter was an amiable and distinguished man who had risen without effort to the degree of inhumanity which his rôle demanded of him. A fanatical nationalism, a fanatical sense of his power and the curiosity of a dilettante were combined in him to form an affable indifference. He was never more dangerous for the accused than when he was interested in them.

He was interested in Pitan. He found him very sympathetic. They had had long, courteous talks together from which he had tried to extract the hemp of the rope to hang him with. But the rope was slim: he had to confess it with a good grace and much regret. The little peddler was a very gentle, enlightened soul, quite inoffensive and entirely disinterested. He talked freely, he was glad to reveal his well-intentioned fantasies, he seemed grateful that any one was willing to listen to him and looked forward to the gallows with the shy jubilation of a bright-eyed dog squinting at a lump of sugar. But nothing could induce him to name any of his accomplices nor to furnish any information about the imputed offenses. Whether from taste or from a naïve and cunning cleverness, he always turned the narrative into a dissertation. He appeared to attach no importance to facts and a great deal to ideas.

The judge showed Franck some letters that Pitan had written from prison to a young friend, together with the young friend's replies. The name of the latter was Marc Rivière. Franck felt a momentary emotion: had this

little imbecile, all by himself, betrayed the secret? With
these Rivières, one never knew what to expect. But he
was reassured when the magistrate read to him in a
melodious voice portions of these letters, written in a beautiful, lyrical style that made one think by turns of the
young Schiller, Flaubert, Rousseau and Rimbaud. Pitan
himself intermingled Bernardin de Saint-Pierre and Ed-
gar Quinet. The young man expressed an exalted affection for the older one, an indignation at the abuse of force
and an ardent desire to share the fate, whatever it might
be, that was in store for the just. The elder paternally
endeavored to calm him, spoke of his tranquil joy, his
peacefulness of mind: one might have gathered that his
prison was the chosen retreat of the wise, a sort of lay
hermitage granted to a thinker by the grace of the State.
Through the window of his high, barred cell, the wind
had brought from the banks of the Seine a blossom from
a chestnut-tree, and the whole Spring had entered with it.
Pitan became bucolic. There was the flower, carefully
spread out between the sheets of the letter which the
magistrate held. And the two Parisians, exchanging an
amused smile, said:

"The good man ought to be pinned up also."

But neither the good man nor the passionate boy had
betrayed what was at the bottom of their minds: the latter's anxiety and remorse about his mother, the former's
desire to reassure the other. They understood each other
by innuendoes, and the Parisians saw nothing in all this
but a dialogue from *Emile*.

The magistrate closed his dossier.

"What does it all come to?" Franck asked.

"Everything boils down to this singular affair of the
escape. I don't quite understand what interest this old

Anacharsis could have taken in it. He didn't know the prisoner personally. We have tracked the young bird into Switzerland. He is being sheltered in a French provincial family."

Franck pricked up his ears.

"Honorable people, beyond all reproach. A wounded son, both the other men at the front, dead or alive, three women: the mother, a married daughter and a nurse-companion. Some reason to believe there is an intrigue between the handsome young man and the married daughter. A very ordinary story. The husband is at the front. In the rear, morality maintains itself as it can. It is a little surprising that such a good patriot should have chosen a German scab. But half a loaf! They probably knew each other before the war."

Franck rose, quite reassured. "At night all cats are gray."

"Of course we are not anxious to reward the zeal of a combatant by making him publicly a cuckold. The public safety is not involved in that."

"But what about the older man?"

"As for the older man, they can hang him if they wish —or, if they wish, they can let him go. There are just about as many reasons for as against in either case. The scales are equal, and whether one of them drops or the other is of no importance. Just as the State commands!"

The "State" was Franck's peculiar sphere. He went to see the "boss."

He had known him for a long time, but who could boast of really knowing him? That human demon always did the opposite of what one expected. A thicket strewn with snares. Franck advanced cautiously.

Chance favored him. Instead of the surly answer with
which the irascible old wild boar ordinarily honored the
young wild boars, he found the animal quite affable. He
had "slept well"; he felt frisky. The man with the
Mongol's mask had returned from a tour of the front.
Everything was going well: people were dying there in
their places according to regulations, without requiring
any pressing. The line of defense had been consolidated,
and once more the German wave seemed to have been
stopped. The violent old man had returned very much
cheered up. Fatigue had no more effect on his hide than
sentimentality. He had just hurried off the mass of
urgent matters which his secretaries had prepared for him;
and now, before the sitting of the Chamber, he was giving
himself a half-hour of recreation. He liked gossip; and
his hangers-on, who knew his taste, always had their
hands full of the scandals of the day. He at once caught
the scent of one in the pockets of Franck as the latter advanced with a circumspect and promising smile.

"So here's the Lord of Frangipane"—he pronounced it
"Francktjipane"—"bringing his merchandise!   Come
along, young man, quick, open your basket!"

Franck, flattered by the familiarity but irritated by the
nickname, which struck home all too well, fell in with the
facetious tone of the "boss." And by way of sounding
the ogre he began to sketch a sympathetic, comic portrait
of Pitan. He did not get very far, for his impatient
auditor cut his description short with a bantering: "A
beautiful soul. Haven't you something else?"

Whereupon the story-teller bethought himself of em-
broidering on the material a few extravagant designs, improvised for the taste of his public, and Pitan became the
bashful lover of a "virtuous" lady who in her turn was

the passionate mistress of the Austrian whom Pitan had helped to escape.

This time the "boss" flared up. "Who is it? Who is it?" he shouted, gripping Franck's arm. "I wager I know her. Do you mean X.'s wife? . . ." (X. was one of his ministers.) Through his little eyes passed a gleam of ferocious malice. "No? . . . No? . . . A pity! I would have put her into Saint Lazare in the name of the *Union Sacrée!*"

He mentioned two or three other women. He would never have stopped if Franck had not blurted out her name. It was not without anxiety, for the risk was great, but it was too late to recall it now, and the babbler was caught—not for the first time!—by his tongue.

At the name of Annette Rivière, the old man exclaimed: "Rivière!"

He had known him, Rivière, the architect, the diner-out, the wit, the free-thinker, the Dreyfusard. They belonged to the same epoch, they had sailed in the same boat, they had had more than one jolly or cynically ironical tilt together. As for the daughter, he had pinched her cheeks when she was a little girl. He had lost sight of her, but she was sympathetic to him because she had made a fool of "that idiot" of a Roger Brissot. (He was sound enough himself to have a mortal hatred of hypocrisy, and he scented it everywhere—even in the truth.) He had been delighted by the consummate blow Annette's fist had dealt to the face of the slimy tribe, leaving their Roger flat as a pancake, his nose in the mud. On the watch for every sort of scandal, he had contributed not a little to spread this abroad, to the suppressed fury of the Brissots, who pretended to know nothing about it. This was one of his happy memories! At this distance, he felt as if there had been two who had acted together in this excellent farce, himself and Annette. He had a feeling of gratitude towards the gallant girl. (For so it was he saw her.) Her new adventure disposed him to be indulgent. "That Rivière! What a Gauloise!"

"But tell me, Frangipane, she can't be very young now. She must be . . . Wait . . . Bah. It's all the better! I like her. She has fire in her. Well, so the affair has ended in this game of billiards? What on earth has politics to do with it? You are not going to drag that good Frenchwoman before Foutriquier-Tinville?" (So he called his Attorney-General.) "He would lick his chops over her. NO! Let her sleep with her Viennese! We shall have one more soldier of the right for the next war! As for old Pitan (another good French name, hail to the regiment!) 'the happiest of the three,' let him enjoy his good luck! You will hush up the inquiry for me, my boy. Throw out the indictment, in heaven's name! And now let's talk about serious things. The Chamber is just going to sit. What shall I say to these cattle?"

So the affair was buried.

And, after they had covered her with mud, Annette was saved.

In the jungle, covering people with mud is a form of sympathy.

*
* *

Happily for her, she knew nothing about all this. A single word from Franck merely informed her that things were going well. She was not satisfied with this. Full of distrust, she had written to the magistrate, demanding to be heard. The magistrate later showed the request to Pitan, when he released him.

Returning home, Annette found Sylvie, who had hurried over immediately, and she told her about her doings. Thereupon Sylvie expressed herself fully and freely. She was beside herself at such idiocy. Annette let her talk, until at last—since the harm was done and there was nothing to do but accept it—Sylvie suddenly stopped short, threw herself on her sister's neck and embraced her. As a matter of fact, she wouldn't, for an empire, have had Annette act otherwise, and knowing that she, Sylvie, would never have done it, she was proud of her big sister. This will, this calmness, impressed her.

From behind the partition, Marc, without understanding much of what was going on, heard the confused murmur of the two sisters, the outbursts of Sylvie's irritated voice, that sank to a low tone at a gesture from Annette, then their furious embraces, then silence. Sylvie blew her nose. This woman whose eyes were always dry had wept. . . .

The two women, as they stood there, with their arms tenderly locked, looked at each other, and Annette, kissing Sylvie's eyes, whispered to her the whole story, Germain's friendship, Franz's escape, the death. It no longer occurred to Sylvie to blame the mad generosity of her sister; she ceased to measure her by the common stature, by her own; she recognized in Annette, in Annette alone, the privilege of acting and existing according to a law superior to the ordinary law. Meanwhile, behind the partition the jealous boy was mortally hurt that they had not taken him into their confidence. He was not going to ask for it. His pride was going to wait until they came and brought it to him.

But he champed his bit on the following day when Pitan arrived. He emerged from his Thebaid. Annette heard the joyous exclamation of her son as he opened the door, and she dropped the work she was holding. Marc cried out in his surprise, crushing the visitor's hands. With his little calm, affectionate cluck, Pitan laughed in his beard. At sight of him Annette rose and threw her arms about him; then, remembering that her son was present, she was embarrassed. Marc, much more embarrassed, disappeared; under the pretext of going to close the door to the stairs, he left them alone for a few minutes. Annette and Pitan rapidly exchanged a few affectionate, happy words; and when Marc returned the conversation of the three went on under a veil of half-innuendo. They tried to keep Pitan for luncheon, but he was already anxious to set out for a run over Paris; he was going to make the round of his comrades. Marc went out with him. As they trotted along together, Marc said: "Pitan, I know what you wrote to my aunt."

"Ah!" replied the old man. And he stopped there.

Marc swallowed. "You risked your life for us. You have been generous."

"Less so than your mother."

"But what did she risk?"

"She hasn't told you anything about it?"

"No."

"Then you wouldn't like me to tell you for her?"

"No." He was annoyed, but Pitan was right. They continued their walk. Marc went on, after an effort: "But I would like to know, at least . . . Is she still in danger?"

"For the moment I believe not. But in these days of cowards and wolves a brave, sincere woman like her is always in danger."

"Can't any one prevent her?"

"One has no right to prevent her. On the contrary, she must be aided."

"But how?"

"By running risks with her.

Marc couldn't say: "Run risks, yes. But how, when I don't know anything about her, when she doesn't tell me anything about her risks and her dangers?" He still felt very bitter for being pushed aside. He repeated to himself: "I am the one she confides in least of all."

As he said no more, Pitan misinterpreted his silence. He said: "My dear boy, you can be proud of your mother."

Marc angrily cried: "Do you think I have to wait for you to tell me to be proud of her?"

He turned his back on Pitan and strode furiously away.

*
* *

Relieved of a great weight, Annette had resumed her calm, inconspicuous life in the household. The war that was going on, the anxiety in people's minds, did not seem to touch her. She was sharing their dangers: she had no desire to share their thoughts. She had enough to fill her mind. Attentive as Sylvie had been—in her absence she had kept an eye over Marc—there were a quantity of very important small details which only a mother's eye could have noticed in regard to her son: his appearance, his health. She went through his linen and his clothes, maliciously delighted when she discovered something amiss that had escaped the critical eye of Sylvie. She had a great deal to do, also, in putting to rights the flat in which, for so long, the dust and the moths had had their own way. Sylvie always found her at work sewing and arranging things. Every evening the two sisters had long talks. Marc, working in the adjoining room, with the door open, watched them, but the young chick's eye that could see backwards did not find in these discussions a single grain to devour. The intimate subjects had been canvassed once for all, and they no longer talked about anything but commonplaces, the affairs of the day, women's trifles, their needlework, the cost of food. Losing his patience, he went and closed his door. How could they keep chattering about these nothings for hours? It was natural enough for Sylvie! But that other woman, his mother, who had just risked her life and was perhaps going to risk it again to-morrow, his mother, in whom, without being able to grasp them, he divined burning secrets, became just as excited over these nothings, the price of bread, the restrictions on butter and sugar, as over that hidden world which she only half concealed from him! For his jealousy saw the gleam in the heart of the lamp. Annette herself was scarcely aware of it all the time that she was silently illumined by it.

Tacet sed loquitur. . . .

Yes, the lamp was burning, noiselessly. In broad daylight one didn't observe it. But under the alabaster covering his falcon's eye caught the silent gleam. Whence had it come? And for what was it burning?

One other soul, in the night, perceived this glow-worm's light, shining in the grass, and prowled about, attracted by it.

Ursule Bernardin, whom Annette had scarcely noticed as she passed her on the stairs, stopped her timidly, touched her arm and whispered: "Pardon me, Madame. Would you let me come into your room and talk to you for a moment?"

Annette was very much surprised. She knew how extremely timid were the two Bernardin girls and what care they had taken, hitherto, to avoid her. In spite of the semi-darkness of the stairway she saw the blush on the confused face; and the gloved hand trembled on her arm. She said warmly: "Come in now!"

The young girl, overcome with apprehension, was already on the point of drawing back and suggested postponing her call until some other day. But Annette took her arm and led her in: "We shall be alone. Come in."

Ursule Bernardin, breathless, stood in Annette's bedroom, motionless and stiff.

"We have hurried up too fast? Excuse me, I always forget. When I'm coming up I run, I simply eat up the stairs. Sit down! No, here, in this corner, away from the light; you will find it better. Get your breath again. Don't be in a hurry to talk. You are actually panting!"

She looked at the young girl, smiling, and tried to reassure her as she sat there awkwardly, frozen with embarrassment, her breast heaving with emotion under the heavy stuff of her dress. For the first time, Annette was able to study this face and this rustic form, narrowed by her bourgeois confinement. Her features lacked refinement and she was clumsily made. But she would have appeared attractive had she been leading a country life, in the normal activity of a farm, surrounded by domestic animals and children, happy and busy. This courageous figure, young and healthy, happy and bustling, under the burning sun, bathed by a summer day, a warm moisture on brow and cheeks, would have had its charm. But the laughter and the sunlight had been placed under lock and key. The blood had ebbed away. What remained were the flat nose, the thick lips, the heavy, lymphatic, shrunken figure that did not dare move and was afraid to breathe.

Seeing that she could not bring herself to speak, Annette, in order to give her time to collect herself, asked her a few friendly, commonplace questions. Ursule found it difficult to reply. She was confused and forgot what she was saying. Her thoughts wandered. She would have liked to broach the subject that was in her mind, but she was terrified at the idea of mentioning it. She was wretched and she had only one wish: "Good heavens, how can I get away?"

She rose. "Madame, I beg you . . . let me go! I don't know what's come over me. Forgive me for having stopped you!"

Annette took her hands, laughing. "Come, compose yourself! Take all the time you like. Is it because you are afraid of me?"

"No, Madame. . . . Forgive me. I would like to go. I can't speak. . . . I can't do it to-day."

"Very well, you needn't speak. I shall ask you nothing —merely to stay a few minutes longer. You have been kind enough to come up to my apartment to see me, and I am going to take advantage of the opportunity. You needn't try to fly away the moment you come in. We have lived so long, almost side by side, without uttering a word to each other! And I am not going to stay here long. I am going away again. Let me just once have a quiet look at you! Come, let me see your eyes! I am showing you mine. There is nothing in them that can frighten you."

Ursule, confused and touched, gradually became re-assured and began to apologize awkwardly for her timid-ity and rudeness. She said she had never forgotten Annette's kind words at the time of their great sorrow the year before; she had been touched by them and had wanted to write her, but she had not dared. Her family did not want her to become friends with strangers.

Annette said in her friendly way: "Of course. . . . Of course. . . . I understand."

Ursule, gradually growing bolder, stammered, began again; then, making a great effort, she said how much she had suffered for four years from this war, from these hatreds and all this spitefulness. Though she had not known Annette, she thought she would disapprove of them also.

(Annette, without speaking, gently took her hand.)

But there was no one in her family to whom she could

breathe these things. Even her parents, who were very
good, were always thinking about vengeance. (She corrected herself.) No! Merciless punishment. The death
of their poor sons had driven them mad. The mere word
"peace" threw them into a fury. The most violent of all
was her sister Justine, with whom she had shared her
bedroom and her thoughts since they were children.
Every night, before she went to sleep, she prayed out
loud: "God, Virgin Mary, Saint Michael, exterminate
them!" It was frightful. She had to appear to join in
these prayers; otherwise they accused her of indifference
to the misfortunes of the country, to the death of the two
brothers.

"Indifferent—I am very far from that. Ah, it is just
because one is unhappy, it seems to me, that one ought to
wish others not to be."

She expressed her ideas clumsily and touchingly. Annette, to whom they were not new, agreed with them;
and she expressed them better. It made Ursule happy to
hear her and, falling silent, she listened. At last she
asked, confidently: "Madame, you are a Christian?"

"No."

Ursule was shocked. "O my God! . . . Then you
can't understand me. . . ."

"My child, one doesn't have to be a Christian to understand and love everything that is human."

"Human! That is not enough! Evil is human also.
And men. They appall me. Look at their cruelties, these
abominations! Nothing but the blood of Christ can atone
for them."

"Our own blood can, the blood of every one—man or
woman—who devotes himself to others."

"If it is in the name of Christ."

"What does a name matter!"

"But this name is a God."

"And what sort of a God would it be who was not in every devoted soul? If a single one of these men—I say a *single one* were where God was not, how narrow would be God's limits! The heart itself would surpass them."

"No, nothing surpasses Him! Everything good is in Him."

"Then the good is enough."

"Who can show it to me if you take God away from me?"

"My dear, I wouldn't for anything in the world take Him away from you! Keep Him! I respect Him in you. Do you think I would unsettle the mainstay of your life?"

"Then tell me, Madame, that you believe in Him also."

"My child, I cannot say that I believe what I don't know. You wouldn't want me to tell a lie?"

"No, Madame, but believe, believe, I implore you!"

Annette smiled affectionately. "I act, my child. I don't need to believe."

"To act is to believe."

"Perhaps. It is my way of believing."

"If Christ does not illumine it, action is always in danger of being either an error or a crime."

"Has Christ been enough, during these four years, to save those who believe in Him from error and crime?"

"Ah, don't say that, Madame! I know how few real Christians there are! That's the most distressing thing of all! I scarcely know two among all those whom I know. It rends my heart; they are killing me. I am full of misery and horror. This life horrifies me. These men horrify me. I want to atone for them. I can't remain among them any longer. I don't know how to act as you do; I am afraid of every kind of action. I wasn't made to live in this world. I wish . . . I am going to retire into a Carmelite convent. My father has given his permission, my mother cries, and my sister disapproves; but I can't stay with my family any longer. Every moment, it seems to me, they make Our Lord Jesus suffer. My God, what have I said? Don't believe me, Madame! They are good, I love them, I haven't the right to judge them. No, don't listen to me. Ah, if you had been a Christian!"

She hid her face in her hands.

Annette soothed her. Laying her hand, maternally, on Ursule's bowed neck, she said: "My poor child! Yes, you are right."

Ursule lifted her head. "You don't blame me?"

"No."

"I am doing the right thing in going?"

"It is probably the best thing for you."

"And you don't disapprove of me for retiring, instead of acting, as you do?"

"That, also, is acting. Every one must have his own form of action. I am not one of those who deny that prayer is one form. It is a good thing that some souls should guard the sacred fire of contemplation which, by a rivulet of blood, keeps open the flood-gates between the Eternal and ourselves. Pray for us, my daughter, for us who act for you! Perhaps we are the blind and you the paralytic."

Ursule leaned over gratefully, to kiss her hands. Annette embraced her and led her back to the door opening on the stairs. Ursule sighed. "Ah, why, why aren't you a Christian?" Then, on the threshold, she said: "You are one."

"I don't think so," said Annette, smiling.

With her eyes beaming, Ursule replied: "God chooses those whom he wishes. You are not consulted about it."

*
* *

Annette had received no letters from Franz since she had left him. She was hurt by this, but she was not surprised. She knew what it meant. The big baby was sulking and wanted to punish her; silence was the best weapon he had for avenging himself, for obliging her to return, perhaps more quickly. Annette was amused by the stratagem and (malice for malice!) pretended not to notice it. She wrote to him every week, calmly, affectionately, playfully, without altering in any way the plans she had arranged. She wanted very much to see him again, but she had found it unreasonable now, with all the duties that held her in Paris. She intended to wait until summer, giving herself as an excuse the mountain trips that would be so beneficial for Marc, who had been shut up too long. But the delay weighed upon her more than she would have liked.

In the middle of the fourth week after her return to Paris, a letter arrived from Franz. At last! With a smile, Annette shut herself up to read it. What reproaches, what anger she was going to encounter!

Franz did not reproach her at all. He was not in the least angry. He was perfectly calm, courteous, well-bred. He was in good health. He urged her to stay on.

As long as Franz had not written, Annette had not been anxious. After reading this letter, she was perturbed.

It would have been difficult for her to say why. She ought to have been happy in finding him so patient, but she was not. But she could not prevent herself from sending him an answer the same day. Of course she did not express the things that filled her mind. Was she even aware of them? She wrote half-humorously: as he

304

was evidently not particularly anxious to see her again, she was not coming back before the end of the year. She expected a protest by return mail. No protest. No more letters came.

Annette began to be impatient. She counted the weeks till summer. She wrote Madame de Wintergrün under the pretext of verifying what Franz had written her about his health. Madame de Wintergrün replied that their dear Monsieur de Lenz was very well, that grief, thank God! passed away quickly at his age, that he was pleasant and gay and was staying now in the same house as themselves, that they regarded him as one of the family.

Annette was reassured, more so than she would have liked to be. She slept badly that night and for several nights afterwards. She shrugged her shoulders and drove back a certain thought. But the thought mutely, tenaciously, returned. Her dignity held out for another week, then one morning, as she was getting up, it surrendered. Annette made up her mind to go. She did not give herself any reasons, she had to go. . . .

During these same days, Marc was burning with a desire to come closer to his mother. He had let the first weeks go to waste. He was counting on some opportunity that had not arrived, and now he tried to force an opportunity. But this can only be done when two are playing, and he was playing alone; his mother paid no heed to the game. He never left her side, he angled for a glance from her, he anticipated her desires. She could scarcely have failed to observe his attentions, he had never before been so prodigal of them. Perhaps she did observe them, perhaps she recorded them mechanically for more propitious days when she should have the time. But she did not have the time now. Her mind was too full. Marc tried in vain to draw back to himself the spirit that had escaped him. He was disheartened. One couldn't go on all by oneself making advances. One had to be helped. Then he would go off into a corner of the room, and there, like one forgotten, he would watch her profile as she sewed on the buttons that had fallen off his clothes. (For she was busy over him all the time that she was thinking of other things. Ah, how much rather he would have had her think of him and let these things go!) He studied the anxious face. What was she anxious about? What memory was it that contracted her cheek? What image was passing like a stream under her skin? At other times Annette, with her hundred eyes, would have seen his glance falling upon her, but now her senses were not there. She worked with fingers half benumbed. When she became aware of herself in the silence, she forced herself to ask Marc some motherly questions, but she received the reply absent-mindedly; or she would ask him to out with her and take advantage of the fine weather. There were the moments when he would have liked to speak. He would get up, distressed. He had nothing to reproach her for. She was gentle with him, and distant. He longed to clasp her in his arms, shake her, bite her cheek or the tip of her ear, even make her cry out. He longed to say to her: "I am here! Put your arms about me or strike me! Love me or hate me! But be here with me! Come back. . . ."

She did not come back.

Then he made up his mind. He resolved to speak— on the following Sunday, in the evening, after dinner.

It was on this Sunday that she suddenly told him, in the morning, that she was going. She had already packed

her trunk. With some embarrassment she gave as a
pretext that she had received news that recalled her to
Switzerland sooner than she had expected. She did not
give him any further explanation, and he did not ask her
to explain herself. He was struck dumb with consterna-
tion.

For a week he had been looking forward to this day.
He had slept badly; during the night he had gone over
and over what he was going to say. And now . . . they
were to separate before he would have a chance to
speak! For he couldn't do it in the hurry of the last day.
He needed time, an evening to collect his thoughts and
have her all to himself. How could she listen, with that
distracted air that followed the hand of the clock, hastening towards the hour of departure!

He was so in the habit of repressing his feelings that
he received without any sign of surprise the news that
overwhelmed him. Silently he helped his mother with
her traveling arrangements. It was not until the last
moment that he was sufficiently sure of his voice to say,
in a detached tone: "You promised to stay until the vacation. You have stolen three months from me." This was
the thought that returned to him bitterly, over and over.

Annette was deceived by his words. She saw it only as
a bit of family politeness, this saying "stay" at the moment
of farewell, when they are sure you are going. She replied in the same tone of friendly pleasantry: "No, I am
making you a present of them."

This injustice hurt him, but he did not answer. What
was the use now? After all, she was saying what he had
thought six months before. How could she know that he
had changed in the interval?

She recalled, later, the serious expression he had had

as he looked at her, standing there, before the door of her railway carriage. Sylvie was there too, talking incessantly. Annette answered her, but all the time she was talking with her sister she was looking at her son, motionless and silent, gazing at her. She carried away this look with her when the two silhouettes—only one waving its hand—vanished in the distance and the night.

Marc walked home with his aunt. She was thinking out loud and it never occurred to her to watch over her words in his presence. She was in the habit—a little too much so—of treating him as a man. She said: "My dear, we don't count for her any more. She has somebody else in her head. She has a wild heart."

Marc could not endure listening to Sylvie. He cut her short. "She has the right."

He had learned by now from Sylvie the story of the prisoner. He knew that Sylvie, like other people, thought there was a love affair mixed up in the adventure, but he was the only one of them all not to believe it, the only one who believed that his mother had obeyed a higher motive. Sylvie's irony offended him, as if one had suspected Cæsar's wife. But rather than discuss the matter he would have taken his mother's side no matter what she did.

"It's her right. . . . We don't count for her any more. It's my fault. I have lost her. *Mea culpa.* . . ."

But when one has confessed, one raises one's head afterwards and says: "What I have lost—sooner or later, by consent or by force, I shall recover."

*

* *

Up to the hour of her arrival Annette was calm. She had now the instinctive faculty of discarding troublesome thoughts; she did not suppress them, she postponed them.

She did not feel any anxiety until she actually arrived. She leaned through the window of the moving train to see the little station she knew so well coming towards her. Yes, everything was just as her memory had left it. The little station was there, but he was not there.

At the frontier Annette had telegraphed word of her return, but in these days of war, the winged heels of Mercury had soles of lead. And then, the dear boy—one could never count on him! Annette was not surprised, but she was disappointed just the same.

She set out on the road to the chalet. In the middle distance she saw Franz coming. Her heart fluttered with joy, but it soon fell. Franz was not alone. Mlle. de Wintergrün was with him. Franz, hastening his steps a little, kissed Annette's hand and politely apologized for being late. Annette joked with him and then became confused; an eye was looking her over. She turned towards Mlle. de Wintergrün. Straight and proud, the young girl was watching her, as if she were affirming that she had taken possession. Annette's eyes encountered the hard, blue eyes that were watching her embarrassment. Smiling coldly, the two exchanged a few pleasant words. Then all three set out again up the road. They were friendly enough. They talked, and Annette hadn't the slightest idea of what they were talking about. When they reached the chalet, the two others left Annette alone under the pretext—which was natural enough—that she

309

would want a rest, and Franz, still most polite, went on with the young girl. They were to meet again in the evening at Madame de Wintergrün's, who had invited Annette to supper.

In her bedroom, Annette stood before the mirror. She had not taken off her hat or her traveling cloak. She looked at herself unseeingly. She was thinking. No, she was not thinking! She had a little nervous smile, and she shook herself out of her hypnotic state only to fall into it again; for she only tore herself away from the mirror to gaze through the window at the mountains and the sky—which she did not see. She did not take off her hat or her gloves. A great weariness had suddenly fallen upon her. She felt a void in herself; she would think to-morrow.

She had to think that evening, at dinner, think how to prevent the others from reading her inner thought, and so she suddenly became aware of it herself. How those amiable remarks weighed on her! They asked her about her journey, about Paris, about the morale there, about the fashions, the cost of food, the probable length of the war. They talked, they talked, and it was so evident that every one, except Franz, perhaps, was lying. Though they both tried to avoid it, Annette constantly caught the unendurable glance of Mlle. de Wintergrün, who was watching her. There was not a wrinkle on her face of which the girl did not take an inventory. But she found fewer than she would have liked to find. Under the stimulus of the battle Annette's fatigue totally disappeared. Her complexion had resumed its mild, golden luster. She smiled, sure of herself, rested, rejuvenated. It was the young girl who seemed to grow older, her features hardened, a tense rigidity took the place of her proud assurance.

She felt the need of displaying her advantage, and in displaying it too much she compromised it.

She talked to Franz with exaggerated familiarity. Annette slightly raised her eyebrows. This was not lost on Erika de Wintergrün. She had scored one point. She hoped to score two. As they rose from the table, she committed the presumptuous mistake of carrying the uncertain, distracted Franz away from Annette, whom he was watching as if he were just discovering her. Leading him into the small, adjoining drawing-room, she monopolized him. Madame de Wintergrün tried to occupy the attention of Annette, who was following Erika with her eyes. Leaning towards Franz's ear, with a forced laugh, the young girl pretended to be confiding malicious secrets to him, and her sidelong glances glided over Annette. Madame de Wintergrün murmured: "Those dear children! They simply can't leave each other. . . ."

While she seemed to be asking Annette about Franz, she showed that she knew all about his financial resources and his family.

Annette, perfectly calm in all of her movements, while she was burning with anger within, strangely lucid about everything that surrounded her, deaf to what was roaring within her, rose quietly. Talking all the time, she examined the photographs on the piano; mechanically, she raised the lid of the instrument as if she wanted to see the maker's name; mechanically, to try it, her fingers ran over the keys. Her hands struck the keyboard. It was not merely the keyboard that was struck. Each of the three received the blow full in the breast. The intruder was whispering in their faces: "I am here."

An imperious gust of wind. Three powerful harmonies. Three cries of irritated passion. Then silence, a lament, rolling down from the peaks in the empty sky, like a train of clouds, in slow descending arpeggios, like a magic net that snared souls in its meshes as it sank.

Caught herself, in catching the others, Annette, leaning over the sonorous abyss, saw emerging from her thoughtless harmonies the *Lamento* that opens the overture of *Manfred*.

Franz hastened forward. A musician by heredity and by nature, he could not resist the magical appeal. Stirred to the depths, he looked at this Circe who was evoking the spirits.

For years Annette had scarcely played. She had been quite a virtuoso in her youth, but she had been obliged to sell her old piano, and her care-filled years, her incessant work, had only permitted her to practice occasionally. Since the war she had felt a sort of repugnance for music; it seemed to her that in yielding to it she was somehow wronging the universal suffering. When she happened to open a piano it was furtively, as if it were a lust of the flesh. But the hold it had upon her was all the stronger because her mind condemned it. At these moments music completely overthrew her; she lay as under the embrace of a lover, motionless, her mouth burning. She felt the torrent beating against her, bearing her away; she retained only enough clearness of mind to watch the shores slipping by and the giddy whirlpools. Her body was bound, paralyzed, and all her power of liberty took refuge in the expression of her eyes.

This troubled expression, this hard expression, at just this moment rose from the waves of the keyboard; it passed heavily over the circle of faces that were watching her; Franz, overcome with emotion, enthralled, the young girl consumed with anger and fear, the bewildered mother who was trying to understand. The glance searched them, while through the hands the demon of the soul spoke.

At that point in the prelude where a fever creeps into the elegiac *Lamento,* where the movement grows quicker, where the passion accumulates and elaboration of the music announces the rush of the flood—at that very second when the flood-gates open, Annette interrupted herself; her fingers stopped short on the crowded keys in the middle of the phrase, while the spirits of the harmonies prolonged their broken flight in the silence. Then the vibrations folded their wings and fell. Annette rose. She thought herself ridiculous.

Warmly and anxiously, Franz urged her to continue. Madame de Wintergrün, without warmth, politely forced herself to insist. Erika remained silent; there was a wicked expression about her mouth and her lips curled. Annette looked at them, smiling coldly, then she said: "I am going home. I am tired." She turned to the submissive Franz. "You will take me home."

As she went out, she saw the anguish and hatred in the young girl's eyes.

They walked along side by side under the frosty stars. They were silent. The gulf of space prolonged about them the gulf of the music. The Erebus of the night and the fiery Pisces. They did not utter a word until they reached the threshold of her door. Darkness. . . . They were part of the darkness. . . . He murmured: "Good night."

Then he saw before him the moving shadow that closed upon him. Their mouths rushed together.

Annette disappeared. He found himself alone before the closed door. He went home through the night.

She had climbed up the stairs without a thought.   She still had no thoughts.

It was cold; it was dark.   She was overwhelmed with fatigue, as if a flagstone had fallen upon her, and the dense rush of the night within her seemed to drown her in a pool of stifling blackness.   She undressed with heavy, hasty hands, without picking up the clothes she had taken off.   With her head on the pillow and the light out, she saw Charles's Wain in the black sky, and in her brain gleamed the lightning of things seen long ago, the past in the formless night. . . . As a stone breaks away. . . . Ah!   She was falling. . . .

But just at this moment (a moment?), the constriction of her heart roused her consciousness with a start.   She became aware of herself again, sitting upright in her bed, with her hands pressing her breasts, and crying: "No, it isn't possible! . . ."

What wasn't possible?   She waited until her pounding heart grew calm.   It became calm and began to beat again. And while she waited she saw Charles's Wain disappear under the horizon, one wheel only emerging over the summit of the mountain.   Soundlessly, her contracted fingers bruised her breast, as she continued to groan. "No!   It isn't possible!"

What wasn't?   She knew. . . .

"But have I deceived myself, then?   Have I allowed myself to be caught?   Again? . . .   Did I love him?"

That maternal tenderness with which she had deluded herself—she saw what it had masked!   So they were right, Marcel Franck, Sylvie, those Parisian roués, whose irony had detected the impurity that lay beneath her devotion!

"But God knows I wasn't thinking of myself; I gave

myself without expecting anything; I thought I was disinterested! And self-interest, like a thief, stole into the house. I was an accomplice. I pretended to be asleep. I heard the furtive footsteps of passion coming in. I said to myself: 'I love him for his own sake.' And I loved him for my own sake! I wanted to possess him! I wanted it! Ah, what mockery! Who was 'I'? Who 'wanted'? I, with my gray hair; I, with my body covered with the dust of the road, my useless experience and my sufferings, twenty years difference between my age and his—and how keenly this child must measure the difference! Shame and pity!"

She was overwhelmed with humiliation, but she raised her head indignantly. "Why? Did I want it? Did I seek it? Why was I stricken? Why was I burned? Why this thirst for love, this famished passion? Why was I given a heart that does not grow old in a body that is growing old?"

She crushed her breasts. This nature that clutched you like a spider, how strike at it? She wanted to make it bleed in her own flesh, but you cannot catch the ocean in a net.

She revolted. "I love. . . . I love. . . . I am worthy of loving still! The jealous fear of that girl told me so. I have taken possession of him, I hold him. It depends on me whether he shall be mine, if I wish it. I do wish it. I love him. It is my right."

Her right? The absurdity of the word struck her. Right, that fiction of man, that fabrication of man's society, that red standard of the revolting slave in the inexpiable war which, since the days of Prometheus, has always ended, always, in annihilation! That hypocrisy of the stronger who crushes the weaker, strikes him down,

while it waits to be struck down in turn! . . . In the
face of nature no right exists. An indifferent force feeds
upon the millions of the living. Annette was one of its
million victims. She could put off for a day, for an hour,
her defeat, at the expense of other victims. But the defeat was sure to come. And was it worth while putting it
off if the other victims had to suffer?

She cried: "Why not? One day, one hour of possession,
one instant—is that nothing? Eternity is in an instant,
as the universe is in one being. And the suffering of the
other victim, of the rival upon whom one avenges oneself,
is that nothing, is that nothing? Nothing, the happiness
that escapes you, that the thieving woman steals from you?
Steal it from her in her turn, make her suffer, destroy
her!"

A whirling flock of wild birds pounced down upon her
with raucous cries; sharp pride, the cruel joys of jealousy
and vengeance. She was deafened by the whirring of
their wings and their clamor. Whence had they come?

"All that in me?"

She had a feeling of both pride and fright, a burning
sensation as of molten lead, a joy in suffering that made
her swoon, a surfeit of agony. She did nothing to drive
the birds away. There was nothing she could do. As
if she lay dying in a field, she watched the mêlée of the
charnel-house birds, quarreling over her, their prey.
They were in two flocks, enemies and equals, the hunger
of Possession and the hunger of Sacrifice. For Sacrifice
has, like the other, a rapacious claw, a voracious beak, and
both the good and the evil—(Which was good? Which
was evil?)—bore the same livery of wild inhumanity.

With her arms folded, naked, stretched out, she lay
waiting like a torn beast under the whirling of the ravens.

And watching, she looked into herself. Nothing, neither fear nor passion, could have kept her from looking. She saw herself in her nakedness. And she saw that she had lied from the very first. She knew that she loved him, she had always known it. Since when? Since Germain had said: "Don't love him too much!"? Long before! Since the escape? Long before! Long before! And her astonishment just now, that virtuous astonishment in discovering her love which she had cherished so long.

"Actress! How you lie! . . ."

She laughed in her self-contempt. In the midst of her suffering her lucid irony reclaimed its rights. There were two in the dialogue: the sentimental part of her that resorted to deceit, and the severe and scoffing that pitilessly removed the mask—and clearly saw.

*
* *

But to perceive passion does not abridge it by a single hour and only renders it more bitter.

The night passed. The daylight drove away the butcher-birds. But they remained perching on the trees round about and continued to utter their threats. None of the flocks gave in. Each of them proclaimed its right. Worn out, stunned, Annette got up. She had decided nothing. There was a roaring in her ears. She sat down and waited.

Until Franz appeared. Through the window, she saw him coming along the road. She had known that he would come.

He came up to the door. He looked at the door. He hesitated. He went by. Thirty paces beyond, he stopped and came back. Through the curtains she saw his anxious features, his burning uncertainty, his confusion. Reaching the door, he paused and stepped forward as if to enter. But he did not enter. His eyes rose towards the window where Annette quickly moved back. She heard nothing now but the tumult of the two hearts. But her own was growing calmer; its great, slow, long beats were finding their equilibrium. She saw him from beneath her closed eyelids: his anxiety, his desire, his weakness. She felt grateful to him. She was sorry for him and a little contemptuous.

When, after a few minutes, she made up her mind to look out over the road again he was no longer there. But she felt certain that he had stopped at some turn of the road, that he was watching the threshold of her door, waiting for her to come out.

Then there came from the sky a sound of heavy wings. The birds were going away. The flock that preyed upon her soul had left her. And her soul was like a dismantled house. The door was open and creatures from without entered. Anguish entered, the shrunken face of Erika de Wintergrün, Franz's blind desire. Annette knew now the extent of her power over these weak children. And she used it. Against herself.

Against herself, but not for them. She studied them with a cold clarity that was trying to judge impartially. But the judgment was harsh, seeking equity without kindness. She weighed Erika and Franz without indulgence. It was in vain, she thought, that she strove to be completely disinterested, to no longer consider anything but the chances the other two had of being happy together. There were plenty of interstices through which her ebbing self-interest demanded its rights again. It did not find Mlle. de Wintergrün beautiful. It did not believe her good. On the state of her health its diagnostic was sharp, harshly pessimistic. It examined her in her nakedness. This was not the woman she would have desired for Franz. Would have desired? What irony! On the other hand, it was no more tender towards him. It passed him through a sieve. How much was lost! It had no confidence in his character. It estimated severely the constancy of his feelings. It could give the future of such a union only a limited credit. But was it really reason alone that was speaking?

The day slipped by. Annette remained in her room the whole morning. She had not in any respect made up her mind. She postponed that for a future hour. Enough of thought! She made herself a blank.

Silence.

Towards the middle of the afternoon she rose and went out. Resolutely her steps carried her to Mlle. de Wintergrün's house.

She found her alone in her drawing-room. The young girl's heart was beating fast, though she did not allow anything to be seen. Her heart shrank. Impeccably dressed, as if she had been expecting the call, helmeted in her pale golden hair, neatly arranged, without a lock in disorder, her brow clear, obstinate, arched, her expression proud and reserved, Erika rose without haste. Responding with a brief "Good afternoon" to Annette's greeting, she smilingly and coldly pointed her to a chair. She was prepared for a battle. But the expert eye of the other knew how to strip people's souls. While they were exchanging commonplace courtesies, this eye saw the narrow throat contracting. The aggressive smile of the young girl shriveled in the crooked corner of her lips; she was unable to control the trembling of her pale mouth, her jerky speech, her anxiety, her spitefulness, her fear, her bitterness. Annette enjoyed it all slowly, consciously, remorselessly; she knew now what the rest of the story was going to be. But the rest of the story depended on her alone, and she was in no haste. They talked about clothes, the new dances, the country, the affairs of the day. And with the tip of her tongue Annette delicately moistened her lips.

She became silent; she was going to take her time. Erika, tensely on guard, was searching the silence for dissimulation, for a trap. Then, having turned over on her tongue the bitter flower of the suspense of these last seconds, Annette, sure in advance of the effect of what she was going to say, enjoying in advance her own compassionate irony, said composedly:

"I am going away again to-morrow morning."

A blush spread over Mlle. de Wintergrün's face. Even the brow reddened, and the tips of her ears were like drops of blood. She lost control of herself; she could not conceal the mad emotion that held her in its grip.

For the first time since her arrival, Annette smiled. Erika, furtively watching her, filled with fear, still defiant, and suspecting some trick, saw that there was nothing hostile in her smile. Annette was contemplating her, still not without irony; but the irony was full of pity. She was thinking: "How she loves him!"

In her confusion Mlle. de Wintergrün bowed her head, and suddenly she leaned her cheek against Annette's arm. Annette placed her hand on the frail neck, the delicate hair, and stroked them with a little affectionate smile. For Annette, now, the girl was only a disarmed child. There was no longer any question of defiance between them. Erika raised her eyes humbly, gratefully, happily. And in her heart Annette said to her: "Be happy!"

Each was reading the other's mind. And they no longer felt shame in having been divined, for they were both needing to be forgiven.

Then Annette asked: "When are you going to be married? It shouldn't be delayed too long."

And she talked to her about Franz. She described him with a lucid affection, and she warned her of the dangers that might be in store for her. Erika was not unaware of them, she was too clear-sighted. They talked without any dissimulation, holding each other's hands. Erika did not conceal what she saw in Franz and her doubts about him, but she showed an iron determination to take and hold this fascinating, fugitive soul which she desired. She accepted in advance all the secret battles, the vigils, the anxious days with which she would have to pay for

the happiness she had conquered, a happiness which would
always have to be reconquered, which would never be
held captive.

As she talked, Annette stroked the girl's nervous hand.
She felt the fierce energy this amorous creature would
have been ready, a moment before, to direct against her,
to defend at any price her threatened happiness, that joy
in living which this invalid, wounded by life, had ceased
to expect.

She thought: "It's just."

She said to herself: "This hand will be able to hold and
lead the man I have entrusted to it."

Erika, with those arctic, blue-green, almost lashless
eyes, under their pale brows, still a little shy, furtively
examined the cheeks, the mouth, the chin, the throat, the
hands of Annette.

"She is beautiful. She is very beautiful."

Her instinct, ripened by her long illness, saw that renunciation was hard for this woman, that it wasn't even
just. But this was only for a moment.

"Just or not, I shall have my happiness!"

Annette rose. She said: "You must send him to me.
I want to talk to him."

For a second Mlle. de Wintergrün hesitated. She was
suspicious again. She gave a startled look at her rival,
who was gazing at her. She saw that Annette was demanding complete confidence. She was obliged to trust
her or break with her. She decided to trust her. And
she said submissively: "I will send him to you."

For a last time the two women looked at each other
fraternally. And on the threshold they exchanged a kiss
of peace.

*
* *

An hour later Franz came.

He was not surprised that Erika had sent him to Annette. He was not used to thinking of other people's feelings; his own absorbed him, and they were very changeable. But even if he had taken the time to study the two women, he would have thought it quite natural that both should be in love with him. It created no obligation for him, he quite sincerely felt. He was always sincere, with that terrible sincerity of a human being who lives only from moment to moment. But he himself never suffered from it.

At the moment he was only thinking of his recent discovery: the hands on the magician's keyboard, the embrace at the door of the house, under the sky. He arrived in a very emotional state, ablaze with feeling, convinced of his good fortune. He was a little timid, and at the same time naïvely vain. And the coldness of Annette's first words disconcerted him.

She did not ask him to sit down. She received him standing, glancing into the mirror, patting her hair, and said: "Let's go out!"

They took a mountain road over which they had walked many a time. They were both good walkers and they strode along at a great pace. Annette was silent. Franz, nonplussed at first, soon recovered his equilibrium. He was gay, light-hearted, enchanted with his new toys, these two women of whose love he felt so certain. How these two loves could be harmonized was a minor question that did not trouble him. He was quite unconscious of his egotism and so filled with himself that, without in the

least wishing to provoke Annette's jealousy, he enumer-
ated to her the perfections of Mlle. de Wintergrün and
frankly delighted in the good fortune that had led him
to this place where he had found his happiness.

Annette's heart contracted and her lips were on the
point of saying: "For this good fortune another person
has paid with his life."

But she did not want to revive this painful memory.
She merely said: "It would have made Germain happy."
Even this was too much. Franz was vexed. He didn't
like to think of that just now. But as he was obliged to
think of it, the shadow of a sincere regret passed over his
face. But it didn't last very long. That ingenious faculty
of escaping from anything that disturbed his peace of mind
seized upon Annette's words and he said:

"Yes, what happiness it would have been to share it
with him!"

His sorrow and his joy were equally sincere; but when
the phrase was uttered only the joy remained. And the
friend's name was not spoken. Annette thought of the
disillusioned remark of the dead man:

"When forgetfulness is slow in coming, one goes to
meet it."

Franz began to prattle again like an amorous poet.
Amorous of whom? He had both of them in mind. But
Annette's presence absorbed his thoughts much more than
the image of the one of whom he was speaking. He could
not take his eyes away from her. His eyes caressed her,
he drank the air over her footsteps. And suddenly he
stopped, arrested by something in the landscape that had
caught the greedy attention of the artist in him; and he
fell into an ecstasy over the outlines of this landscape, their
harmonious nuances. Annette did not stop. She walked

on, proud, inattentive, without turning her head, her eyebrows raised. She felt an irritated disdain for these in-
consistent artistic spirits in whom every minute banishes
the preceding minute, and through whom life and death
pass as through a sieve.

She clambered up a steep slope that led to a rocky platform, narrow and elongated, shaped like a saddle. In
one breath she ran up it. Above, the sky was clear and
hard, like Mlle. de Wintergrün's eyes, but the spring
wind, sweeping fresh and strong over the peaks, streamed
across the slope, bending the stems of the long grasses. It
beat Annette's face and that of her companion. In the
hollow made by a landslip, in the shelter of a little wood
of dwarfed and twisted trees, they sat down on the mountain slope. The pastures fell away steeply towards a
stream at the bottom. About them the circle of the white-
metal sky, hemmed in at the edges by a fringe of sombre
clouds, drifted like waves breaking on the cliffs of the
peaks.

Annette sat down on the wild mint and the stubble,
warmed by the last rays of the setting sun. Her cheeks
had turned purple under the lash of the cold north wind
and under the gale of anger that had risen in her heart.
Side by side with Franz, she did not look at him; she
looked straight in front of her, her head high, with a
grimace of smiling disdain. She radiated strength and
pride. Franz studied her and his prattling ceased. There
was a burning silence. From the scornful distance to
which she had retired, she became aware of the fire in the
glance he fixed upon her body. She continued to smile.
But a final gust of passion broke over her, like the wind
breaking over the heads of the trees which she saw without looking at them: "So, you have discovered me at last!"

And silently addressing the absent rival, down there, below her feet, whose infirm limbs would have not been able to climb the steep slope, she cried out: "I have him . . . if I wish! Come and get him back!"

But she did not wish it.

A wave of blood passed before her eyes, with the fire of the setting sun, then the silent frenzy fell as the sun slipped behind the mountains. She shivered for an instant, rose, stood up on the plateau, in the wind, and turned to Franz, who was following her like a dog. The young man's eyes watched her, imploring her for a glance, but, catching one at last, they met nothing but a distant coldness. Annette saw his discomfiture and smiled. Then, unbending, she studied him with a calm, maternal benevolence.

"Franz," she said, "you are not bad at heart but you cause a great deal of harm. Do you know it? It is time you did know it, my boy. You are not the only one. I, too. We all cause harm as an apple-tree produces apples. But we must eat this fruit of our tree alone. Don't give it to others!"

Discountenanced, he tried to escape the meaning of these words, and the glance that looked him through, but the glance was firm and the words pierced him. His malleable nature submitted to the imprint of every strong hand. How long would such impressions last? Annette was under no great illusion, but she knew that she held him in her hand and she kneaded this heart with a tender severity. There was something sweet in feeling under her fingers, for the first time, the trembling weakness of this living clay.

"Erika loves you," she said, "and you love her. Very well. But be careful, for you have a dangerous capacity

for causing those who love you to suffer. In all innocence,
of course! That's the worst thing about it! You must
unlearn it. You know that I have all too much affection
for you. I can't lie, and why should I lie? You know
what I am telling you. I look upon you as a son—something
more perhaps. I want you to be happy. But I
would rather see you unhappy all your life than playing
with love and wounding, out of sheer light-headedness,
this child who has been entrusted to you. She brings you
infinitely more than you are giving her, everything she
has, her whole self. As for you, you can only give part
of yourself. You men keep the best part, the lion's share,
for that caged monster, that ogre, your brain, for your
visions, your ideas, your art, your ambition, your action.
I don't blame you for it. If I were you I should do the
same thing. . . . But this portion you give us must be
pure! It must be sure! Don't take it back when you
give it! No cheating! We ask little of you, but that
little we want! Are you sure you are able to give it to
her? Sound your nature, test your heart! You desire
her? You love her? Take her! But be taken yourself!
Gift for gift! Learn to take and keep—and to endure!
Cloudy soul! Windy spirit!"

He had stopped short, his head lowered under these
harsh words and these eyes in which a smile was stirring.
Then laughing outright, she loosed her grip and said:
"Let's go back."

They climbed down in silence. She led the way. His
eyes were fastened upon the golden-brown back of her
head. He wished the descent would never end.

Before they reached the first houses, Annette stopped.
She turned and held out her hands to him. Just as on
that first evening in the prison-camp, he bent over them

and covered them with kisses. Annette withdrew them, placed them on Franz's shoulders, looked him in the eyes and said:

"Good-by, my child!"

She went home alone, and she did not wait till the following morning, as she had promised. She left that night.

The next day, Erika and Franz came to bid her farewell. They found the cage empty. They were very sorry, and they were relieved.

*

* *

PART V

NNETTE did not take the train to Paris. She stopped *en route* at an out-of-the-way station where no one would think of looking for her. She was in a state of collapse. She had to retrieve her losses alone. She had to regain her bearings. The fatigue of the last months had suddenly overwhelmed her. That continued tension, that final shock which had reawakened the poignant sense of her irremediable age and the vain need of love, the complete love that she had never had. A melancholy that was without form and utterly exhausting. All this gift of herself— what had been the use of it? Now that she had given everything and given up everything she found herself terribly free. Her ties were broken. And how could she hold herself if they did not hold her? She had nothing left to cling to. The worst of all was that she was no longer *she*. She no longer believed in herself, she no longer believed in her belief in humanity. That was the worst disaster! How much worse than not to believe in humanity itself? When a faith is lost, the vigorous soul makes another, rebuilds its nest. But when your soul itself abandons you? It had turned to sand, it had collapsed. In her passionate sincerity the uncompromising Annette stamped her own brow with the seal of falsehood. Humanity had filled her mouth, but behind the curtain egotism, the greedy heart, had lain in wait for its prey.

329

Humanity, for her, was man. Man, that amiable, insignificant first-comer. How ridiculous! She had thrown away her energy upon him in transports of faith and devotion—and all those dangers, her own and those of the others whom she had drawn into danger with her—to go and let herself be caught by such a bait! Her enthusiastic sacrifice, for that lure, that boy (he or another, it was all chance)—she had dressed him up as an idol, decked out her desire, that her pleasure might be complete, with that tinsel finery of faith, of ideas, with that sacred name, that false name of humanity.

She was in a rage. She slandered herself. Bowing down, with her chin upon her clenched hands, her elbows drawn back, she pressed her sides in the humiliation of her defeat.

She had found a burrow in a little town in the midst of open country. She did not even know its name. She had stopped off there in the night, quite by chance, and had entered the first inn she had happened upon. It was one of those great Bernese hostelries with a vast roof overhanging the smallest of windows, with divided panes, filled with flowering geraniums.

Behind this red screen, in the shadow of a large pentroof, her agitated soul slowly regained its calm, and slipped back into its accustomed path, though more than once it bruised itself against the enclosing barriers. In vain she said to herself: "That's enough! I throw down my arms. I defend myself no longer. I am vanquished. I accept it. Haven't you had enough?"

She had not had enough. Nature reminds you, by sudden attacks, that the treaty is not valid until she has signed it. For more than one day Annette had to resume the combat against the triple grief of that absurd passion, that eternal subjection, that spent youth, the illusory fire, the mocking stake, the ashes of life. Morning found her worn out, mute, obliterated, after the frenzies of the night. She was not the only one. How many calm figures there are that seem, during the day, torpid and remote, while behind the curtains the battle with the soul goes on every night!

At last she reached the end of her reckoning. She was bankrupt. She laid aside her balance-sheet. Against this humanity flushed with hatred, that tore itself and bayed after death, she had wanted to oppose her woman's soul, free and alone, resisting hatred, resisting death, sanctifying life and, without wishing to make a choice between the hostile brothers, opening its motherly arms to all its children. It was all arrogance. She had overestimated herself. She was not free. She did not have the strength to be alone. She was not the mother who forgets herself for her children. She had forgotten her own child, the child of her blood. She was the eternal dissembling slave who secretly and avidly follows her desire like a dog. That beautiful disinterestedness! Her idealism was nothing but the bait that nature had used to make her enter the kennel under the whip. She was not big enough to free herself from the whipper-in.

"Well, so be it! I must learn to be humble now. I have wished . . . I have not been able. . . . But it is something, at least, to have wished! I have not been able. Some day, perhaps, another, a better, a stronger, can . . .

Defeated, and accepting her defeat, though this was not to say that she might not revolt in future, she decided to return to Paris.

In her railway-carriage she found herself alone with

two men, two Frenchmen. One was a young lieutenant
who was wounded in the face, with a black band over his
eyes and his head bandaged. A hospital attendant accompanied him, a robust, indifferent countryman who had lost
all feeling for suffering. (He had seen so much of it!)
After roughly arranging a place for his patient in a corner,
he paid no more attention to him. He began eating
slices of ham, drinking out of a bottle he carried with
him. Then, taking off his clumsy boots, he stretched out
at full length on the seat opposite and began to snore.
The wounded man was sitting on the seat with Annette.
She saw him grope about, rise painfully, search in the net
above his head and, not finding what he wanted, sit down
again with a sigh.

"You are looking for something? Can I help you?"

He thanked her. He wanted a powder to quiet the
shooting pains in his forehead. She brought it to him
in a little water. It was impossible for either of them
to sleep. They tried to talk, amid the roaring of the train,
as it jolted along. Sitting beside the sick man, she did
her best to shield him against the shocks, and she stretched
a coverlet over his chilly knees. He felt revived by this
compassionate presence. And as most of the wretched do,
when a pitying woman bends over them, he very soon
began to confide in her like a child. He told her what
he had never told any man—what he would not have
told her perhaps if he had been able to see her.

A ball had gone through his temples, from one side to
the other. He had been left for two days, blind, on
the battle-field. Slowly the light had seemed to come
back. And then it waned again. It had gone out for
good and all. Losing it, he had lost everything. He was
a painter. It was his joy and his livelihood. And he was

not sure that even his brain was not affected. He was living in torture.

But this was nothing. In his night, he wept, without tears, sweating blood. He had nothing left. Everything had been taken away from him. He had gone into the war without any feeling of hatred, through love for his own people, for humanity, for the world, for sacred ideas. He was going to put an end to war. He was going to free humanity from it. Even his enemies. He had dreamed of bringing them liberty. He had given everything. He had lost everything. The world had made sport of him. He had seen too late the enormous iniquity, the ignoble calculations of those who played at politics— in which he had been a mere pawn on the chess-board. He had ceased to believe in anything. He had been tricked. And he lay there, broken, with no desire even to revolt. . . . To sink down as swiftly as possible into the quick-sand, where one ceased to exist, where one no longer even remembered that one had existed—at the bottom of the abyss of eternal oblivion!

He talked without emotion, almost without feeling, in a dull, tired voice that filled Annette with a sense of sisterly grief. Ah, how like they were in their wholly dissimilar destinies! This man who had seen in the war nothing but love, as she had seen nothing but hatred,— and both sacrificed, to whom, to what? The tragic insanity of all these sacrifices! And in spite of everything, in spite of everything, in the excess of the bitterness of it —(in the presence of such a disaster she scarcely dared to confess it to herself)—what a tragic pleasure! No, it is not for nothing that we are lacerated, stamped upon and crushed, like a bunch of grapes! And even if it is for nothing, is it nothing to be the wine? That Force which

drinks us—what would it be without us?   What a terrifying grandeur!

Leaning over the blind man, she said, in a low, burning
voice: "All devotions are betrayed. Perhaps . . .
Well, it is better to be betrayed than to betray. I have
been so too. I am going to begin again. And you?"

The words struck home. "I shall also!"

They clasped hands.

"At least, we two have not thriven on the deceit. It is
beautiful to be deceived."

The train stopped. Dijon. The attendant, waking up,
went off to the buffet to get some refreshments. Annette
saw the wounded man trying to lift his bandage.

"What are you doing? Don't touch it!"

"No, let me!"

"What do you want?"

"To see you before the night comes for me."

He had got the bandage off, only to groan: "Too late!
I can't see you."

He hid his face in his hands. Annette said to him:
"My poor boy! You would not see me any better with
your eyes. I didn't need mine to understand you. Touch
my hands! Our hearts have touched."

He gripped her wrist as if he were afraid to lose her.
He said: "Speak again! Speak to me! Speak!"

For his dead eyes the voice was like a silhouette on the
wall. He gazed at it greedily while Annette spread out
in miniature the image of the forty years of hopes and
desires, renunciations, defeats and recommencements—
the forty years of reality and dream (everything is a
dream) that had left their stamp on her face.

"Yes, they have modeled it well," he thought. "The
soul is overflowing."

He saw it now, the most beautiful of his pictures. He alone saw it.

She stopped speaking. They said no more until the night was over. Just before they arrived she withdrew her hand, which she had left in his, and said: "I am only a companion in your misery. But I bless your poor eyes. I bless your body and your thoughts, your sacrifice and your goodness. And you, in turn, must bless me. When the Father forgets his children, the children must be fathers to one another."

*

* *

Marc had received, one morning, the telegram announcing his mother's return. His heart leapt with excitement. Since Annette's departure she had only sent him a line on a post-card, on her arrival in Switzerland. He had written to her every day. But Annette had not read one of his letters. They were stranded at the *poste restante* of the little Swiss town which Annette had left the day following her arrival; and in her confusion she had not thought of leaving an address or having anything forwarded. This silence, which he thought was intentional, struck a chill into him.

He was living in the abandoned apartment. In spite of Sylvie's entreaties, he had refused to live with her again. He insisted that he was old enough to live by himself. He remained there with the absent one. She was all about him, but he tried in vain to regather her invisible traces upon these objects, this furniture, these books, her bed. He suffered from the indifference his mother had shown him. But he was not angry with her because of it; for the first time in his life he did not resent a wrong that had been done to him. He was angry with himself; he said to himself over and over that she had once been his and that he had allowed her to be carried away. His heart was chilled. He went and placed his head on her pillow so that he could think of her better. And the more he thought of her the more he felt the difference between her and all the others whom he loved.

He had tried to take up again some of his friendships. He had made things up with Pitan, wishing to find out what was at the bottom of his mind. Ah, how fantastic

it was, that bottom! That faith, that heroism, that dog-
like devotion—how utterly they lacked the personal note!
What darkness, what a reflected light! When one tried
to get him to explain himself, to follow exactly the thread
of his phantom-like thought, one saw the water-spaniel,
pointing, his eyes glued to the brilliant words: one might
have beaten him to death where he stood without his moving his round, glassy eyes. (Needless to say, Marc was unjust. He was so by nature. Like every one for whom
to love is to prefer, Justice was the last thing he thought
of. Marc had no liking for people who were slaves of
constraint. This little Diogenes was in search of a man
who was Man, a man who was himself, every moment of
his life, and not an echo. And women were not to be
thought of! They were the eternal servers-of-the-master.
They found all their pleasure in catching others, intwined
with themselves, in the sticky snare of the illusion of the
Species, that blind, big-bellied monster.

But there was one person at least (or perhaps he imagined it?) who, as far back as he could remember, had
fought against the snare, ripping it to pieces, escaping,
and, though captured again, never giving up the struggle,
—his mother! In these days of lonely self-communion,
shut up in the empty apartment, which she seemed to
have abandoned forever, he strove with all his might to
reascend the river of memory, to reconstruct the existence
of that woman during the last years, that solitary life,
unknown in its sufferings and joys, the passions and the
combats that peopled it. For he had now discovered
enough about that soul to know that it was not empty for
a single moment. He had left her alone, in her inner
world: what rights had he at present over this world? She
was used to fighting alone, to conquering, to being con-

quered, and she pursued her way alone. Where was this
road leading her now—far from him? He was thinking
so much of this, he was thinking so much of her that he
no longer thought of himself. He only wanted to smooth
her road if he could.

This was the state of mind into which the telegram fell.
Like one of those explosions that punctuated the days of
the besieged city. He read it over and over to convince
himself that it was true. This return, which he had ceased
to hope for, filled him with a fearful joy. What was
bringing her back? He carefully refrained from thinking that it was for his sake. The last disappointments
had made him modest. A superstitious sentiment whispered to him the belief that the best means of obtaining
what one desires is not to expect it.

Annette, on her arrival, did not find her son waiting
for her. The train was eight hours late; it did not reach
the Gare de Lyon till the middle of the afternoon. Marc
had come and gone away again, discouraged, after a long
wait. But he did not go home to stay. When at last Annette reached the house he had just left. He had hurried back to the station again. She climbed up to her
apartment and waited for him there. It touched her to
see that he had put some flowers in her bedroom. She sat
down and rested her head on the back of her chair. Very
tired, she listened anxiously to the sounds of the street and
the house. She felt drowsy. In a haze she heard a step
climbing the staircase at a run. Marc entered. As he
opened the door of the apartment he uttered a cry of joy.
Annette, still in a torpor, smiled, thinking: "Is it possible
that he loves me?"

She made an effort to get up and meet him. Her legs

gave way. She was in her chair again when he rushed into the room. She held out her arms to him. He threw himself into them:

"Ah, how I have been waiting for you! How did you come?"

She did not answer. She stroked his cheeks and his hair. At a glance he saw the fatigue and pain on the exhausted face, and an instinct warned him. He did not ask her any more questions, he stopped the words that were on his lips. In his embrace he had lifted her out of her seat. (How strong he had become all of a sudden! While she, how weak she was!) She found her feet and, leaning upon him, took a few steps with him towards the window. The yellow twilight discolored her features.

"You must go to bed at once," he said.

She protested, but her head was swimming, and she allowed herself to be led, almost carried, to her bed. He forced her to lie down, took off her shoes, helped her to undress. She did not resist. It was good to surrender herself to some one who willed for her and loved her.

Loved her? Then he did love her? She was tired of thinking! She would put it off till the next day. He was glad enough to have a reason for waiting to explain himself. One question alone was urgent. He turned it over on his tongue. He had not yet uttered it when his mother, in bed, apologized for being so tired.

"It is shameful to come and let oneself be coddled! Forgive me, my dear! I, who used to be so strong! But I can't stand up any longer. I haven't slept for several nights. Sit down beside me. Tell me what you have been doing to-day, how you missed me when I arrived."

He told her confusedly of his comings and goings. She did not follow the thread of his phrases. Before long, even the meaning of the words escaped her; but the sound of his voice soothed her. Her eyes closed. She fell asleep. He stopped talking, got up, looked at her, and reluctantly stole out of the room. His question was still burning him. He came in again, hesitantly, and leaned over the sleeper. She opened her eyes again. He arranged her pillow awkwardly and hastily asked: "Are you going to stay, this time?"

Not understanding him, she looked at him in surprise. He asked her again, trying to seem unconstrained: "Are you going to stay?"

She smiled: "I am going to stay."

And she fell back, asleep.

He walked out, relieved.

*
* *

He had left the door of her room ajar. He heard his mother's regular breathing. He said to himself: "She is there. . . . I have her. . . . There is time enough."

During this night there was another alarm of enemy aëroplanes. The sirens began to screech, and the usual commotion followed among the inhabitants of the house as they got out of bed and ran downstairs. Marc sprang up and went into his mother's room. She was sleeping so well that he decided not to awaken her. He thought: "The bomb can fall now. We are together."

On the other nights when the alarm had sounded and he was alone he had vainly put on a bold front; he had been afraid. But this time (Why?) it was almost a pleasure.

The following morning, Sylvie, who was anxious about him, dropped in. She called him "little cur" when she found that Annette had arrived. (He had jealously concealed the telegram from her in order to have his mother all to himself, the first day.) But Annette was still asleep, and Marc stood like a dragon at the door of the bedroom. The noise of their dispute woke her and Sylvie came in. She had a great deal to say, but at the first glance she, too, saw that many rains and winds had agitated her Rivière, and wisely, as always, when there was any question of the welfare of those she loved, she avoided speaking of anything that might disturb her. Her experience of life had taught her that when a soul is stirred to its depths the first remedy is to leave it alone, so that little by little the sand may sink, by itself, to the bottom. She laughed at Annette for the heavy sleep that had kept her from hear-

ing the explosions of the night, and she scolded that little
beast of a Marc who had persisted in sleeping in his
mother's apartment ever since Annette's departure, instead
of staying with her.   She pretended to suspect him of
plotting nocturnal escapades, but he grew angry, said he
had given his word to behave, and that he would allow no
one to question it.   If he had wanted to amuse himself
against Sylvie's wishes he was old enough to have told
her so to her face.   He was sorry at once that he had
spoken so before his mother, and he went out ashamed.
After he had gone, Sylvie said proudly to Annette: "What
an obstinate boy!   How like us he is!"

Annette asked herself: "Is he really like me?"

She tried to resume her household work, but the lacera-
tion her feelings had undergone was not effaced for a
long time.   She was exhausted very quickly.   Marc did
what he could to lighten her labor.   He was not obtrusive,
but he was always there to save her from overtasking herself, to move the furniture or climb the step-ladder to put
up a curtain.   These attentions were something new—for
him, as for her.   Like all very sincere people, he was
afraid that he was exhibiting too much zeal, a sort of family hypocrisy.   Consequently, he was very careful to appear very detached in everything he did.   Annette,
touched, embarrassed, would end her thanks more coolly
than she had begun them.   They both held themselves on
an expectant, attentive, affectionate level, speaking little,
observing each other out of the corners of their eyes. . . .
Was the other going to speak?   Each feared that if he
spoke first he would again be disappointed.   Marc still
avoided questioning his mother about her journey to
Switzerland and her sudden return.   And if, sometimes
unawares, she fell into one of her dejected reveries, he

became silent and turned away his eyes, as if through a modest apprehension of reading her thoughts. He would even withdraw into the adjoining room so as not to embarrass her. But when Annette asked her son about what he had done during her absence, he was pained by certain questions to which he had replied in advance in his letters. If she had read them so carelessly, she couldn't love him very much.

She would still have been ignorant of the existence of those poor letters if Sylvie had not told her about them. Sylvie, who came to see how the "little ménage," as she called it, was getting on, and who had sworn, so as to leave to them the whole joy and the whole pain, not to intervene in the mutual discovery of these two hearts that understood each other so little, thought they were very slow about it. She tried to help them out of their little difficulty. One day, when Marc was out, she jokingly referred to them as lovers. Annette protested.

"I'm not talking about you, hard heart," said Sylvie, laughing. "You like to make people suffer. It's your rôle."

"Oh, you're a fine one to talk!" said Annette.

Sylvie stuck to her subject, she went on: "But your little lover wrote to you every day you were away."

Annette did not hear anything else she said. He had written to her every day! It had never occurred to her to go for those letters that had been left lying way off there! Yes, Sylvie spoke the truth, she had a hard heart. She wrote at once to bring the exiles back. But Marc mustn't know anything about it! The packet mustn't get into his hands through the post! Annette watched for the mail. It was days in coming, but by good luck she was able to snatch the letters from the hand of the con-

cierge just ahead of Marc who was only a few steps behind her. She waited until he had gone out before she
read them.

There were eight of them, a treasure! As she read the
first lines, Annette's eyes were filled with tears. She
wanted to read them all at once, and she could not read
them at all. She made up her mind at first to arrange
them in order and read them slowly, one by one, but she
was unable to stick to her decision. She devoured them
at one gulp, at random, racing ahead, leaping over the
lines, stopping, greedily going back to the tender phrases.
Afterwards, when her first hunger was a little appeased,
she was able to place them in their proper order and she
lingered over them with delight. She blushed with love
and confusion. What a wrong she had done him!

Not that he was effusive. He loathed sentimentality.
(All the more because he was afraid he was infected by
it.) Even in his letters he stiffened himself against the
tender words that were on the tip of his tongue. But for
a mother who knew him so well this self-imposed restraint
was all the more touching. He even avoided using the
word "dear" in writing to her. His first letter said:

"My mother, you do not love me. . . ." (Annette's
heart shrank.) "I don't love myself any more. I have
done nothing to make any one love me, so it's only just.
But I am your son all the same! And I feel closer to you
than to any one else. I have not been able to tell you so.
Let me write it to you! I need a friend. I haven't one.
I have nobody. I need to believe that you are one, even
if you are not. Don't answer this! I don't want you to
tell me that you are, out of kindness or pity. I detest
kindness. I don't want to be humiliated. I don't want

to be deceived. I don't love you because you are good.
I don't know whether you are good. I love you because
you are sincere. Don't answer this! Whatever you think
of me, you are my friend; and I must tell you so in writing. Even if my mother is not my friend I am writing
to my friend. I am not writing to my mother. I must
confide in some one. My heart is heavy. I am too lonely,
I am too stupid! Help me! I know that you help others.
You can surely help me too! Just by listening to me. I
don't ask you for any reply. I have a great deal to tell
you. I am not what I used to be. For a year I have been
changing, I have been changing. In beginning this letter
I wanted to tell you about what I have been doing this
year, about what has changed me. But I don't dare now:
there are too many shameful things to tell. I am afraid
of alienating you all the more, and you are already so
far away! But I must tell you everything some day, even
if you despise me. I should despise myself still more
if I did not tell you. I shall tell you. But later. Some
other day. This is enough for to-day. I have given you
enough to-day. I embrace you, my friend."

This tone of imperious love tightened Annette's heart,
disturbed her, mastered her. The letters that followed
showed the same indomitable, violent spirit. He could
not make up his mind to confide to her whatever it was
that weighed most heavily upon him. In each letter he
said:

"Will it be this time? No, I can't yet. I absolutely
cannot. I need to forget that you are a woman. My
friend . . . Will you be my friend? Can you? You
are a woman. And I distrust women. I haven't much of

an opinion of them. Forgive me! With you it's different. But it hasn't been for very long! Up to this last year I thought you were like the others. I had an affection for you (I have not shown it to you), for all that I owe you; but I had no confidence in you. That is changed now. A great many things have changed, many things that I have seen, that I have learned, that I believe I have divined. In you, in me, in other people . . . You see, I have learned much . . . too much! And, among all these things, things that are not beautiful, and that have hurt me. But I say to myself that it is better that I should know them, because they are true. The world is ugly. I haven't much of an opinion of women. I despise men. And I despise myself. But I respect you. I have learned to see you. I have learned about you things that you have not told me (you haven't told me much!) and that my aunt has told me. And I have learned more about others which my aunt has not told me because she is not aware of them. She is a good woman, but she doesn't understand these things. I do understand them. (Or I think I do. . . . No! . . . I am sure!) And this has made me understand many things in myself which I could not explain. . . . Ah, how confused all this is, all this I have written!"

His pen, in his vexation, stuck and dug holes in the paper.

"How difficult it is to express oneself, at a distance or nearby! One's tongue gets tied into knots. It seems to me that I could explain myself better if I had you before me. But again, no! I don't know. Your eyes, when you look at me, indulgently, protectingly or mock-

ingly, madden me . . . or else they are absent-minded.
. . . You are thinking of other things. Look at me, into
my heart, straight to the bottom, look at me as your son, as
your friend, as a man!"

Annette saw this look gazing at her, exacting and severe,
and she turned away her eyes, intimidated. Her son, a
man! That had never occurred to her. A mother always
sees the child in her child. In these boyish letters, abrupt,
uncertain, angry, she caught the tone of a master. And,
as in ancient times, when the widowed mother fell under
the guardianship of her oldest son, she bent her head.

But she soon raised it again.

"My son. The man whom I have made. My work.
He is my equal."

*
* *

She went on reading in the darkness, without having observed that the night had come. He came in again. With a turn of her hand she swept the letters from the table and tossed them under it. She did not want him to catch her reading them. She had sworn to herself not to confess to him that she had not read them before.

He was surprised to find her without a light and was going to turn it on. She stopped him. They walked over to the window and stood there talking awkwardly. They looked down into the street: the house-fronts gleamed with lights, shadows hurried by. They were embarrassed. She was trying to get in order this new stream of hitherto unsuspected feelings. He was distrustful of her, filled with a secret bitterness because she had never alluded to any of those things he had told her. They talked coldly and confusedly, with many pauses. He told her what he had heard during the afternoon: the news, the war, the battles, the deaths. Nothing interesting! She did not even listen.

And suddenly in the silence she threw her arms about him.

He submitted, frozen with astonishment.

She said to him: "Turn on the light!"

He pressed the button of the electric lamp. And he saw the letters strewn over the floor. She showed them to him. She confessed everything to him, everything which, the moment before, she had resolved to hide from him. She begged his pardon. And she said: "My friend . . ."

But he was no longer the man who had displayed in his

letters an irritated pride. He was a little boy, running into his bedroom to hide his emotion.

She did not follow him. She had to conquer her own feelings. Standing on the same spot where he had left her, she was as silent as he was on the other side of the partition.

Sylvie's arrival broke the spell that bound them. The three of them dined together; but Sylvie, who was always on watch, did not divine what they were thinking. They were calm and distant.

After she had left, however, they still sat on at the table. Hand in hand, they spent hours unbosoming themselves to each other in whispers. And they continued to do so later, from one room to the other, when they at last decided to go to bed. Then, in the middle of the night, he got up and went in his bare feet into Annette's room. He sat down in a low chair by her bedside. They did not talk any more. They only needed to be near each other.

In the silence rose the tormented soul of the house. The sorrows and the passions of that burning house. From the floor below, from the Bernardin family, who had lost their sons, a *de profundis clamat* mounted to the eternal silence. Two floors below, Monsieur Girerd, who had lost his only son, was eating himself up with the patriotic idolatry that was his only recourse against despair. On the floor above, in the young Chardonnet household, the haunting secret, shameful, unconfessed, burned like red-hot iron in body and mind: for all time it had made strangers of these two who loved each other and were bound together forever. Even in Annette's apartment, on the other side of the passage, an empty room, with a door closed as in fear, still preserved the fiery breath of the incestuous woman who had killed herself. The house was a smoking torch, half consumed. And of all these living beings who lay there, at this hour of the night, not one slept. Their fever, their grief, their obsessions were devouring them.

The son and the mother alone swam on the crest of this ocean of scorched souls. A few words showed them that they were both thinking of it. They avoided speaking of it; but they held each other's hands as if they were afraid of losing each other. They were escaping together in the conflagration of the Borgo.

She became the mother again. She said to her little Æneas: "Now go back to bed! This isn't sensible, my child. You will catch cold."

But he shook his head obstinately and said: "You have watched over me long enough. It's my turn."

The dawn came. He was asleep in his chair, his head leaning against the bedclothes. She got up and laid him, half dressed, on her bed. He did not wake up. And in the armchair by the window she awaited the day.

*
* *

In these conversations of the evening and the night they had said scarcely anything—only the essential thing, that they had found each other again and were going to march along side by side. They had put off confessing precisely what was in their hearts and minds and they continued to put it off during the days that followed. But Annette gradually learned how, during the year, her son's mind had developed in regard to the war and society. And she read with emotion between the words—(for it embarrassed him to tell it as much as it embarrassed her to hear it)—the discovery that he had made of his mother's soul and the adoration that he felt for her.

But Marc could not make up his mind to express the painful things that weighed upon his heart. Annette refrained from urging him to do so. But when she realized how they would continue to obsess him until he could bring himself to speak of them, she helped the uneasy spirit to deliver itself.

One evening, in the twilight—the hour for confidences, when people can scarcely see themselves—she said to him, as they sat by the window: "Your heart is heavy. Let me carry it for you."

Lowering his head, he said: "I want to, but I can't."

She drew him towards her, covering his eyes with her fingers, and said to him: "You are alone with yourself."

He began to speak, with difficulty, in whispers. He told his experiences of the last years, the good and the evil. He had made up his mind to speak firmly as if he were talking about somebody else. But at the hard places his voice faltered and broke off and he did not know if

351

he had the courage to go on. She was silent. Under her fingers she felt his burning eyes and his shame. The pressure of her fingers said to him: "Say it! I take the shame."

She was not surprised at what she heard. What he confessed, what he kept back, she felt she had always known. It was *that,* the world—the world into which she had cast her son—into which she had been cast by an unknown force! She felt pity for him, she felt pity for herself. Come! Let's stand on our feet again! This is the way things are. Let us accept it!

When he had finished he was afraid of what she was going to say. She bent over her son's lowered head and kissed it. He said: "Can you forget it now?"

"No."

"Then you despise me?"

"You are myself."

"But I despise myself."

"Do you imagine that I don't despise myself also?"

"No. Not you!"

"We are human, we are proud, we are vile."

"No. Not you!"

"My child, my life is not pure. I have erred, I am still erring. And not only in my acts. For beings like ourselves the inner judgment is not a mere police that only punishes our deeds. What we wish, what we desire, what we have caressed with the fingers of the mind is not less humiliating than what we have done. And it is terrible, all we have thought!"

"You too? But then I knew it."

"You knew it?"

"Yes, I believe it's because of this . . . it's because of

this that I love you. I don't think I could have loved any one who did not also feel, think, wish, this forbidden world."

Sitting behind him, with her arms resting on his shoulders, she embraced him without speaking. After a moment he said with a sigh: "I understand confession now. I feel relieved."

"Yes, when one can tell everything and the other can listen to everything. But to whom can I make my confession? I am not allowed to speak."

"You don't need to speak."

In the silence and the night he recited:

"You have come, your hand holds me—I kiss your hand,
With love, with fear, I kiss your hand."

She trembled. This voice from the past! "O God! How did you know that?"

He did not reply. He went on:

"You have come to destroy me, Love . . ."

She shut his mouth with her hands: "Be silent!"

She blushed. That was so long ago! "Was that I? Somebody else . . . I was that other one. She is dead."

"I kiss her hands," said Marc.

"How did you know this?"

He was silent.

"How long have you known it?"

"Since *she* told me. I have learned it by heart."

"You know it by heart, you have known it when you were with me, all these years? What treason!"

"Forgive me!"

"You are a strange boy."

"And don't you think you are a strange woman?"

"What do you know about women? You don't know anything about them."

He protested indignantly. She smiled: "Wretched little boaster! Don't be proud of your knowledge! Your lamentable knowledge . . . What you know about them, what you think you know about them prevents you from knowing them. A man only knows woman as his own plaything, as something that is useful to him. To know her truly he must be able to forget himself. That isn't possible at your age. What I am, my friend, thousands of women are. I am not exceptional. Those women who read what is in me recognize themselves. But they shut themselves up behind the blinds of their own houses; and those who live near them do not take the trouble to see through them. What is going on within does not interest them. You, little rascal, have seen, you have peeped through the chinks. And what you have seen seems to you strange. The strange thing is that you have seen it. And what you have seen is woman, my friend."

"Well then, *that* isn't simple."

"Neither are you. There are many persons in each of us."

"But just the same they are one."

"Not in everybody."

"In you. In me. And it is that *one* I love in you. And I wish you could love it in me."

"We shall see! I promise nothing."

"You say that to pique me. But I shall force you to!"

"You know that despotism has no hold over me."

"But you love it at bottom."

"If I love the despot."

"You will love him."

He felt very strong now! It was vain for her to pre-

tend to treat him as a child any longer. She could not
deceive him!   He had asserted his advantage over her.
She let him assume an authority in their common life.
And she found a secret pleasure in submitting to it.

*
* *

He did what all men do. He had scarcely conquered this authority before he began to abuse it.

He had just come in. She was sitting there, sewing. He went over to her and kissed her. He had something on his mind. He looked at her, stepped away, seemed to be searching for some book in the bookcase, glanced out of the window, came back, sat down at the table in front of her, opened the book and turned over the leaves as if he were reading. Then, stretching out his arm, he grasped his mother's hand and said hastily: "I have something to ask you."

It was something he had wanted to say for a long time, but he had not dared to say it. That was why he was in such a hurry to say it this time. The moment he had come in, Annette had felt the question burning on his lips; and while she could not divine it she was afraid of it. She tried to evade it. She got up, pretending to look for something, and said, with an air of indifference: "Come, ask me your question, my dear."

But he held her firmly, by the wrist. She had to sit down again. He did not let her go; his eyes were lowered. He forced himself to assume an air of assurance.

"Mamma," he said abruptly, "there is one thing we have never talked about. All the other things are your own, and I haven't the right to ask you about them. But this one I have the right to ask. It concerns me too. Tell me about my father!"

He was in a very emotional state. The suffering caused him by his irregular birth was no recent matter. In his contacts with society it had brought him many a slight at which his susceptibility had bristled. But he was too proud to admit them.

Ever since his first months at the Lycée he had received, not without returning them, many a wound. They were not deep, however. Parisian school-boys have too many other things on their minds to bother about the behavior of fathers and mothers—especially during the war that upset all morals and the whole of society. In their greedy contempt for women, most of these urchins considered them only good enough to sleep with. They did not reproach them for the liberties they took, they would have feared to seem backward themselves. Marc had only to submit to a few coarse but good-humored remarks, without any real spite in them, from one or another little blackguard who perhaps thought he was making him a compliment. He had not taken them that way. He quivered at every allusion that was aimed, even remotely, at his mother; he was a great deal more touchy about Annette's honor than she would have been. His replies were terrible. Knock-out blows.

Later, during the fortnight's visit which he made his mother in the country, he noticed the glances of his schoolmates, who used to whisper as they watched the two of them, and that some of the townswomen pretended not to see them as they passed. He had not mentioned any of these impressions to his mother. But they had contributed not a little to his aversion for the country and his firm intention never to go back again.

But all this amounted to very little. When one doesn't respect people one can easily dismiss what they think. It

no more exists than so much dust.   You are rid of it for
brushing your shoes, spitting on the leather, so as to clean
it the better.   But those to whom one is attached?   Those
for whom one's heart hungers?

Marc had entered his eighteenth year, and for several
months his footsteps had been crossing the golden shadow
of love.   A tender sentiment had found its way into this
young, untouched, restless heart.   He thought he had
fallen in love with the sister of one of his school friends
whom he had met several times—in the street with her
brother, then alone.   They had both tacitly arranged
things so that their paths crossed; the attraction was recip-
rocal.   Marc had gone to see his friend at his house.   But
he had never been invited there.   He might not have felt
the affront so acutely perhaps if his friend had not
thoughtlessly led him to expect an invitation.   Since then,
the brother's embarrassment, his awkward eagerness to
avoid Marc, had revealed the insulting nature of the intended slight.   The family meant to keep the undesirable
young man at a distance.   This cutting blow led Marc to
discover—invent, perhaps—other signs of contempt that
he had never suspected.   He realized that he had never
been admitted into various bourgeois households where his
friends went.   He had never seriously wished to enter
them.   But it seemed to him now that their doors were
closed in his face.   And he felt insulted.   He had a convulsion of revolt against this society.

But while he furiously took his mother's side against it,
he had a secret grudge against her because of these affronts.   And his wounded mind was always returning to
this question: "Who was his father?   Why had he been
defrauded of him?"   He knew that he wronged his
mother in asking her about him.   But he had been

wronged himself.   Each deserved his share.   He wanted
to know.

Annette had foreseen what Marc was going to say.
And yet she hoped that he would not say it.   It was quite
true that she owed him these secrets of the past; she had
promised herself to reveal them to him before he asked
for them.   But she kept putting it off, she was afraid.
And now she had allowed herself to be taken by surprise.

"My dear," she said, anxiously, "he has never known
you.   For—I have told you that I am not without reproach in the eyes of the world—I was separated from
him before your birth."

"No matter!" said Marc.   "I ought to know who he is.
I have the right."

His right?   He too?   Was he going to take exception
to her?   . . .   She said: "You have the right."

"Is he still alive?"

"He is alive."

"What is his name?   Who is he?   Where is he?"

"Yes, I shall tell you everything.   But wait a moment. . . ."

Her heart was heavy.   He was sorry, but he wanted to
know.   He said, coolly: "Mamma, there is no hurry.
Let's talk about it some other day."

She was not deceived by his ill-disguised impatience.
She did not wish to accept the respite he offered her.   She
recovered her will and said: "No, this evening.   You are
anxious to know.   And I want you to know.   Just as you
have said, this thing belongs to you.   I am keeping it.   I
have owed it to you too long.   And this evening I have
been reminded of my debt."

He tried to apologize.

"Be quiet," she said. "I am going to tell you this evening."

Now that she was actually going to speak, he almost wanted not to hear it.

"Turn on the light," she said, "and lock the door! No one must disturb us!"

She had scarcely begun when some one knocked. Sylvie, no doubt. The door remained closed.

Without apparent emotion, Annette outlined the story of her past, the broken engagement. She expressed herself with a proud modesty that betrayed nothing which belonged to herself alone but concealed nothing that she should and wished to say. What was he thinking as he listened? She tried to drive the obsession away, and he revealed nothing of what he felt. He listened as if paralyzed. It was as if the son and the mother were both strangers to the far-away events whose image passed on the screen. God knew, however, with what anxiety she awaited a wave of sympathy, though she would do nothing to appeal for it. He remained impenetrable to the end of the story. And then, as she waited for the verdict he was going to deliver, he made this sole remark:

"You have not mentioned his name."

She had given his Christian name alone. She said: "Roger Brissot."

Her son's coldness had frozen her heart.

He caught nothing but the name she had uttered. It was very familiar to him. He cried: "The Socialist deputy!"

His surprise concealed ill—did not conceal at all—his joy.

Brissot had won a brilliant renown among parliamentary speakers. He fascinated the young. This fascination An-

nette read in her son's eye, and she trembled. But she
was too proud to show it and too loyal to depreciate the
adversary, so she said: "Yes, his name is famous. You
have no reason to blush for it."

She had scarcely said this when she read on her son's
lips: "Then why have you deprived me of it?"

But he did not say it. He had risen; he walked to and
fro through the room, without speaking. She followed
his movements. She was reading his mind. She lost all
desire to defend herself. If he did not defend her, what
would be the use? She marched straight into the danger,
not warding it off but inviting it. She asked: "You would
like to know him?"

"Yes."

"You can. I haven't told you everything. He knows
of your existence. He knows that you are his son. And
no doubt he will be ready to welcome you as his son."

Marc cried angrily: "And you have never told me!"

Annette, very pale, closed her eyes. Then she opened
them again and, fixing them upon those of her son, she
said: "I was waiting, before telling you, until you were a
man. I see that you have become one."

Marc did not feel her proud bitterness. He asked:
"Where does he live?"

"I don't know, but it will be easy for you to find his
address."

Marc continued to stride up and down the room. He
was not thinking of her any longer. He was only thinking
of himself. He considered himself wronged. He said
pitilessly: "I am going to see him to-morrow."

*

* *

Why are the hearts of young people so cruel? Once in his room, alone, Marc felt a twinge of conscience; but he enjoyed it. He knew that he had hurt a being who loved him—whom he loved—and he was not without remorse. But the sharpness of the remorse added to the pleasure. He was avenging himself. For what? For the wrong she had done him? Or because she loved him? If she had loved him less, he would have been less avenged. He would not have been avenged if he had not been loved. She had told him everything without in any way defending herself. He had taken advantage of her. And he excused himself for taking advantage of her, for his unconfessed pleasure in doing so, by telling himself that he was able to fling the whole thing up whenever he wished. But, once they have begun, how many have been unable to stop!

Annette was suffering. She had loved him too much. Yes. Too egotistically. How could one love without egotism?

"That being I made out of myself. He is myself. How can I forget myself in loving him? But it's got to be done. I wasn't able, and I'm not able. I am well punished."

For a long time she had known this day was coming. And the day had come. She had waited too long. She had trembled for fear of losing this son whom she had jealously monopolized. And she had lost him. One single minute had been enough to detach him from her. She was terrified. In the hearts of these young men a whole life of maternal devotion is forgotten for one moment of possession or passionate hope. She had had a frightened prescience of this. But the reality surpassed the presentiment. He didn't have a single tender word for her, not one gesture of respect. He had thrown her overboard with one turn of his hand! No consideration of the past! He was only thinking of to-morrow. She spent the night picturing to herself this to-morrow, and the following night when it would be all over. She was vanquished in advance.

She did not try to struggle any more. Let him go his own way! Whatever he might decide, she placed herself at his service. If she could not keep him any longer, she was going to help him to the last.

In the morning, when she saw him again, she did not recur to what had been decided upon. She got ready his best clothes for him, helped him with his toilet, left for a moment to serve breakfast; and while they were at table—she, forcing herself to eat so that he would not think she wanted to be reproachful, he, eating hastily and voraciously because he was thinking of the hours that were coming and was anxious to reach them—she told him that she had procured the address he wanted. She advised him to look for Brissot not at his home but in his law-office. She had good reasons for this and she spoke composedly. He acquiesced. He was grateful to his mother for the effort she had made, though he did not show it. It did not enter into his plan to allow himself to be troubled now by an emotion. He wished first to see for himself and form his own judgment. As for her who had to wait for his judgment and suffer, well, she would have to suffer. A few hours more or less! She was used to it!

He would be tender afterwards. Yes, so he promised himself: it was for him to decide. And because she had suffered she would enjoy all the more the happiness that he was going to bring her. He was too sure of his power over her now. She could wait. He had plenty of time!

*

* *

Since 1900 Roger Brissot had enjoyed a brilliant career. His resounding cases, his success at the Palais de Justice and then in Parliament, had carried him to the first rank. In the Chamber, he kept within the limits of the Radical and Socialist parties, watchful lest either spring a leak, always ready to pass from one boat to the other. Minister several times and of all the portfolios, public instruction, labor, justice and even, once, the Navy. Like his colleagues, he was as comfortable in one seat as another, they fitted every one. After all, whatever the department may be, it is all the same machine under the same management. When one knows how to handle it, the rest—the personnel under one's administration—is of little importance. The only thing that counts is the administration.

In treating so many subjects, he had enriched his store of ideas, or, more exactly, his repertory of words—without learning much that lay beneath them, for he was too busy talking to have the time to listen. But he talked very well. On one point, however, his knowledge was really profound, the breeding of the electoral cattle and their exploitation. On this subject several statesmen of the Third Republic were past masters; they had the keyboard of the masses at their finger's ends, they had the secret of touching its weaknesses, passions, and manias. But no one was a more accomplished virtuoso, no one could set vibrating with more sumptuous sonorities the sovereign chords of democracy, the brazen-tongued ideologies that overlaid, evoked and over-excited the virtues of the race and its hidden vices, than the honorable Bris-

sot. He was the great parliamentary pianist. His party,
his parties—for he permitted himself to claim more than
one!—appealed to his talents on every occasion for resounding discourses, those chamber-concerts, the music of
which, spread out on the great white placards (voted by
acclamation, at the expense of the electors), made the
tour of France. He never refused; he was always ready.
He was equally competent on all subjects—aided, of
course, by active and well-informed secretaries. (He had
a whole crew of them.) His devotion to his party—to his
parties—and to his own glory was only paralleled by his
lungs. The latter were never tired.

This zeal and this voice, equally magnificent, were very
useful to the Republic during the Great War. The war
mobilized them. Roger Brissot was charged with convinc-
ing the world and the people of France of the high truths
for which they were driving themselves to ruin. He was
sent on missions to distant parts. He had taken the pre-
caution to resume, at the beginning of the war, his stripes
as a Major of Reserves in the cavalry; and in this quality
he was even attached for some time to the General Head-
quarters, solidly seated in the Château de Compiègne.
But they led him to understand that he would serve the
country more efficaciously in the trenches of America; and
he had lavished his breath there without ever exhausting
it. For the rest, on his numerous journeys and voyages,
to London and New York, in Turkey, in Russia, in almost
all the neutral or allied countries, he had encountered a
few serious dangers. Brissot's courage was beyond all
question; he would have done just as well fighting in the
Argonne and Flanders. But he understood the duties
that his genius imposed upon him. In order to preserve
himself for the nation he had allowed himself to take

shelter. And in the talking service he spent himself in volley after volley. His great voice filled the ears of the world. They heard it in London, in Bordeaux, in Chicago, in Geneva and in Rome, even in St. Petersburgh before the Revolution, in all the towns of France, at the front and in the rear, at funeral ceremonies and at anniversaries. Abroad, he was the incarnation of French eloquence. He was in the great cabinet that was grouped about Clemenceau. They abominated each other. Brissot could not endure the unscrupulousness and lack of principle of the man with the Mongol's face. And Clemenceau unkindly chaffed him as "the loud-speaker."

But all hostilities were destroyed in the presence of the invasion. And the rivals of yesterday, uniting their wisdom, divided the cake between them, forming—Millerand and Briand, Brissot and Clemenceau—a radiant constellation about that fixed star of Revenge—Poincaré, the chicaner. The unforgettable epoch of the Union Sacrée—too soon passed!—in which the political heads of all the parties, and even those without a party, like the brothers Aymon, bestrode the same croup of that old horse of labor and combat, France—resolved to hold on until the animal perished.

Brissot's career had been unclouded—save for the clouds that envious rivals tried to throw over his oratorical past, which was marred by a few ardent flights, certainly a little imprudent, towards the empyrean of international pacifism. But it is fatal for a man who is always talking to talk about everything, and one cannot expect him to be bound by every one of his words: he would be drawn and quartered by more than four horses. And then pacifism is, as its name indicates, a harmless potion the use of which is lawful in times of peace—prohibited only

when war has sounded: for only then would it be effica-
cious. That was what the great orator had no difficulty
in demonstrating—except to his faithless enemies whom
nothing could convince, not even the burning zeal that
Brissot used in denouncing his former companions as infatuated pacifists, disguised Germans, who maintained
their right to pursue their game in times of war at the risk
of unnerving a fatigued people and taking away from
them the costly fruit of victory. But it is the right of
great men to be calumniated, and Brissot was strong
enough not to allow himself to be overclouded by injustice. He laughed at it, with that broad Gallic laugh
which his admirers compared to Danton's. (An inap-
propriate comparison, for Brissot lacked—let us say!—
that style of the market-place and that disorderly tone.)
Finally, he had no rancor and was ready to oblige his enemies to-morrow. The essential thing was that he had got
the best of them.

Everything has to be paid for here below. Brissot ex-
piated his political good fortune at home. He was not
happy in his domestic life. The woman he had married,
rich, colorless, plump, anemic, a fat pullet stuffed with
good bank securities, was, from all points of view, an inadequate consort for a man like Brissot. She had few
resources either in mind or in feeling. Lacking in person-
ality, and unhappily lacking also what some other nobodies
have, the faculty of knowing how to efface herself, she en-
cumbered the horizon with her nonentity. She grumbled
unceasingly and she admired nothing, not even the talents
and the glory of her husband. She had that distressing
and no doubt unhealthy gift of never getting out of a
life rich in advantages anything but the disagreeable ele-
ments. She was always blaming everything and every-

body. In a way, this was her mission in life. For the rest, she made no effort to change anything. She spread over everything her own dull, sticky fog, like an October downpour. Every one who approached her caught cold from her. It can easily be imagined that such a climate did not suit the robust Roger Brissot. He reduced his sojourns in it to the strictly necessary, and he escaped from it with vigorous sneezes. He went in search of happier climates, and the fame of his success only added to the dreary gloom of the house.

His "extras," however, had not prevented this dutiful man from punctually rendering his spouse her due. It was not his fault that the parsimonious creature only provided him with one daughter. Brissot was very fond of her. But the child, pleasant, full of laughter, very healthy, with plump cheeks and happy eyes, died. Suddenly, from an operation that was not dangerous, or, more exactly, from an anesthetic from which she did not awaken. She was thirteen years old. The Brissot household fell to the ground. The wife had reasons this time for accusing the world. She carried her lamentations to the foot of altars and into confessionals. She became a devotee. This greatly embarrassed Brissot in his politics: clericalism had not yet come into fashion again! The poor man had neither a God nor men of God to console him. He was hard hit; and in his solitude, facing the portrait of the little girl that stood on his work-table, he poured out bitter tears. The war brought him a diversion. Frantic activity gave him a refuge from thought. He fled from his house, his wife and his dead daughter. He fled them, alas, even into pleasures in which he ended by using up the excess of strength which his political labors did not consume. His toadies found here another trait of re-

semblance to Danton and his sprees. But Brissot was not
appeased by anything of this kind. He was a family man,
like almost all Frenchmen; he needed domestic affection.
Nothing could take its place. Ambition, glory, pleasure,
of which he seemed so avid, were at bottom nothing but
an *Ersatz*. Brissot could not be consoled for not having
a son.

He knew that Annette's son was his. Before his daughter's death he avoided thinking of this. The memory of
Annette was not agreeable to him. He dismissed it. A
secret spite kept bringing it back to him: the scar of a
wound to his *amour-propre*, and perhaps his love, that had
not been healed. He had lost sight of this woman; but he
had not been able to prevent himself, two or three times,
from indirectly informing himself of what had become of
her. Without wishing her evil, he was not displeased to
know that her life had been a failure. This was not to
say that he would not gladly have helped her, if she had
appealed to him; but he knew very well that she would
never accord him this secret revenge.

Two or three times, in fifteen years, he had met her,
in the street, with her son. She made no effort to avoid
him. It was he who had pretended to pass without seeing
her. He had retained a painful impression of her which
he preferred not to analyze. What was this far-away story
to him, this woman he had possessed and who had become
a stranger to him, this obscure passer-by—what was she to
him, who had everything! But, alas, one can have everything and believe one possesses everything, and not be able
to prevent a regret from surging up out of the depths of
the past, a poisonous remorse for a mere nothing that one
has lost! And this nothing becomes everything. And
the everything becomes nothing. It is like a fissure, an

imperceptible crack in the side of the vase of life, and everything crumbles and falls.

Happily, these recollections of the past were rare, and Brissot was sufficiently used to insincerity to be able to persuade himself that he did not hear them. When one leaves behind one an inglorious hour the best thing is to tell oneself that it has never existed. Brissot would have succeeded in obliterating it from the panorama of his busy life if it had only contained the silent shadow of this woman and his own enlaced with hers. But there was that other that would not let itself be effaced—the son.

Ever since his little girl had died, this living child had pursued him. He was always encountering him now on the streets of his mind. He did not know what he looked like. On the two or three occasions when he had met Annette, he had not been able to look at the boy closely, and he was not sure that the image he had caught in passing was exact. Once only he had thought he recognized, in the autobus, a few seats ahead of him, the young boy whom he had seen on Annette's arm and whose eyes, skimming over him, were much more interested in a pretty girl on a neighboring seat. Brissot watched him tenderly: his son ought to be like that. But could he be sure?

How he wanted this son! For himself, for his household, for his need of affection, for the natural joy of transmitting to one of his own blood his name, the glory he had won, his possessions and his mission so that he could give the pass-word to the doleful, "What was the use?"—to the Charon who refuses to carry across to the other bank the man without a son, the family without a future, the being who is going to die and will never be reborn.

But these are the sort of sorrows one does not mention,

and no one would have known about it if, by chance, one night in 1915, when he was at a gay party with some obliging ladies, inquisitive, honest creatures, none of them professionals, he had not met Sylvie. (It was during the brief but crowded period when she went from spree to spree.) She was with a man whom Brissot knew. At supper the two men exchanged their companions. Brissot had not recognized Sylvie, but Sylvie took it upon herself to refresh his memory. He manifested an unexpected feeling at meeting her again, despite the fact that in the old days he had not thought much of the dressmaker sister-in-law and had taken little pride in her. Sylvie was well aware of this, but the adventure amused her. Her partner was in a condition in which one has little control over one's words. Brissot melted towards this gay companion, who agreed with everything he said. He questioned her eagerly about Annette and Marc. Without concealing a certain bitterness against the former, too lively not to reveal both vexation and regret, he showed a hungry interest in the child. He asked her about his health, his work, his success and his means of livelihood. Sylvie praised her nephew, of whom she was proud, and his paternal feeling was still more aroused by this. Brissot confided to Sylvie the joy it would give him to see his son, to have him near him, with him, and he expressed his desire to look after the boy's future.

The next day Sylvie reported this to her sister. Annette turned pale. She made Sylvie promise not to speak of it to Marc. Sylvie had not the least desire to speak of it. She was as jealous of Marc as her sister was, and she did not want to lose him. She said:

"Do you imagine I'm going to tell him? He would only blow us up."

Annette flared up. She was unwilling to admit that she had "defrauded" the boy. (Sylvie had harshly used this word, laughing as she did so. "Well, what of it? each for himself?") If she wanted to keep him to herself it was to save *him*. She wanted to protect him from anything that might destroy the ideal she had formed in him. But she knew very well that she was protecting herself also! To have sheltered him for fifteen years with so much effort, through so many sorrows—more precious to her than the joys—to have made a man of him and then to see him carried off by this other person who, without having had the anxiety would have the benefit—this man who had never bothered about his duties and who was coming now to plead his rights, the rights of blood. The enemy! Never!

"Am I unjust? . . . Very well! Unjust, unjust . . . Yes, I am. . . . It's for the sake of my son, it's for his welfare! . . ."

*

* *

What his welfare was, young Marc was going to decide for himself alone! And he was not going to forgive others for prejudging it for him.

There still remained in his heart a certain grudge against his mother when he set out coldly on this strange adventure, the "quest" of his father. He was more anxious than he appeared. What was he going to find? He had little assurance of what the result of the day was going to be: With every step, as he advanced, he was seized with a desire to turn back. The audacity of his procedure seemed to him preposterous now. But he said to himself:

"I am going. It may be audacious, it may be impudent. Shameful or not, I don't care. I want to see him. I am going to see him."

He was not very far away from the address indicated when his eye was caught by a name on a placard. His name, the name of the man he was looking for! It was the announcement of a meeting that very afternoon. Roger Brissot was to speak.

He went to the appointed place. A great hall that was used as a riding-school. He had several hours to wait. Rather than return home he sat down on a bench in the street; and, with his back turned to the passers-by, he thought over what he was going to do. How was he going to approach the man whose voice he was about to hear? At what moment? What would he say to him? There were not going to be any preliminaries. He would say to him, straight out: "I am your son."

As he said these words over to himself, his tongue was

paralyzed with fear. And—could one believe it?—in the midst of his emotion, he thought of Monsieur de Pourceaugnac, that little Gaulois! He burst out laughing. A ruse, no doubt, of the repressed instinct that was seeking a diversion. The absurdity of the scene obtruded shamelessly upon his emotion. Whistling, he went off after a cup of black coffee. But from the corner of the terrace where he was sitting he did not lose sight of the door of the riding-school. And when it opened he was one of the first to enter.

He managed to slip up to the first row, near the platform. The seats were reserved. He allowed himself to be pushed back, once, twice, three times, as many times as they tried to push him, but he returned, tenaciously: he had become thick-skinned. He was standing up, to see better, leaning against an iron pillar, just below the platform, when Brissot entered. He was so excited, in spite of his assumed air of indifference, that he did not see Brissot until after he had taken his seat. He felt the shock that comes when a long-awaited event has taken place: he was quite different from what he had imagined—had no resemblance to it. But the reality gave him such a relief that everything he had imagined collapsed, bursting like a paper hoop. It was no longer: "Is he going to be like this . . . or like that?" He *was*. He was there in front of one, of the same flesh and blood as oneself; and for all eternity it was no longer possible for one to change him.

"He! . . . That man! . . . My father! . . ."

What a blow! At first a rebellious something said, "No!" He had to have time to get used to it. And then, suddenly, his mind was made up. There was nothing more to discuss. The fact was there. "I accept it. *Ecce Homo!*"

"And this man is myself. Myself?"

His eager curiosity fastened upon this face, upon all the features in detail, tried to discover itself in him.

This big, stout man, with his large smooth-shaven face, the fine brow, the strong, straight nose, the affable nostrils that were as used to the scent of dung as to that of roses, the plump cheeks and chin full of good health, the head thrown backward, the broad chest thrown out—a mixture of the actor, the officer, the priest and the gentleman-farmer . . .

He shook hands right and left. He waved to the people in the hall whom he recognized, his eyes exploring his audience while he seemed to be listening to those who were beside him. He expanded, he laughed, he responded gayly, at random, to every volley of applause with a manner that seemed good-natured, unctuous and cavalier by turns and all at once. The tumult and hubbub in the hall made it impossible for any one to hear what he was saying. Nothing could be heard but the sound of the bell. He was in his element.

"Myself! Myself! That! . . . That mass of flesh! That laugh, those handshakes!"

The slim little Marc, pale and proud, looked at this big man, so florid and exuberant, with very severe eyes. But he was fine-looking, just the same! There was something very attractive about him that did not escape Marc. But he distrusted it. Without being able to recognize the odor, he seemed to catch a certain scent in it. He would wait till the man spoke.

Brissot began to speak. And Marc surrendered to him.

Brissot, with great skill, was careful to begin on a low note. Calmly, simply, *sotto voce*, he placed his instrument at the proper pitch. He knew that for true virtuosos

one of the ways of obtaining silence in a bustling hall is to
play softly. Others set out imperiously, with resounding
chords, at the very start; but they can do no more and attention soon flags. When the note of authority is sustained too long it grows wearisome. But he came to meet
you, quite frankly and simply, a man like yourself, a
comrade. You gave him your hand; and when he had
got you . . . then you would see! . . .

Marc saw nothing. He was too busy drinking things in.
At first, he did not hear the words. All he heard was the
voice. It was warm and cordial, breathing the soil of
France, evoking the perfume of the familiar fields. Marc
recognized the rolling Burgundian r's which his mother
had studiously taught him to avoid. It was a secret bond
that was suddenly revealed between them. That mark of
the tribe which is most intimately embedded in the flesh
and most indelible: the tongue. The rustic intonations,
virile and endearing, took hold upon him, as a father takes
his child upon his knees. He was filled with affectionate
gratitude. It was good. He was happy. He smiled with
pleasure at the speaker.

And Brissot began to observe the young boy whose eyes
were devouring him.

It was his custom, in speaking, to look about the hall for
one or two auditors who would be good reflectors of his
eloquence.

He heard himself through them. He could estimate
the effect, the resonance of his words, and, swift to seize
the meaning of these signs, he steered by them the course
of his speech, improvising as he went on, according to the
general plan of a scenario—except for a few big morsels
that were like the cadence and the *raplapla* of the or-
chestra in a concerto. Marc, who was directly in front of

him—the burning eyes smiling in the feverish face—was a superb reflector.

Seeing himself in this mirror, Brissot was elated. Then suddenly the reflector became dull. . . .

Marc had heard the words he was uttering.

Brissot had broken the spell. The flight of his eloquence had just revealed to the keen eyes of the boy that the wings were artificial. The open-mouthed wonder of the public, as they followed the speaker, had the immediate effect of placing Marc on his guard and making him react against his own emotion. He was one of those who are always instinctively on the defensive against the contagion of crowds. He was vexed at having allowed his feelings to be carried away, as they had been, by that beautiful voice. He stiffened, and from that moment he ceased to permit anything to pass from the other's mouth and heart into himself without submitting it to an aggressive criticism.

Before his captivated public Brissot sounded the clarion of the Immortal Principles. He sang the heroic mission of the land of France. It was the eternal anvil on which worlds were forged, the table of the sacrifice, the victim offered up for the other nations. The Battle of Poitiers, the Marne and Verdun, Pétain, Bayard, Mangin, Charles Martel, Joffre and Jeanne d'Arc . . . Tirelessly it offered itself for the salvation of men. And, twenty times immolated, it had risen again twenty times. Alone in the universe, in defending itself it defended the universe. . . .

Brissot spoke of the gold and iron circle of the Allies. Their love encircled France as his valiant knights had encircled Charlemagne. Brissot had visited them all. He could attest with his own eyes the sublime disinterestedness of the Sister-Republic of the star-spangled banner which, without asking for anything, was hastening to pay the debt of Lafayette and avenge the Right. . . . Magnanimous England . . . Incorruptible Italy . . . Since the days of the Crusades no such spectacle had been seen! But instead of Crusades fighting for the tomb of a Christ, the greatest of the Crusades, that of to-day, was the new Christ, opening the tomb of an enslaved humanity. . . . Etc. . . . Etc. . . .

"The immense infamy for which the monstrous Boche Empire was solely to blame and uniquely responsible was going to be crushed utterly, along with the empire. All political and social crimes came from that sink, and from that alone: vile despots and degraded masses, Junkers, false Socialists, slaves, bullies, Krupp, Hegel, Bismarck, Treitschke and Wilhelm II. Bestial ferocity, the frenzy of Sardanapalus, Nietzsche, who thought he was God and went around barking on four paws. . . . The moaning peoples and the smoke of ruins. Innocent Belgium and sacred Poland, Rheims, Louvain, black vultures hovering over helpless towns, massacring women and children without pity. But the white birds of France were pouncing upon the beasts of prey, breaking up their flocks and crossing the Rhine, scattering punishment over the guilty race. Liberation was coming. The enfranchised peoples of Europe, Asia, Africa, under the affectionate Ægis of free France and free England, were going to drink at the fountain of Liberty. The last continental Empire was collapsing. The Republic was spreading its wings. The angel of Rude. The genius of the Arc de l'Étoile. . . . Forward, children of the Fatherland!

"I have come back from the front. Marvelous! Those children laugh. The dying laugh. They say: 'Short and sweet! I haven't wasted my day.' When they are urged to return to the rear, they reply: 'Never! Hang me on the barbed wire! I shall prevent them from passing.' "

Marc blushed with shame and his expression froze. How he drove these cattle! These hollow words, these vulgar ways, these filthy lies! He gazed with a cold contempt at the orator, who was streaming with sweat and eloquence. And Brissot, without understanding it, was aware that some drama was taking place in the mind of this auditor. He set all his snares to catch his bird again. He was disconcerted by this glance that was judging him and he did not dare to seek it any longer. But while he continued to shout, "France, unanimous France," displaying his arpeggios, without any effort, like a well-trained virtuoso, he could not dislodge from the corner of his brain the image of the young boy. For he had met him before; he tried to recollect where he had seen him. But in the transports of his well-balanced phrases he could not stop to follow the tracks of his memory.

He concluded with a resounding harmony that re-echoed a hundred times over in the clamor of the hall. The audience stood up, shouted, acclaimed him, rushed up to the platform to shake the hand of the great citizen. They were purple with excitement, they called to each other, they laughed, and there were tears in their eyes. Brissot, happy, unbending, threw a glance towards the recalcitrant one.

"Does he admit that he's vanquished?"

The place was empty. Marc had disappeared.

He had not been able to endure to the end the stench of this eloquence. He had left abruptly. But he was still at the door of the hall when the thundering applause broke loose. He turned around, his lip drawn up in disdain. For an instant he looked at the delirious hall and the triumphant orator. Then he went out. Once in the street he spat with disgust. He spoke out loud. He took an oath:

"I swear, ignoble crowd, never to deserve your applause."

At that moment, Brissot, who, in the hall, was talking very loudly and laughing with his admirers, replaced in its exact compartment the image that tormented him. He had just remembered the young man of the autobus.

*

* *

Marc walked along with great strides. He was running away. He was running away from the spot where he had been disillusioned. But his disillusionment clung to him. Good God, how the world had changed since he had come up that same street that very morning! Even though in coming, that morning, he had tried not to hope too much, what hope had risen in him! What joy, what passionate expectations of the man he was going to find! What a need he felt for loving and admiring that man! When he had heard his voice he had been ready to run to him and throw his arms about him. To throw his arms about him! Disgusting! He wiped his lips as if they had touched him!

That repulsive rhetorician, that Pharisee, that hypocrite! Liar, liar, liar!—deceiving France and himself. . . . As for France, it was her own affair if she liked lies, if she wanted to be deceived! But himself! . . . That was unpardonable! It was the last degradation. Disgusting, disgusting for him, disgusting for me! . . . For I was made out of him. I am the son of that lie. That lie is in me!

He strode along like a madman. He reached the Seine. He leaned over the embankment. He wanted to wash himself, to wash his blood, to wash his flesh, to remove the fetid impurity. He did not reason, he had no pity. He was in the sort of passion one has at seventeen. Not for a moment did it occur to him that this man might be good, might be simply weak, like the average man, that if he had known his son he would have been fond of him; for, like the average man, he concealed under a

382

mass of weaknesses, lies and filthinesses a sacred recess full of pure sentiments and inviolable truth. It did not occur to him that that generation of old-fashioned scholars, rhetoricians, babblers about the antique (the false antique, the Gallo-Roman stuff), had been habituated from their childhood to the worship of words, that they were the victims as well as the comedians of words . . . *"Commediante. . . . Tragediante. . . ."* They would not have been able, even if they had wished, to recover contact with the real under the mountain of words that smothered them. . . .

But this was the very thing that Marc was least able to forgive! A young man of good blood who sets out in pursuit of life prefers crime to abject impotence and babbling. For if crime kills, the other is born dead. . . . "Of good blood." . . . Marc's blood was the blood of this liar.

"Never!"

He knew it, he felt it, he recognized now in himself the other man's impostures, he surprised himself in the act of repeating the gestures, the intonations he had caught from the other; he remembered having made use of them on his own account before he had even suspected the existence of the model whom he had unconsciously reproduced. He rejected in vain the heritage of this man. He carried it in him.

"Never! Never! Nothing between us! Nothing of him! If, in spite of myself, I were his understudy, if he repeated himself in me, if I began from him, I should kill myself."

He wandered about wearily for several hours, without eating. The night had come. He did not dream of going

home. How could he show himself? Confess his disillusionment?

He passed close to a severely wounded man, mutilated
in the face, with his eye scooped out, one cheek with a
great hollow in it, as if molten lead had fallen upon it.
A woman of the people with gray hair held his arm,
watching him tenderly with sad, loving eyes. He pressed
against her. And in Marc's feverish mind *she* reappeared
—the Mother. Her proud image and her silence, her
life, full of trials and passions that were not profaned, that
soul of hers, with its integrity and straightforwardness,
her contempt for words, the depths of her uncompanioned
solitude and that uncompromising will against which he
had rebelled, which he had hated, which he blessed to-
day, her inflexible law of truthfulness. She grew and
grew in his eyes beside the man whom he had just found
out and disowned, the man of the crowd. And now he
understood, he cherished her jealous passion in fighting
for him against his father, her injustice.

"Unjust! Unjust! *'I kiss your hands.'* Bless you!"
And the memory of his harshness towards her, last
evening, this morning, struck him in the face. He began
to run. Back to her. He had caused her suffering. He
was going to atone for it. Thank God, there was time
enough. . . .

*
* *

He reached the foot of the staircase. The concierge stopped him. "She has had a close shave. . . . Your mother has been injured."

He heard nothing more. He ran up the stairs, four steps at a time. Sylvie opened the door. Her face was severe. Breathless, he asked: "Mamma?"

She said: "You decided to come home? We've been waiting for you all day."

He pushed her aside without paying any attention to her and went in. He opened his mother's door. She was in bed with her head enveloped in bandages. He uttered a muffled cry. Seeing his anxiety, she said to him quickly: "It's nothing, my dear. I was a fool. I fell."

In his anguish Marc touched her with trembling hands. Sylvie drew him away.

"Come! Don't disturb her! Don't agitate her still more!"

Then, bitterly, she told him what had happened. With her eyes fixed upon her son's face, Annette corrected the details of the story, made light of the accident, tried to joke, blamed herself.

What she did not tell him was that after her son had gone out she had lost her head. She said to herself over and over: "He is going to leave me."

She had lost all hope. In order to pass the time till evening came, she forced herself to work. She said: "Whether he abandons me or not, I shall not abandon myself."

In spite of her extreme fatigue, she set to work cleaning

and sweeping. She scrubbed the floor, she polished the brass, she cleaned the glass. Climbing up on a little folding step-ladder, she was wiping the panes of the open window that looked out on the street; she was staring at the curtains. Did the step-ladder slip? Did she faint for a few seconds? Was it because of her great weariness and the thought that filled her mind, or perhaps one of those strange lapses of consciousness that sometimes occurred without her being aware of them—they were so rapid? She found herself on the floor. She might have been thrown into the street, but the step-ladder, in slipping, turned over sideways and closed the window, breaking the glass. Annette's forehead and wrist were bleeding; and, when she tried to get up, a pain in her ankle told her that her right foot was dislocated. At the sound of the broken glass falling into the street, the concierge came up. Sylvie was summoned.

Serious as her injury was, Annette felt it less than the annoyance. This was the last day she would have wanted to have an accident. She did not want to be in need of help to-day; above all, she didn't want to seem to be making an appeal for Marc's pity. It seemed to her odious and degrading, for him as well as for her. She exerted all her energy to hold herself on her feet, but the pain was too stinging and her heart failed her; she was obliged to allow herself to be put to bed. She was humiliated. She repeated over and over to herself: "What is he going to say to me—think of me—when he comes back?"

And, as suffering makes one less master of oneself, Annette allowed her sister to wring from her the secret of her anxiety. Sylvie learned that Marc had set out to find his father. She did not want to remind herself that she had been the intermediary. She thought Annette was very stupid to have revealed everything to her son. But this was no time to treat her harshly; all her irritation turned against Marc. She doubted no more than Annette that the boy would abandon them. She knew how egotistical he was, how vain, how ready to sacrifice others for his own pleasure. She did not love him the less for this. She loved him all the more for it. She recognized herself in him. That was why she could not forgive him. She would never forgive him if he abandoned them. If? The thing had happened. For since he was so long in coming, was it not evident that he had stayed at Brissot's house for dinner? She could not see any other excuse, any other possibility. She alone was more unjust than Annette and Marc together.

Her animosity was evident in every one of her glances, in every word she uttered, now that he was there. The impatient Marc bristled with hostility against this hostility. But Annette humbly thought of nothing but begging his pardon. One might have thought she was to blame for being obliged to take to her bed. Sylvie's manner hurt her more than Marc. She bade her be silent.

"Come!" she said. "Enough! Enough talking about me! That isn't the important thing."

What was important? Marc knew. Annette also. Sylvie just as much. But she was determined to stay; and Marc was unwilling to speak as long as she was there. Annette besought her with her eyes. Sylvie pretended not to understand. And then, suddenly, she threw down the napkin she was holding, got up without a word and went out.

The mother and the son were alone. They waited. How, where were they to begin? Marc looked at Annette. She looked away, she was afraid, and she did not want her eyes to betray her, she did not want to weight the decision of her son.

Marc walked up and down the room. He gulped before he began to tell about his day. He threw another glance at his mother who lay there, motionless, gazing at the window facing her bed. He stopped. . . . He went straight up to her, he fell on his knees, and with his mouth against the bed-clothes, kissing her hidden knees, both his arms stretched over the woman's body, he said:

"You are my father and my mother."

Annette turned towards the wall and wept.

*

* *

EPILOGUE

"You command the ship of Humanity.
 Then cross the river of Sorrow!
 Madman, this is not the moment for sleeping."
                    —BODHICARYAVATARA.

EPILOGUE

LL the sluices, all the veins of the flood-gate were open. The embankments of mankind were thrown down. The twenty-year-olds had set out. The nine-teen-year-olds had been summoned. The eighteen-year-olds would be summoned to-morrow. Marc's turn was coming.

The mother and the son were both thinking of this. But they did not talk about it. Annette was not afraid of the war alone; she was afraid of Marc's silence. She was afraid of knowing what was in his mind. And she was afraid of it because she knew what it was.

To whom could she confide her fears? If it had been something that concerned her alone, she could have kept it to herself. But it concerned him. To whom could she go for advice? Sylvie? At her first words, Sylvie cried out in her usual way:

"The war? It will be over in six months. The Boches are at the end of their rope."

Annette replied: "You have been saying that all these last six months."

"This time it's the truth," said Sylvie, with assurance.

"Your confidence is not enough for me," said Annette.

"Nor for me either," said Sylvie, "now that it concerns Marc. As long as it was only a question of other people one could easily fool oneself. It wasn't of any conse-quence! But for our young man, a mistake is a crime. You are right. If the war is going to go on! With these

idiots, can one ever know? When everything seems to
be over, they begin again. Look at Brother Jonathan now,
just joining in the dance! It will be China and the Papu-
ans next! Well, let them dance as long as they like!
But our Marc isn't going to join in their dance!"

"How can he help it?"

"I don't know. But they are not going to get him.
When the war devours our husbands, friends, lovers, we
let it: they made their own times. But our children—
we brought them into the world for ourselves. I'm going
to protect him!"

"All the mothers are giving their sons."

"But I am not going to give mine."

"Yours?"

"Ours. He belongs to both of us."

"But tell me how?"

"There are a thousand ways."

"I am asking for one."

"We have plenty of friends. Your Philippe Villard.
There he is, a surgeon-major, inspector-general of the
army! It would be easy enough for him to find some safe
place for Marc."

"You don't imagine I would ask him?"

"And why not? You mean it would cost you something? Pride! I can think of plenty of others too! If
it were necessary, to save my boy, do you think I would
hesitate to give myself to any man in the street?"

"There is no pride, just or unjust," said Annette, "that
I am not ready to trample under foot for my son! For
my son, for his good."

"Isn't it for his good?"

"It wouldn't be good for him if I dishonored myself.
For I am he. He would never forgive me. And I should

never forgive myself if I did something that humiliated him."

"Is it humiliating him to save him?"

"If I were saved that way I should be humiliated."

Sylvie flew into a passion. "There's a fine mother for you! Much I would care if I were humiliated, that he would not forgive me, so long as I had saved him. Well, if you don't do it I shall do it myself."

Annette cried: "I shall prevent you!"

"You can't prevent me."

"Ah!" said Annette. "Do you think it is enough to remove him from danger?"

"What are you afraid of?"

Annette was afraid that Marc would go to seek it.

*
* *

He shut himself up with his books and his thoughts. In spite of the warm intimacy that now united the hearts of the mother and the son, Marc spent his days in his own room, without speaking; and Annette respected his retreat. She would wait for him to come and find her. She was aware of the great travail through which he was passing. A travail of maturation and purification. The crisis of four years was finding its solution.

He was determined to carry his rigorous self-examination through to the end, and he judged himself, as he judged others, without pity. In order to tear himself free from the burning solicitations of his nature, which was very refractory, he had imposed upon himself a rigid discipline: a strict life and strict thinking. The last combats in which he engaged were not the least violent. He came out of them bruised and burned, as from a bath of passionate shame and molten conscience. But from the ashes emerged the hard core, compact, incorruptible.

He had put to the test all the thoughts that had beset his boyish brain, which had matured too early: those of his books, his philosophers, the chorus-leaders of his generation. Very few had stood the test, and they had stood it badly. Hardly anything was left of them. They were all phrases. They had no body. Not one of these Words had been made flesh. Or only one, made of smelted and hammered iron, a product of the machine age that had made of humanity another machine without any freedom. One group crushed the other, blindly, as with a pestle. No free act. No act of the soul. No free soul that surpassed the act. No will that disengaged itself from the thought-cloud and the agglomerated mass of moving matter—like lightning.

But the fire ran under the cloud, and under the cool bark, in the air, in the earth and in the water. . . .

One evening he took up his Händel. (He was reading the sacred books through him.) In the *Israel* he read the phrase:

"*Er sprach das Wort.*"

He heard it. . . .

*
* *

Drop by drop the house was losing its blood.

A fever for lucre had for four years possessed the tenant of the ground-floor—Numa Ravoussat, wine-merchant and dealer in wood. He fed it well. The jovial soul was larded with a triple layer of red, sweating fat, and bawling jovially, flapping about in his old shoes, he was bursting with gold and good health. Now that he had made his pile he had nothing more to live for, before he retired, like Philopœmen, on the land he had bought, but the return of his son. And his son didn't return. His Clovis's body was left hanging one day on the barbed wire. On the morning when the news arrived, they heard ascending from below a sound like the bellowing of a bull clumsily beaten to death by a butcher. It had all gone for nothing, all that effort and that money he had earned! A stroke of apoplexy had struck down the big man. Afterwards he had got better, but he lay propped up, thick of speech, one eye deformed. Now they never heard his voice. The hogshead was broken.

Next came news of the gentle Lydia, carried off by the epidemic of influenza in the hospital of Artois, where under the cross-fire of the two armies, she was nursing the wounded. She had gone to meet her fiancé. She had been waiting for that hour so long! Alas, if she could have believed this as she wished to believe it! But things are not, as these poor souls think, simple affairs of the will! The will opens the doors of the vestibule of the soul but stops at the last door, and this is the only one that counts for souls that count! God, if one could only be sure of even a hell, or of burning forever with one's beloved! Sure or not, now, she was delivered. Was that tender flower, her body, returned to-day to the earth, going to form with its flesh the flesh of new flowers that the jaws of death were going to devour anew?

Then the Cailleux boy (Hector) came back, gloriously wounded, without a nose, and without a jaw. (The State had generously given him another, patented, guaranteed for two years, perhaps three, depending on how carefully he used it.) His hands shook and his legs trembled like those of a child who is learning to walk. But he had a decoration. His mother swaddled him with her kind, pitying eyes, happy, in spite of all, and proud. He leaned on the old woman's arm when they went out, limping along, resuming their customary walk. They had very little to live on. But with patience they succeeded in making ends meet. And the Cailleux mother and son thought they were very lucky.

Then there was Joséphin Clapier, who had become inspector of morale in the rear and was using his precious health and even his reason in this noble service to which he was ordained. The great fault of renegades is excessive zeal. By dint of puffing himself up over his new mission and badgering his former companions for their pacifist faith and the doctrines that had been his own, he ended by complaining that he was persecuted. When those whom he pursued paid no attention to him and turned their backs on him, he began to shout that the country was insulted in him. This was dangerous for the others. It was dangerous for him too. It was not long before he changed his residence for the madhouse.

Brochon, however, was prospering—the keeper of the house who, like the Eumenides, was called by antiphrasis the keeper of the peace.

Marc, passing before his office, said to his mother: "It's just as if we were in Père-Lachaise. Do you see the guardian of the cemetery? Come, Mamma, let's climb up again to our dove-cote!"

"Yes, let's go up, my pigeon!" said Annette.

In half-spoken words they confided to each other their sorrows, pity for this one, disgust for that, for the den of Polyphemus—the house, the city, the world—in which every one of these imprisoned souls was patiently waiting for his turn to be devoured.

"And now," said Marc, "my turn has come."

Annette gripped his arm. "No! Don't say that!"

And then she was sorry she had not let him speak. She must know at least what his plans were.

Marc watched her, in silence, sitting before her, at her feet, in the bedroom, on a low foot-stool, his knees raised and his hands clasped about them. He gazed at her for a long time, his eyes full of determination. And she looked tenderly at him. Heavens, how completely she was his! But he was not going to take advantage of her any more. She was his wealth.

He smiled at her and said: "It's strange! Before the war neither of us was a pacifist."

"Don't utter that word!" said Annette.

"True enough. They have dishonored it. Those who used to have it in their mouths have denied it."

"If they only had the frankness to deny it! But they have been false to it, they simply go on dressing themselves up in it."

"Let them keep it," said Marc. "But we, who disown the war, did not use to be against it. I remember it made me very happy when it began. And you accepted it. What has changed us?"

"The baseness of it," said Annette.

"Its falseness," said Marc.

"When I see," said Annette, "that contempt for the weak, for the unarmed, for prisoners, for human suffering, for sacred sentiments, that exploitation of the basest instincts, that oppression of consciences, that cowardice in the face of public opinion, those sheep who are painted as heroes and become so in their very sheepishness, those good people who are driven to killing that feeble mass which does not know itself and allows itself to be led by a handful of misled men—my heart sickens with shame and misery."

"When I see," said Marc, "this ignoble war that hides its snout, this troop of masqueraders, these merry-andrews of a rapacious Right who, behind their backs, pick the pockets of the world, this atrocious slavery that imagines it is fooling us by gargling its throat with that empty word Liberty, that hypocritical heroism—I laugh in all their faces!"

"Don't provoke them," said Annette. "They are the majority."

"Naturally! The basest of tyrants is a million base people together."

"They know not what they do."

"Until they have learned it, let them stay in their chains!"

"You are too hard, my child. One must have pity. They are in chains! They have always been. That is why democracy is such a sell. They are told and they believe that they are the Sovereign People, and they are handed about like animals at an auction."

"For their Sovereign Stupidity I can't have any pity."

"The most stupid of them all is my brother."

"Brother—that doesn't mean anything! I am the brother of the dog who ransacks that heap of refuse in the street. But what have he and I in common?"

"Life."

"Yes, the life that dies. That's not enough."

"What else is there?"

"You ask me that, you who have it? There is that which neither life nor death can destroy: the grain of eternity."

"But where is this grain? Alas, I don't see anything eternal in me."

"But everything you do, everything you are, you would not do it, you would not be it if it were not in you."

"You are too clever for me, my child. I do what I feel. I do it honestly, and I am often mistaken. But I confess that at my age I still don't understand it. And I am not sure that I need to understand it."

"But I do need to understand it. I need to see where I am going in order to go where I want to go."

"To want to go where you are going."

"No matter! I want to see."

"Well, what do you see? What do you want? Where are you going?"

He did not reply.

Annette gathered together all her courage, and with a choke in her voice she asked him: "If the war comes for you, what are you going to say to it?"

"I am going to say 'No!'" said Marc.

Annette was waiting for the blow. And when she had

received it, she stretched out her hands, too late to ward it off. "Not that!"

Marc said calmly: "Would you like me to say 'Yes'?"

Annette protested: "Not that either!"

Marc looked at his mother, who was struggling with herself. And yet for so long a time she might have had a reply ready! With respect, with pity, he waited for her to make up her mind. But she had no arguments, she had nothing to offer him but a passionate anxiety.

"No, no, don't decide anything! You can't know and judge for yourself yet. Wait! It would be a crime to risk your whole life on the premature negation of a child who has not yet lived!"

"But you, who have lived?"

"I am a woman. I don't know. I am not sure. There is no one to direct me. I have only followed my heart and my instinct. That is not enough."

"No, that is not enough. But when will anything be enough? Even at the end of his life, what man could ever say that he knew, that he was certain, that he had examined everything? Is he condemned, then, always to wait for to-morrow in order to act? By postponing things day after day, you reach the last day debased, degraded, prostituted, like the majority of those who live. When am I going to have the right to exist?"

Annette did not wait to hear him. (She understood too well!)

"You have no right to destroy yourself."

"I don't want to destroy, I want to construct."

"Construct what? And for whom?"

"For myself, in the first place. A clean house where I can breathe. I couldn't endure living like these other people in their filthy den of deceit. But I have forced the

note in what I have said to you just now. You call me
hard. I am. One must be hard if one wants to be able
to help these men whom you have pitied. And it is for
them also that the house must be built."

"That is not the work of a day. To build one must
endure."

"The foundations must endure. The highest building
begins with one stone. *Eris Petrus.* I am a stone."

"You are Marc. You are mine."

"I am *of* you. I am what you have made me."

"But you are sacrificing me. You have no right to do
it."

"Mamma, that's your fault. You have wanted me to
be true. Wanted me to be a true man, a man indeed.
I don't know whether I can be. But I want to try. Let's
be frank! All evil comes from the fact that no one dares
to be sincere beyond the line where his own interests and
passions are threatened. When people reach this line,
they find some subterfuge, they play some trick with themselves, like these pacifists. You have wanted me to be
sincere, but you have not wanted me to be so at the risk
of my happiness and yours. Is that good? Is it frank?"

Annette was obstinate. "Yes!"

"Do you mean you think it's frank?"

"It's good."

He took her hands, which tried to escape from him.
But he had a firm grip. "Look at me! You are not saying what you think! I want you to look at me. Answer
me! Am I wrong? Which is frank, of the two of us?
You or I?"

She kissed his head and said, "You."

But immediately afterwards she cried: "It's mad! I
don't want it."

She had collected herself enough to give him her arguments. She tried to discuss the question with him.

"Frankness consists in being frank in all one's thoughts, in not deceiving any one, especially oneself, about what one believes. But it doesn't demand from us the impossible: only that we should always and entirely act in accordance with what we believe. Our spirit alone is free. Our body is enchained. We are slaves of society. We submit to its order. We cannot destroy it without destroying ourselves. Even when it is unjust we have no resource but to judge it. But we must obey it."

"Mamma, you are denying your life. Do you imagine I don't know your revolts, your struggles, your inability to submit to injustice for yourself and for others? My great breaker of laws! . . . If you had not been one, I should not have loved you so much!"

"No, don't follow my example! Ah, this is my punishment! It is not fair. . . . I have told you, as you know, that I have lived blindly. I have nothing to guide me but this inner feeling, these feminine passions, a too exalted heart that starts up in the night at the least touch. A man —the man I have made—must not model himself on a woman. He can, and therefore he should, extricate himself from the mud of nature. He should see both more clearly and further."

"Wait! We shall come to that in a moment. When we have reached it, you will ask me perhaps to turn back. For the moment, tell me whether you deny your own 'disobediences'?"

"Every one makes some evasion."

"But every evasion is (confess it!) a deliverance."

"Ah, I have only changed my chains in bruising my-

self. They are innumerable. One escapes from one only
to fall into another. Perhaps chains are necessary."

"You are speaking against yourself. I can see you
filing at your chains up to the last day of your life."

"But what if I am wrong? What if, in trying to shake
them off, the circumscribed instinct runs the risk of causing
more harm to oneself and others? What if one is obliged
to purchase order by renunciation?"

"Mamma, don't try to apply to yourself the words of
the genial egoist who loves the order of the universe more
than the good of his neighbor and the tranquillity of his
contemplation more than a dangerous activity against the
evil that exists! What is permitted to Goethe is not permitted to us. The eternal order is not enough for us.
We breathe the order of this world. And when it is
vitiated by injustice our duty is to break the glass partition
in order to breathe."

"You cut your veins open."

"If I fall into the breach, well and good! I have made
the breach. Others will breathe the better for it."

"My dear, you don't believe in humanity. You have
told me so a hundred times. Why do you talk now of
sacrificing yourself for it? Haven't you often made fun
of me for my faith in it—my poor faith which has received so many buffets that it is not very proud any longer,
nor very sure of itself?"

"Forgive me! I have never made fun of you! As for
what you believe, you are, in my eyes, more than what you
believe. . . . But it's true that I have never loved this
'humanitarianism,' this 'humanity,' all those hollow shams,
those ideologies, those wordy illusions. I see men, men,
droves of them, going astray, crowding together, running
into one another, going to the right, to the left, ahead, be-

hind, and stirring up under their feet the dust of ideas. I see in life, in theirs, in ours, in that of the universe, a tragi-comedy of which the *dénouement* has not yet been written: the scenario is composed, improvised, by the wills that conduct the attack. And I am one of the attackers, I have been marked out for it; and because I am your son, because I am Marc Rivière, I can't withdraw now. My pride is involved in it. And whether my team loses the match or not, I am going on to the end of the match without giving in!"

"What is this match? On which side are you? In the new camp? The old camp? Who knows? How can one be sure? Perhaps the past will command the future. Perhaps the future will command the past. Who is going to enlighten us? Often, in the mental isolation in which I used to live, when I suddenly felt myself overflowing with certitude, I have said to myself: 'How could I feel this way if the conqueror (the God to come) were not in me!' But afterwards, when I saw other men, whole peoples, equally certain, different and opposed, when I saw these mad faiths of patriotism or religion, art or science, order or liberty, even love, in which blind, frantic life wears itself out, how could I have the vanity to say to myself obstinately: 'My certitude alone is good'?"

"My certitude alone is mine. I cannot have two."

"I have all those of the people I love. And my certitude is in loving them."

"Do you love so many? Are there so many to love?"

"To love or pity. They are the same thing."

"I don't want to be pitied. I want another love, a love that chooses, a love that prefers."

"I prefer you only too much, cruel child! I would give all the rest of the world to keep you."

"Well, be with me and be like me: choose! You dream too much. You drift, like the ebb and flow of the tide that comes in and goes out again, without advancing. One must advance, cost what it may. Destroy, in order to go straight ahead on one's own way."

"But if it leads into a stone wall? If one finds oneself alone there? If the rest of the world is on the other side?"

"Whoever takes the lead goes alone. And if one goes alone, it is because one is a pioneer. Every advance that a single man makes becomes the road of the whole world."

"That is a creed, and there are almost as many as there are men. I believe in men almost more than in creeds. And I would like to embrace all these madmen with the same indulgent maternity."

"They don't want it. They don't want the breast. They have been weaned. We are obliged to believe, act, destroy, march forward, struggle, but advance. . . . You know the phrase about one's country: 'An encampment in the desert!' . . . Let us go further, bearing on our backs the pegs and the canvas of the tent."

"My encampment is fixed. It is the law of the heart. All the social duties, which vary and refute each other, count for little in my eyes beside the sacred affections— love, maternity—immutable, eternal. Whoever wounds them wounds me. I am ready to defend them wherever they are menaced. But I can't go further."

"Well, I am going further! When social duty begins to wound natural sentiments, another social duty, larger and more human, must be substituted for it. The time is ripe. The whole of society, its moral code and its cate- chism, must be made over, and it is going to be. Our whole being demands it: our reason, our passions, protest

against the oppressive error of a social contract that is
out of date to-day. So many of those great forces which
stir the hearts of men are condemned by law and become
a cause of pain, sometimes a crime, but only through the
inhumanity of the laws and of the system which imposes
on nature a system that has become an instrument of torture. If thousands of young people welcomed the war
as a deliverance, if my own heart bounded wildly at the
sight of it, it was because we hoped it was going to liberate us. The strangling constraint of an outworn order
of thoughts and conventions, of sordid prosperity and
mortal ennui, glossed over with disgusting idealisms: in-
sipidity, hypocrisy! (Your old time pacifism, your humanitarianism) atrophied nature, and killed in us the
joy of living, that strong, healthy, holy instinct. *Sanctus.*
We thought that the accursed bond was going to break.
Worse luck! Nothing has been offered to us in the way of
deliverance but a filthy war, engulfing everything in useless and ignoble suffering and death! And the bond
grows tighter, and our youth is enchained, standing on its
feet, bent over, in a cage like that of La Balue! We must
break, break the dead and murderous order, the unnatural
order, the order that is falser than disorder. It must be
broken so that we can build up a higher, vaster order, pro-
portioned to the men who are coming, who have come—
the men, ourselves! Air! More air! Let us have a
wider conception of good and evil! They have grown
larger with us."

"Where do you see these men? I don't see any of
them about me except my big child. And I am afraid for
him. Why did I bring him into the world at this bitter
moment of history?"

"Don't regret it! Don't be sorry for me! It's a

stormy time. Long life to the gale! And long life to
you who have made my lungs and my wings! Do you
remember that 'Last of the Vikings,' that Norwegian fish-
erman whose modern saga we read? When, at the end,
saved from death, he deserted the storms of the Lo-
foden Islands for the motionless air of the towns, he could
not be happy any longer. Come! I would rather belong
to my generation than yours. Yours dreamed power-
lessly of a cold human progress. Against this back-screen,
the picture that you cast of the present was dull and uniform. The privileged class enjoyed themselves in a poor
sort of way, without any appetite. Pallid joys, pallid
sorrows, a monotonous irony and sweetness. Ennui, ennui.
For the workers—for us—it was turning an everlasting
wheel in the darkness. To-day, the hurricane is blowing,
the house is in ruins but the daylight has entered our
cellar along with the wind. And without any illusion
about life and men and the moment that is coming, we
live rashly on the brink of the preposterous and magnificent abyss. Whether it endures or falls, we carry on our
shoulders our own universe of a day."

"We? Who has seen these 'we'? Where are they?
Who are they?"

"The first one who acts. The others will be born from
him."

"But he will die."

"Yes."

"I don't want it to be you!"

"You have just been talking about this maternity that
dreams of reaching out to all the sons of men. Here is
some use for it! Carry to others the love you have for
me!"

"I was boasting. I can't. Ah, who could ever do that?

It would be inhuman. I love others in you. I love you in others. It was you whom I was seeking in them before I had you. And now that I have you am I going to sacrifice you? I don't need them any longer. You are my universe."

"But the universe draws us, and it has its destiny to fulfill. You must follow it with me. Even if it leads to the cross. Remember the Mater Dolorosa!"

"Even she didn't want it! She was coerced."

"We are all coerced. You and I."

"By what?"

"By the law of our nature."

"Why should I submit to it if it is against me? I revolt against it, I reject it, like the other laws."

"You can't. You wouldn't be sincere."

"Well then, I shall lie!"

"You can't. And I don't want you to do so."

He looked at his mother, stopped, then said, in a trembling voice: "You see, there are two things, Mamma, that I don't want: not to be sincere and not to be brave. Perhaps . . ." (He hesitated.) "Perhaps because I am not brave and because I am a liar."

Annette took his face between her hands: "You a liar?"

He closed his eyes and said, in a low voice: "Yes. For, deep down, I am afraid. . . ."

Annette threw her arms about him. He made no movement to release himself. He remained there, the son's cheek resting on the mother's breast. In their weakness each felt strong in the weakness of the other.

Marc drew himself away and said to Annette: "It's absurd for you to say that you lie!"

"I deceive myself."

"You don't deceive yourself. You are deceived."

"Does one ever know the tricks one's mind plays? Haven't I lied to myself over and over?"

"If you have, it's because no man can live altogether without deceit."

"If deceit disappeared entirely from life, would not life itself disappear? Isn't that the thing which keeps up the great Illusion?"

"If it cannot exist without it, if it is the great Illusion, that is because it is not the true life. The true life is beyond. It must be found again."

"Where is it?"

"In me, in you, in this need for the truth. How could it possess us if it did not breathe in us?"

Annette was struck by her son's words, but she stiffened herself. It was a matter of life or death for him.

"I implore you! I implore you! Don't put yourself in danger for nothing! What would be the use of it? You know very well that you can not change men! Whatever one may do for them, they will remain the same, with the same passions, the same prejudices, the same blindness, which they call reason or faith, and which is never anything but a stone wall—their snail-shell. They must have it in order to live. They never emerge from it. You can't break it. You will only be broken yourself. Preserve the truth! Do not unveil it before eyes that cannot endure it! What would be the use? What would be the use? It kills those who reveal it."

"What is the use? What is the use of your life? Haven't you lived according to your sense of truth? Haven't you listened to your truth, even if it was dangerous? Are you sorry that you have listened to it? Answer! Answer! . . . Are you sorry?"

Annette struggled with herself, but she replied: "No."

She was overwhelmed. She thought: "It is I who have killed him."

Her son looked at her tenderly, and there was a grave smile on his young face. He said: "Mamma, don't torment yourself. Perhaps it will never come, perhaps nothing will happen, perhaps the war will end before. Nothing is decided yet. I don't know what I am going to do. I don't know anything. The only thing I know is that when the moment comes I shall be sincere. At least I shall try. Help me, and pray!"

"I am praying, but to whom?"

"My source, your soul. I am the spring that flows from it."

*
* *

After weeks of waiting and solitary anxiety (they had not mentioned this subject again in their talks, but both were thinking of it and secretly watching the face of the other, and Annette's anxious ear was awaiting the vibrations of the air, the whirring of the aeroplane of the deadly hour that was going to carry off her child) one morning the guns of the city thundered and a clamor rose in the street, like a flood.

Before they even realized it, both hearts leaped, and Sylvie came in, out of breath, crying: "The armistice is signed!"

They threw themselves into each other's arms. Then Annette drew back and turned aside with her face in her hands to hide her emotion.

The two others, respecting the veil with which she had covered herself, did not make any movement to take it off. They waited in silence until she was calmer. Then they both tenderly approached Annette; and Marc, his arm about her, led her with short steps towards the French window and made her sit down on the edge of the balcony, seating himself beside her. And Sylvie, at their feet, her legs crossed beneath her, like a Buddha, looked at them, smiling.

They were sitting, the three of them, over a world in ruins.

Annette, with her eyes closed, heard the bells, the cries, the singing in the street, and she felt against her cheek the cheek of her boy. She was dreaming. The nightmare was over. The nightmare of the menace that threatened this dear head, and that of the human suffering that weighed upon her heart. The monstrous ordeal, the war, was ended. But she couldn't be sure yet. Timidly she was reacquiring her taste for the air. She could breathe. . . .

Marc was relieved also. He had taken little pleasure in the sight of the approaching menace. His pride had prevented him from doing anything to avoid it. But he was not sure of his strength and his faith. He heard this incoherent crowd shouting and laughing. He knew very well that the ordeal was only postponed. . . . But a few years saved, at his age, are a whole world! He relished the breathing-space. He could enjoy the life that lay ahead of him. He was dreaming.

Sylvie watched them dreaming. She thought neither of the past nor of the future. The moment was sweet and her joy was running over. All three of them had finished the dangerous voyage; the oars hung loose along the sides of the boat, sleeping now on the pacified sea. She was dreaming. What a beautiful evening!

But the house was silent in its mourning, and its tragic silence was in contrast with the merry kermess in the street.

On the second floor, Professor Girerd, the man whose heart had hardened in his grief, the man of stone, decked his windows with flags. And now the implacable goal was attained, and the desert of his life no longer had an object, he could collapse. On the third floor, the Bernardins had closed their shutters; the daughters and the father were at church, in the shadow of a chapel. But the mother remained in bed, slowly dying. Sickness had come in the train of her grief; and Bernardin himself, who was praying, was unaware that his sallow flesh, no longer able to defend itself, already harbored a cancer. On the ground-

floor there was a copious supply of wine. But Numa was
not to be seen at the bar. The master had shut himself
up in the back room. He was alone, and he was drinking.

Annette heard ascending, in a single harmony, the grief
and the sorrow of these destroyed lives, together with the
blind exultation of the swarming crowd. All of them,
with her, were in the snare of the Illusion, swallowed up
in it, with their heads bowed, sunk under the red cloak of
the matador. For some it was the flag, the sacred frenzy
of patriotism. For others, the flame of faith in the broth-
erhood of men and in love. And her son, who pretended
that he was not deceived by anything, the scorner of the
"illusions of words," was he not the most deluded of all,
he who was ready to sacrifice himself and her to the
chimera of being true in spite of all the world? That passion for truth, by far the greatest illusion of all! All
were intoxicated by their own visions. They were dreaming!

Then she perceived, like a sudden gust of rainbow-
colored vapors, the universal dream in which she was im-
mersed. She raised her head a moment above the water.
She shook off its insidious, violent grip. Was she going
to awaken? For one second the awakening beat its wings
in her dream. In the summits of her mind, through the
gaping cranny, one ray of light slipped in.

But against her cheek she felt the warmth of the cheek
—the flesh, fruit of her flesh—the son who held her captive, through love and pain, the ordeals to come, the fate
that was waiting and bound them.

("I know, I know . . .")

. . . Of the Mater Dolorosa . . .

("I don't shrink from it. Behold me once again! . . .")

And her eyes returned to him, her son, to the dear

dream.   She was caught again by the eyes of the living.
She smiled and fell back. . . .
   "*Warte nur . . .*"
Soon we shall awaken.

END OF THE THIRD VOLUME OF
The Soul Enchanted.

20 May, 1926.